Day Dark, Night Bright

DAY DARK,
NIGHT BRIGHT

FRITZ LEIBER

OPEN ROAD

INTEGRATED MEDIA

NEW YORK

Time Fighter - *Fantastic Universe* 1957, Femmequin 973 - *Science Fiction Stories* 1957, Night Passage - Original to this collection, Moon Duel - *Worlds of If* 1965, Later than you Think - *Galaxy* 1950, Mirror - *Fortune Magazine* 1965, The 64-Square Madhouse - *Worlds of If* 1962, All the Weed in the World - *Playboy* 1961, The Mutant's Brother - *Astounding* 1943, The Man who was Married to Space and Time - *Seacon Programme Book* 1979, Thought-*Astounding* 1944, The Crystal Prison - *Galaxy* 1966, Bullet with his Name - *Galaxy* 1958, Success - *The Magazine of Fantasy & SF* 1963, To Make a Roman Holiday - *Esquire* 1943, Bread Overhead - *Galaxy* 1958, The Reward - *Fantastic* 1959, Taboo - *Astounding* 1944, Business of Killing - *Astounding* 1944, Day Dark Night Bright - *Infinity Four* edited by Robert Hoskins 1972

Copyright © 2002 by the Estate of Fritz Leiber
Introduction © 2002 John Pelan

ISBN 978-1-4976-4217-1

This edition published in 2014 by Open Road Integrated Media, Inc.
345 Hudson Street
New York, NY 10014
www.openroadmedia.com

Day Dark, Night Bright

ACKNOWLEDGMENTS

THE EDITOR WOULD LIKE TO ACKNOWLEDGE THE invaluable assistance of Susan Chernauskas, Richard Curtis, Stefan Dziemianowicz, Allen Koszowski, Brian Metz of Green Rhino Graphics, Kathy Pelan, & David Read in the preparation of this volume.

CONTENTS

Introduction   7

Time Fighter   13

Femmequin 973   19

Night Passage   31

Moon Duel   51

Later Than You Think   63

Mirror   71

The 64-Square Madhouse   75

All the Weed in the World   115

The Mutant's Brother   121

The Man Who Was Married   137
    to Space and Time

Thought   147

Crystal Prison   161

Bullet with His Name   169

Success   201

To Make a Roman Holiday   205

Bread Overhead   213

The Reward   227

Taboo   237

Business of Killing   249

Day Dark, Night Bright   265

THE MAN WHO MADE
SCIENCE FICTION GROW UP

WE GIVE A LOT OF CREDIT TO THE DOUR AND penurious Hugo Gernsback for being the father of modern SF (at least in magazine format), a good bit of credit is accorded to John Campbell for putting the *science* into "science-fiction" and piloting *Astounding* through decades of stories where supremely competent and confident engineers filled to the very brim with "the right stuff" solved problems that would have baffled anyone save that select group of people that subscribed to *Astounding*...

Fritz Leiber made Science Fiction grow the hell up, and despite the trophy-room full of awards that the field bestowed on him, he's never really been given quite enough credit for that... Just as he dragged the Jamesian ghost story wailing and moaning into the Atomic Age, he made the Science Fiction genre take on a new relevance by proving time and time again that it was valid forum for *literature,* not just clever tales that extrapolated on scientific theory. Fritz Leiber wrote about *people,* and what's more, his choices for subjects were as colorful and diverse as the settings that he placed them in.

When did science fiction grow up? When *Dangerous Visions* was published in 1967? No, despite being a very good anthology, it really wasn't really all that dangerous even in 1967. How about when Phil Dick's novels of paranoia begin to hit the market? Again no, Dick was an amazing visionary; an amphetamine-fueled mystic that became progressively more profound over the years, but he really wasn't instrumental in the evolution of the genre.

No, the first shots of the SF revolution were fired long before in Britain by John Wyndham who frequently dared to suggest that just because you have the cause of right on your side, and just because you behave in a heroic manner, in the final analysis that maybe just won't matter. Where others touted success through science and good old American know-how, the cynical Brit had his despairing heroes committing suicide on Mars rather than face a ruined world. In the US the opening salvo might well have been in 1950 when Fritz Leiber gave us "Coming Attraction".

Was it the first story of "The New Wave"? Perhaps not, but Leiber blazed a trail that was followed by a number of other authors and it could just as well be said that 1950 was when Science Fiction began to grow up. A turning point for the whole genre? All with a single story? Of course not, but one can certainly point to 1950 and Leiber's amazing tale as one of the major turning points in the genre.

Not all the stories in this book are as perversely dystopian as "Coming Attraction", but all are excellent examples of Leiber playing the genres of fantasy and science fiction like a master of improvisational jazz, taking familiar riffs and transforming them into something new and different.

Not for Leiber was the jut-jawed Heinleinian competent man conquering the universe armed with a slide rule and a sense of manifest destiny as obnoxious as any of the novels of Colonial Britain. No, Leiber's characters are jewelers, chess players, smalltime gamblers and grifters, lonely middle-aged men, and even aliens and robots with all-too-human foibles and failings. Leiber, like his contemporary Theodore Sturgeon wrote about the human condition and in doing so transformed an entire genre of fiction.

Assembling this book came about almost accidentally. I'd launched a program with our Midnight House imprint to release at least three volumes of Leiber's horror fiction and in preparation for this project began to dig (via long distance) through the Leiber archives at the University of Houston. I didn't know what (if anything) I'd find, after all, someone had already discovered the manuscript for *The Dealings of Daniel Kesserich* and TOR Books had done a handsome edition of same. I thought it was unlikely that any unpublished material was housed in the archive... Still, the index of titled manuscripts looked intriguing...

As readers of our Midnight House collections already know

the outcome of digging through the archives far exceeded my wildest expectations and several completely polished, ready for publication Leiber tales were discovered. The other circumstance that quickly became clear as I studied the existing Leiber bibliographies was just how haphazard had been previous publishing efforts in preserving his short fiction! Scores of tales had either never been collected in book form or had appeared only in long out-of-print anthologies, other stories had made appearances only in paperbacks many years ago and were, for all practical purposes inaccessible to the modern reader.

A situation easily remedied with the kind support of Richard Curtis and Leiber's heirs, but another problem manifested itself... Much of this lost material was very much a part and parcel of the SF genre and would perhaps not be as enthusiastically welcomed by collectors of classic horror fiction as the two Midnight House collections had been. Thus a new imprint was necessary. Leiber blazes a trail yet again, setting a publishing company on a new and challenging path to do the same for classic works of SF and fantasy as we've done in the horror and weird fiction genre.

The reader may well find a few tales to quibble over, stories that just as easily could've been presented by our sister imprint without raising an eyebrow. Sure, stories like "Bullet With His Name", "Night Passage" and so on wouldn't be out of place in a horror collection, nor would his classic "Femmequin 973". Stories such as "Time Fighter", "The Mutant's Brother", "Bread Overhead" and the titular story could perhaps appear nowhere else than this collection labeled as "SF". Other quirkier tales like "All the Weed in the World" and "Success" find their home here alongside the ultimate take on the gentle madness of tournament chess and those that play it, which he covers so masterfully in "The 64-Square Madhouse".

It's an eclectic mix, stories taken from very different times and places in Leiber's long and productive life. For reasons which will be obvious, I could think of no finer way to inaugurate this collection (and by extension the Darkside Press imprint) than with the story "Time Fighter". Leiber opens his tale with the classic line *"A real science-fiction enthusiast has to be a little crazy and a little sane, a little dreamy and a little skeptical, a little idealistic and also a little hard-headed"* This line, written in the year I was born, for a story that appeared in *Fantastic* is as accurate today as it was then. Leiber had been approaching the genre from the standpoint of possessing all these qualities ever since he's sold "The Automatic Pistol" seventeen years earlier. Leiber approached SF as he did fantasy, not content to simply retread the same ground that others had walked, he was wildly experimental in his approaches, in fact, in my opinion, of his contemporaries, only a handful of authors were quite the innovators that Leiber was.

"Femmequin 973" is also an under-reprinted tale from that golden year of 1957 it's as much a horror story as it is science-fiction, and I almost utilized it in *Smoke Ghost and Other Apparitions*. I hope you'll agree that it's perfectly at home in this volume.

"Night Passage" is an original, discovered during my researches through the Leiber papers. From tone and style it appears to have been targeted for *Esquire,* while never quite as lofty a market as *Playboy, Esquire* was an excellent market and one that Leiber targeted throughout his career. Both this story and "The Enormous Bedroom" (from *Smoke Ghost*) were likely passed over due to their length. Since both tales are charged with an underlying eroticism, they were probably "too strong" for the SF digests of the 1950's and likely remained in Leiber's files unsubmitted elsewhere.

"Moon Duel" is a more typical SF tale, taken from the pages of the late, lamented *Worlds of If* this amazingly enough marks the first time the story has appeared in a collection of the author's work. The story was selected by Judith Merril to appear in her prestigious *Year's Best SF* series from Delacorte in 1966 and inexplicably vanished after that one lone appearance in book form. I'm pleased to be able to present this with other fine examples of Leiber's SF.

"Later Than You Think" is another well thought of yet strangely orphaned story. Despite several anthology appearances (including August Derleth's *Far Boundaries* In 1951 and most recently in *100 Astounding Little Aliens,* it's another example of a story that failed to find it's way into one of the author's collections. A short piece, but very effective despite its brevity.

Many of the stories contained herein are genuine rarities, stories that show Leiber at his most daring and experimental such as "All the Weed in the World" and interesting pieces such as "Success" and "To Make a Roman Holiday" from the pages of *Esquire*. And then there's my favorite, *Bullet With Name* a story that would have been perfect for John Campbell's *Unknown* fifteen years earlier. Is it SF or fantasy? Certainly it maintains the aura of SF with super-science as its explanation, but at heart it's an examination of the theme of being careful what you wish for, (though in the case the wishes aren't even consciously voiced). Other tales in the book may have a more familiar ring to them, *The 64-Square Madhouse,* very likely the last word on playing chess with a computer. "The Man Who Was Married to Space and Time" is another tale likely to be familiar to Leiber fans, a mature and poignant character study. Is the authorial voice behind old Guy Manning, somewhat autobiographical? Perhaps it is, as readers of fantastic literature I think that there's likely a little Guy Manning in all of us. A little dreamy and a little skeptical, and stories like these still touch that sense of wonder within us all.

John Pelan
Midnight House
July 2002

TIME FIGHTER

A REAL SCIENCE-FICTION ENTHUSIAST HAS TO BE A little crazy and a little sane, a little dreamy and a little skeptical, a little idealistic and also a little hard-headed. George Mercer inclined toward the first of each of these three pairs, which was why he fell for Dave Kantarian's time-traveling swindle.

George was well into middle age, rather tiredly married, and ran a small watch-repair and jewelry shop. The jewelry he made by hand satisfied only a fraction of his desire for self-expression, his wife did little to feed his yearning for romance, while voting once every two years did nothing to slake his thirst to be in on some great, undefined act of world-saving. The magazines he read and shelved meticulously left him restless, not sated. So he was ripe for becoming the victim of an adventurous, do-gooder swindle.

Not that Dave Kantarian wasn't an ingenious swindler, even though he chose an extremely bizarre field of operations. As one of the Treasury men later said, "Boy, if he had only stuck to uranium stock, cosmic-power generators, and gasoline from water!"

Dave turned up at the local science-fiction club with a half dozen magazines under his arm and a readiness to argue about the relative merits of anything from the Gray Lensman to *Playboy*. Next meeting he showed around a Heinlein manuscript and a Freas original It was several weeks before he began to hint to George about super-normal powers and a mysterious mission. And it was only in George's room behind the shop, after carefully drawing the blinds and extracting a promise of secrecy, that he delicately parted his blond pompadour to expose two quivering golden antennae capable of sending and receiving thought-messages across time (but unfortunately for test purposes, not across space).

Evidently Dave was a reasonably good parlor magician and mechanical gimmicker, for he made several small objects disappear into the future to Dave's satisfaction and he caused two clocks in Dave's shop to first gain and then lose ten minutes without any detectable intervention. Before George managed to check the clocks against anything but Dave's wristwatch the brief trip in time was over and Dave didn't repeat that demonstration; but the future smelled different, George averred.

After baring his antennae, Dave told all, which was simply this: Dave was a man from five thousand years in the future, fighting on the good side of an interstellar war which was being lost because the home base of Terra had run out of certain absolutely essential metals. These turned out to be nothing really difficult to obtain, such as uranium-235 or berkelium, but simply silver and gold, which Seventieth Century technology could transform into a non-corrosive armor far stronger than steel and harder than diamond. Dave had been briefed telepathically, presumably across a short time-span, in the languages and customs of the Early Atomic Age and hustled back across the millennia to garner a supply of the desperately needed metals before they were impossibly dispersed by use. Now would George care to drop a suitable contribution into the time machine?

To understand why George fell for this story, one must remember his stifled romanticism, his sense of personal failure, his deep need to believe. The thing came to him like, or rather instead of, a religious conversion.

Also, one must not under-rate the patient artistry of Dave's build-up, his fanatical attention to plausible touches, such as occasional lapses into an unintelligible and presumably future speech, his fierce looks of concentration as he received unheralded time-messages, and his assurance that George would eventually get a concrete token of gratitude from the embattled futurians—a token which by its very nature would convince George that his contributions were really helpful. Indeed, the ingenuity Dave Kantarian lavished on a not very profitable swindle constitutes a secondary problem: was he really shrewd or merely devious?

For instance, was it sheer lack of imagination or a brilliant stroke of understatement that the contribution box for time-traveling riches was nothing but a cheap modern alarm clock with most of the mechanism removed, a hand-drawn diagram pasted inside, and a rather crude trap-door built in the top? Anything more elaborate might have aroused suspicion and Dave claimed that the gutted clock was simply a lens that focused his mental power to send objects into the future—a power sufficient without focusing for short trips across time, but not a five-thousand-year voyage.

At any rate George came to believe and regular contributions of the purest silver and gold he could buy were put into the clock. Then Dave would carefully set the hands, his gaze would become trancelike, the clock would be hidden and Dave would depart, still glassy-eyed. The time transit might take place at once, Dave said, or in several hours, but the next morning when George opened the clock in Dave's presence, he would always find it empty and experience a deep thrill at the thought that the futurians were a little bit nearer winning the ultimate war against the powers of evil. On some mornings Dave seemed to share his sentiments completely, on others he was mysteriously irritated, almost as if he suspected George of tampering with the time-machine during the night.

Nevertheless, this generally blissful state of affairs might have continued indefinitely, except that the Treasury Department became interested in the tenfold increase in George's gold purchases and at about the same time George's wife noticed their depleted bank balance, got no satisfaction whatever from her husband, fumed and spied for a few days, and finally consulted a lawyer.

When the Treasury men interviewed George early one morning at his shop, he denied everything and made a pitiful effort to conceal his extreme terror, for Dave had repeatedly warned him that the futurians' enemies were capable of sending back time-spies and saboteurs, who might appear in any guise. Since unlike most swindlers there was no obvious way in which the victim could hope to profit from it himself, the Treasury men assumed that George was motivated by an unwillingness to admit that he had been duped. Despite their serious doubts of his sanity, they reasoned with him at length. They showed him what they had dug up about Dave; an unsavory record of petty confidence games, personal betrayals, generally unstable behavior, and grandiose schemes. They hinted that Dave had been preparing to pull the same swindle on other members of the science-fiction club. Still Dave stuck to his story—Dave was just a fellow science-fiction enthusiast—so the Treasury men called in his wife and things became quite nasty when she flatly called him a childish fool who had doped his mind with lurid magazines and finally fallen for a fairy tale and given away their savings to a cheap crook.

Then things got a bit nastier when the Treasury men sprang the news that late last night Dave had been scraped from a sidewalk in the local skid row and that there were indications he might have been pushed, perhaps by an enraged victim of his swindles, from the high window of a cheap hotel where he roomed. They threw down on George's small, glass-topped desk a duplicate key to his store which had been found on Dave and also the thought-transmitting antennae.

At this point George broke down and spilled the whole story: Dave's incredible claims, the quest for gold and silver to be transformed into metals harder than diamond, the alarm-clock time machine, everything. Fortunately George was able to refute the hinted accusation of murder. True, Dave had visited the shop early the previous evening, they had even put a contribution in the clock and Dave had set it; but after he departed some of George's regular science-fiction friends had dropped in and been with him at the moment Dave had hurtled downward with a howl that one frightened bum on the sidewalk below described as sounding more like rage than fear.

But while George was making these helpful admissions, he was also doing something that confirmed the Treasury men's suspicions of his sanity. While admitting that Dave was an out-and-put swindler and had used the duplicate key to come back secretly each night to loot the time machine, George maintained that the dead crook was still an agent of the futurians.

According to the new version, George had always sensed that there was something partly fishy about Dave's claim. Really the futurians couldn't time-travel themselves at all, they could merely send their thoughts ranging back across the centuries and sometimes manage small shipments of metal if there were a suitable sending station at the other end. They had fixed on Dave as such a suitable station. Without realizing that he was merely following their powerful mental suggestions, Dave set up his swindle.

This would account, George pointed out excitedly, for Dave's fits of irritation and suspicion, which must have corresponded to the occasions when the time-traveling setup had actually worked, and also Dave's suicide, induced by the realization that he, the supercriminal, was being inexplicably rooked.

The Treasury men were not buying anything like that, though they didn't tell George so right out. They even went along with him a bit, pretending to round out details and making a serious business out of examining the alarm clock, which had been filled with silver and gold the previous night. Sure enough, it was empty.

"No, wait a minute, there's something in it," one of them said, and extracted a tiny star-shaped button of dull metal with a pin attached to the back of it. He examined it, blinked, and put it down on the desk.

He wanted to say, "That Kantarian was certainly a crazy stickler for details. He told you, Mercer, that you would get a token of gratitude from the good guys, and sure enough he has a cheap button ready with 'Time Fighter' engraved on it. Really pitiful, Mercer, the way he made you look like a kid sending off to a TV program for a spaceman's badge."

Instead he glanced at George's face and yielded to a rather unprofessional impulse. "Maybe you'd like to keep this," he said softly, shoving the button at him.

At that moment a puzzled look came into his face, but a second later he shrugged and followed the other man out of the shop.

George didn't miss it, however, because the light was right from where he was sitting. And because he didn't miss it, he was able to stand up bravely to the loss of his savings and even the endless reproaches of his wife. When things got rough, he merely would smile and glance inside his breast pocket, where he had pinned the cheap little "Time Fighter" button, now with a flat diamond set in the center of it—the dull metal star, one point of which had a golden gleam and, when lightly shoved across the desk, had made a deep scratch in the glass, and later, when George tested it, in the flat diamond.

FEMMEQUIN 973

You WOULD HAVE KNOWN THAT THE GLEAMING skeleton hanging from the black work-rack was going to be a girl, although the steel bones were thinner and fewer, the platform for the electronic brain was in the chest and not in the head, and the pelvis held not a womb but a large gyroscope.

The skeleton had that air and attitude; it *was* that enticing, provocative gesture that means woman—whether it turns up in a fashion-magazine advertisement or a Stone Age carving.

It was a room like a cave, black except where bright lights beat on the work-rack and the silvery skeleton. A stooping man was touching a limb of the skeleton with a tool that made a faint grrr.

Behind the man, unseen by him, was a real woman, clothed in flesh and embellished with clothes—except that after seeing that dangling skeleton you would always doubt a little whether any woman was real and warm and alive. And this woman's face was straight out of a fashion magazine in its cold inscrutable pride, and deadly purpose. She advanced toward the unknowing man. The silvery skeleton got more distinct to her, she could see the cables of its muscles, thin as threads. She could make out on its gleaming limbs—tiny humps, to which a substitute for flesh would later be attached. She could discern the disdainful curves of the latticework making up its metallic skull. She could see the black motors and batteries crowding its slender waist.

The stooped man also became clearer. He was short, even allowing for his stoop. The two lines going up between his eyebrows looked as if slashed by a black pencil He seemed to be trembling a little, but never when he touched the gleaming skeleton. The *grrr* had stopped and he was stroking a silver limb with a pad of rouge.

The woman hesitated for a moment. Then she said, "Chernik!" and at the same instant touched his shoulder. He jumped as if her two fingers were the fangs of a poisonous snake.

Harry Chernik had one of the oddest jobs in one of the strangest and most secret businesses in the modern world. He was an assistant engineer and final tune-up man in a femmequin factory.

Harry owed his job to the intervention of a friend and his own unusual mechanical talents. It was he who cut the cams that gave the pale suede-rubber shoulders of the shimmying femmequins such a delectably lazy wriggle. It was his itch for perfection that kept the powerful electric motors inside the dainty torsos as silent as shy innocence, and the tungsten-steel cables that went down to each rosy toe and fingertip—as quiet in their sheathes as blasé experience. And as for the quartz-crystal inner ear which controlled the gyroscope that kept the femmequin in perfect balance in all attitudes (replacing the less reliable mercury type), he was actually its inventor, though there was no question of patents on such a device, any more than there was on the reciprocating, contractile, variable pulse gadget that was the central feature of each femmequin.

In fact, Harry Chernik was far more important to the company than Mr. Jones, the chief engineer, though he was never told this by Mr. Bissel—the man who shipped the femmequins to the very wealthy individuals (or the clubbed-together slightly less-wealthy men) buying them, and who also raked in the profits.

But Harry Chernik would never have stayed on at his peculiar job for a lifetime except that he believed himself to be a very ugly man, and as such incapable of arousing love in any woman. His work was a substitute for the tender relationships that life denied him, or that he denied himself. When he was mounting a motor— whether a powerful one in the molybdenum-steel ribwork of a femmequin, or a feather-weight one in the armored skull to tighten the delicate ring of cable that puckered the lips—he was possessed by an intense and unwearying excitement that was more than that generated by the exercise of fine craftsmanship.

* * *

When a millionaire customer asked for some new and almost undevisably realistic feature in a femmequin, Harry could be depended upon to work five nights running without the prod of extra money. Mr. Bissel and Mr. Jones were well aware of how their assistant engineer was wedded to his work, and how much of their own financial success was due to the passion of this marriage; being wise, if not generous men, they gave him no hint of this. Indeed, they pretended to find a great deal of fault with his work and even after twenty years were not above hinting that he might shortly be discharged. They believed, and quite accurately, that fear of losing a job that meant much more to Chernik than money would drive him to a higher pitch of inventiveness.

Mr. Bissel would sometimes explain frankly to his intimates, "You can't turn out a really good product unless you love it. Now most of us here are just a little bit contemptuous of our girls, and of the boobs who buy them. In the selling end, that doesn't hurt; but in the production end it does. We have only two people here who really love our girls, and Chernik is one of them."

It must not be thought that Harry Chernik's position allowed him to enjoy the ingenious robot caresses of the femmequins he labored to perfect, and that such crass privileges were the final tie between him and his job. Quite the opposite was the case.

After the femmequins left him in the form of eerie steel skeletons, to receive their suede-rubber flesh and have their eyes and tongues and other details mounted, he was hardly permitted to touch them. More than once at final tune-up Mr. Bissel had said, "Not you, Harry. Your hands are oily, you'll smudge her," and it would be Rita Bruhl's or Joe Novak's fingers which would burrow into the invisible slit in the femmequin's back and unzip the large window there. Only when this was fully open, and the rest of the femmequin draped in a protective shroud, would Harry be allowed to approach and work his magic on the motors, making the final corrections that first testing had shown necessary.

He was invariably dismissed before final testing. This delicate job was the prerogative of Joe Novak, who nevertheless dressed like a fashion plate and was handsome in a beefy way. Mr. Bissel put a great deal of trust in Joe's judgement, believing him to have had a wealth of amatory experience in real life. (This last assumption was quite untrue, but there were limits even to Mr.

Bissel's sagacity. In any case Joe's judgements were vindicated in terms of customer satisfaction.)

Yet, Harry Chernik's ardor was not dampened by the fact that he knew vastly more about the insides of his girls than a surgeon knows about the insides of his repeater patients, without enjoying anything of a surgeon's dignity and prestige. A real skeleton would have horrified a prospective customer less than a glimpse of one of the femmequins in the extremely undressed state in which Harry Chernik worked on them. But Harry, viewing them, was ravished by titillations invisible to other eyes. He saw the languorous undulation of a hip in the curves of a cam, the inviting turn of a haughty head in the routing of a cable, the unswerving glance of wide blue eyes in the adjustment of a photoelectric cell. In fact, Harry might have outgrown his job except for the exceedingly devious nature of the satisfactions he found in it. As in the case of normal love, distance added enchantment.

There was, of course, a more personal reason for Harry Chernik's strange pattern of life than these general considerations. Long ago, he had fallen utterly in love. More important, Louise had been submissive, and more easily hurt than himself, so that for once he had managed to conquer his terrible dread of ridicule and really think of asking someone to marry him. She had returned his love; he had been about to propose, when she had been snatched away from him by an exceedingly handsome and brilliant young man, who had overwhelmed her by imaginative romantic attentions and then actually gone on to marry her. It had always seemed unjustly cruel to Harry that John Gottschalk had deprived him of Louise; Gottschalk had the equipment to win any girl, no matter how beautiful, proud and vixenish. Why should John insist on a mousy and gentle creature like Louise?

It was after this catastrophe, that a guarded message about "an interesting job opportunity" had come from, of all people, Rita Bruhl.

Rita was an exceptionally handsome, but always severely-dressed girl, who had been John Gottschalk's companion on double dates with Louise and Harry, before the attraction between John and Louise had shown itself. Harry had always thought of Rita, with impersonal bitterness, as the sort of girl whom men like John should take the trouble to win. He would never have dreamed of risking any advances himself, and was quite startled that she should remember him at all, let alone do him a favor.

It turned out that Rita worked for a firm manufacturing dress shop mannequins, according to the story she first told him. She introduced him to Mr. Bissel, who, after sounding him out carefully and seeing some evidence of his mechanical ability, bound him to secrecy and then revealed to him that they were bringing out a line of animated mannequins, which a chain of big department stores planned as its smash advertising surprise for next year. Harry found pleasure in discussing the means whereby the movements of wheels and levers and tiny pneumatic pumps could be translated into the flexures and swellings of a chilly pseudo-flesh. (That was before he knew that the femmequins were temperature-controlled to human normal.) Taken to the machine shop, he saw the fleshless steel forms in all their surrealist beauty. Inspecting them more closely, he spotted mechanical crudities that made his fingers and mind itch to be tinkering. He took the job.

It wasn't many weeks before he realized that the story about department store advertising had been a blind. But by that time he loved his "skelegirls" (as he sometimes called them) a bit too much.

Indirectly he heard enough about John Gottschalk to know that both he and his marriage were prospering, though with some setbacks, as when Louise's first and only child died at birth—a tragedy which happened to coincide with Harry finishing work on the first femmequin which he felt to be stamped with his own individual craftsmanship.

What he did hear about John Gottschalk was also enough to keep his hatred alive. Once in a while, Rita Bruhl made use of Chernik, curtly asking secret favors. He made no other friends at the factory.

And so Harry Chernik worked for more than twenty years in his shadow-land of steel houris, nursing his fear of Mr. Bissel; his awe of Rita Bruhl; his contempt for Joe Novak; his hatred of John Gottschalk, and his thin, unreal love for Louise.

These desires and anxieties, and also his despairs, naturally created a considerable degree of nervousness in Harry Chernik, so that when Rita Bruhl stole up behind him in his workshop and stung him on the shoulder with two fingers, he jumped the earthbound equivalent of half a mile.

"Rita!" he protested gaspingly, "you make me think it's Mr. Bissel, you make me think it's the Federal Bureau of Morals. Why, Rita? We're friends, Rita. Why?"

Rita's eyes were like marble as she looked at him. The pupils and irises were almost lost in the expanse of white.

"Because there is a special reason," she said. "Because I want you to make a special femmequin for a special customer."

"Do we ever do anything besides that, Rita?"

"No," she said, "but Femmequin 973 must have motors many times as powerful as any of the others, it must have cables many times as strong, the gadget must be specially armed—I mean equipped. And I must impress my own voice on the wires."

"But that's against the safety rules," Chernik protested. "Our femmequins are built to crack up at that point where they could hurt a customer. Besides, Rita, although you dub in a word here and there, you're not supposed to do whole wires. And as for fooling with the central gadget—"

"Yes," Rita said, "but Femmequin 973 is for a very special customer." And she smiled thoughtfully.

Rita Bruhl went to work for Mr. Bissel just as any other attractive career girl might join the staff of a couturier or fashion magazine. And her work was very much the same. It was to style the femmequins, to decide from her studies of cafe society and fashion art as to whether legs should be made a trifle longer, waists a bit slimmer, breasts full or budding. In compliance with her recommendations, the suede-rubber faces were given a haughty look one year, a palsy-walsy one the next, or perhaps a dewily-innocent expression—or even an intellectual one.

In her early days with the company, such expressions were molded into the suede-rubber. Later, as Harry Chernik's inventiveness bore fruit, they came to depend on the tensions of tiny systems of wires rooted in the suede-rubber, or the inflation and deflation of balloon-like cavities in the cheeks. Expressions became living instead of fixed; variety and a greater degree of naturalness were achieved. Frequently she, and Mr. Jones, and Harry would analyze motion-picture close-ups of glamorous actresses, breaking down a sultry or outraged expression into all its split-second stages; then Harry would go off to cut a miraculous new cam. Sometimes, when they couldn't get just what was wanted, Rita herself would emote for Harry; he would watch carefully, and the resultant cam would be even more of a masterpiece.

Frequently Rita's styling assignments involved individualizing a femmequin: that is, making it a duplicate of some famous screen or TV star, or of a popular advertising model or society girl. In this case, she would have to do a little research to get the exact measurements and characteristic attitudes and gestures. It would also be necessary to run through a great deal of recorded vocal material from radio broadcasts and the like by the desired star, in order to piece together—from sentences, phrases and even single-words—the saucy and tender utterances to be impressed on the magnetic wires in the femmequin's voice box. But Rita was a good mimic; she often used her own voice in difficult cases, even when the needed material might have been otherwise obtained.

Of course such individualizing upped the price of a femmequin considerably, but that was all right with Mr. Bissel.

On rare occasions, a customer might ask for a copy of some girl not in the public eye. In this case, it would be necessary for Rita to contact the girl—frequently by posing as the representative of a fashion house that wanted to popularize its products by giving them away to selected individuals. Then she got the necessary data by means of tiny hidden cameras and recorders, and by her amazing memory for female mannerisms and behavior.

Mr. Bissel was uneasy about accepting orders of this sort, ever since one had almost involved him in a murder case. The customer had asked for a duplicate of an obscure strip-tease dancer. Some weeks later, the newspapers were screaming about the murder of a very wealthy relative of this same dancer. The girl was under suspicion, since she inherited a fortune, but she had an unbreakable alibi; she had been performing at the burlesque bar at the crucial time. Mr. Bissel was convinced that the girl herself had ordered the femmequin, and used it to perform her act; but there was nothing he could do about it—especially as his business was much more profitable than blackmail. Afterwards, similar orders always worried Bissel, but he could hardly refuse them; they brought the most money of all.

* * *

The reason the duplicate would have been able to put on a convincing strip act was that this was an accomplishment of all the femmequins. Harry Chernik's cams for this were wonders of intricacy, and Rita Bruhl worked with him closely in styling the clothing of the femmequins—the more expensive came with elaborate trousseaus, like costly dolls—just as she styled every other particular of their equipment and behavior.

And like Harry Chernik, Rita derived intense secret satisfaction from her work—giving herself to many men in many guises, without the unpleasantness of physical, or the responsibility of emotional contact. High priestess of the cult of her own beauty, she was preoccupied with the preliminary stages of sexual attraction. The later stages were quite repulsive to her.

Naturally, her work permitted Rita to satisfy completely her obsession with nubile female beauty; it was as if she ran a charm school with the added incalculable privilege of creating her pupils from the toes up. But she always put something wholly of herself into her creations—some phrase or gesture or expression that was hers alone. It was for this reason that she so often impressed her own voice on the wires and that she so frequently modeled emotions and postures for Harry Chernik. And she felt a stab of shivery excitement whenever a femmequin was shipped off in its coffin. Coffins were really used for shipping femmequins. It permitted the shipment to be accompanied by a personal representative of the firm, militating against detection. Also, modern coffins, with their rosily quilted interiors, were appropriate and pleasantly expensive jewel-cases for the robot girls.

The little signatures that Rita inscribed on the femmequins were not always unmalicious. She frequently had interviews with men ordering femmequins and during these interviews (when she always behaved with the impersonality of a lawyer or architect) she was able to spot the chinks in the armor around the client's ego—the things that would be most apt to shake his self-confidence. Then, if anything about the client annoyed her (and it generally did), she would insert into the femmequin's voice wires some seemingly innocuous remarks calculated to give the client a bad moment or two. But she was careful never to carry this practice so far that complaints came back to Mr. Bissel; in fact, it probably added to the life-likeness and success of the femmequins.

Also, like Harry Chernik, Rita Bruhl had her private reasons for finding her life's satisfactions in a peculiar occupation, and they were concerned with the same man—John Gottschalk, and the same woman—his wife Louise. John had been one of the very few men, almost the only one, with whom Rita had contemplated falling in love. She sensed in him enough hidden weaknesses, especially a great need to be admired. Rita had definitely decided to say "Yes"—eventually—when he would begin asking her to marry him.

It therefore came to her as a tremendous shock when John shifted his attention to an insignificant, merely pretty girl like Louise and then, monstrously, went on to propose. She could only conceive that he had done it to be revenged on her, because she had not instantly thrown herself into his arms.

The passing years brought no obvious change to Rita. At forty-five her beauty seemed as fresh and unwrinkled as at twenty-five. She became a trifle slimmer—that was the only difference. It was almost as if she herself were one of her metal protégées, immune to age. Occasionally even Mr. Bissel sensed this and almost shuddered—though oddly enough, John, smiling at her across the luncheon table, never seemed to notice.

But there was change in Rita. Deep inside the perpetual youth of her maidenhood, a worm gnawed. And it was the worm that shaped her words and licked her lips as she patted Harry Chernik's trembling shoulder, down by the work-rack and said, "Don't worry so, Harry dear. You've put all sorts of other special features into femmequins. This one you're working on has seven fingers on each hand, hasn't she? And that one there in the coffin is over six feet tall. So why not one with stronger motors and cables, and with a specially armed gadget, and with only my voice on its wires? Come on, Harry."

But Harry pulled away from her reluctantly, until he was half in the shadows. "I can't do it, Rita," he mumbled. "If Mr. Bissel ever found out I had broken the safety rules…"

"He won't find out, I'll take care of that," Rita assured him.

"And what is this… arming, you call it, for the central gadget?"

"I'll tell you when the time comes to install it."

"But if something should happen to the customer..." Chernik whined desperately.

Rita laughed. "I don't think you'd mind having anything happen to this customer, Harry," she told him. "You see, Femmequin 973 is for John Gottschalk."

John Gottschalk's secret was that he was afraid of women, far more so than Harry Chernik. That was why he married Louise; he could be certain she would never desert him or taunt him in any fashion. She would be an unfailing refuge to which he could return...

For of course there were other women, but his ego became more insecure with each new conquest—he had that much more to lose.

He continued to be a thoughtful husband to Louise, within reasonable limits. It did not occur to him that, as regards himself, anyone could object to reasonable limits and demand everything.

With Rita Bruhl he maintained a luncheon-relationship, nothing more. She showed toward him a dispassionate yet untiring interest deeper, it sometimes seemed, even than love.

John always laughed appreciatively at the bits of information Rita let slip about her unusual job. Gradually he inferred the true nature of Mr. Bissel's femmequins and maintained an attitude of slightly contemptuous interest. Though when Rita told him about Harry Chernik's employment in the same business and about Harry's increasing eccentricity and withdrawal, John would merely smile and shrug.

With the passage of years, John Gottschalk's curiosity about Mr. Bissel's femmequins became by imperceptible degrees more marked. Inevitably so, since John's nervous single-mindedness in his affairs made him look more and more on mental and emotional qualities as merely troublesome.

So it happened that John and Rita began to talk jokingly about what qualities he would like in a femmequin.

When he finally did come to place the order, he felt a sudden twinge of uneasiness, but this was dispelled by Rita's impersonal but approving manner—like a Jeeves when his master has decided to order just the proper wardrobe.

And so, since Harry Chernik was a faithful and inspired workman, since Rita Bruhl was a stern and much-interested task-mistress—and since Mr. Bissel was not an overly-inquisitive boss, the femmequin for John Gottschalk got delivered in its canvas-covered coffin.

But John was out. It was his wife Louise who timidly opened the door and showed the two delivery men to John's bedroom. The delivery man, who was Mr. Bissel's representative, never for a moment thought that Louise was Mr. Gottschalk's wife; her manner and her clothes convinced him that she was a servant. He even had his assistant strip the canvas from the coffin, and he smiled knowingly at Louise as he departed.

Afterwards, Louise went back to the bedroom and sat looking at the coffin.

Louise Gottschalk had never thought of herself as an attractive woman and could never understand why John had chosen her; she adored him, made a god of him, and found that the hallmark of a god is that he demands sacrifices. John's affairs sharpened her sense of inadequacy.

And now she sat looking at the strange box shaped so much like a coffin. She wondered if John had taken up an interest in statuary or model spaceships. After looking at the box for a long while, she touched its side.

It opened at once.

A slim, beautiful woman whom Louise knew sat up stiffly and looked at her. The woman was dressed delectably from the male viewpoint, plunging neckline and all.

"Miss Bruhl... Rita," Louise said astoundedly, edging back.

"My little timid one, my frightened darling," Femmequin 973 exclaimed, suddenly standing up in the coffin. "You see, I know you are frightened, for I know you're afraid of all women, and of me especially."

Louise shrank away. "Please, Rita, please don't be silly," she croaked faintly.

Femmequin 973 leaned forward, so that the plunging neckline plunged farther. "Don't run, darling. I know you're very surprised and very frightened, but you can't get away from me now." The femmequin suddenly jumped out of the coffin and slowly advanced.

Louise tried to shrink away farther, but the wall was at her back. "Rita, Rita, this is terrible," she gasped.

The slim hands of Femmequin 973 went to its waist and the plunging neckline plunged. "Look at me," she commanded. "I'm very beautiful, aren't I, and even more frightening. I'm afraid this is going to scare you very much; and it's going to hurt you, too." And the arms of Femmequin 973 stretched out and suddenly clasped tight around Louise.

Then Louise finally screamed and fought and shouted, "Stop, Rita, stop!" but Femmequin 973 did not stop. It clasped and loosed and clasped again, for what seemed to be hours of torture, all the while murmuring in Louise's ear. Finally, clutching her tighter yet, Femmequin 973 drew back its exquisite triumphant face and said, "This is what scares you the most, isn't it? This is what you're afraid women will do to you, you..."

Fainting in the steel and suede-rubber embrace, Louise hardly heard the faint clashing and grinding sound, as Femmequin 973 breathed, "... you eunuch."

NIGHT PASSAGE

THE LARGE GOLD COIN RANG AND SETTLED ON THE green felt where the newly arriving young lady crying out "Eight!" had pitched it and the ivory marble clicked against the diamond-shaped silvery point in the darkly gleaming mahogany bowl while a voice called, "No more bets. Game closed." The golden coin's worn face faintly revealed to my glance a circle that was horned and had a pendant cross. Then the ivory ball clattered into a slowly revolving metal square.

"Eight. Black," the croupier called and the banker's large, meaty, well-manicured white hand with wiry black hairs sprouting from its back closed on the coin and lifted it off the eight square.

"That bet came too late. Sorry," he said and tossed it back.

The young lady did not pick it up, but stared across the table at the house.

The banker and the croupier stared back—and the pit boss too, come up opportunely behind them.

For a moment they made an arresting tableau of challenge. The young lady very slender and standing tall, dark hair piled high, profile neat as one on a coin, wearing a thin, thigh-length cotton dress (snug but not tight around the narrow waist) of black and carnation red, both colors harmoniously faded. The three men oldish young, gone beefy around the necks like tomcats, leaning a little toward her aggressively. All three in evening dress with the blank, stupid faces of athletes and ward politicians, but with a diamond glint deep in their eyes.

Beside me, the thin old man who looked like a bad-tempered

high school physics teacher volunteered, "I heard the ball click out before the bet landed. It was too late."

The banker started a smile, then changed it tentatively to a frown as I said, "I heard it the other way. First the bet landed. Then the ball clicked out."

Immediately two ladies across the table, who looked the sort who are always eager to back up authority, said together, "No, the bet was too late. We were watching," and three other players nodded.

The banker's smile blossomed after all. "Sorry," he repeated.

The young lady snatched up her coin, turned her back, and walked away swiftly.

I had won a small wager split between eight and eleven. I cashed in my violet roulette chips and shoved the general house chips I got in return into the right-hand side pocket of my jacket, which I needed—the air conditioning made the Zodiac's casino almost frigid despite the moderate crowd and the furious Mojave heat outside; early that morning I'd opened my bedroom door, which faced the east and let onto an outside balcony, and the radiance of the new risen sun had been like a physical blow—as if it had been trying to knock me over with one sneaky shot.

I asked the old man beside me (he seemed sharp eyed at least), "Did you notice what kind of coin that was she bet?"

"That was no coin," he told me as if I were one of his poorer students. "That was a yellow ten-dollar chip."

I wandered up and down the luxurious aisles, wondering whether to have a go at blackjack, or rest a bit while making a few keno bets, or even more sensibly take a long nap before my night-long drive. I glanced at my wrist, but I'd left my watch in my room. I started to look around before I remembered that there are no clocks in Vegas, at least anywhere in the casinos.

They keep it a timeless place so one won't be reminded of appointments that should be kept, whether for business or food or sleep or work or love, and so be tempted to cut short a winning streak before it turns into a losing one, or the latter ever, but I like to fancy it makes time travel possible—enter the timeless world from anywhen and later exit at any time future or past one chooses.

Off in a shadowy corner I saw a slender patch of harmoniously faded black and carnation red. They'd put a small bar there. I eased myself onto the stool beside her and ordered a scotch and water.

She turned dark eyes on me. "Thank you for your support," she said and smiled.

"It didn't help," I reminded her with a shrug. "Tell me, isn't a horned circle with a cross below—a horned ankh, one could almost say—a sign of Mercury?"

"I think so," she replied, wrinkling her neat, straight, rather short nose a little as the dark eyes studied me. "But that's not so strange. We're on the edge of Astrological Territory." She said it with capitals just like that, as one would say Western Reserve or Hopi Reservation... or Eldorado."

"Right in the middle of the Zodiac," I agreed. "I thought of the planet Mercury this morning when the sun looked in my bedroom door as I opened it and almost floored me—how the people on Mercury must live in capsules of chilliness to make the heat endurable."

"Yes, the sun's glance can be deadly, his diamond eye," she said oddly. "So you're not surprised at the idea of planet people?"

"I can't afford to be," I told her. "I write science fiction stories for a living."

"And you think the Zodiac Hotel is like a Mercurian capsule, only bigger?"

"Exactly. Aren't you chilly?" I asked, looking down at her thin dress. Although it was completely opaque, she seemed to be wearing little under it.

She picked up the pony of brandy in front of her and drained it, the tip of her tongue slipping out to capture the last drop.

"Not after that," she said.

There was nothing else in front of her on the bar and she wasn't carrying a purse. In fact, she was clean from her small flat ears fully revealed by her unswept, high-piled hair to her toes looking out of the ends of her flimsy shoes through finely textured dark stockings. I wondered where she kept the gold piece.

"Would you have dinner with me?" I asked.

"I'm sorry," she said pleasantly, "but I'm driving south tonight soon as I take a nap."

"That's a coincidence," I said. "So am I too, as far as Lordsburg. Perhaps we could combine—"

Her dark eyes (they were blue) which had been smiling at mine looked past me and grew serious. I looked around.

The pit boss from the roulette table was looking serious too in his beefy way. I thought he was going to speak to her, but instead he took a small green notebook out of his pocket and handed it to me.

"You left it at the table," he told me.

It was mine, all right, though I'd have sworn I hadn't taken it out of my left-hand jacket pocket. "Thanks," I said.

"No trouble," he assured me and walked on. It occurred to me it might have been lifted off me—God knows why, maybe to check on my antecedents. In that case they'd found nothing suspicious except the behavior of two Martians when confronted by an emissary from Galaxy Center. The notebook was for story notes as they occurred to me.

I looked back. The young lady was gone, nowhere in sight, but by the pony glass was a curled-up green bill.

"That was funny," the bartender observed to me as he spread it open. It was a two. "She had it in her hair."

Oh well, not everyone wants to know you better, I philosophized grumpily, but why does it always have to be svelte, long-limbed young ladies with gold pieces tucked away in their high-piled dark hair?

I went and put my wristwatch on and had my nap. When I woke it was fully dark outside, but still oven hot and my car had no refrigeration—one of the reasons that I drove at night. I dressed in brown cotton pyjamas that almost looked like slacks and shirt, but were a lot cooler, then checked out. Dunkirk (my little Datsun station wagon) was like a furnace. I opened her up and gave her a chance to get less hot before I got in.

Over the parking lot, despite the upward glare of the casinos along the Strip, the desert night showed some bright stars: the triangle of Vega, Deneb, and Altair, and to the south red Mars in Sagittarius. Vega from Vegas? The asphalt under my feet was baking hot.

On a slightly higher section of the parking lot near its exit, beyond an intervening row of cars, light spilling sideways from the Zodiac showed two white roadsters with tops down parked next to each other. Beside one was a slender figure with head held as if in thought or meditation. Even at the distance there was no mistaking that profile and she was still wearing the harmoniously faded red and black cotton dress.

As I considered strolling over, she quickly scurried around to the other white roadster and got behind the wheel and then just before driving out she seemed to look straight at me and she lifted her hand and waved twice, rather solemnly.

Perhaps, I thought, my spirits rising, we'd meet somewhere along the lonely way. I got in Dunkirk (the seat was still hot) and started her and let her run quietly while I checked that my maps and flash and tissue were on the dashboard, my pocketbook, notebook, and pens in my pyjama pockets, Dunkirk's tank full, her hot oil coursing, and her lights all working.

We took off softly. Just before the exit I glanced at the open white roadster with the empty space beside it. From a point near the center of the white hood—from the car's heart, you might say—a single intense highlight reflected by God knows what or from what source, dazzled my eyes so that I flinched them away. It made me wonder, but I didn't try to look back—and wouldn't have even if I'd wanted to, because where was an empty spot coming in the traffic ahead that I wanted to catch, and did.

A quarter mile farther on I heard fire sirens behind me. Looking quickly back, I saw a shaft of intense white flame shooting up from somewhere close to the Zodiac. I wondered if there could have been a connection and if it were the white roadster burning. No, I told myself, the highlight and the shaft of flame could have had no relation.

Just the same, a black spot was still dancing in front of my eyes. That highlight had been *bright*

I soon turned out of the traffic streaming toward California and Los Angeles once the narrower, emptier route leading to Boulder Dam and Arizona. The night stayed hot. At Boulder City I checked Dunkirk's tires, letting out some air. I also checked the oil and water, filled my plastic two-gallon bottle of the latter, and topped off the gas tank.

I kept a sort of watch (not a very serious one, I told myself) for a white roadster and on a straight stretch just beyond Boulder City I thought I glimpsed one disappearing around the far bend, its red tail lights winking. I speeded up, but when I came to the next straight stretch, a much longer one, there wasn't any car ahead at all, though I thought I saw a car, maybe a white one, sneaking away from the highway down a wooded sideroad.

Well, if that were she, I told myself, she hadn't been driving very far south.

Boulder Dam, when I got to it, was magnificent in a monstrous way. The highway went across the top of it, from Nevada into Arizona, but it was so wide and very brightly lit that one could see little of its surrounds and nothing of the Colorado River. There was also much heavy mesh wire fencing. The smell of security was very strong, so that one got the feeling it had been built not for Herbert but for Edgar Hoover. There were several great squat chunky towers, like banks or forts—in fact, to me with my peculiar imagination, it had the feeling of a fortress on Jupiter, built for a heavier gravity than ours. It had a Jovian look, or a Vulcanian.

The shouldering crags at either end were correspondingly hulking, and on them were short, burly, immensely strong-looking openwork towers of steel beams bearing on their huge insulators the thick heavy copper wires that carried off the power the dam generated.

This is electricity's heartland, I told myself, a castle of the lightning. From here the stuff goes out to the great military and space establishments and to the myriad industrial complexes and to the multi-million lights of the Vegas Strip challenging the stars. It somehow made my liberal heart feel lonely and oppressed. Dunkirk the Datsun seemed to feel it too—a little Japanese bowing nervously to giants as she scurried past them.

On the other side it got rapidly darker and the empty road led steadily down and the night got better still. I reminded myself that the county containing this corner of Arizona is called Mojave—I checked it by my map. On my right were Black Canyon and the Eldorado Mountains, on my left the Cerbats with Mount Wilson and Squaw Peak—but you can't see such things in the dark from a car with a top.

The shoulders of the road widened for a little settlement. I slowed down and then pulled up across from a small old cafe that was still open. Better get a little to eat, I told myself, it was a long empty stretch ahead. And some coffee, too, despite the heat.

I got out. The stars crusted the desert night so luxuriously that one almost forgot they marched in unalterable order. Deneb, Altair, and Mars were merely brighter points in the great, eddying river of the Milky Way. Only Vega was still somewhat lonely.

There was a counter with two Indian women behind it. The older, who looked toothless, cooked. The younger (but not that young) was very stolid and taciturn in dark shapeless clothes. I told her coffee and a beef enchilada. She went back and leaned by the older woman. Whatever culture they belonged to, it was apart.

The screen door creaked and a modern cowboy (I took him to be) walked in stiffly. His blue Levi's were caked with whitish dust. So was his wide-brimmed black hat, which he didn't remove. So were his sunken cheeks. And he was very bowlegged. He wearily settled down and ordered tacos. He looked every bit as authentic as the Indian women.

Our food came. The coffee was strong and bitter. My enchilada tasted all right but was too heavy, while orange grease dripped from the end of the cowboy's huge taco, which he munched steadily. I made some notes in my little green book.

I heard another car draw up across the road, but no one came in.

I finished my coffee and some of my enchilada, paid (including a tip), and went out. As I passed the cowboy, he said to the Indian woman and the cafe in general with the solemnity of William S. Hart, "That was the best taco I ever ate, and I've eaten many a taco."

The white roadster was parked off the road on the wide shoulder, but *she* was standing close beside Dunkirk, looking toward me quite gravely. But as I crossed the highway she started to smile, and when I got to her, she said, "You were saying, 'Perhaps we could combine—' and I'm accepting your offer."

I *had* to chuckle. I had been saying exactly that... some six hours ago.

"My car konked out," she explained quickly. "A vapor block. I'm leaving it here—I can send back for it tomorrow. But I must get south tonight."

"Where are you going?" I asked.

"To Gila Peak beyond the Superstition Mountains. That's just beyond Globe and the San Carlos Indian Reservation south of the Apache. I'll get out at Geronimo." She added anxiously, "You are going to Lordsburg by that route?"

"I can," I temporized. (National Interstate 10 through Tucson might be quicker.) It had just occurred to me that this all fitted a classic hitch-hike situation—the girl the bait. You agreed to give her a lift, then the boys appeared, bent on... who knows what?

But I had met her in Vegas at the Zodiac. Besides... I was very aware of her dark, very slender height so near to me, of her slim fingers...

"Of course I can," I said with a smile. "Get in."

She gave me a smile in return and obeyed me quickly, walking around Dunkirk.

"Hey, wait a minute, what about your car?" I asked, ducking my head and looking at her through the driver's window.

"It's locked, it'll be all right," she assured me with another smile from where she was already sitting neatly and decorously in the shadowy interior. "Come on, let's drive."

I opened the door and started to get in. "But where's your luggage?" I asked.

"Locked in the trunk. I've got everything I need. Get in." Her eyes were dark pools, her smile was sure, but her voice was anxious.

I had a last try as I complied. "You're sure you wouldn't like some coffee? We could—"

"No, that's why I waited outside. Let's drive."

I toed the starter and nosed Dunkirk out. At least no guys had appeared. As I shifted to second, my hand on the short stick between our feet, I glanced toward her white roadster sliding past and saw in the heart of the hood that same damn dazzling diamond headlight I had seen in Vegas.

Her fingers touched my forearm briefly but peremptorily. She said, *"Keep driving."*

For a moment I had no intention of doing anything else. The black spot was dancing in front of my eyes again, worse than the first time, and I was busy shifting up. Then I started to look back but—

"That gold coin I bet was a genuine Mercurian double eagle," she said rapidly. "I was surprised you spotted it."

She almost took my mind completely off whatever it was that was happening behind. Besides, there was a curve coming up ahead and from beyond it there were the lights of an approaching car. But then I caught a white flash in the rearview mirror.

"I'm a Mercurian, you see, Mercury person," she went on desperately, "and I play a special game with some Jovian dealers there—Jupiter people. But today—"

But despite that and her slender, wiry fingers touching me again, I did manage to look back very briefly, as we went around the curve and see—

It was almost my last look too, for the curve was sharper than I'd anticipated and I'd let Dunkirk drift toward the center of the two-lane highway and the approaching car came around the curve very fast and in *my* lane, so it was only by dodging very sharply over into *his* lane and passing him on the wrong side that I missed him—and even at that there was a great *whoosh* of squeezed air and Dunkirk shook at the nearness of his passage. If I'd done the automatic thing and tried to dodge him by getting back into my lane and out onto my shoulder—ugh!

I was "real shook" myself, needless to say, and for a bit I was very busy getting Dunkirk straightened out and back where she belonged and making sure there weren't any more bats coming out of hell. Then I started to slow down, but—

"Zowie! that was close," my passenger said with girlish excitement, not to say enthusiasm. "Wow! but he'll sure be mad. Better not stop."

She touched two of my weak spots there: my tendency always to blame myself first for anything and my dread of getting into any sort of strident and wearisome confrontation (perhaps the two are related). Besides, by now what I'd seen (or thought I'd seen) in that one glimpse back was all mixed up with those blinding headlights hurtling at me from ambush and the way Dunkirk had rocked. It took me time to get them sorted out. And while I did that I continued to drive on.

What I believed I'd seen (and it was very clear-etched when I got it) was a pillar of bright white flame going straight up from the roadside across from the Indian cafe and standing in the middle of the road, staring at it and silhouetted by its glare, my taco-stuffed cowboy. He was quite tiny with distance, but the hat, bent back, and bow legs were unmistakable—almost too good.

I drove on for a while, thinking about it and wondering how much if not all of her wild story had been impromptu diversion and how much of it one of those strange bags someone is always opening up for you in these changing days of flamboyant individuality—and giving her a chance to continue her wild story, only she didn't, but stayed strangely (in view of its hysterically swift opening) or perhaps strategically silent. But all the while I was feeling this deep-down thankfulness that I was getting farther away every second from possible trouble and that there were no cars chasing me and that things were smoothing out quietly, just as I always like it.

Meanwhile the heat became really quite astonishing. I found I had to keep Dunkirk down to forty miles an hour, or else the temperature pointer on the dash would lean dangerously toward the red. Soon I was driving by the feel on my face of the air pouring in the side window. If it cooled a bit, Dunkirk would spring ahead. If there were a warm wash, Dunkirk would lag.

Finally on one of the latter occasions I let her keep lagging until she stopped and I looked around at my young mystery lady, sitting beside me like a bundle of gleaming slim shadows and I demanded, "Now just what is all this nonsense about planet people and gold coins brought here from the planet Mercury?"

"Oh, they're not imported from Mercury," she protested. "That *would* be ridiculous. No, they're struck here from gold mined here or made here by the old prenuclear alchemy for local use by Mercury people temporarily in residence here, mostly for gambling with other planet people, but for ritual and diplomatic purposes too."

"Oh, really!" I said, unable to keep back a little laugh. "You don't expect me to believe that all you planet people shift around here among us Earth folk, even gambling against each other, and conducting all sorts of interplanetary intrigues..."

"Yes, that is exactly what I expect you to believe," she countered. "The different worlds aren't nearly so separated, at least in Arizona, as you seem to imagine. As I told you, this is Astrological Territory. They all drift here, star folk and planet people."

"... and even waging interplanetary wars," I continued, "or at least serious skirmishes *in which you burn each other's cars?*"

"We *never* burn cars, we Mercury people!" she denied vehemently. "It's only the barbarous Solarians who do that—" She broke off and looked at me reproachfully. "You tricked me into saying that," she said, "but perhaps that is because I never thanked you properly for standing up for me at the roulette table," and she advanced her hand along the curve of my jaw on either side until her fingers touched my ears and she drew my face to hers and kissed me rather briefly but emphatically and then she then sat back and said, "There. Drive on."

I obeyed thoughtfully. That kiss had tingled like electricity and as for her fingers—well, fingers are really the most amazing erotic tools, except that they have so many other uses that their sexual one is somewhat overshadowed.

When I did speak again, it was to tell her my impressions of Hoover, or Boulder Dam.

"You really are quite intuitive," she said with interest, almost with respect. "Hoover Dam actually was designed and built under the influence of Jovians. Jupiter men had most of the Vegas casinos in those days and for a long while afterwards. That was when I got hooked on roulette. The Jupiter men were sort of rough, of course, but in a nice and genial—I might say jovial—way, like good bears. But the last year or so the Solarians started moving in and taking over—"

"Solarians—that would be Sun people, wouldn't it?" I interrupted. "Now, really, how can you have people at a temperature of millions of degrees?"

"Some people can be awfully tough," she assured me, "as if they were made of nothing but asbestos. That's the Sun men for you—very macho and rough (You saw them!) but in a mean and nasty way, like bad bears. Each of them carries in his asbestos heart a tiny spark of killing nuclear fire, which puts the diamond glint into their eyes and which their eyes, like two burning glasses, can focus on things and make them white hot—if they concentrate."

"In New York City they call it a double whammy, I believe," I commented.

"Well, if you're going to joke..." she murmured huffily and leaned back and looked straight ahead.

Really it was a strange mood I was getting into, though not unpleasant, listening to her wacky fairy tales and letting my own mind drift between the real and the unreal. On the black road ahead there appeared a wavy white line that wriggled like a snake as it went under Dunkirk's hood. It ended in a white arrowhead that pointed at a rectangle of road that had been filled in with gravel but not yet resurfaced, which, now forewarned, I dodged around. It occurred to me that a timeless mind had invented that warning.

After a while there was another white snake and then more kept coming and suddenly there was a detour sign which in this case did not mean a change of road but only that for a stretch it became one of unsurfaced, wicked-looking gravel that forced cars to go very slow. I got the impression that a whole people (men, women, and children) had toiled for centuries to find all the pointiest (though well worn) little rocks, all the tetrahedrons, and pack them carefully, point up, like caltrops of stone, to hurt the hoofs of unshod horses and barefoot poets and pop the tires of speeding cars.

I had to go so slowly that I could try to make out the inky

horizon in the torrid night, the Black Mountains on her side, the Cerbats still on mine, guessing at hills and gaps, drawing reflexively back from breaths of hotter wind. But it was hard to tell whether the lowest stars were stars at all or the lights of low castles topping invisible crags. Everywhere I could sense the working of that timeless mind, that ancient culture. I began to feel that the Indians still secretly ruled Arizona, patiently tolerating the ephemeral White Man, catering to his crazy cars and other childish whims, and succoring dusty cowboys.

I even entertained the fancy that my young mystery lady with her high-piled dark hair, sitting in her gloomy corner of the front seat, was one of them. It was decades of blinding sun and dry winds that had made her so slim and shadowy, such a wraith.

I told her all that I'd been fancying.

"You're being quite intuitive again," she said still somewhat grumpily (at first) but with a certain respect. "Ancienter peoples *are* in charge down here, most secretly, only they came here (from up there) a long time before the Indians. They were drawn to Arizona because it's always had a lot of magic in it, especially at night under the moon, as you could see for yourself if the moon weren't new. They all revered *(pace* the Solarians!) the Moon Goddess. They had their little differences, of course, their little feuds, but settled them all by high diplomacy, codes of civilized behavior as old as the stars. And when the Indians came wandering down at last from the far north, the planet people got along fine with them and they had hardly any more difficulty adapting themselves to the White Man, gold-crazy Latinos from the south full of pot and loco weed and drunken Anglos from the east and west.

"But then those brutal, vicious Sun men began to turn up with their diamond eyes, who burn cars and ignore the age-old usages of diplomacy and *hate* the Moon Goddess and us Mercury people especially because our planet is closest to their huge hairy home and we sneer at all their macho heat, safe in our cool, cool capsules."

"Is that how they spotted you at the Zodiac," I interjected, "when you flashed that Mercury gold piece."

"Of course," she said. "I thought they were three Jupiter men and we could play the old game we always do right under the eyes of you terrestrials. The Zodiac was supposed to be Jovian still, although most of the other casinos are Solarian now. In fact, there's a big interplanetary conference scheduled for the Zodiac day after tomorrow. I'm on the Mercurian delegation, but I'd gone up early to play roulette.

"But as soon as those three hulking bastards (whom I'd taken for Jovians) refused to honor my bet (you *know* it wasn't late!) and I saw the diamond glint in their eyes, I *knew* they were Solarians and that I'd have to get back south and warn my people before the whole conference was ambushed and wiped out (their obvious intention) but I also knew that they knew and would do their damnedest to stop me!"

"But if the Sun men have as little regard for rule as you say," I objected, "why didn't they kidnap you or (excuse me) rub you out while you were still at the Zodiac where they're top dogs?"

"Even the Sun men can't afford to do anything that openly inside the Zodiac with all you square around. Besides, they did try to burn me in my car (they're *great* at burning cars) right in the parking lot, only I fooled them into thinking my car was another that looked just like mine. And it worked. When I got outside the Vegas city limits I looked back and could see it burning."

"But why couldn't you have warned your people simply by telephone or special short-wave radio or something?" I asked.

"My God, you must think we are really stupid if you think we'd ever go around breaking cover like that," she fumed at me, subsiding. "Short-wave radio!"

"Or couldn't you just use telepathy?" I persisted, "—you being so astrological and occult and all?"

"For your information, the planet people do not happen to be telepathic," she informed me and lapsed into an offended silence, only shifting position from time to time to look behind us.

We went through Kingman, which seemed all asleep, and then east on National Interstate 40 for a bit, where we met some cars and were passed by a couple, and then south on U.S. 93 again for another lonely, long, quite straight flat stretch along the Sandy River between the Mualapai Mountains on her side and the Aquarius Mountains on mine. I mentioned the last to her.

"I told you we were in the heart of Astrological Territory," she said shortly.

The long, rather slight curves in the road were all marked with little round reflectors that were born like little yellow stars at the first touch of Dunkirk's headlights beam, or like tiny rockets born on their blasting pads that did not move at first, then slowly toward us, and then took off swiftly as we passed them by. I got my timeless-intelligence kick again and thought of worn fellahin fingers patiently teasing apart with cracked dry fingernails the sheets of yellowish mica to make the reflectors.

I saw a new star, as bright as Sirius, on the horizon ahead. Then it winked out. After quite a bit it flashed on again, somewhat brighter, then off again, then on again, brighter still, and came on steadily. I'd just decided (with some amazement) it was the headlight of an approaching motorcycle, when it divided into two and I realized it was the headlights of a car, but first seen so far away through the incredibly clear desert air that they merged into one. The first bright flash must have come when we were aimed exactly at each other from the tops of almost imperceptible hills many miles apart. That really seemed quite amazing to me, worth commenting on.

My sulking (or merely sleepy?) companion appeared to digest the information I gave her and then remarked in rather lofty tones (and somewhat repetitiously), "For your information, I have been observing the same phenomenon behind us. There appears to be a car hanging on there a few miles back." She subsided.

"And?" I said.

"Its merged headlights have a peculiar diamond glint, to my eye."

"And?" I persisted.

"The Solarians do not give up easily," she observed dispassionately.

"You think some people from the Zodiac are chasing us?" I asked.

She shrugged, somewhat elaborately.

A *diamond glint?*—I thought with a little shiver that surprised me. But the merged headlights of that approaching car I'd watched had been startlingly bright, too, and the same thing could work in the opposite direction, surely.

Nevertheless after a half minute or so, I speeded up. It was getting a bit less hot anyway and I no longer needed to hold Dunkirk down so much.

Twice more I saw horizon stars ahead that changed to cars.

My companion looked back from time to time, but didn't offer any information as to whether we'd shaken the car behind and I didn't ask her.

My science-fiction mind dredged up something that seemed worth repeating.

"If you were out on Pluto, the sun would be just a point of light like any other star, and yet it would be many, many times brighter than the whole full moon. A single point of light, but painfully intense. That sounds to me quite like your diamond glint."

"Um," she said in recognition of my speaking. If I'd scared anyone, it was myself. I lit a cigarette and offered her one and she took it. Lighting it off a match from a book of them she had tucked in her hair, she bent close to the dashboard and saw "Dunkirk" taped there. I told her it was the car's name and she asked me why.

I said, "Because I figure I can always depend on her to get me out of really desperate situations."

"You know, I'm relieved to hear that," she said shortly.

I saw her point. We both smoked quite a bit off and on after that, and didn't talk much. We both had, I think, that sense of shared monotony and watchfulness that comes with any long drive, but intensified here by the heat and the loneliness and the dark and whatever it was that hung behind us and we weren't talking about so much any more. Darting fantasy had given way to a sort of wakeful trance.

We passed through Wikieup, a sort of ghost place in the small hours, and then through Wickenburg, somewhat bigger, the Date Creek Mountains on my side now and the Vulture Mountains on hers. The last of Wickenburg's lights, industrial, showed me a forest of Joshua trees. The tall, twisted cactuses reminded me of something on a moon of Saturn and I told her so.

She said "Um" again and, after a bit, "The Saturnians are the oldest planet people. Very conservative. They're on our side."

Sometimes I was very conscious of her long slim youthfulness, but sometimes as she leaned back in the shadows I got the impression that she was ages old, desiccated by the centuries, the slender mummy of an ancient princess.

The desert gave way to scattered dark settlements and then I saw great openwork towers covered with colored lights.

"My God," I said, startled for a moment, "It almost looks as if we were back on the Vegas Strip again."

"No," she said, "they're cracking plants for petroleum, not casinos." (I'd realized that by then.) She added, "The planet people—Martians especially—had a lot to do with determining the form of both sets of structures."

"There's no accounting for tastes," I said, shaking my head. "Perhaps they're supposed to resemble space-to-space vehicles."

Soon we were into Phoenix, quiet a couple of hours or so

before the dawn. I stopped at a sleepy station to top off Dunkirk's
tank again, add water and a pint of oil, and get us two cups of
coffee apiece out of a machine (she vetoed breakfast and I didn't
argue). She drank her coffee thirstily, but seemed preoccupied
until we were rolling again. I studied my map.

When we were out in the desert countryside again, more
rolling now, heading east, I said cheerily, "The Superstition
Mountains and the Tonto National Forest should be coming up
soon on my side. Then Globe and the Indian Reservation and
Geronimo under your Gila Peak—all in an hour or so!"

"Yes," she agreed, somewhat dubiously, "in an hour or so."

I thought gaily, intoxicated by coffee, yes, she's a somber Indian
princess, all right, no pleasing her, and when she's mummified,
they'll lay her pet Gila monster, reddish and black to match her
little tunic, at her feet, mummified too.

But it was distinctly cooler now. She'd closed the window
on her side, and I cranked mine halfway up. Dunkirk became
sprightly and began to thumb her nose at Arizona's sixty-mile
speed limit. All night she'd been frightened and rather miserable,
her tires tender and her heart careful for itself in the heat, a
lonely Japanese in an arid, gritty land most unlike her moist
and mountainous Honshu, ducking away from rocky phantoms,
watching for poisonous snakes and dry furry big spiders (and gila
monsters). But here with wooded hills to the north at least and
now that it was cooler she could imagine she was home in Japan
and foot it lightly.

I found myself feeling livelier too (although underneath there
was a great weariness) and taking a livelier and more detailed
interest in my companion. She had high cheekbones and, under
her short straight nose, a rather wide, very mobile mouth. The
upper lip was a bit fuller than the lower. I remembered the
electricity of that single emphatic kiss. Her hands were narrow
with long restless fingers and thumb that narrowed at their tips.
She had a way of playing with her cigarette close by her face, as
if it were a tiny baton orchestrating her thoughts, and sometimes
she held it almost alarmingly close to her high-piled dark hair.

She was becoming livelier (or uneasier?) herself. She'd look
ahead, then back, then off to the side, then light another cigarette
(I had two packs on the dash), never at rest. But she didn't seem
to want to talk.

Dunkirk was climbing now. Globe was faintly astir as we

ghosted through, although even astronomical twilight seemed hardly to have begun. And now the way was down and Dunkirk fairly leaped and then the way got straighter and more deserty again as we traversed the Indian Reservation.

I was running out of time with her, I knew, and now I felt impelled to make a move.

"Do you realize," I said, really struck by it, "that we haven't told each other our names?"

She'd been looking back. "I'm sorry," she said, twisting around, her eyes wide with excitement or fear, or both, "but now I'm sure of it—it must be them. They've been behind us again ever since Globe and now they're closing in."

"Who are?" I asked. Then after a moment, "Those Sun men?"

In my more immediate interest in her I'd actually almost forgotten that game we'd played. I suddenly felt very furious with her and had a shockingly strong impulse to grab that flimsy dress at the neck and—

"Yes, the Solarians, who else?" she said sharply. "What's more, I'm certain they've put a mental tail on us, so that we've got to blank our minds or think of something different to mislead them—anything except about them!"

"A *mental* tail?" I exploded. "Those dumb macho Sun men with asbestos brains? Besides, you told me none of the planet people are telepathic."

"The Solarians are star folk, not planet people," she countered angrily. "And all star folk are highly telepathic. Or didn't they teach you in third grade the Sun's a star? Now listen to me closely, dumbbell, I know this territory like I know my crotch, and we've got only one chance now to stay alive, or at most two. Behind each of the next two rises a side road goes off sharply to the left. You whip around the first one and douse your lights and stop, quick as you can start thinking for all you're worth of something very different—I'll tell you what."

During the last part of that she had been lighting a cigarette with very nervous fingers. She took a deep, furious drag now and started to cough. Then I was yelling, "Like hell I will!" and we were going over the rise and she was yelling "Turn here!" between coughs and I wasn't turning and then suddenly there was a bright white flash, a needle of very intense white light lancing through Dunkirk's rear window and I smelled the stink of something burning and then I was steering with my left hand while I clamped the palm of my right to the side of her head to put out the fire in her hair there—a ghostly blue flame traveling swiftly upward.

Somehow that put a different complexion on the whole business and incidentally scared me half to death. I managed to get the fire out (my palm stung, but I hardly noticed) and keep the car on the road and even to speed up. And when we topped the next rise I braked sharply and followed her first orders exactly, and no mistakes. She needn't have shouted, "Then turn *here*, dumbbell!" The side road was there, all right, just as she'd said, and I was down it and Dunkirk's lights were out and she was stopped— and *she* was in my arms and pressed against me and her lips were giving those electric kisses (the shock is greater when there's moisture, as you'd expect) and her fingers were busy with me and mine with her—one of my hands was near the neck of her dress, but it wasn't tearing it—and I had realized what the "something different" thing was we were to think about exclusively.

There is really something very special about fingers, they're so deft and clever, they *know* so much more than any other parts of the body, even the lips and tongue. And there is also something very special about skin felt through thin clothing, even two layers of it, say cotton and fine silk. The three textures move against each other most interestingly. Together they provide a very special sort of enjoyment that can go on and on. It is an argument for bundling, when you think about it.

After quite a long while (the sky was pale, the stars were gone except for Sirius) she murmured softly, "You know, my dear, we *know* we can't have been thinking about anything else, either of us, or they'd have come back and got us."

It occurred to me that I hadn't once even seen the Solarian car. I started to tell her so, but she put her lips down on mine and turned on the electricity again, gently at first.

When I woke again, it was because a bright red ray of sun was poking me in the eye just as it had yesterday morning, and just like then, only worse. I felt I was being shot at. Were Sun men out by day, like their star was? I turned to ask her that, but she was gone.

Well, there's not much to tell after that. I didn't find her then and I haven't found her since, my slim Mercurian. She's gone completely back into Astrological Territory, I guess. Did the Solarians actually set her hair afire, or was it her cigarette? I really have no way of knowing. While cars burn up on our highways every day.

Anyhow, I was still about seventy-five miles from Lordsburg and very tired and all hot again and somehow very uneasy about that sun up there, getting higher and hotter every minute.

So after a bit I headed towards Lordsburg, fast as I dared. Dunkirk met a surprising number of light Datsun trucks used by the farmers thereabouts and wanted to linger and gossip with them about Japan, but I wouldn't let her. That sun was really bothering me and making me nervous, I wanted to get entirely away from it and the heat, and sleep.

I stopped at the first refrigerated motel I spotted at Lordsburg— they call them that instead of air conditioned to distinguish them from the old breeze-and-hanging-wet-blanket type. The manager gave my pyjamas an odd look, but let me register, paying in advance—maybe he figured they proved I just wanted to sleep.

The shades were drawn in my cabin, the lights off, and the refrigeration on. I didn't change any of those—it was so great to get out of the sun and heat. I made my way through the gloom to the bathroom and there I did need light—it was just too dark. So I flicked the switch.

No light came on, but *heat* struck the top of my head and the back of my neck. I got the damnedest, eeriest, most frightened feeling that the sun had come inside after me and I'd never be able to get away from him. She'd said the Sun men were very persistent. And now there began to come a dark, reddish glow.

I glanced from where I'd flinched down and saw three of those flat-faced infrared bulbs set in the ceiling, to warm a person while he washed or shaved on chilly mornings. I'd just flicked the wrong switch.

MOON DUEL

First hint I had we'd been spotted by a crusoe was a little *tick* coming to my moonsuit from the miniradar Pete and I were gaily heaving into position near the east end of Gioja crater to scan for wrecks, trash, and nodules of raw metal.

Then came a *whish* which cut off the instant Pete's hand lost contact with the squat instrument. His gauntlet, silvery in the raw low polar sunlight, drew away very slowly, as if he'd grown faintly disgusted with our activity. My gaze kept on turning to see the whole shimmering back of his helmet blown off in a gorgeous sickening brain-fog and blood-mist that was already falling in the vacuum as fine red snow.

A loud *tock* then and glove-sting as the crusoe's second slug hit the miniradar, but my gaze had gone back to the direction Pete had been facing when he bought it—in time to see the green needle-flash of the crusoe's gun in a notch in Gioja's low wall, where the black of the shadowed rock met the gemlike starfields along a jagged border. I unslung my Swift (all-purpose vacuum rifle named for the .22 cartridge which as early as 1940 was being produced by Winchester, Remington, and Norma with factory loads giving it a muzzle velocity of 4,140 feet, almost a mile, a second) as I dodged a long step to the side and squeezed off three shots. The first two shells must have traveled a touch too high, but the third made a beautiful fleeting violet globe at the base of the notch. It didn't show me a figure, whole or shattered, silvery or otherwise, on the wall or atop it, but then some crusoes are camouflaged like chameleons and most of them move very fast.

Pete's suit was still falling slowly and stiffly forward. Three dozen yards beyond was a wide black fissure, though exactly how wide I couldn't tell because much of the opposite lip merged into the shadow of the wall. I scooted toward it like a rat toward a hole. On my third step, I caught up Pete by his tool belt and oxy tube while his falling front was still inches away from the powdered pumice, and I heaved him along with me. Some slow or over-drilled part of my brain hadn't yet accepted he was dead.

When I began to skim forward, inches above the ground myself, kicking back against rocky outcrops thrusting up through the dust—it was like fin-swimming. The crusoe couldn't have been expecting this nut stunt, by which I at least avoided the dreamy sitting-duck slowness of safer, higher-bounding moon-running, for there was a green flash behind me and hurtled dust faintly pittered my soles and seat. He hadn't been leading his target enough. Also, I knew now he had shells as well as slugs.

I was diving over the lip three seconds after skoot-off when Pete's boot caught solidly against a last hooky outcrop. The something in my brain was still stubborn, for I clutched him like clamps, which made me swing around with a jerk. But even that was lucky, for a bright globe two yards through winked on five yards ahead like a mammoth firefly's flash, but not quite as gentle, for the invisible rarified explosion-front hit me hard enough to *boom* my suit and make the air inside slap me. Now I knew he had metal-proximity fuses on some of his shells too—they must be very good at mini-stuff on his home planet.

The tail of the pale green flash showed me the fissure's bottom a hundred yards straight below and all dust, as 90 percent of them are—pray God the dust was deep. I had time to thumb Extreme Emergency to the ship for it to relay automatically to Circumluna. Then the lip had cut me off from the ship and I had lazily fallen out of the glare into the blessed blackness, the dial lights in my helmet already snapped off—even they might make enough glow for the crusoe to aim by. The slug had switched off Pete's.

Ten, twelve seconds to fall and the opposite lip wasn't cutting off the notched crater wall. I could feel the crusoe's gun trailing me down—he'd know moon-G, sticky old 5-foot. I could feel his tentacle or finger or claw or ameboid bump tightening on the trigger or button or what. I shoved Pete away from me, parallel to the fissure wall, as hard as I could. Three more seconds, four, and my suit *boomed* again and I was walloped as another green flash showed me the smooth-sifted floor moving up and beginning to hurry a little. This flash was a hemisphere, not a globe—it had burst against the wall—but if there were any rock fragments they missed me. And it exactly bisected the straight line between me and Pete's silvery coffin. The crusoe knew his gun and his Luna—I really admired him, even if my shove had pushed Pete and me, action and reaction, just enough out of the target path. Then the fissure lip had cut the notch and I was readying to land like a three-legged crab, my Swift reslung, my free hand on my belted dust-shoes.

Eleven seconds' fall on Luna is not much more than two on Earth, but either are enough to build up a velocity of over 50 feet a second. The dust jarred me hard, but thank God there were no reefs in it. It covered at least all the limbs and front of me, including my helmet-front—my dial lights, snapped on again, showed a grayness fine-grained as flour.

The stuff resisted like flour, too, as I unbelted my dust-shoes. Using them for a purchase, I pulled my other arm and helmet-front free. The stars looked good, even gray-dusted. With a hand on each shoe, I dragged out my legs and, balancing gingerly on the slithery stuff, got each of my feet snapped to a shoe. Then I raised up and switched on my headlight. I hated that. I no more wanted to do it than a hunted animal wants to break twigs or show itself on the skyline, but I knew I had exactly as long to find cover, as it would take the crusoe to lope from the notch to the opposite lip of the fissure. Most of them lope very fast, they're that keen on killing.

Well, we started the killing, I reminded myself. *This time I'm the quarry:*

My searchlight made a perverse point of hitting Pete's shimmering casket, spread-eagle, seven-eighths submerged, like a man floating on his back. I swung the beam steadily. The opposite wall was smooth except for a few ledges and cracks and there wasn't any overhang to give a man below cover from someone on top.

But a section of the wall on my side, not fifty yards away, was hugely pocked with holes and half-bubbles where the primeval lava had foamed high and big against the feeble plucking of lunar gravity. I aimed myself at the center of that section and started out. I switched off my headlight and guided myself by the wide band of starfields.

You walk dust-shoes with much the same vertical lift and low methodical forward swing as snow-shoes. It was nostalgic, but hunted animals have no time for memory-delicatessen.

Suddenly there was more and redder brightness overhead than the stars. A narrow ribbon of rock along the top of the opposite wall was glaringly bathed in orange, while the rim peaks beyond glowed faintly, like smoldering volcanoes. Light from the orange ribbon bounced down into my fissure, caroming back and forth between the walls until I could dimly see again the holes I was headed for.

The crusoe had popped our ship—both tanks, close together, so that the sun-warmed gasses, exploding out into each other, burned like a hundred torches. The oxyaniline lasted until I reached the holes. I crawled through the biggest. The fading glow dimly and fleetingly showed a rock-bubble twelve feet across with another hole at the back of it. The stuff looked black, felt rough yet diamond-hard. I risked a look behind me.

The ribbon glow was darkest red—the skeleton of our ship still aglow. The ribbon flashed green in the middle—a tiny venomous dagger—and then a huge pale green firefly winked where Pete lay. He'd saved me a fourth time.

I had barely pushed sideways back when there was another of those winks just outside my hole, this one glaringly bright, its front walloping me. I heard through the rock faint *tings* of fragments of Pete's suit hitting the wall, but they may have been only residual ringings, from the nearer blast, in my suit or ears.

I scrambled through the back door in the bubble into a space which I made out by crawling to be a second bubble, resembling the first even to having a back door. I went through that third hole and turned around and rested my Swift's muzzle on the rough-scooped threshold. Since the crusoe lived around here, he'd know the territory better wherever I went. Why retreat farther and get lost? My dial lights showed that about a minute and a half had gone by since Pete bought it. Also, I wasn't losing pressure and I had oxy and heat for four hours—Circumluna would be able to deliver a rescue force in half that time, if my message had got through and if the crusoe didn't scupper them too. Then I got goosy again about the glow of the dial lights and snapped them off. I started to change position and was suddenly afraid the crusoe might already be trailing me by my transmitted sounds through the rock, and right away I held stock still and started to listen for *him*.

No light, no sound, a ghost-fingered gravity—it was like being tested for sanity-span in an anechoic chamber. Almost at once dizziness and the sensory mirages started to come, swimming in blue and burnt and moaning from the peripheries of my senses— even waiting in ambush for a crusoe wouldn't stop them; I guess I wanted them to come. So though straining every sense against the crusoe's approach, I had at last to start thinking about him.

It's strange that men should have looked at the moon for millennia and never guessed it was exactly what it looked like: a pale marble graveyard for living dead men, a Dry Tortuga of space where the silver ships from a million worlds marooned their mutineers, their recalcitrants, their criminals, their lunatics. Not on fertile warm-blanketed Earth with its quaint adolescent race, which such beings might harm, but on the great silver rock of Earth's satellite, to drag out their solitary furious lives, each with his suit and gun and lonely hut or hole, living by recycling his wastes; recycling, too, the bitter angers and hates and delusions which had brought him there. As many as a thousand of them, enough to mine the moon for meals and fuel-gases and to reconquer space and perhaps become masters of Earth—had they chosen to cooperate. But their refusal to cooperate was the very thing for which they'd been marooned, and besides that they were of a half thousand different galactic breeds. And so although they had some sort of electronic or psionic or what-not grapevine—at least what happened to one maroon became swiftly known to the others—each of them remained a solitary Friday-less Robinson Crusoe, hence the name.

I risked flashing my time dial. Only another thirty seconds gone. At this rate it would take an eternity for the two hours to pass before I could expect aid *if* my call had got through, while the crusoe—As my senses screwed themselves tighter to their task, my thoughts went whirling off again.

Earthmen shot down the first crusoe they met—in a moment of fumbling panic and against all their training. Ever since then the crusoes have shot first, or tried to, ignoring our belated efforts to communicate.

* * *

I brooded for what I thought was a very short while about the age-old problem of a universal galactic code, yet when I flashed my time dial again, seventy minutes had gone somewhere.

That really froze me. He'd had time to stalk and kill me a dozen times—he'd had time to go home and fetch his dogs!—my senses couldn't be *that* good protection with my mind away. Why even now, straining them in my fear, all I got was my own personal static: I heard my heart pounding, my blood roaring, I think for a bit I heard the Brownian movement of the air molecules against my eardrums.

What I hadn't been doing, I told myself, was thinking about the crusoe in a systematic way.

He had a gun like mine and at least three sorts of ammo.

He'd made it from notch to fissure-lip in forty seconds or less—he must be a fast loper, whatever number feet; he might well have a jet unit.

And he'd shot at the miniradar ahead of me. Had he thought it a communicator?—a weapon?—*or some sort of robot as dangerous as a man...?*

My heart had quieted, my ears had stopped roaring, and in that instant I heard through the rock the faintest *scratching.*

Scratch-scratch, scratch-scratch, scratch, scratch, scratch it went, each time a little louder.

I flipped on my searchlight and there coming toward me across the floor of the bubble outside mine was a silver spider as wide as a platter with four opalescent eyes and a green-banded body. Its hanging jaws were like inward-curving notched scissor blades.

I fired by automatism as I fell back. The spider's bubble was filled with violet glare instantly followed by green. I was twice walloped by explosion-fronts and knocked down.

That hardly slowed me a second. The same flashes had shown me a hole in the top of my bubble and as soon as I'd scrambled to my feet I leaped toward it.

I did remember to leap gently. My right hand caught the black rim of the hole and it didn't break off and I drew myself up into the black bubble above. It had no hole in the top, but two high ones in the sides, and I went through the higher one.

* * *

I kept on that way. The great igneous bubbles were almost uniform. I always took the highest exit. Once I got inside a bubble with no exit and had to backtrack. After that I scanned first. I kept my searchlight on.

I'd gone through seven or seventeen bubbles before I could start to think about what had happened.

That spider had almost certainly not been my crusoe—or else there was a troop of them dragging a rifle like an artillery piece. And it hadn't likely been an hitherto-unknown, theoretically impossible, live vacuum-arthropod—or else the exotic biologists were in for a great surprise and I'd been right to wet my pants. No, it had most likely been a tracking or tracking-and-attack robot or some sort. Eight legs are a useful number, likewise eight hands. Were the jaws for cutting through suit armor? Maybe it was a robot pet for a lonely being. Here, Spid!

The second explosion? Either the crusoe had fired into the chamber from the other side, or else the spider had carried a bomb to explode when it touched me. Fine use to make of a pet! I giggled. I was relieved, I guess, to think it likely that the spider had been "only" a robot.

Just then—I was in the ninth or nineteenth bubble—the inside of my helmet misted over everywhere. I was panting and sweating and my dehumidifier had overloaded. It was as if I were in a real peasouper of a fog. I could barely make out the black loom of the wall behind me. I switched out my headlight. My time dial showed seventy-two minutes gone. I switched it off and then I did a queer thing.

I leaned back very carefully until as much of my suit as possible touched rock. Then I measuredly thumped the rock ten times with the butt of my Swift and held very still.

Starting with ten would mean we were using the decimal system. Of course there were other possibilities, but...

Very faintly, coming at the same rate as mine, I heard six thuds.

What constant started with six? If he'd started with three, I'd have given him one, and so on through a few more places of pi. Or if with one, I'd have given him four—and then started to worry about the third and fourth places in the square root of two. I might take his signal for the beginning of a series with the interval of minus four and rap him back two, but then how could he rap me minus two? Oh why hadn't I simply started rapping out primes? Of course all the integers, in fact all the real numbers,

from thirty seven through forty one had square roots beginning
with six, but which one...?

Suddenly I heard a scratching...

My searchbeam was on again, my helmet, had unmisted, my
present bubble was empty.

Just the same I scuttled out of it, still trending upward where
I could. But now the holes wouldn't trend that way. They kept
going two down for one up and the lines of bubbles zigzagged.
I wanted to go back, but then I might hear the scratching. Once
the bubbles started getting smaller, it was like being in solid black
suds. I lost any sense of direction. I began to lose the sense of
up-down. What's moon-gravity to the numbness of psychosis? I
kept my searchlight on although I was sure the glow it made must
reach ten bubbles away. I looked all around every bubble before I
entered it, especially the overhang just above the entry hole.

Every once in a while I would hear somebody saying Six! Six?
Six! like that and then very rapidly seven—eight—nine—five—
four—three two one—naught. How would you rap naught in the
decimal system? That one I finally solved: you'd rap ten.

Finally I came into a bubble that had a side-hole four feet
across and edged at the top with diamonds. Very fancy. Was
this the Spider Princess' boudoir? There was also a top hole
but I didn't bother with that—it had no decor. I switched off
my searchlight and looked out the window without exposing my
head. The diamonds were stars. After a bit I made out what I
took to be the opposite lip of the fissure I'd first dove in, only
about one hundred feet above me. The rim-wall beyond looked
vaguely familiar, though I wasn't sure about the notch. My time
dial said once hundred eighteen minutes gone as I switched it
off. Almost time to start hoping for rescue. Oh great!—with their
ship a sitting duck for the crusoe they wouldn't be expecting. I
hadn't signaled a word besides Extreme Emergency.

I moved forward and sat in the window, one leg outside, my
Swift under my left arm. I plucked a flash-grenade set for five
seconds from my belt, pulled the fuse and tossed it across the
fissure, almost hard enough to reach the opposite wall.

I looked down, my Swift swinging like my gaze.

The fissure lit up like a boulevard. Across from me I knew
the flare was dropping dreamily, but I wasn't looking that way.
Right below me, two hundred feet down, I saw a transparent

helmet with something green and round and crested inside and with shoulders under it.

Just then I heard the *scratching* again, quite close.

I fired at once. My shell made a violet burst and raised a fountain of dust twenty feet from the crusoe. I scrambled back into my bubble, switching on my searchlight. Another spider was coming in on the opposite side, its legs moving fast. I jumped for the top-hole and grabbed its rim with my free hand. I'd have dropped my Swift if I'd needed my other hand, but I didn't. As I pulled myself up and through, I looked down and saw the spider straight below me eyeing me with its uptilted opalescent eyes and doubling its silver legs. Then it straightened its legs and sprang up toward me, not very fast but enough against Luna's feeble gravitational tug to put it into this upper room with me. I knew it mustn't touch me and I mustn't touch it by batting at it. I had started to shift the explosive shell in my gun for a slug, and its green-banded body was growing larger, when there was a green blast in the window below and its explosion-front, *booming* my suit a little, knocked the spider aside and out of sight before it made it through the trap door of my new bubble. Yet the spider didn't explode, if that was what had happened to the first one; at any rate there was no second green flash.

My new bubble had a top hole too and I went through it the same way I had the last. The next five bubbles were just the same too. I told myself that my routine was getting to be like that of a circus acrobat—except who stages shows inside black solidity?—except the gods maybe with the dreams they send us. The lava should be transparent, so the rim-wall peaks could admire.

At the same time I was thinking how if the biped humanoid shape is a good one for medium-size creatures on any planet, why so the spider shape is a good one for tiny creatures and apt to turn up anywhere and be copied in robots too.

The top hole in the sixth bubble showed me the stars, while one half of its rim shone white with sunlight.

Panting, I lay back against the rock. I switched off my searchlight. I didn't hear any scratching.

The stars. The stars were energy. They filled the universe with light, except for hidey holes and shadows here and there.

Then the number came to me. With the butt of my Swift I

rapped out five. No answer. No scratching either. I rapped out five again.

Then the answer came, ever so faintly. Five knocked back at me.

Six five five—Planck's Constant, the invariant quantum of energy. Oh, it should be to the minus 29th power, of course, but I couldn't think how to rap that and, besides, the basic integers were all that mattered.

I heard the *scratching*...

I sprang and caught the rim and lifted myself into the glaring sunlight... and stopped with my body midway.

Facing me a hundred feet away, midway through another top-hole—he must have come very swiftly by another branch of the bubble ladder—he'd know the swiftest ones—was my green-crested crusoe. His face had a third eye where a man's nose would be, which with his crest made him look like a creature of mythology. We were holding our guns vertically.

We looked like two of the damned, half out of their holes in the floor of Dante's hell.

I climbed very slowly out of my hole, still pointing my gun toward the zenith. So did he.

We held very still for a moment. Then with his gun butt he rapped out ten. I could both see and also hear it through the rock.

I rapped out three. Then, as if the black bubble-world were one level of existence and this another, I wondered why we were going through this rigmarole. We each knew the other had a suit and a gun (and a lonely hole?) and so we knew we were both intelligent and knew math. So why was our rapping so precious?

He raised his gun—I think to rap out one, to start off pi.

But I'll never be sure, for just then there were two violet bursts, close together, against the fissure-wall, quite close to him.

He started to swing the muzzle of his gun toward me. At least I think he did. He must know violet was the color of my explosions. I know I thought someone on my side was shooting. And I must have thought he was going to shoot me—because a violet dagger leaped from my Swift's muzzle and I felt its sharp recoil and then there was a violet globe where he was standing and moments later some fragment *twinged* lightly against my chest—a playful ironic tap.

He was blown apart pretty thoroughly, all his constants scattered, including—I'm sure—Planck's.

* * *

It was another half hour before the rescue ship from Circumluna landed. I spent it looking at Earth low on the horizon and watching around for the spider, but I never saw it. The rescue party never found it either, though they made quite a hunt—with me helping after I'd rested a bit and had my batteries and oxy replenished. Either its power went off when its master died, or it was set to "freeze" then, or most likely go into a "hide" behavior pattern. Likely it's still out there waiting for an incautious Earthman, like a rattlesnake in the desert or an old, forgotten land mine.

I also figured out, while waiting in Gioja crater, there near the north pole on the edge of Shackleton crater, the only explanation I've ever been able to make, though it's something of a whopper, of the two violet flashes which ended my little mathematical friendship-chant with the crusoe. They were the first two shells I squeezed off at him—the ones that skimmed the notch. They had the velocity to orbit Luna and the time they took—two hours and five minutes—was right enough.

Oh, the consequences of our past actions!

LATER THAN YOU THINK

OBVIOUSLY THE ARCHEOLOGIST'S STUDY BELONGED to an era vastly distant from today. Familiar similarities here and there only sharpened the feeling of alienage. The sunlight that filtered through the windows in the ceiling had a wan and greenish cast and was augmented by radiation from some luminous material impregnating the walls and floor. Even the wide desk and the commodious hassocks glowed with a restful light. Across the former were scattered metal-backed wax tablets, styluses, and a pair of large and oddly formed spectacles. The crammed bookcases were not particularly unusual, but the books were bound in metal and the script on their spines would have been utterly unfamiliar to the most erudite of modern linguists. One of the books, lying open on a hassock, showed leaves of a thin, flexible, rustless metal covered with luminous characters. Between the bookcases were phosphorescent oil paintings, mainly of sea bottoms, in somber greens and browns. Their style, neither wholly realistic nor abstract, would have baffled the historian of art.

A blackboard with large colored crayons hinted equally at the schoolroom and the studio.

In the center of the room, midway to the ceiling, hung a fish with iridescent scales of breathtaking beauty. So invisible was its means of support that—also taking into account the strange paintings and the greenish light—one would have sworn that the object was to create an underwater scene.

The Explorer made his entrance in a theatrical swirl of movement. He embraced the Archeologist with a warmth calculated to startle that crusty old fellow. Then he settled himself on a hassock, looked up and asked a question in a speech and idiom so different from any we know that it must be called another means of communication rather than another language. The import was, "Well, what about it?"

If the Archeologist were taken aback, he concealed it. His expression showed only pleasure at being reunited with a long-absent friend.

"What about what?" he queried.

"About your discovery!"

"What discovery?" The Archeologist's incomprehension was playful.

The Explorer threw up his arms. "Why, what else but your discovery, here on Earth, of the remains of an intelligent species? It's the find of the age! Am I going to have to coax you? Out with it!"

"I didn't make the discovery," the other said tranquilly. "I only supervised the excavations and directed the correlation of material. *You* ought to be doing the talking. *You're* the one who's just returned from the stars."

"Forget that." The Explorer brushed the question aside. "As soon as our spaceship got within radio range of Earth, they started to send us a continuous newscast covering the period of our absence. One of the items, exasperatingly brief, mentioned your discovery. It captured my imagination. I couldn't wait to hear the details." He paused, then confessed, "You get so eager out there in space—a metal-filmed droplet of life lost in immensity. You rediscover your emotions..." He changed color, then finished rapidly. "As soon as I could decently get away, I came straight to you. I wanted to hear about it from the best authority—yourself."

The Archeologist regarded him quizzically. "I'm pleased that you should think of me and my work, and I'm very happy to see you again. But admit it now, isn't there something a bit odd about your getting so worked up over this thing? I can understand that after your long absence from Earth, any news of Earth would seem especially important. But isn't there an additional reason?"

The Explorer twisted impatiently. "Oh, I suppose there is. Disappointment, for one thing. We were hoping to get in touch with intelligent life out there. We were specifically trained in techniques for establishing mental contact with alien intelligent life forms. Well, we found some planets with life upon them, all right. But it was primitive life, not worth bothering about."

Again he hesitated embarrassedly. "Out there you get to thinking of the preciousness of intelligence. There's so little of it, and it's so lonely. And we so greatly need intercourse with another intelligent species to give depth and balance to our thoughts. I suppose I set too much store by my hopes of establishing a contact." He paused. "At any rate, when I heard that what we were looking for, you had found here at home—even though dead and done for—I felt that at least it was something. I was suddenly very eager. It is odd, I know, to get so worked up about an extinct species—as if my interest could mean anything to them now—but that's the way it hit me."

Several small shadows crossed the windows overhead. They might have been birds, except they moved too slowly.

"I think I understand," the Archeologist said softly.

"So get on with it and tell me about your discovery!" the Explorer exploded.

"I've already told you that it wasn't my discovery," the Archeologist reminded him. "A few years after your expedition left, there was begun a detailed resurvey of Earth's mineral resources. In the course of some deep continental borings, one party discovered a cache—either a very large box or a rather small room—with metallic walls of great strength and toughness. Evidently its makers had intended it for the very purpose of carrying a message down through the ages. It proved to contain artifacts; models of buildings, vehicles, and machines, objects of art, pictures, and books—hundreds of books, along with elaborate pictorial dictionaries for interpreting them. So now we even understand their languages."

"Languages?" interrupted the Explorer. "That's queer. Somehow one thinks of an alien species as having just one language."

"Like our own, this species had several, though there were some words and symbols that were alike in all their languages. These words and symbols seem to have come down unchanged from their most distant prehistory."

The Explorer burst out, "I am not interested in all that dry stuff! Give me the wet! What were they like? How did they live? What did they create? What did they want?"

The Archeologist gently waved aside the questions. "All in

good time. If I am to tell you everything you want to know, I must tell it my own way. Now that you are back on Earth, you will have to reacquire those orderly and composed habits of thought which you have partly lost in the course of your wild interstellar adventurings."

"Curse you, I think you're just trying to tantalize me."

The Archeologist's expression showed that this was not altogether untrue. He casually fondled an animal that had wriggled up onto his desk, and which looked rather more like an eel than a snake. "Cute little brute, isn't it?" he remarked. When it became apparent that the Explorer wasn't to be provoked into another outburst, he continued, "It became my task to interpret the contents of the cache, to reconstruct its makers' climb from animalism and savagery to civilization, their rather rapid spread across the world's surface, their first fumbling attempts to escape from the Earth."

"They had spaceships?"

"It's barely possible. I rather hope they did, since it would mean the chance of a survival elsewhere, though the negative results of your expedition rather lessen that." He went on, "The cache was laid down when they were first attempting space flight, just after their discovery of atomic power, in the first flush of their youth. It was probably created in a kind of exuberant fancifulness, with no serious belief that it would ever serve the purpose for which it was intended." He looked at the Explorer strangely. "If I am not mistaken, we have laid down similar caches."

After a moment the Archeologist continued, "My reconstruction of their history, subsequent to the laying down of the cache, has been largely hypothetical. I can only guess at the reasons for their decline and fall. Supplementary material has been very slow in coming in, though we are still making extensive excavations at widely separated points. Here are the last reports." He tossed the Explorer a small metal-leaf pamphlet. It flew with a curiously slow motion.

"That's what struck me so queer right from the start," the Explorer observed, putting the pamphlet aside after a glance. "If these creatures were relatively advanced, why haven't we learned about them before? They must have left so many things— buildings, machines, engineering projects, some of them on a large scale. You'd think we'd be turning up traces everywhere."

"I have four answers to that," the Archeologist replied. "The first is the most obvious. Time. Geologic ages of it. The second is more subtle. What if we should have been looking in the wrong place? I mean, what if the creatures occupied a very different portion of the Earth than our own? Third, it's possible that atomic energy, out of control, finished the race and destroyed its traces. The present distribution of radioactive compounds throughout the Earth's surface lends some support to this theory.

"Fourth," he went on, "it's my belief that when an intelligent species begins to retrogress, it tends to destroy, or, rather, debase all the things it has laboriously created. Large buildings are torn down to make smaller ones. Machines are broken up and worked into primitive tools and weapons. There is a kind of unraveling or erasing. A cultural Second Law of Thermodynamics begins to operate, whereby the intellect and all its works are gradually degraded to the lowest level of meaning and creativity."

"But why?" The Explorer sounded anguished. "Why should any intelligent species end like that? I grant the possibility of atomic power getting out of hand, though one would have thought they'd have taken the greatest precautions. Still, it could happen. But that fourth answer—it's morbid."

"Cultures and civilizations die," said the Archeologist evenly. "That has happened repeatedly in our own history. Why not species? An individual dies—and is there anything intrinsically more terrible in the death of a species than in the death of an individual?"

He paused. "With respect to the members of this one species, I think that a certain temperamental instability hastened their end. Their appetites and emotions were not sufficiently subordinated to their understanding and to their sense of drama—their enjoyment of the comedy and tragedy of existence. They were impatient and easily incapacitated by frustration. They seem to have been singularly guilty in their pleasures, behaving either like gloomy moralists or gluttons.

"Because of taboos and an overgrown possessiveness," he continued, "each individual tended to limit his affection to a tiny family; in many cases he focused his love on himself alone. They set great store by personal prestige, by the amassing of wealth and the exercise of power. Their notable capacity for thought and manipulative activity was expended on things rather than persons or feelings. Their technology outstripped their psychology. They skimped fatally when it came to hard thinking about the purpose of life and intellectual activity, and the means for preserving them."

Again the slow shadows drifted overhead.

"And finally," the Archeologist said, "they were a strangely haunted species. They seem to have been obsessed by the notion that others, greater than themselves, had prospered before them and then died, leaving them to rebuild a civilization from ruins. It was from those others that they thought they derived the few words and symbols common to all their languages."

"Gods?" mused the Explorer.

The Archeologist shrugged. "Who knows?"

The Explorer turned away. His excitement had visibly evaporated, leaving behind a cold and miserable residue of feeling. "I am not sure I want to hear much more about them," he said. "They sound too much like us. Perhaps it was a mistake, my coming here. Pardon me, old friend, but out there in space even *our* emotions become undisciplined. Everything becomes indescribably poignant. Moods are tempestuous. You shift in an instant from zenith to nadir—and remember, out there you can see both.

"I was very eager to hear about this lost species," he added in a sad voice. "I thought I would feel a kind of fellowship with them across the eons. Instead, I touch only corpses. It reminds me of when, out in space, there looms up before your prow, faint in the starlight, a dead sun. They were a young race. They thought they were getting somewhere. They promised themselves an eternity of effort. And all the while there was wriggling toward them out of that future for which they yearned... oh, it's so completely futile and unfair."

"I disagree," the Archeologist said spiritedly. "Really, your absence from Earth has unsettled you even more than I first surmised. Look at the matter squarely. Death comes to everything in the end. Our past is strewn with our dead. That species died, it's true. But what they achieved, they achieved. What happiness they had, they had. What they did in their short span is as significant as what they might have done had they lived a billion years. The present is always more important than the future. And no creature can have all the future—it must be shared, left to others."

"Maybe so," the Explorer said slowly. "Yes, I guess you're

right. But I still feel a horrible wistfulness about them, and I hug to myself the hope that a few of them escaped and set up a colony on some planet we haven't yet visited." There was a long silence. Then the Explorer turned back. "You old devil." he said in a manner that showed his gayer and more boisterous mood had returned, though diminished, "you still haven't told me anything definite about them."

"So I haven't," replied the Archeologist with guileful innocence. "Well, they were vertebrates."

"Oh?"

"Yes. What's more, they were mammals."

"Mammals? I was expecting something different."

"I thought you were."

The Explorer shifted. "All this matter of evolutionary categories is pretty cut-and-dried. Even a knowledge of how they looked doesn't mean much. I'd like to approach them in a more intimate way. How did they think of themselves? I know the word won't mean anything to me, but it will give me a feeling— of recognition."

"I can't say the word," the Archeologist told him, "because I haven't the proper vocal equipment. But I know enough of their script to be able to write it for you as they would have written it. Incidentally, it is one of those words common to all their languages, that they attributed to an earlier race of beings."

The Archeologist extended one of his eight tentacles toward the blackboard. The suckers at its tip firmly grasped a bit of orange crayon. Another of his tentacles took up the spectacles and adjusted them over his three-inch protruding pupils.

The eel-like glittering pet drifted back into the room and nosed curiously about the crayon as it traced:

RAT

MIRROR

HOOKING HIS THUMB TO THE MIRROR-BRIGHT PANE to provide a fulcrum for his weightless, maimed finger, Wolfe pushed the final button. Ions swirled invisibly around the transparent sphere holding Barr and himself.

While the ions built the field, he looked out at the globe of Earth, about as big to his eye as a breakfast grapefruit, but his grapefruit was powdered with clouds and set before him on a black tablecloth of stars.

Barr said, "Twenty thousand miles of hard vacuum should be enough insulation." Wolfe nodded absently at Barr's reflection in the panel.

If the new equations had been read rightly, the climax field would plunge them into the hypothetical spherically-curved, four-dimensional world wherein our whole universe is only a quivering globular surface. Then it would whisk their thin three-dimensionality through the hypersphere as a crack speeds across glass and as swiftly as a man can swing a flashlight from one star toward another.

Finally it would pop them out off the Riemannian hyper-continuum into unoccupied space two light years from the solar system and in the direction of the tiny constellation of the Pleiades. After they had made brief confirmatory observations, a simple reversal of the process would bring Wolfe and Barr back near their starting point—if the new equations had been rightly read.

As the ionic swirl became a blizzard, a dull black, dense mono-molecular layer built up from the positive to the negative pole of the transparent sphere. This opaque outer plating was an unavoidable side-effect of the process. First Earth, then Luna, then Sol was blotted out and the stars around them. The last constellation to be obscured was the Pleiades. Wolfe said a silent farewell to the Seven Sisters, though out here he and Barr could see sixteen.

The field neared climax. Wolfe gently rubbed the lopped-off first joint of his right forefinger—which was his only outward expression of tension.

A nervous grin quirked Barr's lips in the mirror. He said, rather loudly, "I don't care how confident the math boys are, we still must be prepared for any species of disorientation. Did you ever read about the German psychologist who wore lenses that turned everything upside down? After a couple of days his brain accommodated and he saw everything—still through the same lenses—as right-side up. Then when he finally took off the lenses..."

A gust of cosmic change swept through Wolfe and Barr with no immediate perceptible effect on them or their vehicle except that two tell-tales on the panel flashed green, one of them blinking.

Wolfe touched another button. The blinking ceased as deplating of the opaque layer began, the molecules flying off in exact reverse of the order in which they had been laid down. The two men watched the spot where the stars would first show.

"The Pleiades!" Then Barr's voice changed. "But something's happened to them." He laughed oddly. "They're not upside down, at any rate!"

"No, but they're reversed right-to-left," Wolfe said quietly. "The translation effect seems to have been somewhat greater than anticipated. We appear to be not two light years away from Earth but 440—twice the distance of the Pleiades—and we are seeing them from the opposite side."

When Barr did not reply, Wolfe continued methodically to spell out the obvious to his comrade. He said, "This is possible with the Pleiades since they are an actual group of stars, physically close to one another. It would not be true of most other constellations, whose member stars differ widely in their distance from Earth. For instance, there is no place on the other side of Ursa Major or Orion whence one can see the Dippers or the Hunter reversed."

Deplating continued. The agelessly familiar constellation of Orion appeared, but to the right of the Pleiades, not to the left as one sees it looking southwest from Earth's northern hemisphere and Bellatrix and great yellow Beteleuse were reversed, and the Sword hung the wrong way from the Belt.

Barr said softly, "This sight is impossible in our home continuum. We appear to have been translated along a diameter of the great Riemannian hypersphere to the mirror-image universe which Muawiya hypothesized as lying at the fourth-dimensional antipodes." And now it was Wolfe's turn not to reply.

Deplating went on. Fierce Sol appeared, and Luna, and then quickly Earth showing the Americas—but Florida hung from the west coast and Baja California from the east, while by the narrow, near-invisible twig of the Isthmus of Panama, South America hung to the left of the northern continent, and the Caribbean opened into what should have been the Pacific.

"Since the mirror universe duplicates ours in detail," Barr said, "our twins must just now have materialized near our home planet—a mirror you and a mirror me."

"Wait," Wolfe said sharply. He was staring at himself in the mirror-bright surface of the panel and holding out his hands. At first he thought all was as it had been: his right forefinger was the one lacking a joint. Then he reminded himself that plane mirrors give a reversed image, and he looked down directly at his hands. His left forefinger was the lopped one.

"Wait," Wolfe repeated to Barr and pointed to the maimed forefinger. "Since we've been mirror-reversed ourselves, we can't be in a mirror universe, because if we were, it would appear normal to us."

"The new equations were misread completely: they don't refer to translation but to reversion. We have only moved through the fourth dimension enough to accomplish a dextro-levo reversal in our bodies—yes, and in our vehicle too, since—look!—the panel's console pattern is still normal to us. But with respect to the Earth we haven't moved a fourth-dimensional micron."

He took a breath. "Besides," he added more cooly, "it better satisfies the Law of the Conservation of Reality to assume a mirror-reversed microcosm than a singularly reversed macrocosm."

Barr sighed, possibly with relief. "And so all we have to do to unkink ourselves," he said, "is to make our 'return journey' as planned."

"Yes," Wolfe allowed, "but I for one don't approve of running needless risks. Besides, I fancy it would be wise to present the math boys with some more physical proof of the mirror-reversal than our unsupported word. They were *so* positive about their reading of the equation. Barr, what happened to your German psychologist when he took off the lenses?"

"Why, he'd got so used to them that the world looked upside down again. But it straightened out, I mean inverted back to normal, after a couple of days."

Wolfe nodded. "We ought to be able to stand mirror-image people and a mirror-image environment for a couple of days, don't you think? He waited a moment, then turned to the panel's communication sector to raise Earth. He added, "If adjustment proves too troublesome we can come out here and unkink, though I'd enjoy always having a complete right hand."

Barr said, "We'll have to remember to tell our doctors our hearts lie to the right now. I'll spend a bit of the next two days simply being thankful I'm not a virtual man on a virtual world."

Wolfe nodded and said, "Let's shake on that." The two men automatically gripped left hands, and a voice came from the panel, saying: "Congratulations!"

THE 64-SQUARE MADHOUSE

Silently, so as not to shock anyone with illusions about well dressed young women, Sandra Lea Grayling cursed the day she had persuaded the *Chicago Space Mirror* that there would be all sorts of human interest stories to be picked up at the first international grandmaster chess tournament in which an electronic computing machine was entered.

Not that there weren't enough humans around, it was the interest that was in doubt. The large hall was crammed with energetic dark-suited men of whom a disproportionately large number were bald, wore glasses, were faintly untidy and indefinably shabby, had Slavic or Scandinavian features, and talked foreign languages.

They yakked interminably. The only ones who didn't were scurrying individuals with the eager-zombie look of officials.

Chess sets were everywhere—big ones on tables, still bigger diagram-type electric ones on walls, small peg-in sets dragged from side pockets and manipulated rapidly as part of the conversational ritual and still smaller folding sets in which the pieces were the tiny magnetized disks used for playing in free-fall.

There were signs featuring largely mysterious combinations of letters: FIDE, WBM, USCF, USSF, USSR and UNESCO. Sandra felt fairly sure about the last three.

The many clocks, bedside table size, would have struck a familiar note except that they had little red flags and wheels sprinkled over their faces and they were all in pairs, two clocks to a case. That Siamese-twin clocks should be essential to a chess tournament struck Sandra as a particularly maddening circumstance.

Her last assignment had been to interview the pilot pair riding the first American manned circum-lunar satellite—and the five alternate pairs who hadn't made the flight. This tournament hall seemed to Sandra much further out of the world.

Overheard scraps of conversation in reasonably intelligible English were not particularly helpful. Samples:

"They say the Machine has been programmed to play nothing but pure Barcza System and Indian Defenses—and the Dragon Formation if anyone pushes the King Pawn."

"Hah! In that case..."

"The Russians have come with ten trunkfuls of prepared variations and they'll gang up on the Machine at adjournments. What can one New Jersey computer do against four Russian grandmasters?"

"I heard the Russians have been programmed—with hypnotic cramming and somno-briefing. Votbinnik had a nervous breakdown."

"Why, the Machine hasn't even a *Haupturnier* or an intercollegiate won. It'll over its head be playing."

"Yes, but maybe like Capa at San Sebastian or Morphy or Willie Angler at New York. The Russians will look like potzers."

"Have you studied the scores of the match between Moon Base and Circum-Terra?"

"Not worth the trouble. The play was feeble. Barely Expert Rating."

Sandra's chief difficulty was that she knew absolutely nothing about the game of chess—a point that she had slid over in conferring with the powers at the *Space Mirror*, but that now had begun to weigh on her. How wonderful it would be, she dreamed, to walk out this minute, find a quiet bar and get pie-eyed in an evil, ladylike way.

"Perhaps *mademoiselle* would welcome a drink?"

"You're durn tootin' she would!" Sandra replied in a rush, and then looked down apprehensively at the person who had read her thoughts.

It was a small sprightly elderly man who looked like a somewhat thinned down Peter Lorre—there was that same impression of the happy Slavic elf. What was left of his white hair was cut very short, making a silvery nap. His pince-nez had quite thick lenses. But in sharp contrast to the somberly clad men around them, he was wearing a pearl-gray suit of almost exactly the same shade as Sandra's—a circumstance that created for her the illusion that they were fellow conspirators.

"Hey, wait a minute," she protested Just the same. He had already taken her arm and was piloting her toward the nearest flight of low wide stairs. "How did you know I wanted a drink?"

"I could see that *mademoiselle* was having difficulty swallowing," he replied, keeping them moving. "Pardon me for feasting my eyes on your lovely throat."

"I didn't suppose they'd serve drinks here."

"But of course." They were already mounting the stairs. "What would chess be without coffee or schnapps?"

"Okay, lead on," Sandra said. "You're the doctor."

"Doctor?" He smiled widely. "You know, I like being called that."

"Then the name is yours as long as you want it—Doc."

Meanwhile the happy little man had edged them into the first of a small cluster of tables, where a dark-suited jabbering trio was just rising. He snapped his fingers and hissed through his teeth. A white-aproned waiter materialized.

"For myself black coffee," he said. "For *mademoiselle* Rhine wine and seltzer?"

"That'd go fine." Sandra leaned back. "Confidentially, Doc, I was having trouble swallowing... well, just about everything here."

He nodded. "You are not the first to be shocked and horrified by chess," he assured her. "It is a curse of the intellect. It is a game for lunatics—or else it creates them. But what brings a sane and beautiful young lady to this 64-square madhouse?"

Sandra briefly told him her story and her predicament. By the time they were served, Doc had absorbed the one and assessed the other.

"You have one great advantage," he told her. "You know nothing whatsoever of chess—so you will be able to write about it understandably for your readers." He swallowed half his demitasse and smacked his lips. "As for the Machine—you *do* know, I suppose, that it is not a humanoid metal robot, walking about clanking and squeaking like a late medieval knight in armor?"

"Yes, Doc, but..." Sandra found difficulty in phrasing the question.

"Wait." He lifted a finger. "I think I know what you're going to ask. You want to know why, if the Machine works at all, it doesn't work perfectly, so that it always wins and there is no contest. Right?"

Sandra grinned and nodded. Doc's ability to interpret her mind was as comforting as the bubbly, mildly astringent mixture she was sipping.

He removed his pince-nez, massaged the bridge of his nose and replaced them.

"If you had," he said, "a billion computers all as fast as the Machine, it would take them all the time there ever will be in the universe just to play through all the possible games of chess, not to mention the time needed to classify those games into branching families of wins for White, wins for Black and draws, and the additional time required to trace out chains of key-moves leading always to wins. So the Machine can't play chess like God. What the Machine can do is examine all the likely lines of play for about eight moves ahead—that is, four moves each for White and Black—and then decide which is the best move on the basis of capturing enemy pieces, working toward checkmate, establishing a powerful central position and so on."

"That sounds like the way a man would play a game," Sandra observed. "Look ahead a little way and try to make a plan. You know, like getting out trumps in bridge or setting up a finesse."

"Exactly!" Doc beamed at her approvingly. "The Machine *is* like a man. A rather peculiar and not exactly pleasant man. A man who always abides by sound principles, who is utterly incapable of flights of genius, but who never makes a mistake. You see, you are finding human interest already, even in the Machine."

Sandra nodded. "Does a human chess player—a grandmaster, I mean—ever look eight moves ahead in a game?"

"Most assuredly he does! In crucial situations, say where there's a chance of winning at once by trapping the enemy king, he examines many more moves ahead than that—thirty or forty even. The Machine is probably programmed to recognize such situations and do something of the same sort, though we can't be sure from the information World Business Machines has released. But in most chess positions the possibilities are so very nearly unlimited that even a grandmaster can only look a very few moves ahead and must rely on his judgment and experience and artistry. The equivalent of those in the Machine is the directions fed into it before it plays a game."

"You mean the programming?"

"Indeed yes! The programming is the crux of the problem of the chess-playing computer. The first practical model, reported by Bernstein and Roberts of IBM in 1958 and which looked four moves ahead, was programmed so that it had a greedy worried tendency to grab at enemy pieces and to retreat its own whenever they were attacked. It had a personality like that of a certain kind of chess-playing dub—a dull-brained woodpusher afraid to take the slightest risk of losing material—but a dub who could almost always beat an utter novice. The WBM machine here in the hall operates about a million times as fast. Don't ask me how, I'm no physicist, but it depends on the new transistors and something they call hypervelocity, which in turn depends on keeping parts of the Machine at a temperature near absolute zero. However, the result is that the Machine can see eight moves ahead and is capable of being programmed much more craftily."

"A million times as fast as the first machine, you say, Doc? And yet it only sees twice as many moves ahead?" Sandra objected.

"There is a geometrical progression involved there," he told her with a smile. "Believe me, eight moves ahead is a lot of moves when you remember that the Machine is errorlessly examining every one of thousands of variations. Flesh-and-blood chess masters have lost games by blunders they could have avoided by looking only one or two moves ahead. The Machine will make no such oversights. Once again, you see, you have the human factor, in this case working for the Machine."

"Savilly, I have been looking allplace for you!"

A stocky, bull-faced man with a great bristling shock of black, gray-flecked hair had halted abruptly by their table. He bent over Doc and began to whisper explosively in a guttural foreign tongue.

II

SANDRA'S GAZE TRAVELED BEYOND THE BALUSTRADE. Now that she could look down at it, the central hall seemed less confusedly crowded. In the middle, toward the far end, were five small tables spaced rather widely apart and with a chessboard and men and one of the Siamese clocks set out on each. To either side of the hall were tiers of temporary seats, about half of them occupied. There were at least as many more people still wandering about.

On the far wall was a big electric scoreboard and also, above the corresponding tables, five large dully glassy chessboards, the White squares in light gray, the Black squares in dark.

One of the five wall chessboards was considerably larger than the other four—the one above the Machine.

Sandra looked with quickening interest at the console of the Machine—a bank of keys and some half-dozen panels of rows and rows of tiny telltale lights, all dark at the moment. A thick red velvet cord on little brass standards ran around the Machine at a distance of about ten feet. Inside the cord were only a few gray-smocked men. Two of them had just laid a black cable to the nearest chess table and were attaching it to the Siamese clock.

Sandra tried to think of a being who always checked everything, but only within limits beyond which his thoughts never ventured, and who never made a mistake...

"Miss Grayling! May I present to you Igor Jandorf."

She turned back quickly with a smile and a nod.

"I should tell you, Igor," Doc continued, "that Miss Grayling represents a large and influential Midwestern newspaper. Perhaps you have a message for her readers."

The shock-headed man's eyes flashed. "I most certainly do!" At that moment the waiter arrived with a second coffee and wine-and-seltzer. Jandorf seized Doc's new demitasse, drained it, set it back on the tray with a flourish and drew himself up.

"Tell your readers, Miss Grayling," he proclaimed, fiercely arching his eyebrows at her and actually slapping his chest, "that I, Igor Jandorf, will defeat the Machine by the living force of my human personality! Already I have offered to play it an informal game blindfolded—I, who have played 50 blindfold games simultaneously! Its owners refuse me. I have challenged it also to a few games of rapid-transit—an offer no true grandmaster would dare ignore. Again they refuse me. I predict that the Machine will play like a great oaf—at least against me. Repeat: I, Igor Jandorf, by the living force of my human personality, will defeat the Machine. Do you have that? You can remember it?"

"Oh yes," Sandra assured him, "but there are some other questions I very much want to ask you, Mr. Jandorf."

"I am sorry, Miss Grayling, but I must clear my mind now. In ten minutes they start the clocks."

While Sandra arranged for an interview with Jandorf after the day's playing session, Doc reordered his coffee.

"One expects it of Jandorf," he explained to Sandra with a philosophic shrug when the shock-headed man was gone. "At least he didn't take your wine-and-seltzer. Or did he? One tip I have for you: don't call a chess master Mister, call him Master. They all eat it up."

"Gee, Doc, I don't know how to thank you for everything. I hope I haven't offended Mis—Master Jandorf so that he doesn't—"

"Don't worry about that. Wild horses couldn't keep Jandorf away from a press interview. You know, his rapid-transit challenge was cunning. That's a minor variety of chess where each player gets only ten seconds to make a move. Which I don't suppose would give the Machine time to look three moves ahead. Chess players would say that the Machine has a very slow sight of the board. This tournament is being played at the usual international rate of 15 moves an hour, and—"

"Is that why they've got all those crazy clocks?" Sandra interrupted.

"Oh, yes. Chess clocks measure the time each player takes in making his moves. When a player makes a move he presses a button that shuts his clock off and turns his opponent's on. If a player uses too much time, he loses as surely as if he were checkmated. Now since the Machine will almost certainly be programmed to take an equal amount of time on successive moves, a rate of 15 moves an hour means it will have 4 minutes a move—and it will need every second of them! Jandorf bravado to make a point of a blindfold challenge—just as if the Machine weren't playing blindfold itself. Or is the Machine blindfold? How do you think of it?"

"Gosh, I don't know. Say, Doc, is it really true that Master Jandorf has played 50 games at once blindfolded? I can't believe that."

*   *   *

"Of course not!" Doc assured her. "It was only 49 and he lost two of those and drew five. Jandorf always exaggerates. It's in his blood."

"He's one of the Russians, isn't he?" Sandra asked. "Igor?"

Doc chuckled. "Not exactly," he said gently. "He is originally a Pole and now he has Argentinean citizenship. You have a program, don't you?"

Sandra started to hunt through her pocketbook, but just then two lists of names lit up on the big electric scoreboard.

THE PLAYERS
WILLIAM ANGLER, USA
BELA GRABO, HUNGARY
IVAN JAL, USSR
IGOR JANDORF, ARGENTINA
DR. S. KRAKATOWER, FRANCE
VASSILY LYSMOV, USSR
THE MACHINE, USA (PROGRAMMED BY SIMON GREAT)
MAXIM SEREK, USSR
MOSES SHEREVSKY, USA
MIKHAIL VOTBINNIK, USSR
TOURNAMENT DIRECTOR: DR. JAN VANDERHOEF

FIRST ROUND PAIRINGS
SHEREVSKY VS. SEREK
JAL VS. ANGLER
JANDORF VS. VOTBINNIK
LYSMOV VS. KRAKATOWER
GRABO VS. MACHINE

"Cripes, Doc, they all sound like they were Russians," Sandra said after a bit. "Except this Willie Angler. Oh, he's the boy wonder, isn't he?"

Doc nodded. "Not such a boy any longer, though. He's... Well, speak of the Devil's children... Miss Grayling, I have the honor of presenting to you the only grandmaster ever to have been ex-chess-champion of the United States while still technically a minor—Master William Augustus Angler."

A tall, sharply-dressed young man with a hatchet face pressed the old man back into his chair.

"How are you, Savvy, old boy old boy?" he demanded. "Still chasing the girls, I see."

"Please, Willie, get off me."

"Can't take it, huh?" Angler straightened up somewhat. "Hey waiter! Where's that chocolate malt? I don't want it next year. About that *ex-*, though. I was swindled Savvy, I was robbed."

"Willie!" Doc said with some asperity. "Miss Grayling is a journalist. She would like to have a statement from you as to how you will play against the Machine."

Angler grinned and shook his head sadly. "Poor old Machine," he said. "I don't know why they take so much trouble polishing up that pile of tin just so that I can give it a hit in the head. I got a hatful of moves it'll burn out all its tubes trying to answer. And if it gets too fresh, how about you and me giving its low-temperature section the hotfoot, Savvy? The money WBM's putting up is okay, though. That first prize will just fit the big hole in my bank account."

"I know you haven't the time now, Master Angler," Sandra said rapidly, "but if after the playing session you could grant me—"

"Sorry, babe," Angler broke in with a wave of dismissal. "I'm dated up for two months in advance. Waiter! I'm here, not there!" And he went charging off.

Doc and Sandra looked at each other and smiled.

"Chess masters aren't exactly humble people, are they?" she said.

Doc's smile became tinged with sad understanding. "You must excuse them, though," he said. "They really get so little recognition or recompense. This tournament is an exception. And it takes a great deal of ego to play greatly."

"I suppose so. So World Business Machines is responsible for this tournament?"

"Correct. Their advertising department is interested in the prestige. They want to score a point over their great rival."

"But if the Machine plays badly it will be a black eye for them," Sandra pointed out.

"True," Doc agreed thoughtfully. "WBM must feel very sure... It's the prize money they've put up, of course, that's brought the world's greatest players here. Otherwise half of them would be holding off in the best temperamental-artist style. For chess players the prize money is fabulous—$35,000, with $15,000 for first place, and all expenses paid for all players. There's never been anything like it. Soviet Russia is the only country that has ever supported and rewarded her best chess players at all adequately. I think the Russian players are here because UNESCO and FIDE (that's *Federation Internationale des Echecs*—the international chess organization) are also backing the tournament. And perhaps because the Kremlin is hungry for a little prestige now that its space program is sagging."

"But if a Russian doesn't take first place it will be a black eye for them."

Doc frowned. "True, in a sense. *They* must feel very sure... Here they are now."

III

FOUR MEN WERE CROSSING THE CENTER OF THE hall, which was clearing, toward the tables at the other end. Doubtless they just happened to be going two by two in close formation, but it gave Sandra the feeling of a phalanx.

"The first two are Lysmov and Votbinnik," Doc told her. "It isn't often that you see the current champion of the world—Votbinnik—and an ex-champion arm in arm. There are two other persons in the tournament who have held that honor—Jal and Vanderhoef the director, way back."

"Will whoever wins this tournament become champion?"

"Oh no. That's decided by two-player matches—a very long business—after elimination tournaments between leading contenders. This tournament is a round robin: each player plays one game with every other player. That means nine rounds."

"Anyway there *are* an awful lot of Russians in the tournament," Sandra said, consulting her program. "Four out of ten have USSR after them. And Bela Grabo, Hungary—that's a satellite. And Sherevsky and Krakatower are Russian-sounding names."

"The proportion of Soviet to American entries in the tournament represents pretty fairly the general difference in playing strength between the two countries," Doc said judiciously. "Chess mastery moves from land to land with the years. Way back it was the Moslems and the Hindus and Persians. Then Italy and Spain. A little over a hundred years ago it was France and England. Then Germany, Austria and the New World. Now it's Russia— including of course the Russians who have run away from Russia. But don't think there aren't a lot of good Anglo-Saxon types who are masters of the first water. In fact, there are a lot of them here around us, though perhaps you don't think so. It's just that if you play a lot of chess you get to looking Russian. Once it probably made you look Italian. Do you see that short bald-headed man?"

"You mean the one facing the Machine and talking to Jandorf?"

"Yes. Now that's one with a lot of human interest. Moses Sherevsky. Been champion of the United States many times. A very strict Orthodox Jew. Can't play chess on Fridays or on Saturdays before sundown." He chuckled. "Why, there's even a story going around that one rabbi told Sherevsky it would be unlawful for him to play against the Machine because it is technically a *golem*—the clay Frankenstein's monster of Hebrew legend."

Sandra asked, "What about Grabo and Kratower?"

Doc gave a short scornful laugh. "Krakatower! Don't pay any attention to *him*. A senile has-been, it's a scandal he's been allowed to play in this tournament! He must have pulled all sorts of strings. Told them that his lifelong services to chess had won him the honor and that they had to have a member of the so-called Old Guard. Maybe he even got down on his knees and cried—and all the time his eyes on that expense money and the last-place consolation prize! Yet dreaming schizophrenically of beating them all! Please, don't get me started on Dirty Old Krakatower."

"Take it easy, Doc. He sounds like he would make an interesting article. Can you point him out to me?"

"You can tell him by his long white beard with coffee stains. I don't see it anywhere, though. Perhaps he's shaved it off for the occasion. It would be like that antique womanizer to develop senile delusions of youthfulness."

"And Grabo?" Sandra pressed, suppressing a smile at the intensity of Doc's animosity.

Doc's eyes grew thoughtful. "About Bela Grabo (why are three out of four Hungarians named Bela?) I will tell you only this: That he is a very brilliant player and that the Machine is very lucky to have drawn him as its first opponent."

He would not amplify his statement. Sandra studied the scoreboard again.

"This Simon Great who's down as programming the Machine. He's a famous physicist, I suppose?"

"By no means. That was the trouble with some of the early chess-playing machines—they were programmed by scientists. No, Simon Great is a psychologist who at one time was a leading contender for the world's chess championship. I think WBM was surprisingly shrewd to pick him for the programming job. Let me tell you—No, better yet—"

Doc shot to his feet, stretched an arm on high and called out sharply, "Simon!"

A man some four tables away waved back and a moment later came over.

"What is it, Savilly?" he asked. "There's hardly any time, you know."

The newcomer was of middle height, compact of figure and feature, with graying hair cut short and combed sharply back.

Doc spoke his piece for Sandra.

Simon Great smiled thinly. "Sorry," he said, "but I am making no predictions and we are giving out no advance information on the programming of the Machine. As you know, I have had to fight the Players' Committee tooth and nail on all sorts of points about that and they have won most of them. I am not permitted to re-program the Machine at adjournments—only between games (I did insist on that and get it!) And if the Machine breaks down during a game, its clock keeps running on it. My men are permitted to make repairs—if they can work fast enough."

"That makes it very tough on you," Sandra put in. "The Machine isn't allowed any weaknesses."

Great nodded soberly. "And now I must go. They've almost finished the count-down, as one of my technicians keeps on calling it. Very pleased to have met you, Miss Grayling—I'll check with our PR man on that interview. Be seeing you, Savvy."

The tiers of seats were filled now and the central space almost clear. Officials were shooing off a few knots of lingerers. Several of the grandmasters, including all four Russians, were seated at their tables. Press and company cameras were flashing. The four

smaller wallboards lit up with the pieces in the opening position—
white for White and red for Black. Simon Great stepped over the
red velvet cord and more flash bulbs went off.

"You know, Doc," Sandra said, "I'm a dog to suggest this, but
what if this whole thing were a big fake? What if Simon Great
were really playing the Machine's moves? There would surely be
some way for his electricians to rig—"

Doc laughed happily—and so loudly that some people at the
adjoining tables frowned.

"Miss Grayling, that is a wonderful idea! I will probably steal
it for a short story. I still manage to write and place a few in
England. No, I do not think that is at all likely. WBM would
never risk such a fraud. Great is completely out of practice for
actual tournament play, though not for chess-thinking. The
difference in style between a computer and a man would be
evident to any expert. Great's own style is remembered and
would be recognized—though, come to think of it, his style was
often described as being machine-like..." For a moment Doc's
eyes became thoughtful. Then he smiled again. "But no, the idea
is impossible. Vanderhoef as Tournament Director has played
two or three games with the Machine to assure himself that it
operates legitimately and has grandmaster skill."

"Did the Machine beat him?" Sandra asked.

Doc shrugged. "The scores weren't released. It was very hush-
hush. But about your idea, Miss Grayling—did you ever read
about Maelzel's famous chessplaying automaton of the 19th
Century? That one too was supposed to work by machinery (cogs
and gears, not electricity) but actually it had a man hidden inside
it—your Edgar Poe exposed the fraud in a famous article. In *my*
story I think the chess robot will break down while it is being
demonstrated to a millionaire purchaser and the young inventor
will have to win its game for it to cover up and swing the deal.
Only the millionaire's daughter, who is really a better player than
either of them... yes, yes! Your Ambrose Bierce too wrote a story
about a chessplaying robot of the clickety-clank-grr kind who
murdered his creator, crushing him like an iron grizzly bear when
the man won a game from him. Tell me, Miss Grayling, do you
find yourself imagining this Machine putting out angry tendrils to
strangle its opponents, or beaming rays of death and hypnotism
at them? I can imagine..."

While Doc chattered happily on about chessplaying robots and chess stories, Sandra found herself thinking about him. A writer of some sort evidently and a terrific chess buff. Perhaps he was an actual medical doctor. She'd read something about two or three coming over with the Russian squad. But Doc certainly didn't sound like a Soviet citizen.

He was older than she'd first assumed. She could see that now that she was listening to him less and looking at him more. Tired, too. Only his dark-circled eyes shone with unquenchable youth. A useful old guy, whoever he was. An hour ago she'd been sure she was going to muff this assignment completely and now she had it laid out cold. For the umpteenth time in her career Sandra shied away from the guilty thought that she wasn't a writer at all or even a reporter, she just used dime-a-dozen female attractiveness to rope a susceptible man (young, old, American, Russian) and pick his brain...

She realized suddenly that the whole hall had become very quiet.

Doc was the only person still talking and people were again looking at them disapprovingly. All five wall-boards were lit up and the changed position of a few pieces showed that opening moves had been made on four of them, including the Machine's. The central space between the tiers of seats was completely clear now, except for one man hurrying across it in their direction with the rapid yet quiet, almost tip-toe walk that seemed to mark all the officials. *Like morticians' assistants,* she thought. He rapidly mounted the stairs and halted at the top to look around searchingly. His gaze lighted on their table, his eyebrows went up, and he made a beeline for Doc. Sandra wondered if she should warn him that he was about to be shushed.

The official laid a hand on Doc's shoulder. "Sir!" he said agitatedly. "Do you realize that they've started your clock, Dr. Krakatower?"

Sandra became aware that Doc was grinning at her. "Yes, it's true enough, Miss Grayling," he said. "I trust you will pardon the deception, though it was hardly one, even technically. Every word I told you about Dirty Old Krakatower is literally true. Except the long white beard—he never wore a beard after he was 35—that part was an out-and-out lie! Yes, yes! I will be along in a moment! Do not worry, the spectators will get their money's worth out of me! And WBM did not with its expense account buy my soul—that belongs to the young lady here."

Doc rose, lifted her hand and kissed it. "Thank you, *mademoiselle,* for a charming interlude. I hope it will be repeated. Incidentally, I should say that besides... (Stop pulling at me, man!—there can't be five minutes on my clock yet!)... that besides being Dirty Old Krakatower, grandmaster emeritus, I am also the special correspondent of the *London Times.* It is always pleasant to chat with a colleague. Please do not hesitate to use in your articles any of the ideas I tossed out, if you find them worthy—I sent in my own first dispatch two hours ago. Yes, yes, I come! *Au revoir, mademoiselle!*"

He was at the bottom of the stairs when Sandra jumped up and hurried to the balustrade.

"Hey, Doc!" she called.

He turned.

"Good luck!" she shouted and waved.

He kissed his hand to her and went on.

People glared at her then and a horrified official came hurrying. Sandra made big frightened eyes at him, but she couldn't quite hide her grin.

IV

Sitzfleisch (WHICH ROUGHLY MEANS ENDURANCE— "sitting flesh" or "buttock meat") is the quality needed above all others by tournament chess players—and their audiences.

After Sandra had watched the games (the players' faces, rather—she had a really good pair of zoomer glasses) for a half hour or so, she had gone to her hotel room, written her first article (interview with the famous Dr. Krakatower), sent it in and then come back to the hall to see how the games had turned out.

They were still going on, all five of them.

The press section was full, but two boys and a girl of high-school age obligingly made room for Sandra on the top tier of seats and she tuned in on their whispered conversation. The jargon was recognizably related to that which she'd gotten a dose of on the floor, but gamier. Players did not sacrifice pawns, they sacked them. No one was ever defeated, only busted. Pieces weren't lost but blown. The Ruy Lopez was the Dirty Old *Rooay*—and incidentally a certain set of opening moves named after a long-departed Spanish churchman, she now discovered from Dave, Bill and Judy, whose sympathetic help she won by frequent loans of her zoomer glasses.

The four-hour time control point—two hours and 30 moves for each player—had been passed while she was sending in her article, she learned, and they were well on their way toward the next control point—an hour more and 15 moves for each player—after which unfinished games would be adjourned and continued at a special morning session. Sherevsky had had to make 15 moves in two minutes after taking an hour earlier on just one move. But that was nothing out of the ordinary, Dave had assured her in the same breath, Sherevsky was always letting himself get into "fantastic time-pressure" and then wriggling out of it brilliantly. He was apparently headed for a win over Serek. *Score one for the USA over the USSR*, Sandra thought proudly.

Votbinnik had Jandorf practically in *Zugzwang* (his pieces all tied up, Bill explained) and the Argentinean would be busted shortly. Through the glasses Sandra could see Jandorf s thick chest rise and fall as he glared murderously at the board in front of him. By contrast Votbinnik looked like a man lost in reverie.

Dr. Krakatower had lost a pawn to Lysmov but was hanging on grimly. However, Dave would not give a plugged nickel for his chances against the former world's champion, because "those old ones always weaken in the sixth hour."

"You for-get the bio-logical mir-acle of Doc-tor Las-ker," Bill and Judy chanted as one.

"Shut up," Dave warned them. An official glared angrily from the floor and shook a finger. Much later Sandra discovered that Dr. Emanuel Lasker was a philosopher-mathematician who, after holding the world's championship for 26 years, had won a very strong tournament (New York 1924) at the age of 56 and later almost won another (Moscow 1935) at the age of 67.

Sandra studied Doc's face carefully through her glasses. He looked terribly tired now, almost a death's head. Something tightened in her chest and she looked away quickly.

The Angler-Jal and Grabo-Machine games were still ding-dong contests, Dave told her. If anything, Grabo had a slight advantage.

The Machine was "on the move," meaning that Grabo had just made a move and was waiting the automaton's reply.

The Hungarian was about the most restless "waiter" Sandra could imagine. He twisted his long legs constantly and writhed his shoulders and about every five seconds he ran his hands back through his unkempt tassel of hair.

Once he yawned self-consciously, straightened himself and sat very compactly. But almost immediately he was writhing again.

The Machine had its own mannerisms, if you could call them that. Its dim, unobtrusive telltale lights were winking on and off in a fairly rapid, random pattern. Sandra got the impression that from time to time Grabo's eyes were trying to follow their blinking, like a man watching fireflies.

Simon Great sat impassively behind a bare table next to the Machine, his five gray-smocked technicians grouped around him.

A flushed-faced, tall, distinguished-looking elderly gentleman was standing by the Machine's console. Dave told Sandra it was Dr. Vanderhoef, the Tournament Director, one-time champion of the world.

"Another old potzer like Krakatower, but with sense enough to know when he's licked," Bill characterized harshly.

"Youth, ah, un-van-quish-able youth," Judy chanted happily by herself. "Flashing like a meteor across the chess fir-ma-ment. Morphy, Angler, Judy Kaplan…"

"Shut up! They really will throw us out," Dave warned her and then explained in whispers to Sandra that Vanderhoef and his assistants had the nervous-making job of feeding into the Machine the moves made by its opponent, "so everyone will know it's on the level, I guess." He added, "It means the Machine loses a few seconds every move, between the time Grabo punches the clock and the time Vanderhoef gets the move fed into the Machine."

Sandra nodded. The players were making it as hard on the Machine as possible, she decided with a small rush of sympathy.

Suddenly there was a tiny movement of the gadget attached from the Machine to the clocks on Grabo's table and a faint *click*. But Grabo almost leapt out of his skin.

Simultaneously a red castle-topped piece (one of the Machine's rooks, Sandra was informed) moved four squares sideways on the big electric board above the Machine. An official beside Dr. Vanderhoef went over to Grabo's board and carefully moved the corresponding piece. Grabo seemed about to make some complaint, then apparently thought better of it and plunged into brooding cogitation over the board, elbows on the table, both hands holding his head and fiercely massaging his scalp.

The Machine let loose with an unusually rapid flurry of blinking. Grabo straightened up, seemed again about to make a complaint, then once more to repress the impulse. Finally he moved a piece and punched his clock. Dr. Vanderhoef immediately flipped four levers on the Machine's console and Grabo's move appeared on the electric board.

Grabo sprang up, went over to the red velvet cord and motioned agitatedly to Vanderhoef.

There was a short conference, inaudible at the distance, during which Grabo waved his arms and Vanderhoef grew more flushed. Finally the latter went over to Simon Great and said something, apparently with some hesitancy. But Great smiled obligingly, sprang to his feet, and in turn spoke to his technicians, who immediately fetched and unfolded several large screens and set them in front of the Machine, masking the blinking lights. *Blindfolding it,* Sandra found herself thinking.

Dave chuckled. "That's already happened once while you were out," he told Sandra. "I guess seeing the lights blinking makes Grabo nervous. But then *not* seeing them makes him nervous. Just watch."

"The Machine has its own mysterious pow-wow-wers," Judy chanted.

"That's what you think," Bill told her. "Did you know that Willie Angler has hired Evil Eye Bixel out of Brooklyn to put the whammy on the Machine? S'fact."

"… pow-wow-wers unknown to mere mortals of flesh and blood—"

"Shut up!" Dave hissed. "Now you've done it. Here comes old Eagle Eye. Look, I don't know you two. I'm with this lady here."

Bela Grabo was suffering acute tortures. He had a winning attack, he knew it. The Machine was counter-attacking, but unstrategically, desperately, in the style of a Frank Marshall complicating the issue and hoping for a swindle. All Grabo had to do, he knew, was keep his head and *not blunder*—not throw away a queen, say, as he had to old Vanderhoef at Brussels, or overlook a mate in two, as he had against Sherevsky at Tel

Aviv. The memory of those unutterably black moments and a dozen more like them returned to haunt him. Never if he lived a thousand years would he be *free* of them.

For the tenth time in the last two minutes he glanced at his clock. He had fifteen minutes in which to make five moves. He wasn't in time-pressure, he must remember that. He mustn't make a move on impulse, he mustn't let his treacherous hand leap out without waiting for instructions from its guiding brain.

First prize in this tournament meant incredible wealth—transportation money and hotel bills for more than a score of future tournaments. But more than that, it was one more chance to blazon before the world his true superiority rather than the fading reputation of it. "... Bela Grabo, brilliant but erratic..." Perhaps his last chance.

When, in the name of Heaven, was the Machine going to make its next move? Surely it had already taken more than four minutes! But a glance at its clock showed him that hardly half that time had gone by. He decided he had made a mistake in asking again for the screens. It was easier to watch those damned lights blink than have them blink in his imagination.

Oh, if chess could only be played in intergalactic space, in the black privacy of one's thoughts. But there had to be the physical presence of the opponent with his (possibly deliberate) unnerving mannerisms—Lasker and his cigar, Capablanca and his red necktie, Nimzowitsch and his nervous contortions (very like Bela Grabo's, though the latter did not see it that way). And now this ghastly flashing, humming, stinking, button-banging metal monster!

Actually, he told himself, he was being asked to play two opponents, the Machine and Simon Great, a sort of consultation team. It wasn't fair!

The Machine hammered its button and rammed its queen across the electric board. In Grabo's imagination it was like an explosion.

Grabo held onto his nerves with an effort and plunged into a maze of calculations.

Once he came to, like a man who had been asleep, to realize that he was wondering whether the lights were still blinking behind the screens while he was making his move. Did the Machine really analyze at such times or were the lights just an empty trick? He forced his mind back to the problems of the game, decided on his move, checked the board twice for any violent move he might have missed, noted on his clock that he'd taken five minutes, checked the board again very rapidly and then put out his hand and made his move—with the fiercely suspicious air of a boss compelled to send an extremely unreliable underling on an all-important errand.

Then he punched his clock, sprang to his feet, and once more waved for Vanderhoef.

Thirty seconds later the Tournament Director, very red-faced now, was saying in a low voice, almost pleadingly, "But Bela, I cannot keep asking them to change the screens. Already they have been up twice and down once to please you. Moving them disturbs the other players and surely isn't good for your own peace of mind. Oh, Bela, my dear Bela—"

Vanderhoef broke off. Grabo knew he had been going to say something improper but from the heart, such as, "For God's sake don't blow this game out of nervousness now that you have a win in sight" —and this sympathy somehow made the Hungarian furious.

"I have other complaints which I will make formally after the game," he said harshly, quivering with rage. "It is a disgrace the way that mechanism punches the time-clock button. It will crack the case! The Machine never stops humming! And it stinks of ozone and hot metal, as if it were about to explode!"

"It *cannot* explode, Bela. Please!"

"No, but it threatens to! And you know a threat is always more effective than an actual attack! As for the screens, they must be taken down at once, I demand it!"

"Very well, Bela, very well, it will be done. Compose yourself."

Grabo did not at once return to his table—he could not have endured to sit still for the moment—but paced along the line of tables, snatching looks at the other games in progress. When he looked back at the big electric board, he saw that the Machine had made a move although he hadn't heard it punch the clock. He rushed back and studied the board without sitting down. Why, the Machine had made a *stupid* move, he saw with a rush of exaltation. At that moment the last screen being folded started to fall over, but one of the gray-smocked men caught it deftly. Grabo flinched and his hand darted out and moved a piece.

He heard someone gasp. Vanderhoef.

* * *

It got very quiet. The four soft clicks of the move being fed into the Machine were like the beat of a muffled drum.

There was a buzzing in Grabo's ears. He looked down at the board in horror.

The Machine blinked, blinked once more and then, although barely twenty seconds had elapsed, moved a rook.

On the glassy gray margin above the Machine's electric board, large red words flamed on:

CHECK! AND MATE IN THREE

Up in the stands Dave squeezed Sandra's arm. "He's done it! He's let himself be swindled."

"You mean the Machine has beaten Grabo?" Sandra asked.

"What else?"

"Can you be sure? Just like that?"

"Of cour... Wait a second... Yes, I'm sure,"

"Mated in three like a potzer," Bill confirmed.

"The poor old boob," Judy sighed.

Down on the floor Bela Grabo sagged. The assistant director moved toward him quickly. But then the Hungarian straightened himself a little.

"I resign," he said softly.

The red words at the top of the board were wiped out and briefly replaced, in white, by:

THANK YOU FOR GOOD GAME

And then a third statement, also in white, flashed on for a few seconds:

YOU HAD BAD LUCK

Bela Grabo clenched his fists and bit his teeth. Even *the Machine* was being sorry for him!

He stiffly walked out of the hall. It was a long, long walk.

V

ADJOURNMENT TIME NEARED. SEREK, THE EXCHANGE down but with considerable time on his clock, sealed his forty-sixth move against Sherevsky and handed the envelope to Vanderhoef. It would be opened when the game was resumed at the morning session. Dr. Krakatower studied the position on his board and then quietly tipped over his king. He sat there for a moment as if he hadn't the strength to rise. Then he shook himself a little, smiled, got up, clasped hands briefly with Lysmov and wandered over to watch the Angler-Jal game.

Jandorf had resigned his game to Votbinnik some minutes ago, rather more surlily.

After a while Angler sealed a move, handing it to Vanderhoef with a grin just as the little red flag dropped on his clock, indicating he'd used every second of his time.

Up in the stands Sandra worked her shoulders to get a kink out of her back. She'd noticed several newsmen hurrying off to report in the Machine's first win. She was thankful that her job was limited to special articles.

"Chess is a pretty intense game," she remarked to Dave.

He nodded. "It's a killer. I don't expect to live beyond forty myself."

"Thirty," Bill said.

"Twenty-five is enough time to be a meteor," said Judy.

Sandra thought to herself: *the Unbeat Generation.*

Next day Sherevsky played the Machine to a dead-level ending. Simon Great offered a draw for the Machine (over an unsuccessful interfering protest from Jandorf that this constituted making a move for the Machine) but Sherevsky refused and sealed his move.

"He wants to have it proved to him that the Machine can play endgames," Dave commented to Sandra up in the stands. "I don't blame him."

At the beginning of today's session Sandra had noticed that Bill and Judy were following each game in a very new-looking book they shared jealously between them. *Won't look new for long,* Sandra had thought.

"That's the 'Bible' they got there," Dave had explained. "MCO—*Modern Chess Openings*. It lists all the best open-moves in chess, thousands and thousands of variations. That is, what masters *think* are the best moves. The moves that have won in the past, really. We chipped in together to buy the latest edition— the 13th—just hot off the press," he had finished proudly.

Now with the Machine-Sherevsky ending the center of interest, the kids were consulting another book, one with grimy, dog-eared pages.

"That's the 'New Testament'—*Basic Chess Endings,*" Dave said when he noticed her looking. "There's so much you must know in endings that it's amazing the Machine can play them at all. I guess as the pieces get fewer it starts to look deeper."

Sandra nodded. She was feeling virtuous. She had got her interview with Jandorf and then this morning one with Grabo ("How it Feels to Have a Machine Out-Think You"). The latter had made her think of herself as a real vulture of the press, circling over the doomed. The Hungarian had seemed in a positively suicidal depression.

One newspaper article made much of the Machine's "psychological tactics," hinting that the blinking lights were designed to hypnotize opponents. The general press coverage was somewhat startling. A game that in America normally rated only a fine-print column in the back sections of a very few Sunday papers was now getting boxes on the front page. The defeat of a man by a machine seemed everywhere to awaken nervous feelings of insecurity, like the launching of the first Sputnik.

Sandra had rather hesitantly sought out Dr. Krakatower during the close of the morning session of play, still feeling a little guilty from her interview with Grabo. But Doc had seemed happy to see her and quite recovered from last night's defeat, though when she had addressed him as "Master Krakatower" he had winced and said, "Please, not that!" Another session of coffee and wine-and-seltzer had resulted in her getting an introduction to her first Soviet grandmaster, Serek, who had proved to be unexpectedly charming. He had just managed to draw his game with Sherevsky (to the great amazement of the kibitzers, Sandra learned) and was most obliging about arranging for an interview.

Not to be outdone in gallantry, Doc had insisted on escorting Sandra to her seat in the stands—at the price of once more losing a couple of minutes on his clock. As a result her stock went up considerably with Dave, Bill and Judy. Thereafter they treated anything she had to say with almost annoying deference—Bill especially, probably in penance for his thoughtless cracks at Doc. Sandra later came to suspect that the kids had privately decided that she was Dr. Krakatower's mistress—probably a new one because she was so scandalously ignorant of chess. She did not disillusion them.

Doc lost again in the second round—to Jal.

In the third round Lysmov defeated the Machine in 27 moves. There was a flaring of flashbulbs, a rush of newsmen to the phones, jabbering in the stands and much comment and analysis that was way over Sandra's head—except she got the impression that Lysmov had done something tricky.

The general emotional reaction in America, as reflected by the newspapers, was not too happy. One read between the lines that for the Machine to beat a man was bad, but for a Russian to beat an American machine was worse. A widely-read sports columnist, two football coaches, and several rural politicians announced that chess was a morbid game played only by weirdies. Despite these thick-chested he-man statements, the elusive mood of insecurity deepened.

Besides the excitement of the Lysmov win, a squabble had arisen in connection with the Machine's still-unfinished end game with Sherevsky, which had been continued through one morning session and was now headed for another.

Finally, there were rumors that World Business Machines was planning to replace Simon Great with a nationally famous physicist.

Sandra begged Doc to try to explain it all to her in kindergarten language. She was feeling uncertain of herself again and quite subdued after being completely rebuffed in her efforts to get an interview with Lysmov, who had fled her as if she were a threat to his Soviet virtue.

Doc on the other hand was quite vivacious, cheered by his third-round draw with Jandorf.

"Most willingly, my dear," he said. "Have you ever noticed that kindergarten language can be far honester than the adult tongues? Fewer fictions. Well, several of us hashed over the Lysmov game until three o'clock this morning. Lysmov wouldn't, though. Neither would Votbinnik or Jal. You see, I have my communication problems with the Russians too.

"We finally decided that Lysmov had managed to guess with complete accuracy both the depth at which the Machine is analyzing in the opening and middle game (ten moves ahead instead of eight, we think—a prodigious achievement!) and also the main value scale in terms of which the Machine selects its move.

"Having that information, Lysmov managed to play into a combination which would give the Machine a maximum plus value in its value scale (win of Lysmov's queen, it was) after ten moves but a checkmate for Lysmov on his second move *after* the first ten. A human chess master would have seen a trap like that, but the Machine could not, because Lysmov was maneuvering in an area that did not exist for the Machine's perfect but limited mind. Of course the Machine changed its tactics after the first three moves of the ten had been played—it could see the checkmate then—but by that time it was too late for it to avert a disastrous loss of material. It was tricky of Lysmov, but completely fair. After this we'll all be watching for the opportunity to play the same sort of trick on the Machine.

"Lysmov was the first of us to realize fully that *we are not playing against a metal monster but against a certain kind of programming* If there are any weaknesses we can spot in that programming, we can win. Very much in the same way that we can again and again defeat a flesh-and-blood player when we discover that he consistently attacks without having an advantage in position or is regularly overcautious about launching a counter-attack when he himself is attacked without justification."

Sandra nodded eagerly. "So from now on your chances of beating the Machine should keep improving, shouldn't they? I mean as you find out more and more about the programming."

Doc smiled. "You forget," he said gently, "that Simon Great can change the programming before each new game. Now I see why he fought so hard for that point."

"Oh. Say, Doc, what's this about the Sherevsky end game?"

"You are picking up the language, aren't you?" he observed. "Sherevsky got a little angry when he discovered that Great had the Machine programmed to analyze steadily on the next move after an adjournment until the game was resumed next morning. Sherevsky questioned whether it was fair for the Machine to 'think' all night while its opponent had to get some rest. Vanderhoef decided for the Machine, though Sherevsky may carry the protest to FIDE.

"Bah—I think Great wants us to get heated up over such minor matters, just as he is happy (and oh so obliging!) when we complain about how the Machine blinks or hums or smells. It keeps our minds off the main business of trying to outguess his programming. Incidentally, that is one thing we decided last night—Sherevsky, Willie Angler, Jandorf, Serek, and myself— that we are all going to have to learn to play the Machine without letting it get on our nerves and without asking to be protected from it. As Willie puts it, 'So suppose it sounds like a boiler factory even—okay, you can think in a boiler factory.' Myself, I am not so sure of that, but his spirit is right."

Sandra felt herself perking up as a new article began to shape itself in her mind. She said, "And what about WBM replacing Simon Great?"

Again Doc smiled. "I think, my dear, that you can safely dismiss that as just a rumor. I think that Simon Great has just begun to fight."

VI

ROUND FOUR SAW THE MACHINE SPRING THE FIRST of its surprises.

It had finally forced a draw against Sherevsky in the morning session, ending the long second-round game, and now was matched against Votbinnik.

The Machine opened Pawn to King Four, Votbinnik replied Pawn to King Three.

"The French Defense, Binny's favorite," Dave muttered and they settled back for the Machine's customary four-minute wait.

Instead the Machine moved at once and punched its clock.

Sandra, studying Votbinnik through her glasses, decided that the Russian grandmaster looked just a trifle startled. Then he made his move.

Once again the Machine responded instantly.

There was a flurry of comment from the stands and a scurrying-about of officials to shush it. Meanwhile the Machine continued to make its moves at better than rapid-transit speed, although Votbinnik soon began to take rather more time on his.

The upshot was that the Machine made eleven moves before it started to take time to "think" at all.

Sandra clamored so excitedly to Dave for an explanation that she had two officials waving at her angrily.

As soon as he dared, Dave whispered, "Great must have banked on Votbinnik playing the French—almost always does—and fed all the variations of the French into the Machine's 'memory' from MCO and maybe some other books. So long as Votbinnik stuck to a known variation of the French, why, the Machine could play from memory without analyzing at all. Then when a strange move came along—one that wasn't in its memory—only on the twelfth move yet!—the Machine went back to analyzing, only now it's taking longer and going deeper because it's got more time—six minutes a move, about. The only thing I wonder is why Great didn't have the Machine do it in the first three games. It seems so obvious."

Sandra ticketed that in her mind as a question for Doc. She slipped off to her room to write her "Don't Let a Robot Get Your Goat" article (drawing heavily on Doc's observations) and got back to the stands twenty minutes before the second time-control point. It was becoming a regular routine.

Votbinnik was a knight down—almost certainly busted, Dave explained.

"It got terrifically complicated while you were gone," he said. "A real Votbinnik position."

"Only the Machine out-binniked him," Bill finished.

Judy hummed Beethoven's "Funeral March for the Death of a Hero."

Nevertheless Votbinnik did not resign. The Machine sealed a move. Its board blacked out and Vanderhoef, with one of his assistants standing beside him to witness, privately read the move off a small indicator on the console. Tomorrow he would feed the move back into the Machine when play was resumed at the morning session.

Doc sealed a move too although he was two pawns down in his game against Grabo and looked tired to death.

"They don't give up easily, do they?" Sandra observed to Dave. "They must really love the game. Or do they hate it?"

"When you get to psychology it's all beyond me," Dave replied. "Ask me something else."

Sandra smiled. "Thank you, Dave," she said. "I will."

* * *

Come the morning session Votbinnik played on for a dozen moves then resigned.

A little later Doc managed to draw his game with Grabo by perpetual check. He caught sight of Sandra coming down from the stands and waved to her, then made the motions of drinking.

Now he looks almost like a boy, Sandra thought as she joined him.

"Say, Doc," she asked when they had secured a table, "why is a rook worth more than a bishop?"

He darted a suspicious glance at her. "That is not your kind of question," he said sternly. "Exactly what have you been up to?"

Sandra confessed that she had asked Dave to teach her how to play chess.

"I knew those children would corrupt you," Doc said somberly. "Look, my dear, if you learn to play chess you won't be able to write your clever little articles about it. Besides, as I warned you the first day, chess is a madness. Women are ordinarily immune, but that doesn't justify you taking chances with your sanity."

"But I've kind of gotten interested, watching the tournament," Sandra objected. "At least I'd like to know how the pieces move."

"Stop!" Doc commanded. "You're already in danger. Direct your mind somewhere else. Ask me a sensible, down-to-earth journalist's question—something completely irrational!"

"Okay, why didn't Simon Great have the Machine set to play the openings fast in the first three games?"

"Hah! I think Great plays Lasker-chess in his programming. He hides his strength and tries to win no more easily than he has to, so he will have resources in reserve. The Machine loses to Lysmov and immediately starts playing more strongly—the psychological impression made on the other players by such tactics is formidable."

"But the Machine isn't ahead yet?"

"No, of course not. After four rounds Lysmov is leading the tournament with 3 ½—½, meaning 3 ½ in the win column and ½ in the loss column..."

"How do you half win a game of chess? Or half lose one?" Sandra interrupted.

"By drawing a game—playing to a tie. Lysmov's 3½—½ is notational shorthand for three wins and a draw. Understand? My dear, I don't usually have to explain things to you in such detail."

"I just didn't want you to think I was learning too much about chess."

"Ho! Well, to get on with the score after four rounds, Angler and Votbinnik both have 3—1, while the Machine is bracketed at 2 ½—1 ½ with Jal. But the Machine has created an impression of strength, as if it were all set to come from behind with a rush." He shook his head. "At the moment, my dear," he said, "I feel very pessimistic about the chances of neurons against relays in this tournament. Relays don't panic and fag. But the oddest thing..."

"Yes?" Sandra prompted.

"Well, the oddest thing is that the Machine doesn't play 'like a machine' at all. It uses dynamic strategy, the kind we sometimes call 'Russian,' complicating each position as much as possible and creating maximum tension. But that too is a matter of the programming..."

Doc's foreboding was fulfilled as round followed hard-fought round. In the next five days (there was a weekend recess) the Machine successively smashed Jandorf, Serek and Jal and after seven rounds was out in front by a full point.

Jandorf, evidently impressed by the Machine's flawless opening play against Votbinnik, chose an inferior line in the Ruy Lopez to get the Machine "out of the books." Perhaps he hoped that the Machine would go on blindly making book moves, but the Machine did not oblige. It immediately slowed its play, "thought hard" and annihilated the Argentinean in 25 moves.

Doc commented, "The Wild Bull of the Pampas tried to use the living force of his human personality to pull a fast one and swindle the Machine. Only the Machine didn't swindle."

Against Jal, the Machine used a new wrinkle. It used a variable amount of time on moves, apparently according to how difficult it "judged" the position to be.

When Serek got a poor pawn-position the Machine simplified the game relentlessly, suddenly discarding its hitherto "Russian" strategy. "It plays like anything but a machine," Doc commented. "We know the reason all too well—Simon Great—but doing something about it is something else again. Great is hitting at our individual weaknesses wonderfully well. Though I think I could play brilliant psychological chess myself if I had a machine to do the detail work." Doc sounded a bit wistful.

The audiences grew in size and in expensiveness of wardrobe, though most of the cafe society types made their visits fleeting ones. Additional stands were erected. A hard-liquor bar was put in and then taken out. The problem of keeping reasonable order and quiet became an unending one for Vanderhoef, who had to ask for more "hushers." The number of scientists and computer men in attendance increased. Navy, Army and Space Force uniforms were more in evidence. Dave and Bill turned up one morning with a three-dimensional chess set of transparent plastic and staggered Sandra by assuring her that most bright young space scientists were moderately adept at this 512-square game.

Sandra heard that WBM had snagged a big order from the War Department. She also heard that a Syndicate man had turned up with a book on the tournament, taking bets from the more heavily heeled types and that a detective was circulating about, trying to spot him.

The newspapers kept up their front-page reporting, most of the writers personalizing the Machine heavily and rather too cutely. Several of the papers started regular chess columns and "How to Play Chess" features. There was a flurry of pictures of movie starlets and such sitting at chess boards. Hollywood revealed plans for two chess movies: "They Made Her a Black Pawn" and "The Monster From King Rook Square." Chess novelties and costume jewelry appeared. The United States Chess Federation proudly reported a phenomenal rise in membership.

Sandra learned enough chess to be able to blunder through a game with Dave without attempting more than one illegal move in five, to avoid the Scholar's Mate most of the time and to be able to checkmate with two rooks though not with one. Judy had asked her, "Is *he* pleased that you're learning chess?"

Sandra had replied, "No, he thinks it is a madness." The kids had all whooped at that and Dave had said, "How right he is!"

Sandra was scraping the bottom of the barrel for topics for her articles, but then it occurred to her to write about the kids, which worked out nicely, and that led to a humorous article "Chess Is for Brains" about her own efforts to learn the game, and for the nth time in her career she thought of herself as practically a columnist and was accordingly elated.

After his two draws, Doc lost three games in a row and still had the Machine to face and then Sherevsky. His 1—6 score gave him undisputed possession of last place. He grew very depressed.

He still made a point of squiring her about before the playing sessions, but she had to make most of the conversation. His rare flashes of humor were rather macabre.

"They have Dirty Old Krakatower locked in the cellar," he muttered just before the start of the next to the last round, "and now they send the robot down to destroy him."

"Just the same, Doc," Sandra told him, "good luck."

Doc shook his head. "Against a man luck might help. But against a Machine?"

"It's not the Machine you're playing, but the programming. Remember?"

"Yes, but it's the Machine that doesn't make the mistake. And a mistake is what I need most of all today. Somebody else's."

Doc must have looked very dispirited and tired when he left Sandra in the stands, for Judy (Dave and Bill not having arrived yet) asked in a confidential, womanly sort of voice, "What do you do for him when he's so unhappy?"

"Oh, I'm especially passionate," Sandra heard herself answer.

"Is that good for him?" Judy demanded doubtfully.

"Sh!" Sandra said, somewhat aghast at her irresponsibility and wondering if *she* were getting tournament nerves. "Sh, they're starting the clocks."

VII

KRAKATOWER HAD LOST TWO PAWNS WHEN THE first time-control point arrived and was intending to resign on his 31st move when the Machine broke down. Three of its pieces moved on the electric board at once, then the board went dark and all the lights on the console went out except five which started winking like angry red eyes. The gray-smocked men around Simon Great sprang silently into action, filing around back of the console. It was the first work anyone had seen them do except move screens around and fetch each other coffee. Vanderhoef hovered anxiously. Some flash bulbs went off. Vanderhoef shook his fist at the photographers. Simon Great did nothing. The Machine's clock ticked on. Doc watched for a while and then fell asleep.

When Vanderhoef jogged him awake, the Machine had just

made its next move, but the repair-job had taken 50 minutes. As a result the Machine had to make 15 moves in 10 minutes. At 40 seconds a move it played like a dub whose general lack of skill was complicated by a touch of insanity. On his 43rd move Doc shrugged his shoulders apologetically and announced mate in four. There were more flashes. Vanderhoef shook his fist again. The machine flashed:

YOU PLAYED BRILLIANTLY. CONGRATULATIONS!

Afterwards Doc said sourly to Sandra, "And *that* was one big lie—a child could have beat the Machine with that time advantage. Oh, what an ironic glory the gods reserved for Krakatower's dotage—to vanquish a broken-down computer! Only one good thing about it—that it didn't happen while it was playing one of the Russians, or someone would surely have whispered sabotage. And that is something of which they do not accuse Dirty Old Krakatower, because they are sure he has not got the brains even to think to sprinkle a little magnetic oxide powder in the Machine's memory box. Bah!"

Just the same he seemed considerably more cheerful.

Sandra said guilelessly, "Winning a game means nothing to you chess players, does it, unless you really do it by your own brilliancy?"

Doc looked solemn for a moment, then he started to chuckle. "You are getting altogether too smart, Miss Sandra Lea Grayling," he said. "Yes, yes—a chess player is happy to win in any barely legitimate way he can, by an earthquake if necessary, or his opponent sickening before he does from the bubonic plague. So—I confess it to you—I was very happy to chalk up my utterly undeserved win over the luckless Machine."

"Which incidentally makes it anybody's tournament again, doesn't it, Doc?"

"Not exactly." Doc gave a wry little headshake. "We can't expect another fluke. After all, the Machine has functioned perfectly seven games out of eight, and you can bet the WBM men will be checking it all night, especially since it has no adjourned games to work on. Tomorrow it plays Willie Angler, but judging from the way it beat Votbinnik and Jal, it should have a definite edge on Willie. If it beats him, then only Votbinnik has a chance for a tie and to do that he must defeat Lysmov. Which will be most difficult."

"Well," Sandra said, "don't you think that Lysmov might just kind of let himself be beaten, to make sure a Russian gets first place or at least ties for it?"

Doc shook his head emphatically. "There are many things a man, even a chess master, will do to serve his state, but party loyalty doesn't go that deep. Look here is the standing of the players after eight rounds." He handed Sandra a penciled list.

ONE ROUND TO GO

Player	Wins	Losses
Machine	5 ½	2 ½
Votbinnik	5 ½	2 ½
Angler	5	3
Jal	4 ½	3 ½
Lysmov	4 ½	3 ½
Serek	4 ½	3 ½
Sherevsky	4	4
Jandorf	2 ½	5 _
Grabo	2	6
Krakatower	2	6

LAST ROUND PAIRINGS
Machine vs. Angler

Votbinnik vs. Lysmov

Jal vs. Serek

Sherevsky vs. Krakatower

Jandorf vs. Grabo

After studying the list for a while, Sandra said, "Hey, even Angler could come out first, couldn't he, if he beat the Machine and Votbinnik lost to Lysmov?"

"Could, could—yes. But I'm afraid that's hoping for too much, barring another breakdown. To tell the truth, dear, the Machine is simply too good for all of us. If it were only a little faster (and these technological improvements always come) it would out-class us completely. We are at that fleeting moment of balance when genius is almost good enough to equal mechanism. It makes

me feel sad, but proud too in a morbid fashion, to think that I am
in at the death of grandmaster chess. Oh, I suppose the game will
always be played, but it won't ever be quite the same." He blew
out a breath and shrugged his shoulders.

"As for Willie, he's a good one and he'll give the Machine a
long hard fight, you can depend on it. He might conceivably even
draw."

He touched Sandra's arm. "Cheer up, my dear," he said. "You
should remind yourself that a victory for the Machine is still a
victory for the USA."

Doc's prediction about a long hard fight was decidedly not
fulfilled.

Having White, the Machine opened Pawn to King Four and
Angler went into the Sicilian Defense. For the first twelve moves
on each side both adversaries pushed their pieces and tapped their
clocks at such lightning speed (Vanderhoef feeding in Angler's
moves swiftly) that up in the stands Bill and Judy were still
flipping pages madly in their hunt for the right column in MCO.

The Machine made its thirteenth move, still at blitz tempo.

"Bishop takes Pawn, check, and mate in three!" Willie announced
very loudly, made the move, banged his clock and sat back.

There was a collective gasp-and-gabble from the stands.

Dave squeezed Sandra's arm hard. Then for once forgetting
that he was Dr. Caution, he demanded loudly of Bill and Judy,
"Have you two idiots found that column yet? *The Machine's
thirteenth move is a boner!*"

Pinning down the reference with a fingernail, Judy cried, "Yes!
Here it is on page 161 in footnote (e) (2) (B). Dave, *that same
thirteenth move for White is in the book!* But Black replies Knight
to Queen Two, not Bishop takes Pawn, check. And three moves
later the book gives White a plus value."

"What the heck, it can't be," Bill asserted.

"But it *is*. Check for yourself. *That boner is in the book.*"

"Shut up, everybody!" Dave ordered, clapping his hands to his
face. When he dropped them a moment later his eyes gleamed.
"I got it now! Angler figured they were using the latest edition
of MCO to program the Machine on openings, he found an
editorial error and then he deliberately played the Machine into
that variation!"

Dave practically shouted his last words, but that attracted no attention as at that moment the whole hall was the noisiest it had been throughout the tournament. It simmered down somewhat as the Machine flashed a move.

Angler replied instantly.

The Machine replied almost as soon as Angler's move was fed into it.

Angler moved again, his move was fed into the Machine and the Machine flashed:

I AM CHECKMATED. CONGRATULATIONS!

VIII

NEXT MORNING SANDRA HEARD DAVE'S GUESS confirmed by both Angler and Great. Doc had spotted them having coffee and a malt together and he and Sandra joined them.

Doc was acting jubilant, having just drawn his adjourned game with Sherevsky, which meant, since Jandorf had beaten Grabo, that he was in undisputed possession of Ninth Place. They were all waiting for the finish of the Votbinnik-Lysmov game, which would decide the final standing of the leaders. Willie Angler was complacent and Simon Great was serene and at last a little more talkative.

"You know, Willie," the psychologist said, "I was afraid that one of you boys would figure out something like that. That was the chief reason I didn't have the Machine use the programmed openings until Lysmov's win forced me to. I couldn't check every opening line in MCO and the *Archives* and *Shakhmaty*. There wasn't time. As it was, we had a dozen typists and proofreaders busy for weeks preparing that part of the programming and making sure it was accurate as far as following the books went. Tell the truth now, Willie, how many friends did you have hunting for flaws in the latest edition of MCO?"

Willie grinned. "Your unlucky 13th. Well, that's my secret. Though I've always said that anyone joining the Willie Angler Fan Club ought to expect to have to pay some day for the privilege. They're sharp, those little guys, and I work their tails off."

Simon Great laughed and said to Sandra, "Your young friend Dave was pretty sharp himself to deduce what had happened so quickly. Willie, you ought to have him in the Bleeker Street Irregulars."

Sandra said, "I get the impression he's planning to start a club of his own."

Angler snorted. "That's the one trouble with *my* little guys. They're all waiting to topple me."

Simon Great said, "Well, so long as Willie is passing up Dave, I want to talk to him. It takes real courage in a youngster to question authority."

"How should he get in touch with you?" Sandra asked.

While Great told her, Willie studied them frowningly.

"Si, are you planning to stick in this chess-programming racket?" he demanded.

Simon Great did not answer the question. "Have you been approached the last couple of days by IBM?"

"You mean asking me to take over your job?"

"I said *I*BM, Willie."

"Oh." Willie's grin became a tight one. "I'm not talking."

There was a flurry of sound and movement around the playing tables. Willie sprang up.

"Lysmov's agreed to a draw!" he informed them a moment later. "The gangster!"

"Gangster because he puts you in equal first place with Votbinnik, both of you ahead of the Machine?" Great inquired gently.

"Ahh, he could have beat Binny, giving me sole first. A Russian gangster!"

Doc shook a finger. "Lysmov could also have *lost* to Votbinnik, Willie, putting you in second place."

"Don't think evil thought. So long, pals."

As Angler clattered down the stairs, Simon Great signed the waiter for more coffee, lit a fresh cigarette, took a deep drag and leaned back.

"You know," he said, "it's a great relief not to have to impersonate the hyperconfident programmer for awhile. Being a psychologist has spoiled me for that sort of thing. I'm not as good as I once was at beating people over the head with my ego."

"You didn't do too badly," Doc said.

"Thanks. Actually, WBM is very much pleased with the Machine's performance. The Machine's flaws made it seem more real and more newsworthy, especially how it functioned when the going got tough—those repairs the boys made under time pressure in your game, Savilly, will help sell WBM computers or I miss my guess. In fact nobody could have watched the tournament for long without realizing there were nine smart rugged men out there, ready to kill that computer if they could. The Machine passed a real test. And then the whole deal dramatizes what computers are and what they can and can't do. And not just at the popular level. The WBM research boys are learning a lot about computer and programming theory by studying how the Machine and its programmer behave under tournament stress. It's a kind of test unlike that provided by any other computer work. Just this morning, for instance, one of our big mathematicians told me that he is beginning to think that the Theory of Games *does* apply to chess, because you can bluff and counterbluff with your programming. And *I'm* learning about human psychology."

Doc chuckled. "Such as that even human thinking is just a matter of how you program your own mind?—that we're all like the Machine to that extent?"

"That's one of the big points, Savilly. Yes."

Doc smiled at Sandra. "You wrote a nice little news-story dear, about how Man conquered the Machine by a palpitating nose and won a victory for international amity.

"Now the story starts to go deeper."

"A lot of things go deeper," Sandra replied, looking at him evenly. "Much deeper than you ever expect at the start."

The big electric scoreboard lit up.

FINAL STANDING

PLAYER	WINS	LOSSES
ANGLER	6	3
VOTBINNIK	6	3
JAL	5 ½	3 ½
MACHINE	5 ½	3 ½
LYSNOV	5	4
SEREK	4 ½	4 ½
SHEREVSKY	4 ½	4 ½
JANDORF	3 ½	5 ½
KRAKATOWER	2 ½	6 ½
GRABO	2	7

"It was a good tournament," Doc said. "And the Machine has proven itself a grandmaster. It must make you feel good, Simon, after being out of tournament chess for twenty years."

The psychologist nodded.

"Will you go back to psychology now?" Sandra asked him.

Simon Great smiled. "I can answer that question honestly, Miss Grayling, because the news is due for release. No. WBM is pressing for entry of the Machine in the Interzonal Candidates' Tournament. They want a crack at the World's Championship."

Doc raised his eyebrows. "That's news indeed. But look, Simon, with the knowledge you've gained in this tournament won't you be able to make the Machine almost a sure winner in every game?"

"I don't know. Players like Angler and Lysmov may find some more flaws in its functioning and dream up some new stratagems. Besides, there's another solution to the problems raised by having a single computer entered in a grandmaster tournament."

Doc sat up straight. "You mean having more programmer-computer teams than just one?"

"Exactly. The Russians are bound to give their best players computers, considering the prestige the game had in Russia. And I wasn't asking Willie that question about IBM just on a hunch. Chess tournaments are a wonderful way to test rival computers and show them off to the public, just like cross-country races were for the early automobiles. The future grandmaster will inevitably be a programmer-computer team, a man-machine symbiotic partnership, probably with more freedom each way than I was allowed in this tournament—I mean the man taking over the play in some positions, the machine in others."

"You're making my head swim," Sandra said.

"Mine is in the same storm-tossed ocean," Doc assured her. "Simon, that will be very fine for the masters who can get themselves computers—either from their governments or from hiring out to big firms. Or in other ways. Jandorf, I'm sure, will be able to interest some Argentinean millionaire in a computer for him. While I... oh, I'm too old... still, when I start to think about it... But what about the Bela Grabos? Incidentally, did you know that Grabo is contesting Jandorf's win? Claims Jandorf discussed the position with Serek. I think they exchanged about two words."

Simon shrugged, "The Bela Grabos will have to continued to

fight their own battles, if necessary satisfying themselves with the lesser tournaments. Believe me, Savilly, from now on grandmaster chess without one or more computers entered will lack sauce."

Dr. Krakatower shook his head and said, "Thinking gets more expensive every year."

From the floor came the harsh voice of Igor Jandorf and the shrill one of Bela Grabo raised in anger. Three words came through clearly: "... I challenge you..."

Sandra said, "Well, there's something you can't built into a machine—ego."

"Oh I don't know about that," said Simon Great.

ALL THE WEED
IN THE WORLD

WHEN YOU FIRST SMOKE MARIJUANA (THE PROFESSOR said) there are all sorts of kicks the old teahounds will try to steer you into to heighten your enjoyment. Some of them are pretty much at the physical level, like getting loaded and eating a cheap cafeteria meal to see how much more intensely good it tastes than your sober imagination of gourmet's feast, or taking a simple amusement-park roller-coaster ride and discovering space flight. Others call on the imagination a little more. There are several pretty obvious ones involving all the most beautiful girls in the world—or if your fellow weed-heads are intellectual you may be guided into imagined converse with all the great musicians of the past and all the great artists and writers. Liszt may play your inner piano, Paganini your violin, Poe may tread behind you on a midnight walk reciting his poetry. Some of these kicks can be very simple. My teacher put his hand lightly on my head as I sipped that first drag and he told me to close my eyes and then he said softly, "You're just a little weed growing in the desert and the wind is blowing through you." Of course he meant the marijuana weed—weed itself.

If you're young and previously unacquainted with drugs and with intense creative activity (the Professor continued briskly), you may take this imaginative bait and have a few memorable bangs before the first flush fades away forever and you quit all drugs if you've got sense. It'll be like you wrote a beautiful poem without ever writing it. If you're older and have done some heavy drinking and so on, you probably won't respond at all and you'll tell your well-meaning mentors that weed is much overrated.

But there's one kick they'll try to give you that will almost certainly work for you at least once, whether you're a fresh kid or a dull codger. It's one of the biggest and best and simplest kicks there is, and it involves another "all". And it's a good kick. (The bad kicks, like knowing that all the cops in the world are just outside that green door, will come whether you're steered into them or not.) This kick is about all the weed in the world—but before I tell it I've got to tell you about the old doctor.

This ancient six-foot-three-inch wreck—a rain-streaked, fire-blackened ruin of a man with a few bats already flitting through his warped and paintless belfry and a few worms already gnawing at his toes inside his size-fifteen shoes with their little black hangnails of peeling leather—this walking catastrophe had got his M.D. from a homeopathic college back at the turn of the century. He'd occupied the same office for forty years—already the building was changing over from offices to slum apartments—and he was to go on occupying it until he died and they tore the building down. And he was a confirmed miser—he had a box of string (each piece coiled like a rattlesnake) and a box of dead rubber bands (maybe the strings had bit 'em) and barrels of pharmaceutical samples going back to 1900, and already the newspapers had started to pile up ominously in the corners. Even by middle-class standards his office was a dark and cluttered hole with sooty green walls, but it was good enough for his dollar patients and for me, who paid him five to write me morphine prescriptions. In fact to me his office was a dim dark restful shrine that soothed my jitters as if the black dust of the walls were loaded with cocaine. Eventually we got to know each other well, and by bits and pieces he told me his story.

In his youth this old stricken eagle, this thunder-blasted tree, had had a great dream to which he had dedicated his whole life. It had come to him while he was interning at a primitive mental hospital—a vision of healing the sick minds of mankind with narcotic drugs alone. Remember this was when even Sigmund Freud briefly thought the newly-discovered cocaine was great for everyday use (at least by a young and vigorous psychiatrist), when the best thing you could do for a mental case was to keep him soothed down and quiet. (They still have that last idea, why else lobotomy?)

Today it is hard for us to visualize how lightly people regarded narcotic drugs then (the Professor said wistfully) and how easy they were to purchase. The Harrison Narcotic Act of 1914 wiped them off the legal market faster than Roosevelt banned dealings in gold.

At any rate, the old doctor (young then) had the inspiration that there must be a specific narcotic drug that in massive doses would cure each recognized form of insanity. He even had them provisionally identified—morphine for mania, codeine for hysteria, cocaine for involutional melancholia, heroin for catatonia, laudanum (though it's no single drug) for dementia praecox, and so on. Somehow the old doctor never got on drugs himself, but his theory was worthy of a King Weedhead—actually it is quite a kick just by itself.

There wasn't much he could do then to test his theory—he didn't have the reputation or a private sanitarium—but he could prepare to test it. At that time the most important preparation was to get hold of an adequate supply of the drugs he'd need. Narcotics were still openly purchasable, but they wouldn't be for long. The Shanghai Conference and the Hague Convention were coming up and the Harrison Act was already a little black cloud on the horizon. The old doctor didn't want mankind to miss out on the boon he was readying for it just because soon even he, a licensed physician, wouldn't be able to get hold of the essential drugs in the large quantities he'd need, so for the next few years he sank all his spare cash in narcotics, purchasing them all over the country and trying to make sure that he had an adequate supply of every known drug—because he couldn't be certain yet just which narcotic would prove to be the specific remedy for each form of insanity. Even after the passage of the Harrison Act, he continued in a small way to build up his stock, especially of newly discovered drugs, through the regular medical channels available to him.

A few years later he got a fine opportunity to test his great theory: his wife went crazy, and a little later their two children took off in the same direction. He shot them each full of what he considered was the right drug. His theory didn't work. One by one, he had to ship them off to the asylum.

That was the little tragedy that finished the old doctor as a dreamer (the Professor said softly). That was the lightning bolt that blackened and blasted him, that started the first bats winging through his lonely belfry, that turned him into a miserly automaton. Being an addict, I often wondered what happened to his great stockpile of drugs, but that was one point where the old doctor got cagey with me. He'd never quite say. I suppose I assumed that he'd sold them or used them somehow in the natural course of things—after all, would he be writing morphine prescriptions for me if he could with greater safety and profit be selling me some? Besides, his great dream had been dead for twenty years or so when we had our little talks.

What I forgot was the degree of his miserliness and the rigidity of his automatism. There were larger and hairier bats in his belfry than I ever guessed.

I soon drifted away from the city and the old doctor (sighed the Professor), partly to take an involuntary cure for my addiction at Lexington. The cure didn't altogether work, but eventually I did make the unusual but not unheard-of transition to alcohol. At any rate, when I got back to the city again I was a wino and (what is almost a tautology) I was broke. I looked up my friend the old doctor and he was dead and they were tearing down the building he'd practiced in for over fifty years.

For the next week or so I camped nights in that half-destroyed building. It was a convenient den and the dead old doctor's dismantled office—still with the same soot-drifted green walls—was a closer approximation to home for me than my other spot in the known world. I remember I dripped a couple of tears the night I dragged myself and my jug up the crazy stairs and came to the familiar doorway—and discovered just in time that they'd knocked the floor out of his place that day. The green wall across from me was still up, though the plaster and laths had started to fall away here and there, but in between was just a pit unevenly floored with rubble two stories down.

That night I camped in the room across the hall, where there was still a floor. It must have been almost dawn when I woke up coughing. The air was full of smoke and the floor was hot and I heard distant sirens. I struggled into the hall and there the heat really hit me.

Light flared through the old doctor's door. Someone (another crazy wino probably) had set fire to what was left of the building. The floor below and the opposite wall were ablaze. And at the very moment I looked in, a big section of flaming lath and green-crusted plaster fell away right across from me, revealing a dark space behind it that had been hidden for decades.

Now pause (the Professor said) and recall that I was going to tell you about a kick involving all the weed in the world. For this kick, you simply imagine that all the weed in the world has been harvested and dried and variously processed and then gathered in one spot close by you—all the reefers, all the joints, all the hemp, all the bhang, kif, takrouri, dagga, charas, mutah, manzoul, maconha, djamba, ganja, esrar, dynamite, tea, pot, stick, gauge, grass, yummy (for those are all names that have been used for marijuana)—and that someone has set fire to this resinous and ecstasy-loaded haystack and that you are sitting at a comfortable distance downwind from it, inhaling the beatific smoke.

Back to the real fire now and to me crouching in the old doctor's doorway and staring across the floorless space at the wall opposite—a wall as far away from me as that of China, as far as my ability to reach it went.

The dark space revealed by the falling lath and plaster was not empty, but neatly lined with shelves, and on the shelves were all manner of boxes and tins and bottles—big bottles with glass stoppers, filled mostly with white powders and crystals. Already one or two of the bottles had burst with the heat and the bold labels were blackening, but I could read enough of them to tell the story—and I'm sure I could have guessed the story without any labels at all.

Even as I watched, a few more bottles exploded and the local flames sprang up more fiercely. Most of the opiates are highly inflammable, you know—people *smoke* opium—they're unsaturated hydrocarbons.

So there I crouched and watched them burn—not fifteen feet away from me but absolutely inaccessible. The white crystalline morphine and heroin and cocaine, great swelling jars of it. The tins of black bubbling opium with the pale blue flames shooting up. Hashish melting and flaming and running like some lava of the Eastern gods. The tall sealed beaker of ruby-red laudanum—*that* really set everything blazing when it burst, for laudanum is opium dissolved in alcohol. The big bottles of melting barbiturate capsules—red Seconal, blue Amytal, yellow Nembutal, phenobarbital, tuinal, Veronal. Oily, hot-burning chloral and paraldehyde. Volatile chloroform and the devil-god ether—*there* were explosions for you! And all the endless others that the old doctor had gathered in his crazy quest—pantopon, paregoric, papaverine, novocaine, thebaine, narcotine, narceine, codeine, Dilaudid, Dicodide, Dionin—all, all burning, burning completely and utterly.

I didn't hear the fire engines arriving or the hoses sizzling into the flames, or the firemen finally clumping up the stairs behind me. I just crouched there witless, staring and sniffling until I blacked out.

The firemen found me in time, though I sometimes think that was the worst thing that ever happened to me. I woke up in the city hospital, telling my story over and over again to anyone who'd listen. I honestly think I was still higher than a kite on the variegated fumes I'd sniffed.

Of course everyone told me the old building burned down completely, and that was so.

All my big mouth should have got me was trouble (the Professor finished) except no one believed that my story was anything but a wino's vision, an old hophead's dream.

THE MUTANT'S
BROTHER

THE CABIN OF THE STEELTON AIRJET WAS LIKE A LONG
satiny box, hurled miraculously through the night. Inside it, the
thunder of the jets was muted to a soothing rumble. Passengers
dozed in the soft gloom, or chatted together in low, desultory
voices.

There was comfort in the cabin, and the warmth of human
security.

But Greer Canarvon turned away from his fellow passengers
and peered out at the wild rack of wind-torn clouds, silvered
by a demon moon. Like shadowy monsters they loomed and
writhed, now bending close around the airjet, now opening
their ranks so that he caught moonlit glimpses of the ragged
Dakota Bad Lands.

Out there, he knew, lay his real kinship—with all that is alien
and terrible and lonely. With the wild forces of darkness and
the unknown. With all that is abnormal and inhuman, though it
wear the mask of humanity.

Hunger to be with one of his own kind—a hunger which
had never been satisfied—rose to a new pitch of poignancy. He
fumbled in his pocket for the radiogram, which already looked
creased and old, although it had popped out of the radioprinter
only yesterday.

CONSOL SKYGRAMS

EXPRESS BEAM   No. 3A-3077-B89
    9/17/1973
GREER CANARVON
209 BUNA TERRACE
COMPTON, OHIO

DEAR BROTHER.
    IT IS TIME WE GOT IN CONTACT. IF YOU ARE
WHAT I THINK YOU ARE, YOU WILL KNOW WE HAVE
MUCH TO TALK ABOUT THAT ONLY YOU AND I CAN
UNDERSTAND. THE ADDRESS IS 1532 DAMON PLACE,
STEELTON. IF YOU COME, HURRY.
                                    JOHN HALLIDANE.

Greer's heart pounded—that heart whose beating always
brought a momentary frown of perplexity to doctor's faces as they
listened to it through their stethoscopes. He felt for a cigarette,
but the package was empty. He glanced at his conventional
radioactive-driven wrist watch. Half an hour yet to Steelton. An
hour perhaps before he got to Damon Place.

His only brother. His twin brother. And, if orphanage records
of their striking similarity could be trusted, his identical twin.
The only person in the whole world whose chromosomes and
genes could carry the pattern of that frightening mutation.

For it must be a mutation. It was unthinkable that his parents
could have possessed his powers and still lived such cramped
and mediocre lives as the brief records showed. Almost equally
unthinkable that such characteristics could have lain dormant in
the germ plasm for generations, submerged by dominant factors,
to be brought to life by one chance mating.

"I'm coming home a day early to please the wife," one of the
men in the seat ahead was explaining jocularly. "This Carstairs
business has made her jumpy."

"A regular city-wide scare," agreed his airjet acquaintance.
"Glad to be back with the family myself."

Home, thought Greer bitterly. The familiar, the cozy, the safe,
the tried-and-true—all he was now cut off from. Should he lean
forward and whisper confidentially, "Speaking of scares, gentlemen,
I have certain knowledge that there is a monster on this airjet."

Though for that matter his own home life had been of the

most pleasantly conventional sort. His foster parents were grand people—apparently he'd been luckier than John in that regard. During childhood and adolescence there had been only the most shadowy intimations of what would some day set him so utterly apart. Doctors had frowned at his heartbeat, had puzzled over something in his eyes and an odd tinge in the color of his skin. They had caught fleeting, almost intangible impressions of *otherness*. But being practical physicians, they had assured themselves that his health was sound, and had gone no further. Or perhaps something—some kind of intuition that shields men from contact with the unnatural—had made them sheer off.

At times he had wondered, with a touch of fear, if there weren't something different about him. But all children do that.

Otherwise, he had grown up as a healthy, normal child in a favorable environment. His ideals and aims and standards of behavior had been those of the children around him—a little better, perhaps, for his foster father was a very upright man.

And all the while that thing—that power—had been silently breeding in his flesh.

The cabin lurched gently, and the rumble of the jets went a tone deeper, as if some vast organ in space were sounding the opening notes of an awesome prelude. The silvery-smoky cloud monsters swooped close.

Awareness of his power had come with the suddenness of a thunderclap. Afterward he remembered the splitting headaches he'd had for weeks, and realized that something might have been growing in his brain. Some new organ for which his skull hardly provided space.

Not all characteristics of an individual, whether normal or mutant, need be present at birth. Some, like sexuality, mature late. His power was like that.

He stared at the ragged cloud monsters. They seemed for a moment to be reeling in a wild dance, perhaps in invocation of the spirit of the grotesque and barren landscape the airjet was traversing. A terror of the abnormality lurking in the cosmos possessed him. Evolution was such a coldly and frighteningly inhuman process.

Mutation worked by chance. It had no pattern or plan. Usually it only botched the normal organism. Sometimes, though rarely, it brought a slight improvement. But it could, conceivably, give rise to—anything.

He realized he was trembling slightly. His face was a tight mask. He automatically fingered for a cigarette, then remembered that the package was empty and crumpled it. He was frightened of his own power, terrified. It was such a darkly inhuman thing, like a survival from myth or primitive sorcery. That was one of the reasons he had not been able to tell anyone about it. It had such immense potentialities. It made a man a king—much more than a king. It clamored to be used. It tempted him, and he wondered if he would be strong enough to resist temptation.

He must talk to someone about it! In less than an hour, he would be with his brother. It would be easier then. Together they could work out some course of action. If only they could have gone together sooner!

Greer had not always known that he had a brother. When his foster parents took him from the orphanage, his twin had already been adopted by the Hallidanes. Later on his foster parents had tried to bring the two boys together, for a visit at least, but the Hallidanes had rebuffed this friendly suggestion.

There were things which his foster parents had not told him about the Hallidanes—unpleasant things, which he had now only discovered through his recent inquiries at the orphanage. How the Hallidanes had been accused of neglect and cruelty with regard to their adopted son, but had successfully fought a legal action. How—final action of what must have been a sordid domestic tragedy—the father had murdered the mother and then killed himself.

That had happened a little less than a year ago. Thereafter the orphanage had lost track of John Hallidane.

For a brief moment the soft lights of the cabin winked out. Chilly moonlight, flooding through a gap in the turbulent clouds, transformed his fellow passengers into a company of ghosts, bound on some ominous mission.

Since Greer had first learned that he had a twin, he had indulged in endless speculations about him. He imagined his twin doing the same things, thinking the same thoughts. Realization that he was a mutant had changed those speculations into a frantic desire for contact. During the past months he had made every conceivable attempt to pick up his brother's trail. All had failed. In the end it was his brother who had gotten in touch with him.

Evidently John Hallidane had been kept completely ignorant of the fact that he had a twin, and had only discovered it by chance. Perhaps he had recently recontacted the orphanage.

Again Greer scanned the terse radiogram. He could read something like his own anxiety between the guarded lines. The same hunger for a kindred being. The same fear of being found out by strangers. "If you are what I think you are—"

Anticipation made Greer's mind almost painfully alive. Speculations about his brother and his brother's life flashed through it more quickly than he could grasp them. There were a thousand things he wanted to know.

"Well, we should be there in a couple of minutes," observed one of the men on the seat ahead, reaching for his hat. "Then we'll be able to get the real dope on this Carstairs business," he added.

"No doubt of that," his companion replied with a faint, nervous chuckle. "Everybody in Steelton must be talking about it."

Only half an hour now—maybe less! As Greer folded the radiogram, he realized that his hands were shaking. His body throbbed—a suffocating feeling.

The muffled thunder of the jets changed to a different key. He pressed his face against the cold transparency of the window. The airjet was slanting down toward a hole in the thinning clouds. Through it, as through a vast reducing glass, he could glimpse the streets and towers of Steelton. A general glow, and the absence of bright points of glaring light, made it seem like a spectral city.

For a moment the emotion he felt was not so much eagerness as fear.

"Package of Camdens," Greer told the girl at the tobacco counter, a tiny bower of garish plastics in the vaulted immensity of the Steelton Terminals.

"Self-lighters?"

He shook his head. While she was getting them, he jerkily tried to analyze what it was that struck him as so peculiar in the behavior of the people around him. There was something set about their expressions, something tense about their movements. They were a little like the robot mannequins parading shimmering garments in the display front opposite. The hum of conversation wasn't as

loud as it should be. The amplified voice of the newscaster rang
out too clearly. From the moment he'd landed, the atmosphere
of apprehension had been as palpable as fog. Steelton was like a
city awaiting attack.

Probably just a reflection of his own nervousness.

Impatiently he turned back toward the counter and caught the
girl staring at him fixedly. He took the package from her hand.
She smiled, nervously this time. As she was getting his change,
she still watched him guardedly.

He lit a cigarette. He heard the newscaster say: "Tonight
Police Director Marly assured a committee of Steelton citizens
that it will only be a matter of time before Robert Carstairs is
apprehended. 'Every police officer is on the alert,' said Marly.
'Our nets are closing in. Robert Carstairs' hours of liberty are
numbered.'"

Suddenly Greer realized that the hum of conversation and the
echoing tramp of footsteps had ceased almost altogether. The girl
at the counter turned away to look at the huge tele-screen. That
was what the rest of them were doing.

"We take this opportunity to repeat a previous statement of
Police Director Marly," continued the newscaster. "It is the duty
of every citizen to aid in ridding Steelton of this menace. Robert
Carstairs is dangerous. As the terrible tragedy at the Carstairs
residence proved only too well, he displays a fiendish talent for
ingratiating himself with his victims and subjecting them to his
willpower. If you see this man, instantly inform the police."

Then Greer saw flashed on the tele-screen what was, in every
detail and particular, a gigantic picture of himself.

What happened next seemed to Greer to happen in slow-
motion. The girl turned around. Her mouth sucked in air for a
scream.

But the scream never came. He exerted his power. He did
not see her thoughts—he seldom could see thoughts. He merely
exerted his power. She stood there, staring woodenly.

Ducking his head so that half his face was masked by hat
brim, he walked away rapidly. He could hold her for perhaps a
hundred feet. By that time—

A big man carrying a black suitcase looked at him sharply,
then looked again. He dropped the suitcase. He turned on Greer,
his hands coming up to grab.

But they never grabbed. Under Greer's control, he picked up the suitcase and walked on.

Several people noticed the incident. They peered at Greer curiously. First two of them, then three, he had to bring under his control, as he saw that they recognized him as the man they had seen on the tele-screen. He didn't know how many he could dominate, because he had never tried. Not more than four or five, he had the feeling.

From behind came a piercing scream, as the girl at the tobacco counter escaped from his influence.

The way everyone jumped at that scream gave him an idea. Distraction. There was a young man approaching in a gray coat and hat not unlike his own. Just as the number of people who recognized him was getting beyond his control, he caused the young man to break into a run, and sent three people after him yelling, "There he goes! There he goes!" Then he continued toward the exit.

He felt a profound thrill of satisfaction. It was good to have to use his power without having time to be afraid of it, to think, to weigh the consequences. He walked purposefully, eyes searching the crowd ahead for the tell-tale signs of recognition, exerting control when he saw them.

Here and there behind him men and women awoke with a jerk—to fear and to the disquieting realization that four or five seconds had vanished unaccountably. They had seen the archcriminal Robert Carstairs. They had been about to do something. Then he had suddenly vanished—as if life were a film and the film had jumped a couple of feet ahead. Had it been an hallucination? Or—what sort of being was this Robert Carstairs. There were stories—stories which the newscasters played down. Around their hearts twined the tendrils of an icy terror.

A surging agitation followed Greer through the crowd, like a wave that lapped at his heels but never quite caught up. He was constantly shifting control from one group of persons to another.

The young man in the gray coat and hat came to himself and began to make profuse, bewildered apologies to an elderly woman he had careened into. His pursuers stopped and stared around, as baffled as he. Individual communicators clicked an alert to the police and detectives stationed in the terminals, as an observer in the gallery sought to fathom the nature of the commotion.

Greer was nearing the exit. But the agitation was increasing, and more and more it was centering around him, closing in. Too many people were staring at him. The situation was getting beyond his control. If he had to hold off a dozen at once, he was done for. Five or six was the limit.

He changed his tactics—caused four men to form a cordon around him, shielding him from view. He had them walk briskly and assume important, official-looking expressions, so that people got out of their way.

There were two policemen at the exit, trim in blue and silver, suspicious-eyed. But as they came within range of Greer's power, their expressions became first blank, then different. They opened the doors for him. He slipped away from his cordon. He kept control of the policemen, causing them to stand at the exit and block off any possible pursuit.

There was a sleek black monocab cruising past the Terminals. He summoned it to the curb. It gave to his weight as he sprang abroad. The gyro brought it smoothly back to even keel as it lunged ahead.

Under his control, the driver turned several corners at random, then headed for the rendezvous at Damon Place.

Since Steelton was a young metropolis, indirect street lighting was the rule. The result was ghostly, unreal—a shadowless city half materialized from the night. It seemed to Greer that there were unusually few people abroad. None of them loitered. Their taut apprehensiveness was more marked even than that of the crowd at the Terminals.

The monocab purred like a satiny cat. Greer felt himself slipping into a mood of black reaction. There was something fundamentally loathsome about using people like puppets. You didn't know where to stop.

Was that what had happened to his twin? Had he yielded to the temptation to use his mutant power to his own aggrandizement, make people his pawns?

Greer's mind veered away from the possibility. Much more likely, he told himself, that his twin had gotten into trouble by unwisely revealing his power. That was enough to make people hate you, fear you, fabricate hysterical accusations, lay all manner of crimes at your door. How else could you expect people to behave toward a mutant with the power of direct hypnotic control?

Yet why the change of name from Hallidane to Carstairs?

Why—He fought the ugly suspicions that crowded up into his mind. Partly from unreasoning loyalty. Partly because he so ached for contact with his own kind, that he could not bear to think of anything standing between them. His brother's attitudes *must* be like his own!

A police monocar droned past. Greer ducked his head, acutely aware that, whatever predicament his brother was in, he was in it, too. For the present, there were two Robert Carstairses in Steelton.

Of course, if he had to, he could prove his identity. Or could he? Steelton's panic was of the hysterical, shoot-on-sight sort. And suppose he did prove that he was Robert Carstairs' identical twin. Wouldn't that only mean two monsters to be exterminated instead of one?

His brother must stand in desperate need of help. Now he could understand the last line of the radiogram. "If you come, hurry."

The monocab swung into a wealthy residential district. The houses drew back, screened themselves with trees. The diminished street lighting was a ghostly counterpart to the cold beams of the high-riding moon. At reduced speed the motor was almost silent. From somewhere far off Greer heard the wail of a siren mount and die away. The face of the driver was placid but very pale. Greer shuddered, although it was his own power which controlled the man. It was too much like traveling under the guidance of the undead.

Quietly, almost furtively, because the driver responded to Greer's present mood, the monocab drew up in front of a yawning archway on which appeared, in glowing metal, the numerals "1532".

Greer stepped out, looking around puzzledly. Something seemed definitely out of key. This was not the sort of neighborhood in which he had expected to meet his brother.

In response to his unspoken question, the driver turned. Moonlight blanched the last color from his features. He enunciated tonelessly, "Yes, I know this place. It is the Carstairs residence."

At that instant Greer's mind darkened with the cloudy telepathic warning that there were minds inimical to himself within his range of control.

From the archway, and from a similar archway across the street, narrow beams of white light struck him like dazzling spears. That such beams traced the course along which police bullets would follow, Greer knew. But the telepathic warning had given him the split second he needed. Before fingers could press triggers, the minds which the fingers obeyed were under his control.

Yet something whipped past his ear with a faint, high-pitched squeal. A gout of momentary incandescence blossomed from the pavement beyond him as an explosive bullet struck. From a roof perhaps a hundred yards away a lone searchbeam was seeking him out, inexorable determining the path of a second shot.

Once again, as at the station, it seemed to Greer that everything was going slow-motion except his thoughts. His mind reached out to overpower that of the police gunman. But, as he feared, the distance was too great. The lone searchbeam seemed to crawl as it swung in on him. Yet its crawl was airjet speed compared to anything he could get out of his muscles. The gunman would get at least two more shots before he could reach cover. Perhaps three. There was only one thing to do.

Almost before he realized it, the searchbeams of the police under his control swung away from him, scattered, reconverged on a high, tiny figure silhouetted against the massed black tubing of a sun-heater. As one, their guns spoke. The lone searchbeam careened wildly. There was a nerve-racking pause. Then the sickening hollow smack of a body hitting pavement.

A spasm of revulsion went through Greer. It was murder he had commanded. The man on the roof hadn't had a chance.

Yet even as he fought that reaction of self-loathing, even as he strained to maintain control of the police, he realized that it was not alone the impulse of self-preservation which had motivated him.

There was a job to be done, a job that only he could do. There was a monster at large in Steelton, and Steelton must be ridded of that monster.

"Not only Steelton. The whole world."

In one dizzy instant, his fears and suspicions crystallized. Only loyalty to his unknown brother, and an aching desire for the companionship of his own kind, could have blinded him to the obvious truth.

Why had his brother summoned him to Steelton, *without even warning him of the deadly danger to which he would be exposed?* For one reason, and one alone—so that Greer Canarvon would be killed. So that Steelton would think that Robert Carstairs had been killed. So that his twin would be free to exploit his power without suspicion—with more caution and subtlety, no doubt, but with infinitely greater danger to mankind.

It was not so much hate that filled Greer, as a cold and unswerving determination. Already he had made his plan. The police under his control were escorting him to their monocar.

His thoughts were coming with a machinelike rapidity. All Steelton was engaged in a man hunt. If his brother's mind worked like his own, there was one very obvious place for his brother to be.

And if he were at that place, Greer knew a very simple way of getting at him.

Once again tattered clouds marched across the moon. Through lonely streets the monocar raced toward its destination, the siren wailing a challenge, like some night-thing. Greer sat between two policemen, and there were two more on the seat ahead. To all intents, he was their prisoner.

One of them was reciting a brief history of the Carstairs case. Only a certain lack of color in his voice indicated that he was under direct hypnotic control—unconscious, yet as obedient to Greer's wordless commands as the man at the monocar controls.

"At first we only thought that an unusually clever pickpocket must be at work. Even at that time there had been a crop of odd suicides, but we didn't connect them up until later. Some of the people who were robbed claimed that their minds had gone blank, usually while strolling down a busy street. They had come to themselves perhaps a half a block later and found their valuables missing. We supposed they'd day-dreamed and that the pickpocket had taken advantage of their abstraction. Later we had to change that opinion, for in two cases witnesses reported having seen the victim hand over his pocketbook to a young man, apparently of his own free will.

"About the same time, there had begun an inexplicable series of burglaries. Householders would go to answer the door chimes, their minds would blank out, later they would recover consciousness and discover that their homes had been ransacked. A newscaster got hold of that and started a wild story about a criminal who used a mysterious gas to render his victim helpless. The police doctors found no support for any such view."

The monocab banked sharply around a corner. But the voice went on without a break, calmly.

"At first we thought the robberies and the other cases were fakes, done to collect insurance or perpetrate similar frauds. But there were too many of them, and the faking wasn't good enough.

"Then a woman came to us with a story that the Carstairs girl had blurted out to her. The Carstairs are about the richest people in town. The Carstairs girl claimed that they were being victimized by a young man who had installed himself in their home and was passing himself off to visitors as a distant relative. He could control their minds, she said, cause them to lose consciousness and make them do anything he wanted them to. He had made very explicit threats as to what he would do if any one of them squealed to an outsider while not under his influence. They were all terrified of him. The Carstairs girl herself was pitiably frightened, but she just had to talk.

"At any rate, that was the story the woman told us. It was pretty wild, like a lot of groundless accusations we'd been getting. But we went to the Carstairs home to investigate, taking the woman along.

"The Carstairs girl denied the whole story. Said the woman had invented it. Yes, their cousin Robert was visiting with them, but he was a completely respectable young man. The accusations were absurd. And so on. We didn't know at the time that Robert Carstairs must have been in the next room.

"She talked in a very calm and reasonable way—there wasn't the slightest indication that she was hiding any fear. That was what was so convincing about it. It was *our* woman who got hysterical.

"But because we were at our wits' end and not passing up anything, a detective was assigned to shadow Robert Carstairs.

"Two days later that detective carefully locked himself in a room and committed suicide.

"A real locked-room suicide, with a note in his own handwriting and everything else. No chance of fake. Still—the coincidence. Police Director Marly started some general inquiries about Robert Carstairs. Very quietly, of course, for the Carstairses had enough influence to stop an inquiry if they got wind of it—and if they *were* under his power that was presumably what they'd do.

"Gradually, adding one bit of information to another, we got at the truth. Friends of the Carstairs complained that the whole family was becoming moody. On some occasions, usually when Robert was present, they would be very pleasant—though there was something unfamiliar about their manner. At other times they would appear very miserable, as if haunted by some secret which they dared not divulge. Some of those same friends mentioned feeling acutely uncomfortable in Robert Carstairs' presence. For some reason they could not define, they were afraid of him. One or two of them spoke of experiencing unaccountable mental lapses in the Carstairs home.

"A discharged servant told an ugly story which indicated that Robert Carstairs' word was law in the household.

"We tried to find out his background, where he came from. We were up against a brick wall.

"Businessmen talked of how old Carstairs was changing the financial policies of his firm. Some of them thought that Robert Carstairs was somehow responsible for this.

"Meanwhile, the crime wave continued. More and more of the crimes seemed to be of a purely wanton sort, done to satisfy a whim or to display power, rather than for the sake of gain. You got the feeling that the criminal was amusing himself with his victims.

"Then a picture of the Carstairs attending a social function went out on the telecasts. One of the witnesses of an early pickpocket episode came to headquarters and identified Robert Carstairs as the young man to whom he had seen the victim hand over his valuables.

"That was all we'd been waiting for.

"Maybe Marly had a hunch about what might happen, for he sent half a dozen men to make the arrest.

"Well—he didn't send enough. Inside the Carstairs home, something happened to their minds. They became insane— homicidally. Up to now, this has been kept out of the newscasts. They killed each other. At least, they were found dead by their own weapons.

"It was the same thing with the Carstairs family, only there the indications pointed at suicide."

Siren moaning a warning, the monocar swung into a brighter thoroughfare, but it brought to Greer no feeling of escape from darkness. His mind was tight and cold. He was remembering how his brother's foster parents, the Hallidanes, had died—a sordid domestic tragedy—the father had murdered the mother and then killed himself.

Suicide—a kind of signature his brother scribbled on his crimes.

Greer understood, almost too well. He knew the temptation to use people, then to go a little further, then a little further still. If he had been brought up in his brother's environment—

His brother had raised a whole city against himself before he realized that there were limits on even a power like his. He could doubtless escape from Steelton, but there would always be that criminal record behind him. How much simpler if a Robert Carstairs died.

As if in agreement with that thought, Greer nodded grimly to himself. The story he had drawn from the unconscious detective had confirmed his own notion about his brother's behavior patterns. When his brother sought power, he had taken control of the wealthiest family in Steelton and had hung on until the last possible moment. Now that his brother was the object of a city-wide man hunt—

The deskman at Steelton Police Headquarters looked up at the newcomers. He saw the prisoner being brought in. His eyes went wide and stayed that way.

"Yes, we got Carstairs," one of the detectives told him. "We're taking him in to Marly."

And they walked up the corridor, two of them on either side of the prisoner, two with their guns in his back.

The deskman stared after them. He'd never really believed that they would get Carstairs. You couldn't—not if you knew what the police did.

And they were being so casual about it!

A little later he remembered he hadn't flashed Marly to let him know they were coming.

Greer felt the tautness growing, in muscle and mind. He sought to dispel it, to empty his mind of thought, to maintain only subconscious-level control of the four men around him. He must avoid giving any sort of warning.

The corridor turned. He caused the four men to walk ahead of him. They quickened their pace in response to the feeling of urgency that surged through him.

Just a little farther now, Greer told himself, just a little farther— and then, in the mental dark, he sensed a glowing brightness, like a living light. It seemed to beat against his mind in ever-strengthening waves. It called to his mind to leap toward it and mingle with it. He strove to resist that call, to take no notice of it.

Ahead of him, the four men were filing through a door. On it he read "Director of Police." Beyond it he saw a gleaming metallic table and a ruddy-faced, gray-haired man, with two policemen in uniform seated beside him.

But behind them was another person. As if in a subtly distorting mirror, Greer looked at himself.

He had guessed right. His brother had done the crazily logical thing that Greer had expected.

Tonight there was a city-wide manhunt for his brother—and his brother was directing it.

And now, face to face with his brother, mind to mind, he was overwhelmed by the thought of what they might have meant to each other under different circumstances, and he hesitated too long in giving the order that he knew must be given.

Before the men under his control could raise their guns, they were cut down by a deafening burst of fire from Police Director Marly and the two officers with him. Human flesh exploded nauseously.

Then, for a third time that night, time seemed to crawl. Greer had flung himself to one side. Out of range—but only for a moment. His turn, he knew, was next. He sought to take control of Marly and the other two. He might as well have tried to control statues. They were his brother's puppets—not his.

He heard the rattling echoes of the gunfire die along the corridor. He saw a ribbon of smoke curl from the doorway. Seconds seemed like minutes.

He could see his brother's purposes so clearly now, read them direct from his mind. Control of the world. And it would be such an easy thing—just a matter of getting to the men who controlled it, or who were in a position to control it, and then controlling them.

And he could have prevented it, if only—

If only—

He struck suddenly at his brother's mind, to control it!

For an instant he thought he had succeeded. Then for an instant he thought he had failed. Mental brightness surging at mental brightness, seeking to extinguish. He felt a paralysis grip his muscles, a darkness closing down on his mind. By a supreme effort, he fought it off.

But deadlock was all he had wanted.

In Marly's room, guns thundered.

Greer did not need to look. He felt his brother's mind die.

In resisting Greer's mental assault, his brother had been compelled to free his puppets.

Dully, Greer wondered if he ought to die, too. He, too, was a dangerous monster. Tonight he had killed a harmless man and been the cause of death for four others.

And he had destroyed the only one of his kind in the wide world, the only one with whom he could speak from mind to mind and be answered. Darkness now. Mental darkness unending.

From Marly's room came a muffled exclamation of crazy amazement. Greer Canarvon realized that if he wished to escape, he must act quickly.

He turned to meet his lonely destiny.

THE MAN WHO WAS MARRIED TO SPACE AND TIME

OLD GUY MANNING WAS IN LOVE WITH SPACE AND time all of his life, not only during the months preceding his mysterious yet oddly unspectacular disappearance. He didn't write poetry about them, although he sometimes spoke of them poetically, and it did not lead him to become a professional physicist or astronomer (the stars being supreme examples of distance and of great use in timekeeping). No, it was altogether a humbler sort of affection and in his last years, after his wife's death (there were no children) and his retirement from his minor editorial job, when he was living alone in a big-city apartment he leased by the year, it had some of the humdrum ailments (ailments of bondage, almost) that one sees in most long marriages. The sort of affection or devotion that kept him interested in science and science fiction all his life, and staring speculatively into the distance more than most people do, and toward the end compulsively concerned with small numbers and with counting (which is, after all, the simplest way we measure both time and space).

And yet this humble, humdrum, rather metaphysical love was so obvious to the few friends of his last years that none of them was exactly startled by the fanciful suggestion made after his casual yet eerie disappearance (though by no means agreeing with the suggestion, of course) that old Guy had somehow melted

away into space and time, become "married" to them in the sense
of becoming merged with them.

And indeed, old Guy Manning's disappearance did have an
unstudied air to it, as if he had simply stood up one day (as if
going to get a drink of water) and walked out of life, or at least
away from life as we know it. Though in what direction that
would be, it's puzzling (or perhaps meaningless) to ask.

It was the girl Joan Miles who made the fanciful "melting into
space-time" suggestion. She was a mildly hippie young person,
unseriously addicted to astrology, white witchcraft, and other
pastel superstitions, who had the distinction of living and keeping
time by her personally-embellished lunar calendar, in which all
the full moons have names, not just the Harvest and Hunter's.
There are the Sower's Moon and the Loner's, for example, the
Ghost's, and of course the Lover's. By her calendar, incidentally,
old Guy Manning disappeared on the night of the Murderer's
(or Adulterer's—Joan liked both names and couldn't choose
between them) Moon, the one nearest the summer solstice, the
full moon that steals across the sky low in the south, latest to
rise and earliest to set, short and dim as a December day. (In
contrast, the Lover's Moon is of course the one nearest the winter
solstice, rising shamelessly high in the heavens and shedding an
intoxicating silver radiance all the long, long night.)

Manning's other young friend (who was also Joan's friend)
was Jack Penrose, a restless chap with a keen interest in both the
occult and science, and with ambitions too of becoming a writer
of fantasy romances. He was the one to whom Manning told
some of his dreams.

Then there was Mr. Sarcander, a sallow and lean-jawed clinical
psychologist working mostly in geriatrics. Originally Manning
had consulted him about his recurrent depressions, but their
relationship had become social also. Those who knew him well
found Mr. Sarcander the most cynical and sardonic man alive,
shockingly harsh in his evaluation of human motives, and they
were occasionally hurt when they found such value judgments
being applied to them or their friends. Such had never learned
or else temporarily forgotten, that Mr. Sarcander was harshest
of all on himself, expending all his optimism, flattery, and merry
mood on his patient-clients, reserving his honesty for the people
he could relax with.

And then there was the amiable and tolerant Dr. Lewison,

Manning's medical doctor with whom he had something more than a purely professional relationship. He had keys to Manning's apartment, as did Jack Penrose.

These four persons had become acquainted while Manning was still alive (undisappeared, rather) and after his vanishing they met a few times to talk about it and him, especially when police investigations developed no leads—or any push at all, for that matter.

Such was the surprisingly small circle of Manning's last friends unless we include (and we probably should) Mr. Breen, a burly, dark, not unhandsome Irishman with permanently bewildered eyes and given to fits of absentmindedness, who was the apartment manager of the building where Manning lived on the top floor. Breen wasn't the first to notice Manning's absence (Joan did) but he made a small discovery in connection with it that became somewhat puzzling as he recalled more of the attendant circumstances.

"I was up on the roof," he said, "when I noticed this small ring of keys sitting on one of the steps leading up to the little room over the shaft that has the elevator motor and relays in it. Right next to the edge of the roof, too. At first I didn't think of Manning specially but then I remembered—You know how he'd go up there once or twice a day, nights too, to check out the weather or the stars, he'd say?—I remembered times when he'd forgotten and left other things in about the same spot—his pipe or matches or a half-filled cup of coffee, and once his binoculars. So I checked out the keys and they were Manning's. Which is sort of funny because you need them to get down from the roof. The one for the front door to the building also unlocks the door in from the roof. The police have them now."

"No," Jack Penrose contradicted, "the lock on the roof door doesn't snap shut unless you make it. He took me up there several times and he always left the door hanging ajar and then pulled it tight shut, so it locked, after we came back in. And even if you were locked out on the roof without a key, you could always climb down the outside ladder to the fire escape."

"That's true," Breen admitted, frowning doubtfully.

Dr. Lewison smiled to himself, thinking of how lightly young people contemplated such athletic feats.

Meanwhile Joan Miles was visualizing an ovoid space shuttle landing as silently as death on the pale, tar-set gravel overhead by the light of the Murderer's Moon. And a door opening in its glassy skin and old Guy Manning bowing courteously toward it and then climbing inside. He wouldn't have needed a key to get down from the roof then, she thought. Or any Earth keys any more, if it were going to be that sort of journey.

What she said was, "He had a way of narrowing his eyes and moving his head around from side to side as he looked out at the city. I wondered about it and then I realized he was lining up things very precisely—buildings, flagpoles, clouds, stars. He'd move his head the same way when he used his binoculars. He was learning all the stars, he told me once, not just the constellations but the smaller asterisms too that make them up and often look so much alike. He said it was a job that would last out his time. He had a geometric mind."

Mr. Sarcander snorted faintly. "Old people," he said, "are forever checking out their eyesight, trying to prove to themselves that it's as good as ever—or even better."

Jack Penrose said defensively, "He was very careful about all his sensations. They were more like observations. He paid attention to details. He watched the city—almost as if that were his special job."

"All old people do that," Mr. Sarcander said. "You see their white faces at windows and in shadowed porches. They watch their little world, their microcosm in which each has been God all of his life, waiting for the cracks to appear and it to crumble. It's the only occupation life has left them."

"Mr. Manning," Joan murmured, mostly to herself, a little primly, "became more and more immersed in distance and duration."

And indeed that was a very fair way of describing the way Guy Manning's life had gone. Early on, he'd traveled as much as he could, experiencing distance that way. He'd liked to watch the sea. Later on this urge had expressed itself in a love of maps. He liked to measure distances on them with a small ivory ruler he carried. When he took walks he'd head for the nearest hill or high place so that he could see distance emerge from the scene around him as he mounted. And always there were the vastly far, infinitely regular stars at night, or in their absence the clouds filling the middle distances. During one period his interest shifted to great *interiors,* those of cathedrals, industrial assembly buildings wherein small aircraft could fly, and huge county-size extraterrestrial structures such as those imagined in Arthur C. Clarke's *Rendezvous with Rama* and John Varley's *Titan*.

As with distance, so with duration. At one time of his life he was greatly interested in clocks, and if he'd had more money he might have become a collector and ended up with a house full of tickings and chimings. But in the long run he was more drawn to the commoner and more ordinary aspects of timekeeping, the adjustment of watches and alarm clocks, the calls to Time of Day, the counting out of seconds accurately, the estimation of the duration of a moment of awareness (that vital surface which patches together the subjective and objective, the mental and material, the microcosm and the macrocosm), and the slow circling march across the sky of the time-keeping stars.

"He never cared for those new digital watches and clocks," Dr. Lewison remarked, "especially the kind that show a black empty face until you press a button. Neither do I for that matter. For a wrist watch or clock he preferred the simplest kind of face: upright black numerals evenly spaced, minute markings around the rim and all three hands."

"I know," Joan Miles agreed. "He said you could see the face of time that way, judge its expression, and sometimes guess what it was up to."

Jack Penrose lifted his eyes. "He once told me a desert dream he had," the young man reminisced. "He was standing on this perfectly flat expanse of fine silvery sand. The illumination was general but he knew he was in a desert. He could feel on his back the infrared rays of a very hot sun beating rhythmically down through a thin cloud layer. And as if in time with the beating of those rays he could feel the hard-packed sand vibrating very rapidly—about five or six tight tiny shakes to every one of his heartbeats, as if the earth beneath were quaking constantly. There was mist all around him, but it was slowly dissipating upward. Yet as it rose, he could at first see nothing but the endless silver (and invisibly vibrating) plain extending out in all directions. He felt terribly lonely.

"Then, as the mist continued to rise by slow stages, there came into view—about two miles away, he judged—a squat dark tower of considerable width—more like a fort, really. Then he noticed two rather thin dark aerial wings jutting out from the tower for miles and miles—an impossible job of cantilevering. He could barely make out the end of one of them in the far distance. And then as he swung his eyes back to the other wing, the longer one, and continued to watch it, he got the impression it was very slowly moving toward him over the silver sand.

"At that point the mist rose another stage. He noticed a shadow rapidly traveling across the plain toward him. He looked up and saw the tower's *third* and highest-set wing slicing through the misty air a quarter of a mile overhead like a gigantic revolving dark scythe. He glanced down at his wrist to time the scythe's speed... and as he saw the skinny sweep second hand of his watch crawling rapidly in infinitesimal five-a-second jerks around the silvery dial, he realized where he was."

"Trapped under a wrist watch crystal," Joan heard herself say. "It's ticking the vibration of the sands? Did the mists clear all away? Was it his room outside? Did *he* peer down?"

"He woke up feeling the watch band gripping his wrist oppressively. He'd forgotten to take it off the night before. He said you became more aware of tiny pressures like that as you grew older." Jack's eyes widened a trifle and then he frowned as faintly—as though what he had just said had reminded him of another memory, one more difficult to disentangle.

"A wristwatch does tick five times a second," Dr. Lewison observed, "though it's harder for me to hear it these days. That compulsion to count... the concern with small numbers—you know, somewhere Guy picked up the habit of segregating his coins in different pockets according to their value (some joke about putting a use to all the pockets in a pair of pants) and then he found he'd acquired the additional habit of reaching in and counting them by touch—"

"A test of tactile acuity," Mr. Sarcander put in sharply. "The elderly reassure themselves that way, filling their empty time with little tasks, so they won't have to think unpleasant thoughts about what's coming."

"He had another habit involving small numbers and counting," Dr. Lewison pressed on. "He'd read or been told by someone (he told me) about how people have been traced down by the characteristic pattern in which they tear matches out of matchbooks. That inspired him to experiment with different patterns of tearing out matches when he smoked his pipe—every other match in a rank, every third one, from in front, from behind, from the sides, from the center out, sometimes (he said) he'd give each match a weight from its position and try to tear them out in such a way that the two sides continued to balance without being symmetrical—"

"Anyone tracing him would have thought he was a dozen different people," Jack couldn't help interrupting, relieved to be able to grin at something.

"He told me about that too," Joan Miles said rapidly. "Eventually he came to think of the matches mostly as people—or actors on a stage, rather with the matchbook cover their backdrop. The trick was to tear them out in such a way that you'd always have an effectively balanced stage, though that consideration only became apparent, mostly, when they'd got thinned down in numbers—"

Mr. Sarcander's small brusque shrug gave his evaluation of such matchbook charades.

Dr. Lewison leaned forward a little. "But the strongest indication by far," he said, "of Guy's obsession with counting and the fascination small numbers held for him, was when he gave up chess for backgammon. In that game you're constantly counting and you're always juggling small numbers in your head, combining and recombining them as you hunt your move. In a way the largest number you work with is six, because there is none higher on a single die.

"One of the reasons (he told me) he made the change," the doctor continued, "was that he'd come to think that backgammon is much more like real life than chess is. In chess you're operating in an ideal universe where all the laws and forces are known to you and you control half of the pieces. You can make the most far-reaching and elaborate plans and nothing can upset them but your adversary. But in backgammon blind chance enters the picture on each move, at every throw of the dice. There are no certainties, only possibilities and probabilities. You can't plan in the same way as in chess. All you can do is make your arrangements so that whatever comes, good or (more often it always seems) bad, you can best endure it or take advantage of it." His voice was growing more animated. "It exemplifies the Pythagorean injunction: Believe that anything that can happen in the world can happen to you. You can only fight on for victory or survival, while chance rains down its blows unendingly." He took a deep breath and settled back.

"He once told me another dream he had," Jack Penrose broke in. "He was on this rather large flat square roof that seemed strangely familiar. It had a parapet a little less than waist high. There was also a wall the same height that went across the middle of the roof, dividing it into equal rectangles—later in the dream he figured it was the roofs of two buildings the same height and shape abutting each other, because the central wall was thicker with a crack down its middle and when he had to cross over that wall (as he did several times in the dream, moving rapidly) he was always afraid there'd be nothing on the other side or that something else drastic would happen.

"It was night with a heavy overcast pressing down and a biting wind that blew irregular splatters of rain, but enough light leaked up from the streets so that he could make out his surroundings. He was wearing some sort of dark gray uniform— it felt uncomfortable and harsh to the skin, like a uniform—but without any insignia he could discover.

"He wasn't alone. In fact, there were quite a few other people on the roof, but they were all crouched down against the outer walls (or at least along three of those walls) just as was himself, some of them alone, some in pairs and small huddles, so that he couldn't see them any too well. In fact, during his whole dream he never got to look one of them in the face—or address a single word to any of them, or they to him—though later on he occasionally got comfort, or at least a sense of safety, from being close to one of them and moving side by side together without their ever looking at each other. They all seemed to be wearing the same sort of nondescript gray uniform as his own, only quite a few of them—about half, in fact—were wearing uniforms of a lighter shade of gray; being near one of the latter never gave him a sense of reassurance.

"Most of the time all of these figures held very still, though watching each other closely, he supposed, as he was doing. But every so often a couple of them would scurry-crawl along the wall they were huddled against for a short (or sometimes quite long) distance and then as suddenly hold still again. If one of them had to cross the central will in the course of his crawling rush, he'd hump over it as swiftly as he could through the chill swooping wind, always keeping a low profile. It struck him that their actions were a lot like those of soldiers practicing to advance across a broken field under enemy fire.

"And every once in a while he'd get the overpowering urge to do likewise. He'd crawl as fast and inconspicuously as he could for as long as he felt the urge. When it left him he'd hold still wherever he happened to be, alone or beside others, but always as close to the wall as he could get. That part was like musical chairs, he said, except there was no music to tell you when to start and stop. It was only the urge that gave you those orders.

"He noticed that the dream soldiers in lighter gray always moved in one direction along and around the walls, while he and the ones in the same darker uniforms always advanced in the opposite direction. When opposing soldiers neared or went past each other, the sense of peril increased. Whenever the light gray soldiers moved, especially if he were alone against the wall, he'd huddle down, trying to hide his head, in horrid anticipation, of one of them landing on his back or just so much as *touching* him.

"Yet whenever in spite of all his efforts that did happen, there wouldn't be any terrible pain or shock such as he anticipated, but only a break in the dream, a momentary black-out, after which he'd be back at the point where the dream had started, or near it, and all that crawling and terrified crouching in the dark windy wet to do again, and no comfort except sometimes a like-uniformed faceless gray soldier to crouch against, shoulder to shoulder.

"It was only when he'd at last made it all the way around and was huddled down with all the other dark gray dream soldiers and they began without warning to vanish two by two (yes, just like that) that he finally realized he was part of a backgammon game being played with living, feeling men—like chess played with living pieces who didn't know they were that. And as he waited his unpredictable turn to be borne off (vanished), there began to build up in him a fear and a pressure—"

Jack snapped his fingers as he broke off. "Pressure!" he said, "—that's what I was trying to remember. Once, *apropos* of nothing special, maybe we'd been talking about science fiction, certainly not backgammon, Mr. Manning asked me if I'd ever had the feeling of being under a kind of pressure that would suddenly squeeze me out of the world altogether, shoot me away in any direction like an apple seed or—"

"—or just melt away into space-time," Joan murmured.

"Seriously, Joan," Jack asked her, "how could something like awareness melt away into the material?"

"Everything has an awareness side, even the atoms, else reality wouldn't balance out. Mr. Manning once said that. And I remember another thing he told me—that a person ought always keep a packed suitcase handy, in case he were called away at short notice. Only I don't remember whether he said he followed his own advice."

Mr. Breen broke in. He'd been listening to everything with the same worried, *hunting* look. "I seem to remember there always used to be a little suitcase at the foot of his bed," he said. "And it's not there now." He continued to look worried and puzzled.

"After you found his keys," Jack addressed him, "I went up and searched every inch of the roof. I found three items that could have been Mr. Manning's—a backgammon doubling cube, a lens cap that fitted his binoculars, and a matchbook with *five* matches left in a pattern of *two* side by side, *one* alone, and *two* one space apart."

"There's *five* of us," Breen groped. He touched the side of his head and winced his eyes. "I *knew* I'd remember," he said guiltily. "When I found the keys they were on a scrap of paper, holding it down. I started to pick the paper up too, though I never thought it might be important then, but it blew off the roof. It was ragged along one side, like it was torn out of a spiral notebook. I *think* it had writing on it, tiny capitals."

They looked around at each other for a while. Then, as though by common consent, they went up to the roof together and watched the rising of the Loner's Moon, which is also often called the Overlapper, linking each year with the next.

THOUGHT

"SO, YOU SEE, THERE IS NO THOUGHT I CANNOT CATCH."

Harborford's chin jutted arrogantly as he said it. He looked rather like a Napoleon of the mental realms, with gray thought-tracings instead of maps scattered across the desk in front of him and showing ghostlike and gigantic in the sunlit projection space behind. Yet mingled with the arrogance was a sincerity that made it difficult to take—or at least to show—offense.

Blacklaw was up against this difficulty.

"That's a large statement," he remarked. "I should think there would always be some cases—"

"No!" Harborford's stumpy hand thumped the pile of tracings, then seized one and pointed at an oddly humped trace which stood out plainly from the shadowy pattern. "See, even when you were thinking that I could not catch your thought, I caught that thought!"

Blacklaw grinned woefully. "I'll admit you plucked out some of my hiddenmost secrets," he said. "An amazing performance, considering the brief time you had for orientation. Still, I have the feeling that you'd eventually run up against certain insurmountable difficulties. It's an elusive point I'm trying to make. I don't know quite how to express it, because—"

"Because it's a false point," Harborford interrupted conclusively. "If I had you back in the projectorium, that would become obvious at once. You could see the inconsistency indications, the breakage lines signifying illogic, for yourself. No, I'm afraid humanity must face the fact that, given time and the proper facilities for research, there is not one of its thoughts which I cannot ferret out." He sat down.

Blacklaw followed his example. He felt a twinge of regret which did not show in his lean, mobile face. It was beginning to look as if he would have to use Harborford's dogmatic challenge for the theme of his article, even though the resultant product would resemble primitive twentieth-century journalism. He had rather hoped to do something quieter for the *Newsbeam*.

He brushed aside these considerations. "Let me see if I have the general outlines straight. Don't want to pull any boners, though of course I'll send you a transcript for corrections before we beam it." Harborford nodded gravely. "Well, as I understand it, thought involves changes of electrical potential throughout the brain. These changes interfere with the uniform sub-photonic beam passing through the subject's brain and are eventually projected as a pattern of grays."

"Making use of the technique of beam-amplification which has revolutionized astronomy," Harborford reminded him.

"Yes. Well, then doesn't a lot depend on the angle from which you take the projection? Wouldn't an arbitrary change in the angle at which the beam passes through the subject's brain make the resultant tracing almost unrecognizable?"

"Only in the case of two-dimensional tracings. Kesserik, would you—" Harborford motioned to the dark, wiry man at the far end of the room. He manipulated some controls. It became black. In the empty space beyond Harborford's desk, a mistiness became apparent, took on thickness, manifested itself as a dome-shaped dancing of lights and shadows.

Harborford stood up. To Blacklaw he was a stubby, square shouldered silhouette, from which came a didactic voice.

"There are, you see, not one, but a series of beams. Each focuses one potential plane in the brain, and one only. These planes are projected as a packet, building up a three-dimensional picture. Very much as, in primitive television, a two-dimensional picture was built from single points of light."

He walked back from Blacklaw until he was in the shadowy dome. Then he turned around. A constantly altering flicker illumined his chinny face.

"I am now standing in such a three-dimensional picture. Dark light, timed to explode into visibility at an exact distance from the projector, does away with the need for a series of screens. The picture is not directly projected, of course, from a human brain present with us now, but from one of the multi-level films made in the projectorium. It comes, however, to the same thing." He spread his arms wide. "I am standing, as it were, in the midst of a thinking human brain. Each flicker is a nerve discharge, or a thought-pattern, or a conscious thought. And I can interpret every one of them. Nothing is hidden—not the faintest twinge of feeling or the subtlest hint of an idea."

His voice was triumphant and raw with emotion, as if all this were very important to him in an intensely personal way. Blacklaw wondered why. As before, he was both impressed and repelled. Bathed in that swirling flicker, Harborford seemed like some evil gnome that had crept into the human brain to strut and mock. Blacklaw knew this was a foolish feeling, yet it was so.

The flicker dwindled. Sunlight returned. The dark, wiry man, who seemed faintly bored, went back to a desk at the far end of the room.

Harborford said, "So, you see, the three-dimensional picture is basic. Two-dimensionals, however, are convenient for reference and comparison. In them the packet of planes is compressed into one plane, with the resultant blending effect. They are generally taken from a frontal position, to insure uniformity."

Blacklaw frowned. He said, "I think I understand that part of it now. But that only leaves you with a very complex and shadowy pattern of grays. I don't quite see—"

Harborford bridled. "A pattern which we can analyze down to the last detail. We can pick out and follow an individual thought-trace as readily as a trained musician, listening to a symphony, can recognize the note of a single instrument—or its pattern in a sound track."

"I didn't make myself clear. Analysis still only leaves you with a pattern of tracings, meaningless by themselves. It's in the interpretation of the tracings that I'd think there'd be room for error."

"Not at all." Harborford was dogmatic. "While the tracings are being made, the subject is presented with various stimuli—pictures, words, and so forth—and he gives us a verbal account of his thought, which is recorded. Stimuli and account are afterwards correlated with the tracings. In a single instance, error or deception would be possible. But when the instances are multiplied, when the same ground is covered again and again, any such possibility cancels out. We know the thought back of each individual trace and can identify it whenever it reappears—whether in the median size and dark gray of a sensation, the light gray of a memory, the isolated black pattern of a so-called unconscious thought, or the large and comprehensive pattern of an abstraction or generalization."

He warmed to his subject. "The whole logical process is open to our view, just as if it were diagramed on a blackboard. For example, you have in mind the knowledge of individual houses and also the general idea 'house'. The former would show as a set of similar small traces, the latter as a large trace covering them all and growing from them—a kind of magnified composite photograph. Similarly, we can identify the traces representing the subject's knowledge of a scientific law and the instances of that law. Most important, if one of the instances does not agree with the law and therefore tends to be suppressed, we can spot it at once—the inconsistency indications are very marked. Ultimately, all scientists and thinkers of any consequence will have their thought processes checked at frequent intervals. In this way they will become truly infallible thinking machines. All cloudiness and freakishness will be eliminated from human thought."

Harborford leaned back and smiled at Blacklaw. His voice was easier now and friendly, marked by that sincerity which tempered his arrogance. "Of course, each person requires detailed study. The brain is very plastic with regard to which set of neurons does which job. Fairly similar thought patterns may mean quite different things in two individuals. Although, after spending years in interpreting tracings, one acquires an amazing knack of catching on to the patterns of a new mind. You saw what I was able to do in your case."

Blacklaw rehearsed his woeful grin.

"However," Harborford continued, leaning forward, stubby finger tapping the pile of tracings strewn across his desk, "there is in the long run no substitute for detailed study of a single individual—sessions running over months and years, until you can interpret every twist and turn of his mind. I have literally hundreds of miles of taped files on single cases." His expression grew suddenly angry and bitter. "Unfortunately I have been rather unlucky in my choice of subjects for detailed study. Each one of them found some excuse to break off the sessions, just as I was getting to know their minds completely." His voice became heavily sarcastic. "They professed to be afraid of losing individuality, of becoming mere mental guinea pigs. They developed or claimed to develop, a wholly unreasoning terror—as if I were some primitive medicine-man trying to trap their souls." He laughed harshly. "Fortunately, I have at least one subject on whom my files are complete—myself. For years now there has not been a single thought-trace taken from my mind that I could not immediately interpret."

For a moment Blacklaw wrestled with the image of Harborford intently studying his thoughts both from inside and out, hour after hour. Then he said, "I believe I can understand the attitude of your subjects. I don't imagine they were insincere. After all, privacy is something that most people prize highly—mental as well as physical. There's something terrible in the thought of not having at least one corner of your mind wholly your own, to which you can retreat."

"Superstition!" Harborford said harshly. "A reversion to primitive attitudes—the secrecy of the hunted or hunting beast! An outcropping of that illogic and lack of realism which has at regular intervals vitiated the progress of human thought—under the guise of mysticism, intuitionalism, inspirationalism, or some other nonsense! Fear of science's light! But I have ended all that."

He threw himself back, breathing heavily. His eyes studied Blacklaw, whose smiling composure remained unbroken. Gradually they changed. The angry glare was replaced by an embarrassed grimace. He leaned forward.

"Pardon me," he said. "But it is a matter on which I feel very deeply. You see, in my childhood I had a very unpleasant experience—"

His voice sank. His hands played aimlessly with the piles of tracings, shuffling and reshuffling them. He murmured, "I don't know why I'm telling you this—"

Blacklaw did. It was because people didn't know why they were telling him things that he was the *Newsbeam's* ace interviewer.

"—but if you've read anything about me, you probably know it anyhow. My parents were Irrationalists—you must have heard of that wild cult, though now it's almost died out. I was an only child, educated, if you can call it that, at home. They looked on me only as someone on whom they could try out their theories—a defenseless new convert to their crazy cause. There were other regrettable circumstances. As a result I spent two years in a mental sanitarium."

His hands went on shuffling the tracings. His eyes stared at them blankly.

"Ultimately the results were very fortunate. My parents lost control of me. My recovery left me with an icy enmity to any sort of mental secrecy—any hobgoblinism—and a burning determination to lay bare all the hidden corners of the mind, my own and others', so that the light of science would bathe them and forever prevent any cancerous thought-growths in darkness. That determination has never left me. It was that which led me to the study of psychology and ultimately to these present researches in a field which others pioneered. It is back of everything I have done. It has—"

The sentence was left hanging in the air. Blacklaw was conscious of a peculiar tremor in the last word—something that lingered and somehow gave him a faint shiver. He looked up.

Harborford's hands had stopped playing with the tracings. Gripping one they were frozen. His eyes were fixed on something. Either he or the sunlight had grown a shade pale.

It was very quiet in the big workroom. From the far end came a faint shuffling noise as the dark, wiry man shifted at his work. Again Blacklaw shivered faintly, without knowing why.

"What is it?" he heard himself ask.

Harborford's voice was almost normal—there was only the tiniest suggestion of a choked, muffled quality.

"This trace... I don't recognize it... I can't interpret it... I don't know what it means—"

Swiftly Blacklaw moved behind the desk, peered over Harborford's shoulder. A stubby forefinger, almost steady as a rock, followed a misty, humped shadow all the way across the mazy pattern. "I don't know how I ever came to miss it."

"One of mine, isn't it?" said Blacklaw quickly.

"No." Harborford paused heavily, "one of *mine.*"

"But it looks so much like that trace you pointed out to me a little while ago—"

"No! Any such resemblance is purely superficial! A layman's mistake!" Angry denial, not untinged with panic, tightened Harborford's throat, then subsided as he returned like one hypnotized to the tracing. "But what I don't understand is how, having had such a thought, I don't remember it... how I came not to record it."

"But a person has so many thousands of thoughts, so many tens of thousands—" Without having intended to, Blacklaw found himself trying to reassure the other.

"Every one of which tens of thousands I have studied and docketed—No!"

"It might have been unconscious—" Blacklaw felt foolish making these amateurish suggestions, yet he didn't stop.

"Impossible! Then the trace would be black and small. This has the faintness and large size of a generalization. It is a master-thought—something I would never forget. I can readily recognize the lesser thoughts from which it springs and which it sums up. They are, in fact, my own cases—those subjects, including myself, which I studied so exhaustively." He feverishly scrutinized the tracing. "There must be inconsistency indications. There must be!"

Suddenly he looked up at Blacklaw. It was as if he had just realized that he was talking to someone and that someone was a comparative stranger.

Blacklaw was faintly aware that there were no more sounds coming from the far desk. He got the impression that the dark, wiry man was peering at them curiously.

A little unsteadily Harborford got to his feet.

"I am sorry," he said, "but this has rather disturbed me. If we could continue the interview at some other time—?"

"We spoke of possibly having another session tomorrow," Blacklaw suggested easily.

Harborford nodded in relief. "That would be better," he said. "Much better."

As Blacklaw went out, his last backward glimpse was of Harborford's bullet head hung broodingly over the tracing.

The press of unexpected work delayed the interviewer's return an additional day. When he entered the workroom, Harborford was sitting with bowed head at his desk. Blacklaw got the eerie impression that he had stayed there in the same position, the whole intervening time.

Kesserik and Madderlee—a large sandy-skinned man, the director of the Institute for Thought Research—were standing by the far desk. They glanced around quickly as Blacklaw came in.

Harborford looked up. His haggardness was shocking. The tired eyes widened. He got up slowly, his hand heavily clutching the desk.

"Mr. Blacklaw? I am glad—"

In a dull sort of way he really seemed to be.

After they had sat down, he appeared immediately to sink back into a deep and unpleasant reverie. Only his eyes showed occasional activity, peering sharply from side to side of a lonely road late at night. Involuntarily Blacklaw followed his glance. Of course there was nothing.

Kesserik and Madderlee quietly left the room.

When Harborford finally began to talk, it was in a fatigued and toneless voice, very low. Obviously any thought of an article for the *Newsbeam* was a million miles away. He might have been talking to the wall.

"I can't interpret that trace. I've tried every way and I've failed."

His full gaze fixed on Blacklaw's pearl-gray tunic, stayed there. He stopped talking. Blacklaw shifted uneasily.

"Mr. Blacklaw, would you kindly smooth out your tunic?" the scientist requested quietly.

Mystified, Blacklaw complied.

Harborford went on, "I've spent hours in the projectorium. I've got several repeats of the trace, but I can't catch the thought that goes with it. My own master-thought, and I can't catch it." Again he stopped and his eyes moved. "Mr. Blacklaw, would you mind shifting your chair a little? Your shadow on that globe— Thank you."

"But, surely," Blacklaw remarked gropingly, "just one thought—It can't be so important—"

Harborford slowly shook his head. "The mind must be completely bare. If only one door is left open for the unknown to slip through, it's as bad as a thousand. And this is a master-thought—my mind's final comment on my most important studies." He paused. "And it must be true. I've searched and searched for inconsistency indications and I can't find any.

"And I don't know what the thought is."

He looked hopelessly at Blacklaw.

Then his eyes started to move again.

As soon as Harborford had made himself decide to go home and get some sleep he felt better. After all, he couldn't stay at the Institute forever. And the workroom was beginning to get on his nerves. It was beginning to get too much *into* his mind, like a room in which a sleeper wakes and lies drowsily peering at the walls.

Of course it was hard to admit even temporary defeat, even harder perhaps than he tried to pretend to himself. But it was no use trying to go on fagged like this. Already he had caught Kesserik and Madderlee giving him queer glances. If only that interviewer fellow had known more about thought-research—somehow he could talk to him. He wished he had stayed longer.

He lingered, puttering aimlessly. Averting his eyes, he arranged the tracings on his desk in neat, meaningless piles.

He was getting middle-aged, he realized. He couldn't stand up to a strain like this as he had once been able to—as when, in a sanitarium bedroom, he had fought the black-shrouded mind-devils.

He shut the door on that memory, leaned against it.

His wife must be worried about him, he told himself. She couldn't have missed the anxiety in his voice when he had called to tell her he was working overnight.

And he really needed the security of home very badly.

Still he lingered by his desk, shifting from foot to foot.

Then he noticed that, with the sunset, shadows had grown in all the corners, were sprouting like vines across walls and floor. Vines all of one peculiar shape.

His footsteps across the room and down the corridor had the rapid, plunging rhythm of panic.

One of the Institute's private jetters was waiting outside with a pilot. But now that he was in the open air, Harborford again delayed, looking around at the panorama, broken at a few places by towering skylons, of forest and low hills, soft in the sunset, trying to let its peace sink into him.

His eyes were heavy and aching with fatigue. He experienced an illusion with which he was familiar and which did not frighten him. Across every object he viewed, as it faintly sketched in mist, was a gray pattern. Just as a person who thinks chiefly in visualized words may see objects accompanied by their names, so Harborford often saw them along with a ghost of their thought-traces.

Another thought-trace tried to creep into his mind—an uglily humped one with five subordinate undulations apparent to the expert and jagged spindles toward either end. Redfield Indications and Harborford-m Halo very marked.

He suppressed it.

He decided that a little of the peacefulness of the landscape was filtering through to him.

Then he noticed darker shadows marching down the hills below the sunset's line of fire, collecting at the edge of the forest, lurking among the trees, gathering strength for a final undulating rush at the Institute. An army of humped shadows, all alike.

He ducked into the jetter. Almost with the first smooth upward swoop, fatigue got in its hammer-blow. He slept.

The soft shock of landing awakened him with jangling nerves, his mind refreshed all too soon.

He told himself it was good to get home.

He thanked the pilot and went inside. His wife greeted him with hardly a trace of anxiety. She knew that he liked her to be very calm and untroubled.

He told her nothing. They talked of inconsequential matters. He began to absorb the feeling of home into him. He began to feel safe.

Halfway through dinner he noticed something repeated at regular intervals in the restful wall-pattern of leaves and branches. An uglily lumped curve in one of the twigs.

He got up and left the room.

His wife followed him to his study. She no longer concealed her anxiety. He felt her arm around him, her cheek close to his, the touch of her lovely hair, graying now.

"What is it?"

He felt close to her. He almost felt he could tell her about it. In fact, he turned and started to.

Then he saw, in the smooth pile of her gray hair, a certain pattern.

That did away with any possibility of confidences. Though they talked for a while in a general way—and at a distance—of his fatigue and need for some sort of vacation.

Being cooped up alone all night in his study was hard. Harborford wished he had not slept in the jetter. But at least the walls were unpatterned, and there was enough light to kill almost all shadows. He wanted to get out his pipe, but that would mean twisting curls of smoke. When he tried to read, weariness made the projected letters run together suggestively.

His mind was abnormally active. It kept visualizing the universe, the world, the past, his life, his researches, his thoughts and their traces. Everything clear as crystal, except for one inscrutable, humped trace that wriggled through them all.

Toward morning he got a little sleep.

He awoke feeling a little more detached. He could see plainly now that he really needed a vacation. He had been plugging away too uninterruptedly at his research. He needed a day of idle roving, free from routine and the sense of driving purpose, time to let his mind run down. Perhaps several days.

It was exciting getting into his flying togs. He hadn't had them on for over a year. He recorded a brief message for his wife and got out before the dew was off the grass.

He gunned his field and the house dropped away as if slipped under a giant's reducing glass. He felt, exhilaratingly, the weight of his blood in his veins and his flesh on his bones. He plummeted up a thousand feet and hung.

The landscape stretched out soft and greeny-gray and faintly hazed, as if still drunk with sleep. In the distance streams of workers were swirling toward the skylons, but here the air was clear.

He had forgotten how good it was to stand on air.

Inland, rolling hills stretched off enticingly toward a horizon mysteriously veiled with low lacy clouds. He headed toward it.

Then in a moment he had swung around in a close, racking semicircle and headed for the sea.

The low lacy clouds had all been of one shape.

A few minutes of blind plunging flight put him over water. He could look down and see shoals of fishes, distinct in the clear depths, and—off to one side—an all-media craft exuberantly porpoise-plunging.

He kept on like a rocket that doesn't know whither or why.

This way the horizon was clear. The low sun turned the long ripple edges into rosy veins. A maze of curves.

All alike.

Just in time he reestablished control over his actions and came out of his breakneck plunge to drift gasping a few yards above the fishes, who scattered from his shadow.

With the suddenness of a revelation, he realized that the whole idea of a vacation had been a mistake. He must get back to the Institute and lick this thing.

As soon as he had made the decision he felt better. The features of the landscape no longer took on shapes that weren't there, as he streaked steadily along. They stood out sharp and real, what they should be and nothing more.

He stripped off his togs and hurried to the workroom without seeing anyone.

He eagerly picked up the first tracing on his desk and stared at it.

He continued to stare at it.

He threw it aside and snatched up another.

And another.

And another.

Black and gray, large and small, dim and distinct, singly and grouped, memory traces, sensation traces, unconscious traces, deduction traces, synthesis traces, writhing, marching, crowding, as if there were no other thought in the whole universe—it was everywhere. That one humped trace.

Kesserik and Madderlee heard the crazy noises and the fall, and came running.

"Then it's fairly certain he will recover?" Blacklaw's voice expressed concern.

"Absolutely." Madderlee's nod was reassuringly emphatic. "He should be out of the sanitarium in a month. Though whether he'll ever return to thought research is quite another matter, since his breakdown seems to have been linked up very intimately with some phase of his work." He glanced curiously at Blacklaw, and Kesserik did likewise. "We're hoping you'll be able to throw some light on that point."

The three men were sitting in the workroom, near Harborford's desk.

Blacklaw hesitated. He said, "Ordinarily you'd be in a position to know much more about it than a comparative stranger like myself."

"Ordinarily. He was not a secretive man. But those last two days—" Madderlee threw up his hands.

Blacklaw addressed them both. "How much do you know?"

Madderlee looked at Kesserik.

"Very little," the dark assistant replied rapidly. "He was very much concerned about some point in his work. We spent forty straight hours here and in the projectorium, mostly taking tracings of his thoughts. He wouldn't tell me what he was after and he didn't give me a chance to examine the tracings. I got the impression he was apprehensive about something. Then he went home. Early next morning he came back and—it happened."

Blacklaw looked at Madderlee. "Did he tell you anything when you saw him yesterday?"

"Only that he would never again have anything to do with thought research. They didn't let me talk with him much, but he was very eager to tell me that. I'd intended suggesting that we take tracings to help in analyzing his case, but his attitude pretty well ruled that out."

Blacklaw turned to Kesserik. "Did you examine those last tracings afterwards?"

"Of course. But they were strangely unhelpful. A lot of thoughts concerning his research and special cases. Marked tension indications and neurotic groupings. But nothing to give me a definite line on what was causing him such anxiety."

Blacklaw stood up and moved behind the desk. "Well, gentlemen," he said, "Harborford *did* tell me a little more than he revealed to either of you. It's my idea that he became obsessed with one of his own thought-traces which he couldn't interpret or consciously recognize."

Kesserik pursed his lips, smiling queerly. "Hm-m-m—barely possible, I suppose. Though I wouldn't think you'd ever get the old boy to admit it."

Madderlee asked, "What trace? You've looked through those on his desk. He had them scattered all over the place when the seizure occurred. Were you able to recognize it again?" he sounded skeptical.

Blacklaw nodded. "Solely because it was identical with a pattern in one of my own thought-tracings, which Harborford made to give me a demonstration. The same circumstances enabled me to make an amateur's stab at interpreting it."

He picked up the top tracing and handed it to Kesserik, indicating a misty, humped curve.

The assistant scanned it intently, then shook his head and broke into a smile, letting the tracing slip to his knee. "No, Mr. Blacklaw, you must be mistaken. This trace could never have puzzled Harborford for a moment. Why, even I can interpret it, and without any reference material." He picked up the tracing.

"It's simply—"

"Wait a minute," said Blacklaw. "If my idea is right, it *is* a trace whose meaning would be very obvious to any thought-research man—except Harborford."

He took a few steps. "I know I'm just a layman," he said, "and what I'm going to say is not at all original, but it's something you fellows probably lost sight of at times, because you're so close to your work.

"Thought is different from every other object of man's research. Stars, atoms, amoebas, even body cells—they're all outside the mind. But in analyzing his thoughts, and is analyzing his own analyzing apparatus. So it always stays one jump ahead of him.

"Let's suppose there was a scientist who knew everything, who understood the whole universe perfectly. Well and good. But then who would understand the scientist? *He* couldn't, because his own understandings of himself would constitute new data requiring analysis. He couldn't ever get ahead of the game."

Madderlee and Kesserik were obviously interested, though they still looked skeptical.

"When Harborford claimed to be able to catch any thought, he was putting himself in the place of that hypothetical scientist—and *without* understanding the whole universe by a long shot. He claimed to be able to keep ahead of the game. He thought he had his thoughts all neatly taped and docketed, and for that affront his thoughts took a revenge—a rather nasty one, because it was so simple.

"He found the trace of a thought springing from his research. It was a master-thought—his mind's final comment on his life's work. There was no evidence of illogic or inconsistency in its pattern—he couldn't get rid of it that way. So because it was a thought which knocked all his arrogant claims into a cocked hat, he tried to suppress it from his consciousness. He refused to recognize its meaning—and as a result it became an obsessive shadow which terrified and eventually overwhelmed him."

An odd thing happened. Madderlee still looked skeptical but Kesserik's attitude had changed completely. He was nodding excitedly.

Blacklaw said, "It was a simple thought. You and I wouldn't have found it in the least unusual or frightening. But I want you to put yourselves in Harborford's position. A man with an almost frantic hatred of any dark corners in the mind, a man who had spent two years in a sanitarium and had an overpowering fear of anything abnormal or hidden in his thought processes, a man who had staked everything on his ability to lay his mind completely bare... and then for that man to find in his mind, springing logically from its experiences, this thought of all thoughts."

He paused. "You interpret it, Kesserik."

Kesserik looked at the trace and read: "There are thoughts in your mind that you will never catch."

CRYSTAL PRISON

"MY GREAT GRANNY WILL TRADE THREE BALLS OF gray string, big as grapefruit," Jack said to the girl. He was an 18-year-old boy—in Oldlands you didn't become a young man or woman until 30, or a voter until 65. The new antibiotics, carcinophages and cell-restorers had upped life expectancy to 350 years. Jack had a narrow sunny face and brown crew-cut hair, but he looked plump because he was wearing a suit lined with thick foam rubber, so he wouldn't break a bone or a priceless chair if he bumped anything, and colored white, so any dirt he got on it would show. A month ago he had discovered in the 3-foot-deep swimming pool that it floated beautifully, but Great Granny had given him the treatment of "You're worrying me into a heart attack before I'm 200." Around his neck was a silver dollar with a glistening listen-whisper jutting up by his jaw.

"My Great Great Aunt will trade her two string-balls, one red, one green, for them," Candy replied. "They're big as the Temple oranges of Holy Florida and the green has a gold thread in it." At 17, Candace had long black hair and a slim face like amused moonlight, but you could hardly see it because of the black burnoose her Great Great Aunt made her wear against sunburn and to assure she'd reach 30 properly modest. She had once tried to give up wearing it indoors, outside her bedroom. But only once. "Little girls of 17 are not to be seen, especially their legs." You could, however, see the gleam of her silver dollar.

"That's trading 300 yards for about 70," Jack objected, prompted by his listen-whisper.

"How many knots have your string-balls got hidden in them?" Candy demanded, prompted by hers.

"1,327," Jack admitted. "Granny had me count."

While their mouths were saying these things, their eyes were saying something else. It was strange.

"Mine have only 19," Candy sneered. "No deal, unless you throw in the broken birdcage... or some tea bags."

"My knots are all square knots—" Jack began, but then his listen-whisper blatted audibly.

"You're possessions-mad, Grace! That would violate senior citizens' fair-trading laws."

"You and your dirty string, all knots!" Candy's blatted back.

The teen-agers faced each other across a road wide enough for two oldsters' electric wheelchairs to pass. Behind each of them was a large handcart piled high with choice oldster treasures arranged very neatly. From their collars silver wires trailed back past de-thorned bushes up de-insected tidy green hills to two sweet cottages, smothered in artificial flowers, which smiled at each other like camouflaged tanks across the narrow road. Behind each cottage stood a larger storage barn.

Some progressive oldsters let their youngsters play and run errands and record diet-and-health gossip and do trading deals on collars only radio-linked to home. But wired collars seemed wisest to most, including Jack's and Candy's guardians. True, a girl had recently been strangled when her wire snagged in a tree she was climbing and she slipped. But she shouldn't have been climbing the tree. You always had to pay a price for safety and freedom from worry.

Besides, although the Oldlands police snagged 99 of 100 runaway youngsters headed for Freeshore, there was always that risk too.

The close-clipped vacuumed landscape was dotted at 100-yard intervals with 125-foot gray pillars like the trunks of giant pines identically lightning-blasted.

Although the sun shone brightly and the blue sky was gay with cirrus clouds, the air was somewhat stuffy, very still, and smelled just a touch of old newspapers, sour milk and soap. This was because of the invisible glasstic roof which was supported by the pillars and kept out of Oldlands all dangerous weather, including draughts.

* * *

"Don't gape and dawdle, Jack," his listen-whisper prompted.

He said to Candy, "I've got all 2,396 back issues of *Garbage Art* and *Junk Beautiful"*

"I've got them too," she retorted. "Your Gran just wants more storage space."

"Liar," Jack said. His hand held at his side, he crooked a finger at the girl. They pulled their carts closer together and knelt down in front of them, so they were hidden from the cottages.

"What are you doing, Candace?" her listen-whisper demanded. "Don't block the road, boy," was Great Granny's contribution.

"About those tea bags," the girl said quickly toward Jack. "I have 57 copies of the *Geriatric Observer* and *Daily Diet* to trade— just the sort of newspaper to spread over plastic tablecloth covers to keep them from getting dull."

"Well," Jack replied loudly, "I have 63 tea bags—used, of course, but dried out nicely." He wasn't looking at Candy, he was letting down a large hinged door in the bottom of his cart.

"Those might be acceptable," Candy bargained. "My Great Great Aunt seldom uses fresh tea bags. The used ones make her feel *more saving.*" She said this reverently, but her lips were laughing, especially when she saw the wrinkled gray tea bags neatly lined up on a shelf of Jack's cart, like mummified mice. Then her eyes became wild with excitement as Jack drew a life-size figure out of the false bottom of his cart and sat it beside him. She clapped a hand over her mouth to keep from exclaiming and she wagged the other hand and her eyes implored.

Jack snatched an antique aluminum coughdrop box from a pocket in his bump-proof white suit. From it he quickly took a bumblebee on a two-inch thread with a square of Stick-Tite tape at the other end, which he rapidly stuck to his collar just by the whisper-listen. The bee buzzed madly and its wings rattled against the silver metal.

"Oh, a bee!" Candy squealed in terror, leaning forward so that her listen-whisper was close to Jack's.

"It must have got in from the Freeshore through the Killing Wall," Jack shrilled frightenedly. Both of them were grinning. "Lovely bee," Candy said with her lips as it buzzed close to them.

From the cottages up the hills came faintly the sound of windows being slammed shut.

* * *

Her voice masked to the listen-whispers by the buzzing, Candy whispered, "Oh, she's beautiful, Jack. I wouldn't have made her nearly as beautiful."

She was referring to the robot duplicate of herself sitting by Jack and dressed in pearl-gray sweater, slacks and sandals.

"No, you wouldn't," Jack whispered back gruffly. "And you would have been wrong, so that's why I had to build her."

"Can I hear her talk?"

"Yes, once, but then you got to work fast," Jack said curtly. He felt the figure's side for a button under the sweater, then pressed.

The robot Candy blinked her eyes and smiled—a little sadly, Candy fancied—and nodded her head and softly said, "Yes."

"That's about all her vocabulary," Jack admitted, "except for repeating things people tell her."

" 'Yes' is the only word she'll need with G-G Aunty," Candy said. "Her repeat-talk will let her do trading and diet-gossip." She was already turned away and letting down a door in the bottom of *her* cart. Jack reached in his secret compartment for what looked like a thick green rug, rolled up tight. Then he looked at the robot, dressed almost identically to the first, which Candy had produced.

"Hey, I'm not *that* good-looking," he objected, his eyes a bit dreamy. At that moment the bumblebee stung him on the chin, but he hardly winced.

"Says you," Candy replied smugly.

"You remember to steal your key?" Jack growled, holding out his hand.

Candy wrinkled her nose and dropped a silver key in his palm, then turned around.

"I made him *look just* like you," she said. "I'll admit I couldn't have installed the servo-motors and batteries without your help."

"I couldn't have done the cybernetic circuits without yours," Jack said. By that time her silver collar had been unlocked from her neck and snapped around her robot's. The robot-Candy looked unhappy at that. Silly, Candy told herself, robots can't feel.

Then she had Jack's key and was fitting it into the tiny keyhole in the back of his collar.

* * *

In a lull in the bee's buzzing, Jack's whisper-listen blatted quaveringly, "Jack, my boy, can you speak?"

"Yes," Jack and his robot replied simultaneously, "Are you dead, son?" the emotional voice went on. "

Yes," the robot-Jack responded, but Jack overrode that with, "No, Great Granny, but that awful bee is still menacing us," whereupon the bee buzzed madly again as if on cue. "Good boy," Jack called to it. His collar was around his robot's neck now.

Candy whipped off her black burnoose while Jack lost time squirming out of his white anti-bump suit. For a moment all four were dressed alike in gray and looked like two pairs of identical twins. Then it was Candy's robot who was dressed like an Arab girl, black-cloaked and hooded, while with some difficulty they wormed the cumbersome foam-rubber suit onto the Jack robot.

Candy looked at the two silver keys in her hand. Somewhere down the road a siren sounded faintly. She slipped one key each into the pockets of the two robots. Jack frowned and almost said something, but instead captured the bumblebee, still straining for freedom, in the antique coughdrop box. "Not until Freeshore, old boy," he told the insect.

"Are you holding out, Candace?" G-G Aunty demanded from the whisper-listen and then at the robot's reply, "Good, just keep your hood shut. It won't be much longer—we've called the police."

"It can't sting you through the rubber. Cover your face with your arms, boy, and pray," Great Granny contributed.

The siren sounded again, much closer now, reverberating against the invisible glasstic sky.

"Come on!" Jack whispered sharply, grabbing up the green cylinder. Together he and Candy wormed their way, like soldiers infiltrating, between the bushes, away from the cottages and the siren, until they had some concealment behind them and a wide long lawn ahead. Then he unrolled the cylinder until it looked exactly like a thick green rug about 6 feet by 4 and the same color as the grass. In one corner was a gray metal square set with two buttons and a joystick.

Jack hit one of the buttons and the carpet stiffened flat and hard.

"It's a bomb, Candy!" Jack cheered softly. "An electronic cyclone. Crawl aboard."

As they did that, Jack explained, "Dad smuggled it to me through a friend of his who's a free trader."

* * *

Jack's widowed father and Candy's divorced mother had both had, separately, to leave Oldlands for Freeshore many years before. They had tried to take their children with them, but there had been a custody fight and as generally happens in the Oldlands courts, the oldest litigants had won out—especially in this case because neither Jack's father nor Candy's mother were yet of voting age; Candy's mother had been under thirty—a child. And because rich Oldlands almost always won out in the courts against money-poor Freeshore.

When he and Candy were stretched side by side, Jack hit the second button. The green carpet lifted four inches and hovered. Air sucked in at the front end of the carpet hissed down through a million tiny holes. The strange ship rocked a little, not much.

Just then a bullet-snouted blue police car nosed into sight on the road behind them, traveling at least 35 miles an hour. With a final blast of its siren, it carefully braked to a stop between the junk carts. Up from it stood four spry oldsters in blue, their heads hooded with mesh, like beekeepers'. One held in his heavily gauntleted hands an insect spray, the second an insect rifle, the third a pinpoint death-ray. The fourth lifted a bullhorn to his masked mouth. His voice rang from the glasstic sky: *"Bee at large! Bee at large! Where's the person around here reported a bee at large?"*

Then he looked down. "Oh, was it you kids?"

Jack and Candy gripped hands and grinned at each other as they heard their robots answer together, "Yes." This was instantly followed by the listen-whispers on the silver rings blatting, "We'll tell you all about it, officers. Come home, Candace. Come home, Jack," and by another two obedient calls of "Yes."

Then Jack pulled back on the joystick, and the carpet leaned forward, air hissed from the back end too, and it went skimming off across the green lawn. It lifted over the bushes and arrowed between the gray pillars and swung wide of the senior citizens' dormitories and cottages that kept whipping into view.

He said in her ear, "You know, I'll miss Great Granny."

"And I'll mist G-G Auntie," she replied. "They weren't really bad, just terribly scared and lonely."

He nodded. "And maybe a little possessive, too," he added, almost doubtfully.

She said, "I'm bothered about our robots. We thought they'd just fool G-G and G-Gran long enough to let us get to Freeshore. But now I think they'll go on fooling them forever. And then—I know this is foolish—they'll be as unhappy as we were."

He said, "If they ever do grow minds, they can escape to Freeshore too. You left them their keys."

And then there was only the rushing wind and the flashing pillars and the dizzying lawns and musty cottages as they sped, faster and faster, toward Freelands and wild bees and wild spiders and wild tigers, and firecrackers and loud jazz and the open life and open sky and danger and spaceships and the stars.

BULLET WITH HIS NAME

THE INVISIBLE BEING SHIFTED HIS ANCHORAGE A BIT in Earth's gravitational field, which felt like a push rather than a pull to him, and said, "This featherless biped seems to satisfy Galaxy Center's requirements. I'd say he's a suitable recipient for the Gifts."

His Coadjutor, equally invisible and negatively massed, chewed that over. "Mature by his length and mass. Artificial plumage neither overly gaudy nor utterly drab—indicating median social level, which is confirmed by the size of his bachelor nest. Inward maps of his environment not fantastically inaccurate. Feelings reasonably meshed—at least neither volcanic nor frozen. Thoughts and values in reasonable order. Yes, I agree, a satisfactory test subject. Except..."

"Except what?"

"Except we can never be sure of that 'reasonable' part."

"Of course not! Thank your stars *that's* beyond the reach of Galaxy Center's keenest telepathy, or even ours on the spot. Otherwise you and I'd be out of a job."

"And have to scheme up some other excuse for free-touring the Cosmos with backtracking permitted."

"Exactly!" The Being and his Coadjutor understood each other very well and were the best of friends. "Well, how many Gifts would you suggest for the test?"

"How about two Little and one Big?" the Coadjutor ventured.

"Umm... statistically adequate but spiritually unsatisfying. Remember, the fate of his race hangs on his reactions to them.

I'd be inclined to increase your suggestion by one each and add a Great."

"No—at least I question the last. After all, the Great Gifts aren't as important, really, as the Big Gifts. Besides..."

"Besides what? Come on, spit it out!" The Invisible Being was the bluff, blunt type.

"Well," said his less hearty but unswervingly honest companion. "I'm always afraid that you'll use the granting of a Great Gift as an excuse for some sardonic trick—that you'll put a sting in its tail."

"And why shouldn't I, if I want to? Snakes have stings in their tails (or do they on this planet?) And I'm a sort of snake. If he fails the test, he fails. And aren't both of us malicious, plaguing spirits, eager to knock holes in the inward armor of provincial entities? It's in the nature of our job. But we can argue about that in due course. What Little Gifts would you suggest?"

"That's something I want to talk about. Many of the Little Gifts are already well within his race's reach, if not his. After all, they've already got atomic power."

"Which as you very well know scores them nothing one way or the other on a Galaxy Center test. We're agreed on the nature and the number of our Gifts—three Little, two Big, and one Great?"

"Yes," his Coadjutor responded resignedly.

"And we're agreed on our subject?"

"Yes to that too."

"All right, then, let's get started. This isn't the only solar system we have to visit on this circuit."

Ernie Meeker—of Chicago, Illinois, U.S. of A., Occident Terra, Sol, Starswarm 37, Rim Sector, Milky Way Galaxy—rubbed his chin and slanted across the street to a drugstore.

"Package of blades. Double edge. Five. Cheapest."

At one point during the transaction, the clerk lost sight of the tiny packet he'd placed on the coin-whitened glass between them. He gave a suspicious look, as if the customer had palmed them.

Ernie blinked. After a moment, he pointed toward the center of the counter.

"There they are," he said, dropping a coin beside them.

The clerk's face didn't get any less suspicious. Customer who could sneak something without your seeing could sneak it back the same way. He rang up the sale and closed the register fast.

Ernie Meeker went home and shaved. Five days—and shaves—later, he pushed the first blade, uncomfortably dull now, through the tiny slot beside the bathroom mirror. He unwrapped the second blade from the packet.

Five shaves later, he cut himself under the chin with the second blade, although he was drawing it as gently through his soaped beard as if it were only his second shave with it, or at most his third. He looked at it sourly and checked the packet. Wouldn't have been the first time he'd absentmindedly changed blades ahead of schedule.

But there were still three blades in their waxed wrappings.

Maybe, he thought, he'd still had one of the blades from the last packet and shuffled it into this series.

Or maybe—although the manufacturers undoubtedly had inspectors to prevent it from happening—he'd got a decent blade for once.

Two or three shaves later, it still seemed as sharp as ever, or almost so.

"Funny thing," he remarked to Bill at lunch. "Sometimes you get a blade that shaves a lot better. Looks exactly like the others, but shaves better. Or worse sometimes, of course."

"And sometimes," his office mate said, "you wear out a blade fast by not soaking your beard enough. For me, one shave with a stiff beard and the blade's through. On the other hand, if you're careful to soak your beard real good—four, five minutes at least—have the water steaming hot, get the soap really into it, one blade can last a long time."

"That's true, all right," Ernie agreed, trying to remember how well he had been soaking his beard lately. Shaving was a good topic for light conversations, warm and agreeable, like most bathroom and kitchen topics.

But next morning in the bathroom, looking at the reflection of his unremarkable face, there was something chilly in his feelings that he couldn't quite analyze. He flipped his razor open and suspiciously studied the bright metal wafer, then flipped it closed with an irritated shrug.

As he shaved, it occurred to him that a good detective-story murder method would be to substitute a very sharp razor blade for one the victim knew was extremely dull. He'd whip it across his throat, putting a lot of muscle into the stroke to get through the tangle, and—*urrk!*

Ridiculous, of course. Wouldn't work except with a straight razor. Wouldn't even work with a straight razor, unless... oh, well.

He told himself the blade was noticeably duller today.

Next morning, he was still using the freak blade, but with a persistent though very slight uneasiness. Things should behave as you expected them to, in accordance with their flimsy souls, he told himself at the barely conscious level. Men should die, hearts should break, girls should tell, nations perish, curtains get dirty, milk sour... and razor blades grow dull. It was the comfortable, expected, reassuring way.

He told himself the blade was duller still. Just a bit.

The third morning, face lathered, he flipped open the razor and lifted it out.

"You're through," he said to it silently. "I've had the experience before of getting bum shaves by trying to save a penny by pretending to myself that a wornout blade was still sharp enough, when it obviously couldn't be. Or maybe—" he grinned a little wryly—"maybe I'd almost get one more shave out of you and then you'd fall to pieces like the Wonderful One Horse Shay and leave me with a chin full of steel porcupine quills. No, thanks."

So Ernie Meeker pushed through the little slot beside the mirror and heard tinkle faintly down and away the first of the Little Gifts, the Everlasting Razor Blade. One hundred and fifty thousand years later, it turned up, bright and shining in the midst of a small knob of red iron oxide excavated by an archeological expedition of multibrachs from Antares Gamma. Those wise history-mad beings handed it about wonderingly, from tentacle to impatient tentacle.

That day, Ernie felt a little sick, somehow. After dinner, he decided it was the Thuringer sausage he'd eaten at lunch. He hurried up to the bathroom with a spoon, but as he clutched the box of bicarbonate of soda, preparatory to plunging the spoon into it, it seemed to him that the box said distinctly, in a small inward-outward voice:

"No, no, no!"

Ernie sat down suddenly on the toilet seat. The spoon rattled against the porcelain finish of the washbowl as he laid it down. He held the box firmly in both hands and studied it.

Size, shape, materials, blue color, closure, etc., were exactly as they should be. But the white lettering on the blue background read:

AQUEOUS FUEL CATALYST

Dissociates H20 into hemi-quasi-stable H and O,
furnishing a serviceable fuel-and-oxydizer mix for most
motorcycles, automobiles, trucks, motorboats, airplanes,
stationary motors, torque-twisters, translators, and rockets
(exhaust velocity up to 6000 meters per second).

Operates safely within and outside of all normal atmospheres.
No special adaptor needed on oxygenizer-atmosphere motors.

DIRECTIONS: Place one pinch in fuel tank, fill with water.
Add water as needed.

A-F Catalyst should generally be renewed when objective
tests show fuel quality has deteriorated 50 per cent.

U.S. and Foreign Patents Pending.

After reading that several times, with suitable mind-checking
and eye-testing in between, Ernie took up a little of the white
powder on the end of a nailfile. He had thought of tasting it,
but had instantly abandoned the notion and even refrained from
sniffing the stuff—after all, the human body is mostly water.

After reducing the quantity several times, he gingerly dumped
at most four or five grains on the flat edge of the washbowl and
then used the broad end of the nailfile to maneuver a large bead
of water over to the almost invisible white deposit. He closed the
box, put it and the nailfile carefully on the window ledge, lit a
match and touched it to the drop, at the last moment ducking his
head a little below the level of the washbowl.

Nothing happened. After a moment, he slowly withdrew the
match, shaking it out, and looked. There was nothing to see. He
reached out to touch the stupid squashed ovoid of water.

Ouch! He withdrew his fingers much faster than the match,
shook them more sharply. Something was there, all right. Heat.
Heat enough to hurt.

He cautiously explored the boundaries of the heat. It became
noticeable about eighteen inches above the drop and almost an
inch to each side—an invisible slim vertical cylinder. Crouching
close, eyes level with the top of the washbowl, he could make out
the flame—a thin finger of crinkled light.

He noticed that a corner of the drop was seething—but only a corner, as if the heat were sharply bounded in that direction and perhaps as if the catalyst were only transforming the water to fuel a bit at a time.

He reached up and tugged off the light. Now he could see the flame—ghostly, about four inches high, hardly thicker than a string, and colored not blue but pale green. A spectral green needle. He blew at it softly. It shimmied gracefully, but not, he thought, as much as the flame of a match or candle. It had character.

He switched on the light. The drop was more than half gone now; the part that was left was all seething. And the bathroom was markedly warmer.

"Ernie! Are you going to be much longer?"

The knock hadn't been loud and his widowed sister's voice was more apologetic than peremptory, but he jumped, of course.

"I am testing something," he started to say and changed it midway. It came out, "I am be out in a minute."

He turned off the light again. The flame was a little shorter now and it shrank as he watched, about a quarter inch a second. As soon as it died, he switched on the light. The drop was gone.

He scrubbed off the spot with a dry washrag, on second thought put a dab of vaseline on the washrag, scrubbed the spot again with that—he didn't like to think of even a grain of the powder getting in the drains or touching any water. He folded the washrag, tucked it in his pocket, put the blue box—after a final check of the lettering—in his other coat pocket, and opened the door.

"I was taking some bicarb," he told his sister. "Thuringer sausage at lunch."

She nodded absently.

Sleep refused even to flirt with Ernie, his mind was full of so many things, especially calculations involving the distance between his car and the house and the length of the garden hose. In desperation, as the white hours accumulated and his thoughts began to squirm, he grabbed up the detective story he'd bought at the corner newsstand. He had read thirty pages before he realized that he was turning them as rapidly as he could focus just once on each facing page.

He jumped out of bed. My God, he thought, at that rate he'd

finish the book under three minutes and here it wasn't even two o'clock yet!

He selected the thickest book on the shelf, an over-poweringly dull historical treatise in small print. He turned two pages, three, then closed it with a clap and looked at the wall with frightened eyes. Ernie Meeker had discovered inside the birthday box that was himself, the first of the Big Gifts.

The trouble was that in that wee-hour, lonely bedroom, it didn't seem like a gift at all. How would he ever keep himself in books, he wondered, if he read them so fast? And think how full to bursting his mind would get—right now, the seven pages of fine-print history were churning in it, vividly clear, along with the first chapters of the new detective story. If he kept on absorbing information that fast, he'd have to be revising all his opinions and beliefs every couple of days at least—maybe every couple of hours.

It seemed a dreadful, literally maddening prospect—his mind would ultimately become a universe of squirming macaroni. Even the wallpaper he was staring at, which imitated the grain of wood, had in an instant become so fully part of his consciousness that he felt he could turn his back on it right now and draw a picture of it correct to the tiniest detail. But who would ever want to do such a thing or want to be able to?

It was an abnormal, dangerous, temporary sensitivity, he told himself, generated by the excitement of the crazy discovery he'd made in the bathroom. Like the thoughts of a drowning man, riffling an infinity-paneled adventure-comic of his life as he bolts his last rough ration of air. Or like the feeling a psychotic must have that he's on the verge of visualizing the whole universe, having its ultimate secrets patter down into the palm of his outstretched hand—just before the walls close in.

Ernie Meeker was not a drinking man, then. A pint had stood a week on his closet shelf and only been diminished three shots. But now he had a good job on the sturdy remainder.

Pretty soon the unbearable, edge-of-doom clarity in his mind faded, the universe-macaroni cooked down to a thick white soup uniform as fog, and the words of the detective story were sliding into his mind individually, or at most in strings of three and four. Which, if it wasn't as it ideally should be in an ambitious man's mind, was at least darn comfortable.

He had not rejected the Big Gift of Page-at-a-Glance-Reading.

Not quite. But he had dislocated for tonight at least the imposed nervous field on which it depended.

For want of a better place, Ernie dropped the rubber tube from the bathtub spray into the scrub bucket half full of odorous pink fluid and stared doubtfully at the uncapped gas tank. The tank had been almost empty when he'd last driven his car, he knew, because he'd been waiting until payday to gas up. Now he had used the tube to siphon out what he could of the remainder (he still could taste the stuff!) and he'd emptied the fuel line and carburetor, more or less.

Further than that, in the way of engine hygiene, Ernie's strictly kitchen mechanics did not go, but he felt that a catalyst used in pinches shouldn't be too particular about contaminants. Besides, the directions on the box hadn't said anything about cleaning the fuel tank, had they?

He hesitated. At his feet, the garden hose gurgled noisily over the curb into the gutter; it had vindicated his midnight estimate, proving just long enough. He looked uneasily up and down the dawning street and was relieved to find it still empty. He wished fervently, not for the first time this Saturday morning, that he had a garage. Then he sighed, squared his shoulders a little, and lifted the box out of his pocket.

Making to check the directions the umpteenth time, he received a body blow. The white lettering on the box had disappeared. The box didn't proclaim itself sodium bicarbonate again—there was just no lettering at all, only blue background. He turned it over several times.

Right there died his tentative plan of eventually sharing his secret with some friend who knew more than himself about motors (he hadn't decided anyway who that would be). It would be just too silly to approach anyone he knew with a more-than-wild story and featureless blue box.

For a moment, he came very close to dropping the box between the wide-set bars of the street drain and pouring the pink gas back in the tank. It had hit him, in a way for the first time, just how *crazy* this all was, how jarringly implausible even on such hypotheses as practical jokes, secret product perhaps military, or mad inventor (except himself).

For how the devil should the stuff get into his bathroom disguised as bicarb? That circumstance seemed beyond imagination. Green flames... vanishing letters... "torque-twisters, translators"... a box that talked...

At that point, simple faith came to Ernie's rescue: in the same bathroom, he *had* seen the green flame; it had burned his fingers.

Quickly he dipped up a little of the white powder on the edge of a fifty-cent piece, dumped it in the gas tank without quibbling as to quantity, rapped the coin on the edge of the opening, closed and pocketed the blue box, and picked up the spurting hose and jabbed it into the round hole.

His heart was pounding and his breath was coming fast. That had taken real effort. So he was slow in hearing the footsteps behind him.

His neighbor's gate was open and Mr. Jones stood open-mouthed a few feet behind him, all ready for his day's work as streetcar motorman and wearing the dark blue uniform that always made him look for a moment unpleasantly like a policeman.

Ernie swung the hose around, flipping his thumb over the end to make a spray, and nonchalantly began to water the little rectangle of lawn between sidewalk and curb.

The first things he watered were the bottoms of Mr. Jones's pants legs.

Mr. Jones voiced no complaint. He backed off several steps, stared intently at Ernie, rather palely, it seemed to the latter. Then he turned and made off for the streetcar tracks at a very fast shuffle, shaking his feet a little now and then and glancing back several times over his shoulder without slowing down.

Ernie felt light-headed. He decided there was enough water in the gas tank, capped it, and momentarily continued to water the lawn.

"Ernie! Come on in and have breakfast!"

He heeded his sister's call, telling himself it would be a good idea "to give the stuff time to mix" before testing the engine.

He had divined her question and was ready with an answer.

"I've just found out that we're supposed to water our lawns only before seven in the morning or after seven in the evenings. It's the law."

It was the day for their monthly drive out to Wheaton to visit Uncle Fabius. On the whole, Ernie was glad his sister was in the car when he turned the key in the starter—it forced him to be calm and collected, though he didn't feel exactly right about exposing her to the danger of being blown up without first explaining to her the risk. But the motor started right up and began purring powerfully. Ernie's sister commented on it favorably.

Then she went on to ask, "Did you remember to buy gas yesterday?"

"No," he said without thinking; then realizing his mistake, quickly added, "I'll buy some in Wheaton. There's enough to get us there."

"You didn't think so yesterday," she objected. "You said the tank was nearly empty."

"I was wrong. Look, the gauge shows it's half full."

"But then how... Ernie, didn't you once tell me the gauge doesn't work?"

"Did I?"

"Yes. Look, there's a station. Why don't you buy gas now?"

"No, I'll wait for Wheaton—I know a place there I can get it cheaper," he insisted, rather lamely, he feared.

His sister looked at him steadily. He settled his head between his shoulders and concentrated on driving. His feeling of excitement was spoiled, but a few minutes of silence brought it back. He thought of the blur of green flashes inside the purring motor. If the passing drivers only knew!

Uncle Fabius, retired perhaps a few years too early and opinionated, was a trial, but he did know something about the automobile industry. Ernie chose a moment when his sister was out of the room to ask if he'd ever heard of a white powder that would turn water into gasoline or some usable fuel.

"Who's been getting at you?" Uncle Fabius demanded sharply, to Ernie's surprise and embarrassment. "That's one of the oldest swindles. They always tell this story about how this man had a white powder or something and demonstrated it once with a pail of water and then disappeared. You're supposed to believe that Detroit or the big oil companies got rid of him. It's just another of those malicious legends, concocted—by Russia, I imagine— to weaken your faith in American Industry, like the everlasting battery or the razor blade that never gets dull. You're looking pale, Ernie—don't tell me you've already put money in this white powder? I suppose someone's approached you with a proposition, though?"

With considerable difficulty, Ernie convinced his uncle that he had "just heard the story from a friend."

"In that case," Uncle Fabius opined, "you can be sure some fuel-powder swindler has been getting at *him*. When you see him—and be sure to make that soon—tell him from me that—" and Uncle Fabius began an impassioned ninety-minute defense of big business, small business, prosperity, America, money, know-how, and a number of other institutions that defended pretty easily, so that the situation was wholly normal when Ernie's sister returned.

As soon as the car pulled away from the curb on their way back to Chicago, she reminded him about the gas.

"Oh, I've already done that," he assured her. "Made a special trip so I wouldn't forget. It was while you were out of the room. Didn't you hear me?"

"No," she said, "I didn't," and she looked at him steadily, as she had that morning. He similarly retreated to driving.

Stopping for a railroad crossing, he braked too hard and the car stalled. His sister grabbed his arm. "I knew that was going to happen," she said. "I knew that for some reason you lied to me when—" The motor, starting readily again, cut short her remark and Ernie didn't press his small triumph by asking her what she was about to say.

To tell the truth, Ernie wasn't feeling as elated about today's fifty-mile drive as he'd imagined he would. Now he thought he could put his finger on the reason: It was the completely... well, *arbitrary* way in which the white powder had come into his possession.

If he'd concocted it himself, or been given it by a shady promoter, or even seen the box fall out of the pocket of a suspicious-looking man in a trenchcoat, *then* he'd have felt more able to *do* something about it, whether in the general line of starting a fuel-powder company or of going to the F.B.I.

But just having the stuff drop into his hands from the sky, so to speak, as if in a crazy dream, and for that same reason not feeling able to talk about it and assure himself he wasn't going crazy... oh, it is rough when you can't share things, really rough; not being able to share depressing news corrodes the spirit, but not being able to share exciting news can sometimes be even more corroding.

Maybe, he told himself, he could figure out someone to tell. But who? And how? His mind shied away from the problem, rather decisively.

When he checked the blue box that night, the original sodium bicarbonate lettering had returned with all its humdrum paragraphs. Not one word about exhaust velocities.

From that moment, the fuel-powder became a trial to Ernie rather than a secret glory. He'd wake in the middle of the night doubting that he had ever really read the mind-dizzying lettering, ever really tested the stuff—perhaps he'd bring from sleep the chilling notion that in the dimness and excitement of Saturday morning he'd put the water in some other car's gas tank, perhaps Mr. Jones's. He could usually argue such ideas away, but they kept coming back. And yet he did no more bathroom testing.

Of course the car still ran. He even fueled it once again with the garden hose, sniffing the nozzle to make sure it hadn't somehow got connected to the basement furnace oil-tank. He picked three o'clock in the morning for the act, but nevertheless as he was returning indoors he heard a window in Mr. Jones's house slam loudly. It unsettled him. Coming home the next day, he caught his sister and Mr. Jones consulting about something on the latter's doorsteps, which unsettled him further.

He couldn't decide on a safe place to keep the box and took to carrying it around with him day and night. Bill spotted it once down at the office and by an unhappy coincidence needed some bicarb just then for a troubled stomach. Ernie explained on the spur of the moment that he was using the box to carry plaster of Paris, which involved him in further lies that he felt were quite unconvincing as well as making him appear decidedly eccentric, even butter-brained. Bill took to calling him "the sculptor".

Meanwhile, besides the problem of the white powder, Ernie was having other unsettling experiences, stemming (though of course he didn't know that) from the other Gifts—and not just the Big Gift of Page-at-a-Glance Reading, though that still returned from time to time to shock his consciousness and send him hurrying for a few quick shots.

Like many another car-owning commuter, Ernie found the traffic and parking problems a bit too much for comfort and so used the fast electric train to carry him five times a week to the heart of the city. During those brief, swift, crowded trips Ernie, generally looking steadily out the window at the brown buildings and black stanchions whipping past, enjoyed a kind of anonymity and privacy more refreshing to his spirit than he realized. But now all that had been suddenly changed. People had started to talk to him; total strangers struck up conversations almost every morning and afternoon.

Ernie couldn't figure out the reason and wasn't at all sure he liked it—except for Vivian.

She was the sort of girl Ernie dreamed about, improperly. Tall, blonde and knowing, excitedly curved but armored in a black suit, friendly and funny but given to making almost cruelly deflating remarks, as if the neatly furled short umbrella dangling from her wrist might better be a black dog whip.

She worked in an office too, a fancier one than Ernie's, as he found out from their morning conversations. He hadn't got to the point of asking her to lunch, but he was prodding himself.

Why such a girl should ever have asked him for a match in the first place and then put up with his clumsy babblings on subsequent mornings was a mystery to him. He finally asked her about it in what he hoped was a joking way, though she seemed to know a lot more about joking than he did.

"Don't you know?" she countered. "I mean what makes you attractive to people?"

"Me attractive? No."

"Well, I'll tell you then, Ernie, and I've got to admit it's something quite out of the ordinary. *I've* never noticed it in anyone else. Ernie, I'm sure your knowledge of romantic novels is shamefully deficient, it's clear from your manners, but in the earlier ones—not in style now—the hero is described as tall, manly, broad-shouldered, Anglo-Saxon features, etcetera, etcetera, but there's one thing he always has, something that sounds like poetic over-enthusiasm if you stop to analyze it, a physical impossibility, but that I have to admit you, Ernie, actually have. Flashing eyes."

"Flashing eyes? Me?"

She nodded solemnly. He thought her long straight lips trembled on the verge of a grin, but he couldn't be sure.

"How do you mean, flashing eyes?" he protested. "How can eyes flash, except by reflecting light? In that case, I guess they'd seem to 'flash' more if a person opened them wide but kept blinking them a lot. Is that what I do?"

"No, Ernie, though you're doing it now," she told him, shaking her head. "No, Ernie, your eyes just give a tiny flash of their own about every five seconds, like a lighthouse, but barely, *barely* bright enough for another person to notice. It makes you irresistible. Of course I've never seen you in the dark; maybe they wouldn't flash in the dark."

"You're joking."

Vivian frowned a little at that remark, as if she were puzzled herself.

"Well, maybe I am and maybe I'm not," she said. "In any case, don't get conceited about your Flashing Eyes, because I'm sure you'll never know how to take advantage of them."

When he parted from her downtown, pausing a moment to watch her walk away with feline majesty, he muttered "Flashing Eyes!" with a shrug of the shoulders and a skeptical growl. Just the same, he ducked his head as he moved off and he pulled the brim of his hat down sharply.

Afternoons, hurtling home in the five o'clock rush, it was not Vivian but Verna who frequently occupied the seat beside him, taking up rather more space in it than the Panther Princess. Verna was another of his newly acquired and not altogether welcome conversation-pals, along with Jacob the barber, Mr. Willis the druggist and Herman the health-food manufacturer, inventor of Soybean Mush—conquests of his Flashing Eyes or whatever it was.

Verna was stocky, pasty-faced, voluble (with him), coy, and had bad breath—he could see the tiny triangles of pale food between her incisors and canine whenever her conversations became particularly vehement and confidential, which was often. She always had a stack of books hugged to her stomach. She worked in a fur-storage vault, she said, and could snatch quite a bit of time for reading—rather heavy reading, it seemed.

It wasn't very long before Verna was head-over-heels (fearful picture!) infatuated with him. Somehow his friendliness had touched a hidden spring in this ugly, friendless, clumsy girl and for once she had lost her fear of the world's ridicule and opened her hulking heart to another human being. It was touching but rather overpowering, especially since she always opened her mouth too. He learned a great deal about herself, her invalid father, Elizabethan and Restoration poetry, paleontology, an organization known as the Working Girls' Front, Mr. Abrusian, and a brassy Miss Minkin who sounded like a fiendish caricature of Vivian.

He felt that deliberately avoiding Verna would be a dirtier

trick than he liked to think himself capable of. Nevertheless there were times when he seriously wished he'd never acquired whatever power it was—except for Vivian, of course. What the devil, he asked himself for the nth time, could that power be?

That night, in the bathroom, the question came back to him and he impulsively switched off the light and looked into the mirror. He gasped and seemed on the point of shrieking out something, but he only grasped the washbowl more tightly and stared into the mirror more intently.

After about a minute, he tugged on the light again. He was pale. He had convinced himself of the actual existence of the phenomenon that was in reality the third of the Little Gifts: Flashing Eyes.

He couldn't notice anything in the light, but in the dark his eyes gave off a faint blue flash about every five seconds, just as Vivian had said, lighting up his cheeks and eyebrows like some comic-book vampire!

It might be attractive by day, when it just registered as an impalpable hint, but it was damn sinister in the dark! It wasn't much, but it was *there*—unless the flashes were inside his head and he was projecting them... blue... something called the Purkinje effect?... but then Vivian had actually seen... oh, damn!

Suddenly he wildly looked around, a little like a trapped animal. Why did it always have to happen in the *bathroom,* he asked himself—the bicarb, the flame, the blade (if that counted), and now this? Could there be something wrong about the bathroom, something either in the room itself or in his childhood associations?

But neither the bathroom walls nor his minutely searched memory returned an answer.

It was dark in the hall outside and he almost bumped into his sister. He recoiled, stared at her a moment, then threw his hand over his eyes, darted into his bedroom and shut the door.

"Is there something wrong, Ernie?" she called after him.

"Wrong?"

The door muffled his voice. "How do you mean?"

"I mean about your eyes."

"My *eyes?*" It was almost a scream. "What about my eyes?"

"Don't shout, Ernie. I mean are they painful?"

"Painful? Why should they be painful?"

"I really don't know, Ernie." She was being very patient and calm.

"I mean did you *notice* anything about them?" He was trying to be the same without much success.

"Just that you put your hand up to them as if they hurt."

"Oh." Great relief. "Yes, they do smart a little. I guess I've been using them too much. I'm putting some eye-drops in them now."

"Can I help you, Ernie? And shouldn't you see an opto... ocu... optha... I mean an eye doctor?"

Ernie answered "No" to both those questions, but of course it took a lot more lying and improvising and general smoothing out before his sister would even pretend to be satisfied and stop her general nagging for the evening. She was getting uncomfortably cagey and curious lately, addicted to asking such questions out of a blue sky as:

"Ernie, when we were visiting Uncle Fabius, did you actually believe that you went out and bought gas?"

That one momentarily brought Ernie's stammer back, something which hadn't troubled him for years.

And when she wasn't asking questions, her quiet studying of him for long minutes was even more upsetting.

Next morning, on the way to the electric train, Ernie made a purchase at the drugstore. When he sat down beside Vivian, she took one look at him and gave a very deliberate-sounding hollow laugh.

"Blackglasses!" she said. "I tell him he's attractive because he has Flashing Eyes and within two days he's wearing black glasses. I suppose I should have guessed it."

"But my eyes hurt," Ernie protested. "Sensitive to sunlight, I think." He wished he could explain to her that he'd bought the glasses not only in case he got caught out at night, but also to convince his sister he hadn't been lying about sore eyes. He hadn't intended to wear them by day and hardly knew why he'd put them on before joining Vivian.

"Spare me your rationalizations," she said. "Your motives are clear to me, Ernie, and they happen to be very commonplace."

She leaned toward him and her voice, little more than a whisper, took on an unexpectedly gloomy, chilling, hopeless tone.

"See these people all around us, Ernie? They're suicides, every one of them. Day by day, in every way, they're killing themselves. People love them, admire them, and it only makes them uneasy.

They have abilities and charms by the bushel—yes, they do, even that man with the wen on his neck—and they only try to hide them. The spotlight turns their way and they goof. They think they're running away from failure, but actually they're running away from success."

Ernie looked at them, he couldn't help it, her voice made him, and the ability of Page-at-a-Glance Reading chose that moment to come back to him, only applied to faces instead of letters, and there seemed to be another ability along with it, unclear as yet but frightening. He felt like a very old detective scanning the lineup for the thousandth time.

The black glasses didn't interfere a bit—the dozens of faces in this speeding electric car were suddenly as familiar as the court cards in a deck—and he had the feeling that, like a bunch of pink pastelboards, they were about to be hurled in his face.

My God, he asked himself, flinching, how could you go on living with so many faces so close to you, so completely known?—each street you turned into, each store you entered, each gathering you joined, another deluge of unique features. Ugly, pretty, strong, weak—those words didn't mean anything any more in this drenching of individuality he was getting, and that showed no signs of stopping.

So he hardly heard Vivian saying, "And it's true of you, Ernie—in spades, for your black glasses," and he hardly remembered parting from her, and when he found himself alone, he did something unprecedented for him at that time of day—he went to a bar and drank two double whiskies.

The drinks brought the downtown landscape back to normal and stopped the faces printing themselves on his mind, but they left him very disturbed, and the suspiciousness with which he was treated at the office didn't improve that, and Ernie began to wish for ordinariness and commonplaceness in himself more than anything in the whole world. If only, he silently implored, there were some way of junking everything that had happened to him in the past few weeks—except maybe Vivian.

Verna on the train home positively terrified him. She was unusually talkative and engulfing this evening and he thought that if the faces-forever feeling came to him just as she was baring her food-triangles and all, he wouldn't be able to stand it. Somehow, it didn't. Yet the very intensity of his distaste frightened him.

Not for the first time, the word "insanity" appeared in his mind, pulsing in pale yellowish-green.

Half a block from home, passing his parked car (with an unconscious little veer of avoidance), he spotted three figures in close conference in front of his house: his sister, a man in dark blue—yes, Mr. Jones, and… a man in a white coat.

Almost before he knew it, he was in his car and driving away. He truly didn't know what he was going to do, only that he was going to do it, and found a trivial interest in trying to guess what it was going to be. Whatever it was, it was going to dim that yellowish-green world, decrease its type-size, make him a little more able to face the crisis waiting him at home… or somewhere.

He had a picture of himself getting on an airplane, another of renting a room in a slum, another of stopping the car on a lonely, treeless country road and getting out and looking up to the coldly glimmering Milky Way—why?

That last picture was the most vivid, and when he realized he had actually stopped his car, it was a moment before it would go away. Then he saw he was parked in front of a demolished old apartment building a few blocks from his home. Only yesterday he'd watched the last wall going down. Now, just across the littered sidewalk from him, the old cellar gaped, flimsily guarded in front by a makeshift rail and surrounded on the other three sides by great hillocks of battered bricks. Tomorrow probably (and in fact that was the way it happened) a bulldozer would tumble them forward, filling the cellar with old bricks and brick-dust, leveling the lot.

Now he knew what he was going to do. He unlatched the top over the windshield and pushed the button. Slowly the top folded back over his head, showing the smoke-dark sky, almost night. He hitched up a little in the seat, reached inside his coat, pulled out the blue box he always carried and pitched it into the dark pit across the sidewalk.

He was driving away almost before it landed. Yet through the hum of the motor he thought he heard something call faintly, "Good-bye!"

The material of the filled-in cellar stayed fairly dry for many years and the atom-bombing, when it finally came, created a partial surface-seal of fused stone over that area. However, the bicarb box fell apart in time; water reached it in little seepings and was accumulated as a non-evaporating fuel-and-oxydizer mix. The amount of this strange fluid grew and grew, eventually invading and filling a now-blind section of the city's old sewer system.

Many tens of thousands of years after that, the buried pool was sensed by the fuel-finders of a spaceship from up Polaris way, which had made an emergency landing on the mined planet. A well was drilled, and the mix pumped up and the centipedal Polarians, scuttling about the bleak landscape, had a fine time trying to explain how such a sophisticated fluid should occur in a seeming state of nature. However, they were grateful to the Cosmic All-Father.

Long before that, Ernie had arrived home in something of a daze. He told himself that he had cast off the most tangible element of his "insanity", but he didn't feel any the better for it. In fact, he felt distinctly apathetic when his sister confronted him and only with an effort did he manage to brace himself for the trial he knew she had in store for him.

"Ernie," she said hesitatingly. "I've come to a decision about something—about a change in our arrangements here, to tell you the truth—and I've gone ahead with it without consulting you. I do hope you won't mind."

"No," he said heavily. "I guess I won't mind."

"I'm doing it partly on Mr. Jones's advice," she added slowly. "As a matter of fact he suggested it."

Ernie nodded. "Yes, I've noticed the two of you conferring together."

"You have? Then maybe you know what I'm talking about."

"Oh, yes." Ernie nodded again and smiled grimly. "The man in white?"

She laughed. "Exactly, the man in white. For a long time I've thought it was just too much bother for either of us to carry the milk home, and the eggs and my yogurt too. So I decided to have the milkman that Mr. Jones uses make deliveries. Mr. Jones brought him over half an hour ago and it's all arranged. Four quarts a week, one dozen eggs, and yogurt Tuesdays and Fridays."

The Invisible Being and his Coadjutor, backtracking for a checkup, summarized the situation.

The latter said, "So he's already thrown away the Everlasting Cosmetic Knife and the Water Splitter; he seems to be trying to reject the third Little Gift and the first Big One, while he still isn't even conscious of the other two Gifts.

"Cheer up," said the Invisible Being. "It's his life and he's doing what he thinks best."

"Yes," the Coadjutor said, "but he doesn't know he's making these decisions for his race as well as himself. Sometimes I think Galaxy Center makes it too hard for chaps like him. For instance, that trick of having the images on the box fade back to the old ones."

"Nonsense! We have to take all reasonable precautions that our activities remain secret. He knew that the powder worked. He should have had faith."

"Sometimes it takes a lot of faith."

"You're right, it does." The Invisible Being smiled, his Cheshire-smile. "You feel a lot for these test subjects, don't you? That's fine, but you've got to remember you can't accept the Gifts for them; that's one thing they have to do themselves, however long they take about it. Which reminds me, I think we ought to set up a recorder here to report the final outcome of the test to Galaxy Center."

"Good idea."

"And cheer up, I say. This test isn't over yet and our featherless biped isn't necessarily licked. If he thinks to link up the third Little Gift with the two Big Ones, he has a pretty sweet setup for making psychic progress—and his race will be Galactic Citizens in a jiffy."

"You're right."

"Moreover, it stands to reason he's soon going to become aware of the Great Gift, and that generally gives a person a jolt and makes him think seriously about other things."

"True enough—though I still have the feeling you intend some sardonic trick in conjunction with the Great Gift. Are you sure you're not planning to leave some other setup here along with the recorder? I notice you've got a spare Juxtaposer in the ship and it bothers me."

"That, dear Coadjutor, is my business. Whatever I do, it won't interfere in any way with the fairness of the tests."

"Sometimes I think the tests are *too* fair," the Coadjutor observed. "I'd like to be able to ease them up a bit in special cases."

"Confidentially, my friend, so would I."

* * *

The Great Gift announced itself to Ernie next morning at 7:53 sharp, when the Special slowed to forty miles an hour to swing past the platform on which he was waiting for the Express.

One moment he was standing morning-weary on the thick wooden planks, looking down through the quarter-inch gaps between them at the cinders five feet below, vaguely conscious of a woman's white-polka-dotted black skirt on one side of his field of vision and a man's brown shoes and briefcase on the other.

Next moment he was in a small cab under which steel rails were vanishing at an alarming speed, and way ahead he could just make out the platform on which he was standing, and something was hurting his head and he was slumping forward and everything was darkening and the cab was leaping forward more swiftly still.

The third moment he was back on the platform, running furiously to get off it. He didn't care who yelled at him or whom he bumped, so long as it didn't slow him down. The people were just blurs anyway and soon he was beyond them. He took in two strides and the short flight of wooden steps leading down off the platform proper and spurted the last sixty feet to the stairs leading down to street level. There he stumbled, recovered himself, and chanced a hasty backward look.

There was a tall man at his heels, hugging a briefcase and panting hard. Then, beyond the tall man, he saw the platform rear up like a wooden caterpillar, spilling people against the bright gray morning sky. There was a cosmic crunch and the battered Special, still coming strong, burst through the upreared platform in a blossoming broken-matchstick crown of planks and beams— and big blue sparks where a writhing power wire, snagged by the uprearing platform, was grounding against the first car.

Ernie ducked his head and plunged down the steps ahead.

(That was how I came to meet Ernie Meeker. I was the tall man. As you can imagine, it's quite strange to be standing in a huddle of fresh-washed morning commuters and have the one beside you close his eyes and slump a little and then take off like a bat out of hell—without a word spoken or a thing happened to explain it. I started to laugh, but then I got the funniest feeling of curiosity and terror and I took off after him. It saved my life.

Afterward, Ernie and I went back to help with the ghastliness, but pretty soon there were more than enough trainmen, firemen, police, and what not, and we got chased off. We had a couple of drinks together and met a few times after and that's how I got some of this story. But my chief sources of information I am not permitted to disclose.)

As the Invisible Being had predicted, Ernie's first brush with the Great Gift gave him a considerable jolt, though he didn't suspect at first that it was a permanent gift.

He analyzed what had happened, quite reasonably, I believe, as a case of second sight. Somehow his mind had been projected into the brain of the motorman of the Special just at the moment the latter had his stroke (the final official explanation too) and blindly put on more speed instead of reducing it for the approaching curve and station. His second sight saved his life by getting him off the platform before the Special jumped the tracks and ploughed through it.

It certainly gave a jolt to Ernie's habit patterns, as it temporarily did of a great many other people. He started driving his car to work, for one thing, and he took to drinking regularly in the evenings, though not excessively as yet.

He also had the feeling, which he did not try to analyze, that his miraculous escape marked the end of the "strange weeks" in his life, when he'd had such odd illusions or been the victim of such odd circumstances; and, true enough, that first week or so there were no recurrences of his chillingly weird experiences.

But jolts have their infallible Law of Diminishing Effects.

After a few days, Ernie found the traffic and parking problems as nervous and wearisome as ever and he grew envious of the snug commuters meditating luxuriously in their electric coaches. Come the first morning of the third week and he was standing on the rebuilt platform, studying the new planks, ties and rails with a pleasantly morbid interest.

Vivian was not in her accustomed seat nor on the train, as far as he could tell, which did not surprise him, though it disappointed him sharply; the Panther Princess had a stronger hold on his feelings, or at least on his imagination, than he'd realized.

But Verna was on the train home all right; in fact, she gave a small whoop of pleasure when she spotted him. And he had barely sat down beside her when who should come prowling smoothly along but Vivian in a charcoal version of her tailored black armor.

Ernie jumped up and blurted out introductions. Vivian accepted his seat with a certain deliberateness and with a smile that seemed to Ernie to say, "So I'm his morning light-badinage girl, but this is the girl Mr. Meeker goes home with. It's another instance of 'black-glasses' behavior, don't you think? He puts her on whenever he gets afraid he's getting attractive."

The two women started to chat easily enough, however, and shortly Ernie got over his confusion and, smiling down at them from where he swayed in his aisle with his hand lightly touching the back of the seat ahead, was even thinking quite smugly that here in one seat, by gosh, were the woman he wanted and the woman who wanted him. Very interesting to be the man in the middle.

Just at that moment, the power came back to him that made everything feverishly real, expanding his center of attention to his visual horizons, and this time it was only a prelude, for a second gateway opened behind the first—a window into all human hearts and minds, the power of human insight fantastically sharpened and enlarged. He could "read minds," or at least he knew the motives—the core of values and consciousness—of any person he cared to look at. Most especially, he knew the motives of Verna and Vivian almost as if he *were* them.

The big thing about Vivian was her fear—no, her conviction, that she wasn't attractive. Every glance her way knocked a hole in the armor of artificial attractiveness she built around herself, and all the hours she devoted to perfecting it, even the desperate worship she lavished on her body, were all utterly lost. A simple relationship with another human being was unthinkable; her armor got in the way and under her armor she knew she was worthless. A man was sometimes attracted to her armor—never to herself—but as soon as he started to scrutinize it, it began to tarnish and crumple.

She hoped that other people, men especially, had a trace of her own weaknesses, and she sniped away at them constantly to get under the armor to find out. Ernie was one in a long series of such men. She was actually in love with him, but only as one loves a dream, not the real Ernie at all. Physically he was disgusting to her, like most men.

Verna, on the other hand, had absolute confidence that she was sufficiently attractive for all practical purposes. She wasn't in love with Ernie at all. She wanted to make an intellectual conquest of him, add him to her private Brain Trust, her cultured entourage that won Mr. Abrusian's seldom-tendered admiration and broke Miss Minkin's heart, and finally get Ernie to join the Working Boys' Front. He was one of her projects. If it became tactically necessary during her campaign, she knew that Ernie would be only too happy to jump in bed with her, food-triangles and all.

Now in other circumstances (who really knows?) Ernie might have found the courage to accept Vivian and Verna as they really were and work on from there, ruthlessly discarding his false pictures of them—and of himself. He might conceivably have found the strength to accept all people not as shadowy projections of himself, fabricated targets of his desires and aversions, puppets in his private chess games and circuses, but as complete persons with inexhaustible surprises and contradictions, each a microcosm, a universe-in-little with his or her own Earth and stars, spaceflight and crawling, heaven and hell.

But under the present circumstances, Ernie was confused. His knowledge of the real Vivian spoiled completely the titillating picture of the Panther Princess, who might submit to him contemptuously in the end—he needed that sex idol more than he needed truth. As for Verna, her stalwart self-reliance and her accurate appraisal of his own motives and possible future behavior were both unbearably humiliating to him. And the delight of really knowing people was completely outweighed, in his tired spirit, by the thought of a lifetime of work that would be involved in adjusting himself to this new knowledge. It was so much more comfortable to work with stereotypes.

The Express was slowing for his station. Both girls were looking at him puzzledly.

"Good-bye, Verna. Good-bye, Vivian," he said in a set sort of voice. "This is where I get off."

He moved stiffly toward the door. They watched him go, and turned to each other with a frown.

That evening marked the beginning of Ernie's serious drinking. He never saw either of the V-girls again. He took his car or the bus to work; then, for a short period, he took taxi-cabs, then he lost his job and was working in another part of the city. He became mixed up with a number of other women and crowds, but they are not part of this or any story.

Among other things, his drinking eventually completely

confused his memories of abnormal personal powers with his entirely normal illusions of alcoholic ones. And it also seemed to be blotting out the former. Once, at a party, he bet twenty dollars that his eyes glowed in the dark. Next morning he was relieved to discover, after making several anxious phone calls, that he'd lost his bet.

When he finally pulled out of it, some five years later, because of a growing aversion to liquor that he only understood later, the two Big Gifts of Page-at-a-Glance and Mind Reading were gone forever.

The Great Gift had a more durable lodgment to him. From his alcoholic years, he brought hazy memories of accidents avoided because of sudden wrong-ended visions of onrushing cars, alley rollings missed because he'd seen himself reeling along a block away through the eyes of lounging hoodlums. Now, sober again, he had a clear confirmation of it when he left a banquet on a trumped-up excuse because of a disturbing vision of inexplicable rodlike shapes—and read the next day that a hundred of the guests, of whom four finally died, had come down with bacterial food poisoning. Another time, hiking in dry woods, he'd smelled smoke that his companions couldn't—and persuaded them to turn back, avoiding a disastrous flash fire that broke out soon afterward.

He had to admit to himself that he certainly seemed to have the gift of second sight, warning him against threats to his life.

"All right," he told himself, "so forget it. Gifts are upsetting. Even as a kid, you sweated more about your birthday presents than you ever got fun out of them."

Our story has already jumped five years; now it must jump twenty. Ernie is living with his sister again; while he was drinking, they pulled apart, and now they're once more pulled together. They're having dinner, have arrived at dessert, a big piece of chocolate cake each with satiny thick creamy frosting and filling.

Ernie looks at his piece—and sees himself climbing stairs and clutching at his heart. He thinks of warning his sister, but she's already halfway through her piece. Then she goes on and eats Ernie's.

Ernie's sister didn't get food poisoning, she only got fat, but the incident of the chocolate cake was for Ernie the beginning of a series of peculiar food revulsions and diet experiments that eventually made Ernie instead of his sister the family yogurt-fiend and a regular customer of his old acquaintance, Herman, the healthfood manufacturer.

Herman had to admit that Ernie had cooked himself up a pretty good longevity diet for an amateur, though there were some items in it that made the old man shake his head—and he always asserted that Ernie was passing up a good thing in Soybean Mush.

Ernie got his diet tailored to fit his tastes and stuck to it. He had a strong suspicion of what had happened, though he tried not to think about it too often; that his gift of second sight had taken to warning him of the longer-range dangers of his existence; after all, chocolate cake can be as deadly as atomic bombs in the long run.

More years passed. Friends and relatives began to remark quietly to each other that his sister was aging faster. Ernie, they had to admit, was a remarkably well-preserved old gent. Ironic, considering what a drunk he'd been and what strange junk he insisted on eating now.

One day Ernie's self-styled health diet began to pall on him. It didn't revolt him; it merely left him unsatisfied, yet with no yearning for any particular food he could think of. He lived with this yearning for some weeks, meditating on it and trying to guess its nature. Finally he had an inspiration. He headed for Mr. Willis' drugstore.

The bent, silvery-haired man greeted him eagerly; somehow there was a special warmth about the friendships Ernie had made during the "strange weeks" (Verna and Vivian excepted) that put them in a different class from any other of his human relationships.

"Now what can I give you, Ernie?" Mr. Willis asked. "Anything in the place within reason."

"I'll tell you, Bert. I'd like to go back in your dispensary—you with me, if you want—and just shop around."

"That's a sort of screwy idea, Ernie. I couldn't sell you any narcotics or sleeping pills, of course—well, maybe a few sleeping pills."

"I wouldn't want any."

"What's the idea, Ernie? Getting interested in chemistry in your old... You know, Ernie, you just don't look your years."

"Secret of mine. Yes, in a way I've got interested in chemistry."

"Won't talk, eh? I remember, when I first met you, I tagged you for an evening inventor. Well, come on back and shop around. Just don't ask me for *elixir vitae, aurum potable,* or ground philosophers' stone."

"Not unless I see 'em,"

Afterward, Bert Willis used to say it was one of the most mystifying experiences of his life. For a good half a day Ernie Meeker studied the rows of jars, canisters and glass-stoppered bottles, sometimes lifting two down together and contemplating them, one in each hand, as if he could weigh the difference. Often he'd take out a stopper and sniff and maybe, asking permission of Bert with a glance, take up a dab of some powder and taste it.

"You know that game," Bert would say, "where someone goes out of the room and you all decide on an object, or hide one, and he comes back and tries to find it by telepathy or muscle-reading or something? That was exactly the way Ernie was acting. Dog on a difficult scent."

A couple of times, especially when the customers came in, Bert wanted to chase him out, except that Ernie was such a special friend and Bert was so darn curious about it all himself.

In the end, Ernie made a good twenty purchases, including a mortar and pestle and two poisons for which Bert made him sign, though the amounts were less than a lethal dose.

"Actually none of the chemicals he bought were very dangerous," Bert would say. "And none of them were terribly unusual. The thing about them was that, put together, they just didn't make sense—as a medicine or anything else. Let me see, there was sulphur, bismuth, a bit of mercury, one of the sulfa drugs, a tiny packet of auric chloride, and... I had 'em all on a list once, but I've lost it."

After that, Ernie always mixed a little grayish paste in his cup of yogurt at suppertime.

Ernie stopped aging altogether.

After his sister's coffin was lowered past the margins of green matting into the ground, Ernie shook hands with the minister, walked Bert Willis and Herman Schover to their car and told them he thought he'd better drive home with some relatives who'd turned up. Actually he just wanted to stay behind a while. It was a beautiful blue-and-white summer day; the tidy suburban cemetery had caught his fancy, and now he felt like a quiet stroll.

Ernie followed his little impulses these days. As he sometimes said, "I figure I've got plenty of time. I just don't feel the pressure like I used to."

The last car chugged away. Ernie stretched and started to stroll, slowly, but not like an old man, now that he was alone. His hair had grown whiter in the last few years and his face for a little wrinkled, but that was due to the very judicious use of silvering and theatrical liner—people's comments about his youthfulness had gotten wearisome and would, he knew, eventually become suspicious.

Keeping himself oriented by a white tower at the cemetery gate, he arrived at an area that had no graves as yet, no trees either, just lawn. He made his way to the center of it, where there was a gently swelling hummock, and sat down in the warm crinkly grass, resting his back against the slope. The sky was lovely, enough clouds to be interesting, but a great oval of pure blue just overhead—a pear-shaped gateway to space.

He felt no grief at his sister's death, only the desire to think a bit, have a quiet look at his past and another at the great future.

Alone like this, he dared to face his fate for a moment and admit to himself that, all wishful thinking aside, it really began to look as if he were going to live forever, or at least for a very long time.

Live forever! That was a phrase to give you a chill, he told himself. And what to do, he asked himself, with all that time?

Back in the "strange weeks," he'd have had little trouble in answering that question—if only he'd known then what he did now and realized what was being offered him. For during his sober decades, Ernie had gradually come to a shrewdly accurate estimate of what had happened to him then. He thought of it in terms of having been offered six Gifts and turned down five of them.

Back in the "strange weeks" and armed with the five rejected Gifts (Page-at-a-Glance and Mind Reading were the only ones that counted, though), he could easily have said, "Live forever by all means! Increase your knowledge and understanding until your mind bursts or is transfigured. Plunge forever into the unending variety of the Cosmos. Open yourself to everything."

But now, equipped to travel only as a snail...

Still, even snails get somewhere. With forever to work with, even four-words-at-a-glance gets you through many, many books. Patient love and dispassionate thought give you human insight in the end, can finally open the tightest shutter on the darkest human heart.

But that would take so very long and Ernie felt tired. Not old, just tired, tired. Best simply to watch the soft clouds—the pear-shaped gateway had become almost circular. To do anything but drift through life, a stereotype among stereotypes, was simply... too... much... work...

At that very moment, as if his thought had summoned the experience into being, another scene filmed over the blue sky and white clouds above him. The sudden humming in his ears—a kind of "audible silence"—informed him that his second sight was at work, warning him of some deadly danger. But this was a more gentle instance of it, for not all his consciousness jumped somewhere else. All through the grassy hummock, of the restful melancholy of the scene around him, and of the sky overhead. The second scene only superimposed itself on the first.

He was poised many hundreds of miles above the Earth, a ghost-Ernie immune to the airlessness and the Sun's untempered beams. At his back was black night filled with stars. Below him stretched the granulated dry brown of Earth's surface, tinged here and there with green, clumped with white cloud, and everywhere faintly hazed with blue.

Up there in space with him, right at his elbow, so close that he could reach out and touch it, was a tiny silver cylinder about as big as a hazelnut, domed at one end, reflecting sunlight from one point in a way that would have been blinding enough except that Ernie's ghost eyes were immune to brightness.

As he reached out to examine it, the thing darted away from him as if at some imperious summons, like a bit of iron, jumping through a magnetic field.

But in spite of its enormous acceleration, Ernie's ghost was able to follow it in its downward plunge. It kept just ahead of his outstretched fingertips.

The brown granules that were Earth's surface grew in size. The tiny metal cylinder began to glow with more than reflected sunlight. It turned red, orange, yellow and then blazing white as atmospheric friction transformed it into a meteor.

Ernie's ghost, immune to friction and incandescence alike, followed it as it dove toward its target—for even though Ernie had never heard of a Juxtaposer and how it brought objects together, he had the feeling, from the dizzy speed of the meteor's plunge, that it yearned for something.

He knew most meteors vaporized or exploded, but this did not, even when Earth's brown surface grew rivers and roads. Suddenly there was a cloudbank ahead; then, in the white, there appeared an almost circular hole toward the very center of which the meteorite plunged.

Everything was happening very fast now, but his ghost senses were able to keep pace. As they plunged through the cloud-ring and the green landscape below grew explosively, he saw the white tower, the trees, the curving drives, and the clearing which was now the target.

There was still time to escape. Lying on the warm grass, with death lancing down from the sky at miles a second, he had merely to roll over.

But it was simply... too... much... work...

Elsewhere near Earth, a recorder sped toward Galaxy Center, a message which ended, "Six Gifts tendered, all finally refused. I will now sign off and await pickup with one Juxtaposer."

A little later, a Receiver in Galaxy Center passed the message to a Central Recorder, which filed it in the Star-swarm 37 section with this addition: "Spiritual immaturity of Terran bipeds indicated. Advise against enlightenment and admission to Galactic citizenship. Test subject humanely released."

Police digging into the turf under Ernie's shattered head two days later found the bright bullet, cold now, of course, and untarnished.

"Looks like silver!" one cop said, scratching his head. "Haven't I heard somewhere that the Mafia use silver bullets? So bright, though."

Lieutenant Padilla, later on, lifting the bullet in his forceps to re-examine it for rifling marks had the same thought about its brightness. By now, however, he knew it was not silver. (What alloy was never satisfactorily determined. Actually it was made of the same substance as the Everlasting Razor Blade.)

This time, although he still found no rifling marks, a tiny dull stretch on the flat end of the cylinder caught his attention. He took up a magnifier and examined it carefully.

A moment later, he put down the magnifier, snatched up the pocketbook found on the dead man and rechecked some cards in it. The bullet dropped from the forceps, rolled a few inches. The lieutenant sat back in his chair, breathing a little hard.

"This is one for the books, all right!" he told himself. "I've heard a lot of people, soldiers especially, talk about such bullets, but I never expected to see one!"

For under the magnifying glass, finely engraved in very tiny letters, he had read the words:

ERNEST WENCESLAUS MEEKER

SUCCESS

THE HERO STOOD IN THE WASTELAND OF GRAY SAND
sparsely dotted with gray boulders and thin clumps of spiny gray-green grass, and he confronted the Wall.

On the Hero's out-thrust left arm, clutching the gloved wrist with dexter talons, stood a Golden Eagle which would have sunk any other arm than his and which the Hero had climbed the sky itself to snare and master. In its sinister talons the eagle held the end of a knotted golden thread, stronger than any rope, woven of the head-hairs of blonde lamias and vampires, and so long that its coilings were a smooth golden hillock at the Hero's foot.

At the Hero's right side stood a Brazen Bull, half again as high at the shoulder as he and which the Hero had crossed limitless flinty plains to challenge and to wear down to his will. The bull's brazen brow was like the ram of a quinquireme and transparent green flames flickered from its nostrils and its quiet heartbeat trembled the ground.

On the Hero's back hung a great Silver Horn, formed from the single poison-tooth of a dragon which the Hero had descended the nethermost abyss called Nadir to rout from its cave and slay.

The Wall was most simply like the hemisphere of night boldly encroaching into that of day, with not an atom of twilight between. In it was set a great shut gate only blacker than itself. The Wall shot up vertically to where the feather-clouds were ending in vast jagged crenelations that from its foot looked tinier than saw teeth. Behind the Wall, the Hero knew, lay all power and wealth and worldly delights.

The Golden Eagle shook out its wings, clashing the glittering pinions, and shrieked at the Wall a challenge that was like a thousand fifes, and the Brazen Bull bellowed one that engulfed the sound and shake of its own heartbeat, and the Silver Horn vibrated against the Hero's back with its eagerness to blow.

The Wall made no answer. No tiniest wicket observably opened in the gate for an eye to spy, no midge-small face looked down the black sheer.

The Hero threw up his left arm with the great weight of the eagle on it, and the bird bated from his wrist and smote downward the air in a great beat that swept the fine gray sand grains aside like a giant's besom, and began rapidly to mount in a tight spiral, trailing the golden thread.

The Hero waited until the golden bird looked no bigger than a winged topaz, then hammered once the Brazen Bull on the great ridge of its shoulder blade and pointed at the door in the Wall. The beast pawed the gray sand delicately, then lowered the ram of the brow. Green jets a yard long and straight as swords shot from its nostrils and it began to move toward the door, slowly at first, then faster and faster, and the pounding of its hooves shook the ground as if it were an earthquake climbed from its strait, leagues-deep lair and charging in the open.

The Hero planted his feet wide, against the ground's heaving and he unslung the Silver Horn from his back and set its poison-point to his lips and blew. The note of the horn was like the eagle's skirling and the bull's roaring commingled, and there was a dreadful pulsation to it which infected the Wall so that black ripples shot up it and off to either side, and it wavered like a black comber about to break, and the Hero exulted in his heart.

But then the ripples returned, as if reflected along the Wall by distant mirrors, and they struck back conjoined at the Silver Horn which had engendered them. The horn stung the Hero's lips with its unbearably multiplied vibrations and suddenly it shattered entire and fell to the earth as a silver dust.

There was a double, earth-transmitted thunderclap as the Brazen Bull smashed head-on against the gate and fell dead on its side.

One afterclap then, as the Golden Eagle, enmeshed in the thread it had carried aloft, plummeted like a golden bolt from a sky-demon's crossbow, and struck a gray target-boulder and did not stir.

Silence swiftly gathered and the Wall was as before.

The Hero dropped to his knees and bowed his head and shoulders low. Almost he abased himself in mind as well as body and worshipped the Wall, for the gathered silence was very terrible, but in that moment of uncertainty he felt a feather-touch on his left little finger.

Glancing sideways he saw a tiny leopard-spider crouching in a gray grass-clump and touching him with right fore-leg.

Now although the Hero had tamed bulls and slain dragons, he had a great fear of spiders, but at this moment his misery was so great that he could feel no fear at all, and so he suffered the touch of the minute monster and the staring of the eight pin-point eyes of its sere golden face.

There was a little scuffing noise and a circlet of sand fell in next to the grass-clump, and from the small hole thus made there poked up toward the Hero the quivering blind snout of a mole, its fur rusty-brazen.

Simultaneously there was the faintest stirring of the sand under the right hand of the Hero, and he lifted a silver-gray pinch of it in his fingers.

Then, in a tiny high voice that was like the sidewise clashing of its golden mandibles, the Spider said, "I carry a line to the top of the Wall."

The Mole quavered ghostlily, "I dig under the Wall."

And, as if impalpable winds stirred it, the Sand in the Hero's fingers sang faintly, "I wear the Wall down."

Moving most gently, so as to affright none of his new allies, the Hero looked up at the Wall and pressed from his lips a smile.

TO MAKE A ROMAN HOLIDAY

ONLY THE MAN IN THE TOGA SAW THE GREAT CAT. HE stopped so abruptly in the stone archway that his gorgeously robed attendants had to dig in their heels to keep from bumping him. Small wonder no one else saw it, for the sand of the practice field was so dazzlingly bright that the shadows of the surrounding portico seemed black as midnight. And the cat's fur blended perfectly with the blackness under the opposite archway.

Its green eyes burned with the madness that comes when jungle nerves are tortured by captivity, hunger and abuse.

But in the eyes of the man in the toga was something infinitely worse. His thin patrician lips curled in a slow smile of anticipation.

The practice field was ahum with activity. A half dozen gladiators were working out under the direction of a little man with red hair. More gladiators lounged on the benches in the portico. Guards dangled hooked clubs from their wrists. Slaves bustled about, lugging weapons and armor to or from the crib.

Twice the cat readied itself for a spring. Twice it hesitated. The man in the toga gnawed his lip delicately.

A great shaggy gladiator with legs like pillars and a bear's chest got up from a bench. He lingered for a moment, one huge arm thrown loosely around the shoulders of a lean, swarthy man with the look of a Greek, who wore a loincloth of leopard skin and had a heavy net folded over his arm. They exchanged words, and the big man pushed the other playfully and thumped him, while the Greek pretended to collapse. Through the sword din came a deep chuckle. Then the big man started across the sand.

The cat's green eyes stopped their roving. As if one of the blacker shadows had suddenly come alive, it streaked into the sunlight and sprang for the naked burly back.

But some god who loves friendship must have whispered to the Greek. Something sent him darting forward. Just as the cat began its spring, the heavy net lashed out. Snarling, the cat spun around and hurled itself at the Greek, who fell away behind his net, drawing up his knees to protect his belly. The cat clawed frantically at the net for a moment not distinguishing between it and the man half underneath.

In that moment the big man acted, with incredible swiftness. He grabbed the cat by the tail, weaved his shoulders away from slashing claws, and then... the cat never came down. It started sailing round and round in a great circle, a contorted knot of black panther, as the big man swung.

A guard ran up with a short stabbing-spear. The big man shook his head impatiently and, in a voice that out-dinned the panther's, bellowed, "Cage!"

It was a full minute before gladiators and guards, working together for once, managed to locate a cage and trundle it out on the sand. All that while the big man pivoted and swung. The panther's scream was a rasping high-pitched tone, unendurably prolonged. With quick headshakes and nods, the big man indicated how the cage should be placed—its open end tangent to the panther's swing. Step by short jolting step he edged over till the flailing claws just missed the bars at each pass. He held it at that for three more swings, estimating distance and speed. He took one last, perfectly gauged step.

The bars shook as the panther slammed against the other end, on the inside. The door clanked down. The locking bar grated into place. The panther hit the door and clawed unyielding iron.

The big man blew out three great breaths, like a diver coming up. Then deep, belly-shaking laughter echoed from the portico.

The tension broke. The men yelled applause and ran up to him shouting, "Ursus! Ursus!"

The Greek hurried to inspect the big man's shoulder for claw marks. The big man's laughter roared afresh and he pointed at three shallow scratches on the Greek's side. They threw their arms around each other, both laughing.

The man in the toga pursed his lips unpleasantly. Then a mask of boredom and contempt settled around his features, but his eyes did not leave the big man. He stepped out of the archway.

"Ursus!" shouted a gladiator on the outside of the circle, "was that the trick you'd never show us? Was that it, Ursus?"

The big man's headshake was emphatic and his voice was serious as he replied:

"No! *That* trick is the one I'm saving for a really tight spot."

The man in the toga advanced. The Greek saw him coming. The circle opened and the gladiators looked at the man who had bought their blood for the games tomorrow.

The man with red hair hurried up, bowing, murmuring, "Lucius Sempronius Albus, we are honored."

"Hello, Spiculus," said the man in the toga, "I'm looking for a workout."

He nodded toward Ursus—and noted that a worried look flashed into the face of the gladiator-master.

"Surely, Your Honor," Spiculus stammered, "but... but why not with one of the others? Ursus is winded."

"I'm not winded," the big man said. "But it's true, someone else could give you a better workout."

The gladiator-master nodded eagerly. "Yes, why not try Serpens here? With that net he's every bit as good as Ursus." The Greek stepped forward quickly.

"No," said Sempronius. He jerked his thumb at Ursus, and began to remove his toga. A slave in a green silk tunic darted up to assist him.

"What's the matter, Spiculus?" he asked lazily.

"Are you trying to tell me he won't go easy on me? I assure you that's just what I want—one who's not afraid to fight a nobleman." His look held contempt.

The gladiator-master said nothing. Sempronius laughed, finished removing his toga and tossed it at Spiculus. One fold enveloped the red head and the gladiator-master staggered comically, trying to keep the white garment from touching the sand. No one smiled, and the slave hurriedly relieved him of the burden.

"I'll take a Thracian's weapon," said Lucius Sempronius Albus, flexing his white shoulders. "He can fight heavy-armed."

The gladiator-master motioned two slaves to get the appropriate stuff from the crib. The slaves raced. The nobleman got crested helmet, small round shield, and a curved sword:

Ursus, breastplate as well, larger shield, and a shorter, heavier sword. Both weapons were blunted.

Spiculus ordered the other gladiators to practice at the far end of the field, but it was obvious their minds were all on one thing.

Only Ursus was calm. Under guise of helping with the buckles, the Greek whispered to him urgently, "For the sake of the gods, let him win!"

Ursus did not reply, but into his rugged face came such a look as must have been on the faces of the first legionaires, when Rome was a farmer's republic. He clapped the Greek's hand twice, and then stepped forward.

Sempronius went on guard, saying, "Now we'll find out about that secret trick."

Like a whip, Sempronius came lashing in, feinting low and following with a cut at the neck on the offshield side. It was a blow to maim or kill, even with practice weapons, delivered with professional speed.

Ursus' shield crossed over the necessary inches to send the curved sword glancing off the bronze with a skirling complaint. The nobleman danced back.

A dozen times then in rapid succession the attack was repeated, with variations always ending with a maiming blow at some point armor did not protect. Each time Ursus contented himself with parrying.

The watchers were worried. Sempronius was good and Ursus handicapped himself with his waiting tactics. The Greek looked worried too, but in his case it seemed to be worry of a more far-seeing sort.

The nobleman used every trick in the gladiator's catalog. He feigned weariness, pretended to slip, scooped up sand and threw it to blind, sidestepped, circled about, struck with shield edge instead of sword. Each time Ursus had the answer. Each time Ursus refused to be drawn.

The nobleman fell back. Desperately then, but still with control, he went in with flailing sword, dealing a frantic hammer-rain of blows. It seemed that Ursus, never counterattacking, must go down before the white whirlwind. But he parried. And then, when the nobleman had ventured a shade too far, his great foot went down on the white instep, his shield met the smaller one, and he pushed.

Sempronius looked up from where he lay sprawled. The fall had jolted off his helmet and there was sand in his ringleted hair.

The slave in the green tunic darted up to brush away the sand. Deliberately the nobleman struck him across the eyes.

He made no move to get up, only glared at Ursus with a sick fury.

Ursus glanced a moment at the slave squatting a few feet away, hands over eyes, writhing soundlessly.

Still Sempronius made no move to rise. His lips began to work.

Ursus cleared his throat and said, in the voice of one who states incontestable facts, "It's no disgrace to be beaten by me. I am the best swordsman in Italy—slave, freed, free, or noble. I have invented seven original strategems—and one more that I have never revealed."

The Greek closed his eyes.

But into the shame-contorted face of Lucius Sempronius Albus—it was as if a drowning man sees a straw and at the same time sees how the straw can be made into a long needle to pierce and kill.

"What is that eighth strategem?" Sempronius asked.

"I will not tell you," said Ursus.

Slowly Sempronius got to his feet. "I have bought you for the games tomorrow," he said, "and you are no better than a slave. I have asked you a question."

Ursus shook his head.

The nobleman's gaze drifted sideways to the anguished Greek, and he smiled.

"Ursus is your best fighter, isn't he, Spiculus?" he inquired.

The gladiator-master nodded.

"But with the net, the Greek there—Serpens—is as good."

Again the master nodded.

The nobleman paused. "It seems to me unfair, Spiculus," he said, "that Ursus should conceal a strategem of interest to the whole profession. There has occurred to me a means of forcing him to reveal that strategem. At the games tomorrow Ursus shall fight Serpens."

He savored the shocked, mute hostility in the surrounding faces. Ursus was stony-eyed. From the Greek's face, oddly, the anxiety had vanished. There was instead a kind of distant sadness. The nobleman's gaze drifted back to Spiculus. "Well?"

Spiculus gulped and his face reddened. "You see, they're friends," he blurted out.

"That won't make any difference," Sempronius said. "They'll fight together tomorrow."

The gladiator-master nodded once and hung his head.

The nobleman motioned curtly. Eyes still watering, the slave hurriedly fetched a blue cloak and draped it over the naked, sand-stained shoulders. Then Sempronius turned on his heel and started for the archway.

The gladiator-master edged over to Ursus, but something in the look with which the big man was watching his recent adversary out made the gladiator-master pause. So it was to the Greek that he muttered, "Everything will turn out all right. You can make it a good fight without getting too badly hurt and you're both so popular that the crowd will be sure to spare the loser."

The Greek smiled, wistfully.

From cages under the arena, came the squall of a panther.

High above the arena, even the crowded tiers of seats, a heavy old shield hung on a pole. An ancient trophy, it was always hung there for gladiatorial games—no one remembered why.

Its bronze was always brightly burnished—so brightly that a silken noblewoman in one of the boxes blinked at its glare and ordered a crouching slave to interpose a fan.

From the gladiator's dugout, Serpens, the Greek, watched. His eyes traveled along the languid patrician ranks and he murmured, "These are our gods."

From the upper tiers the crowd booed an unpopular decision. Spiculus stopped his nervous pacing, took his hand out of his red hair, laid it on Serpens' shoulder.

"See," he said apologetically. "Sempronius has spared another man against the crowd's wishes. I'm sure he has repented of his flurry of anger yesterday."

The Greek looked up at the white figure in the central box standing with arm stretched out and thumb turned up. "He spares four men against the crowd's wishes," he said. "Of those four, three at least deserved the death-stroke. But Albus is not tender-hearted. I see a possibility..."

Cheated of their prey, the black-masked guards retired to their position by Dead Man's Gate in the end wall. Three arena-slaves made a great show of scattering fresh sand over a tiny sprinkle of blood. The vanquished gladiator began to hurry away, as if the crowd's hostility were a tangible and irresistible pressure.

Serpens reached for his trident and net. Hearing snarling pandemonium he remarked, "Not the most agreeable audience."

Ursus strode up from the other end of the dugout. He put down his big shield and helmet and gripped the Greek's hand. Suddenly they embraced.

Then Ursus pushed him away, held him at arm's length, and looked in his eyes. The Greek's features strengthened, as if he were absorbing something from the other, and his chin went up. Ursus gave a brief nod, caught up helmet and shield, and clambered out of the dugout.

The Greek started to follow him, but once again the gladiator-master touched his shoulder.

The Greek turned around. "You've been a pretty good master, Spiculus," he said. "Not exactly courageous, but then you men in the middle never can be."

Without waiting for a reply, he vaulted onto the sand. The sun made the sand a burning white floor, against which the masked guards in black, with their whips for driving on cowards, their hooks for dragging out the dead, and their spears for other contingencies, stood out sharply. The blinding ray from the old shield moved with the sun, and a nobleman in a center box put his hand to his eyes.

Ursus put on his helmet. Serpens glanced up at Sempronius, where the glorious giver of the games was chatting casually with a companion. The Greek seemed to be looking for a smile that he knew he would not be able to see.

Ursus lifted his shield. Serpens carefully draped his net over his left forearm, swished it twice to get the feel, gripped his trident, then darted in.

It was a fight to please the gods. The net whirled and whistled. A dozen times Ursus barely escaped the meshing folds. Twice its leaden-pelleted edge caught on the points of his armor or shield but he managed to fight his way clear. The body of the Greek slipped in and out of range of the ever-dangerous sword like something charmed.

It was serpent against bear—deadly speed against shaggy ferocity.

And there was blood enough. It dripped form trident-gouges in Ursus' shoulder and thigh, and streamed crimson from Serpens' trident-arm.

Slowly the cat-calls died. Eager shouts replaced them. The

crowd was on its feet, cursing when its sight was blocked for an instant. Even the patricians were tense.

The end came suddenly. Serpens dared too far, the heavy sword crunched down, his net-arm dangled. Leaping back, his feet tangled in the net, and he fell. Ursus planted his foot on the naked chest, looked up at the crowd and smiled, awaiting their opinion. That generous smile would have turned the trick. The crowd, knowing courage and swordsmanship when they saw it, was friendly.

But without pretending to wait for the crowd's opinion, Sempronius rose quickly in the center box, his thumb half-upturned.

The upper tiers saw it. Their generous impulse forgotten, they remembered only that this was the man who had over-ridden decisions all day. They began to yell and all the tiers took it up.

Sempronius looked around at if surprised. Wherever he looked there came hostile jeers. Finally, shrugging his shoulders, he turned down his thumb. Nine-tenths of the crowd roared approval.

Serpens looked up at Ursus. There came into their faces the warmth of unfailing comradeship. Then the Greek's features stiffened and he drew back his head, baring his throat. The sword came down.

The shouts slackened abruptly. Ursus threw his shield aside and turned around facing the central box, holding his hands up for silence. One of them still held the sword with the Greek's blood on it.

Then in a loud, clear voice, he said, "Yesterday I was asked to demonstrate a certain strategem in swordsmanship, which I have never revealed. I refused. Here and now, freely before you all, gladly I will demonstrate it."

The crowd craned forward. There was a stir in the boxes. Sempronius stood up, his hands gripping the barrier rail. In that instant the beam from the rugged, ancient, brightly-polished shield, moving a fraction further with the sun, flashed into his eyes.

He drew back a little, blinking.

Ursus spun. The heavy-ended sword, a streak of silver and scarlet, flashed through the sunlight. Sempronius threw up his hands, writhed agonizingly, then flopped across the barrier rail and hung there, skewered meat.

Ursus dropped his hands to his sides and waited. Spear points gleaming, the black guards closed in.

BREAD OVERHEAD

As a blisteringly hot but guaranteed weather controlled future summer day dawned on the Mississippi Valley, the walking mills of Puffy Products ("Spike to Loaf in One Operation!") began to tread delicately on their centipede legs across the wheat fields of Kansas.

The walking mills resembled fat metal serpents, rather larger than those Chinese paper dragons animated by files of men in procession. Sensory robot devices in their noses informed them that the waiting wheat had reached ripe perfection.

As they advanced, their heads swung lazily from side to side, very much like snakes, gobbling the yellow grain. In their throats, it was threshed, the chaff bundled and burped aside for pickup by the crawl trucks of a chemical corporation, the kernels quick-dried and blown along into the mighty chests of the machines. There the tireless mills ground the kernels to flour, which was instantly sifted, the bran being packaged and dropped like the chaff for pickup.

A cluster of tanks which gave the metal serpents a decidedly humpbacked appearance added water, shortening, salt and other ingredients, some named and some not. The dough was at the same time infused with gas from a tank conspicuously labeled "Carbon Dioxide" ("No Yeast Creatures in Your Bread!")

Thus instantly risen, the dough was clipped into loaves and shot into radionic ovens forming the midsections of the metal serpents. There the bread was baked in a matter of seconds, a fierce heat-front browning the crusts, and the piping-hot loaves sealed in transparent plastic bearing the proud Puffyloaf emblem (two cherubs circling a floating loaf) and ejected onto the delivery platform at each serpent's rear end, where a cluster of pickup machines, like hungry piglets, snatched at the loaves with hygienic claws.

A few loaves would be hurried off for the day's consumption, the majority stored for winter in strategically located mammoth deep freezes.

But now, behold a wonder! As loaves began to appear on the delivery platform of the first walking mill to get into action, they did not linger on the conveyor belt, but rose gently into the air and slowly traveled off downwind across the hot rippling fields.

The robot claws of the pickup machines clutched in vain, and, not noticing the difference, proceeded carefully to stack emptiness, tier by tier. One errant loaf, rising more sluggishly than its fellows, was snagged by a thrusting claw. The machine paused, clumsily wiped off the injured loaf, set it aside—where it bobbed on one corner, unable to take off again—and went back to the work of storing nothingness.

A flock of crows rose from the trees of a nearby shelterbelt as the flight of loaves approached. The crows swooped to investigate and then suddenly scattered, screeching in panic.

The helicopter of a hangoverish Sunday traveler bound for Wichita shied very similarly from the brown fliers and did not return for a second look.

A black-haired housewife spied them over her back fence, crossed herself and grabbed her walkie-talkie from the laundry basket. Seconds later, the yawning correspondent of a regional newspaper was jotting down the lead of a humorous news story which, recalling the old flying-saucer scares, stated that now apparently bread was to be included in the mad aerial tea party.

The congregation of an open-walled country church, standing up to recite the most familiar of Christian prayers, had just reached the petition for daily sustenance, when a sub-flight of the loaves, either forced down by a vagrant wind or lacking the natural buoyancy of the rest, came coasting silently as the sunbeams between the graceful pillars at the altar end of the building.

Meanwhile, the main flight, now augmented by other bread flocks from scores and hundreds of walking mills that had started work a little later, mounted slowly and majestically into the cirrus-flecked upper air, where a steady wind was blowing strongly toward the east.

About one thousand miles farther on in that direction, where a cluster of stratosphere-tickling towers marked the location of the metropolis of NewNew York, a tender scene was being enacted in the pressurized penthouse managerial suite of Puffy Products. Megera Winterly, Secretary in Chief to the Managerial Board and referred to by her underlings as the Blonde Icicle, was dealing with the advances of Roger ("Racehorse") Snedden, Assistant Secretary to the Board and often indistinguishable from any passing office boy.

"Why don't you jump out the window, Roger, remembering to shut the airlock after you?" the Golden Glacier said in tones not unkind. "When are your high-strung, thoroughbred nerves going to accept the fact that I would never consider marriage with a business inferior? You have about as much chance as a starving Ukrainian kulak now that Moscow's clapped on the interdict."

Roger's voice was calm, although his eyes were feverishly bright, as he replied, "A lot of things are going to be different around here, Meg, as soon as the Board is forced to admit that only my quick thinking made it possible to bring the name of Puffyloaf in front of the whole world."

"Puffyloaf could do with a little of that," the business girl observed judiciously. "The way sales have been plummeting, it won't be long before the Government deeds our desks to the managers of Fairy Bread and asks us to take the Big Jump. But just where does your quick thinking come into this, Mr. Snedden? You can't be referring to the helium—that was Rose Thinker's brainwave."

She studied him suspiciously. "You've birthed another promotional bumble, Roger. I can see it in your eyes. I only hope it's not as big a one as when you put the Martian ambassador on 3D and he thanked you profusely for the gross of Puffyloaves, assuring you that he'd never slept on a softer mattress in all his life on two planets."

"Listen to me, Meg. Today—yes, today!—you're going to see the Board eating out of my hand."

"Hah! I guarantee you won't have any fingers left. You're bold enough now, but when Mr. Gryce and those two big machines come through that door—"

"Now wait a minute, Meg—"

"Hush! They're coming now!"

Roger leaped three feet in the air, but managed to land without a sound and edged toward his stool. Through the dilating iris of the door strode Phineas T. Gryce, flanked by Rose Thinker and Tin Philosopher.

The man approached the conference table in the center of the room with measured pace and gravely expressionless face. The rose-tinted machine on his left did a couple of impulsive pirouettes on the way and twittered a greeting to Meg and Roger. The other machine quietly took the third of the high seats and lifted a claw at Meg, who now occupied a stool twice the height of Roger's.

"Miss Winterly, please—our theme."

The Blonde Icicle's face thawed into a little-girl smile as she chanted bubblingly:

"Made up of tiny wheaten motes
And reinforced with sturdy oats,
It rises through the air and floats—
The bread on which all Terra dotes!"

"Thank you, Miss Winterly," said Tin Philosopher. "Though a purely figurative statement, that bit about rising through the air always gets me—here." He rapped his midsection, which gave off a high musical *clang*.

"Ladies—" he inclined his photocells toward Rose Thinker and Meg—"and gentlemen. This is a historic occasion in Old Puffy's long history, the inauguration of the helium-filled loaf ('So Light It Almost Floats Away!') in which that inert and heaven-aspiring gas replaces old-fashioned carbon dioxide. Later, there will be kudos for Rose Thinker, whose bright relays genius-sparked the idea, and also for Roger Snedden, who took care of the details.

"By the by, Racehorse, that was a brilliant piece of work getting the helium out of the government—they've been pretty stuffy lately about their monopoly. But first I want to throw wide the casement in your minds that opens on the Long View of Things."

Rose Thinker spun twice on her chair and opened her photocells wide. Tin Philosopher coughed to limber up the diaphragm of his speaker and continued:

"Ever since the first cave wife boasted to her next-den neighbor about the superior paleness and fluffiness of her tortillas, mankind has sought lighter, whiter bread. Indeed, thinkers wiser than myself have equated the whole upward course of culture with this poignant quest. Yeast was a wonderful discovery—for its primitive day. Sifting the bran and wheat germ from the flour was an even more important advance. Early bleaching and preserving chemicals played their humble parts.

"For a while, barbarous faddists—blind to the deeply spiritual nature of bread, which is recognized by all great religions—held back our march toward perfection with their hair-splitting insistence on the vitamin content of the wheat germ, but their case collapsed when tasteless colorless substitutes were triumphantly synthesized and introduced into the loaf, which for flawless purity, unequaled airiness and sheer intangible goodness was rapidly becoming mankind's supreme gustatory experience."

"I wonder what the stuff tastes like," Rose Thinker said out of a clear sky.

"I wonder what taste tastes like," Tin Philosopher echoed dreamily. Recovering himself, he continued:

"Then, early in the twenty-first century, came the epochal researches of Everett Whitehead, Puffyloaf chemist, culminating in his paper 'The Structural Bubble in Cereal Masses' and making possible the baking of airtight bread twenty times stronger (for its weight) than steel and of a lightness that would have been incredible even to the advanced chemist-bakers of the twentieth century—a lightness so great that, besides forming the backbone of our own promotion, it has forever since been capitalized on by our conscienceless competitors of Fairy Bread with their enduring slogan: 'It Makes Ghost Toast'."

"That's a beaut, all right, that ecto-dough blurb," Rose Thinker admitted, bugging her photocells sadly. "Wait a sec. How about?

"There'll be bread
Overhead
When you're dead—
It is said."

Phineas T. Gryce wrinkled his nostrils at the pink machine as if he smelled her insulation smoldering. He said mildly, "A somewhat unhappy jingle, Rose, referring as it does to the end of the customer as consumer. Moreover, we shouldn't overplay the figurative 'rises through the air' angle. What inspired you?"

She shrugged. "I don't know—oh, yes I do. I was remembering one of the workers' songs we machines used to chant during the Big Strike—

"Work and pray,
Live on hay.
You'll get pie
In the sky
When you die—
It's a lie!"

"I don't know why we chanted it," she added. "We didn't want pie—or hay, for that matter. And machines don't pray, except Tibetan prayer wheels."

Phineas T. Gryce shook his head. "Labor relations are another topic we should stay far away from. However, dear Rose, I'm glad you keep trying to outjingle those dirty crooks at Fairy Bread." He scowled, turning back his attention to Tin Philosopher. "I get whopping mad, Old Machine, whenever I hear that other slogan of theirs, the discriminatory one—'Untouched by Robot Claws.' Just because they employ a few filthy androids in their factories!"

Tin Philosopher lifted one of his own sets of bright talons. "Thanks, P.T. But to continue my historical resume, the next great advance in the baking art was the substitution of purified carbon dioxide, recovered from coal smoke, for the gas generated by yeast organisms in-dwelling in the dough and later killed by the heat of baking, their corpses remaining *in situ*. But even purified carbon dioxide is itself a rather repugnant gas, a product of metabolism whether fast or slow, and forever associated with those life processes which are obnoxious to the fastidious."

Here the machine shuddered with delicate clinkings. "Therefore, we of Puffyloaf are taking today what may be the ultimate step toward purity: we are aerating our loaves with the noble gas helium, an element which remains virginal in the face of all chemical temptations and whose slim molecules are eleven times lighter than obese carbon dioxide—yes, noble uncontaminable helium, which, if it be a kind of ash, is yet the ash only of radioactive burning, accomplished or initiated entirely on the Sun, a safe 93 million miles from this planet. Let's have a cheer for the helium loaf!"

Without changing expression, Phineas T. Gryce rapped the table thrice in solemn applause, while the others bowed their heads.

"Thanks, T.P.," P.T. then said. "And now for the Moment of Truth. Miss Winterly, how is the helium loaf selling?"

The business girl clapped on a pair of earphones and whispered into a lapel mike. Her gaze grew abstracted as she mentally translated flurries of brief squawks into coherent messages. Suddenly a single vertical furrow creased her matchlessly smooth brow.

"It isn't, Mr. Gryce!" she gasped in horror. "Fairy Bread is outselling Puffyloaves by an infinity factor. So far this morning, *there has not been one single delivery of Puffyloaves to any sales spot!* Complaints about non-delivery are pouring in from both walking stores and sessile shops."

"Mr. Snedden!" Gryce barked. "What bug in the new helium process might account for this delay?"

Roger was on his feet, looking bewildered. "I can't imagine, sir, unless—just possibly—there's been some unforeseeable difficulty involving the new metal-foil wrappers."

"Metal-foil wrappers? Were *you* responsible for those?"

"Yes, sir. Last-minute recalculations showed that the extra lightness of the new loaf might be great enough to cause drift during stackage. Drafts in stores might topple sales pyramids. Metal-foil wrappers, by their added weight, took care of the difficulty."

"And you ordered them without consulting the Board?"

"Yes, sir. There was hardly time and—"

"Why, you fool! I noticed that order for metal-foil wrappers, assumed it was some sub-secretary's mistake, and canceled it last night!"

Roger Snedden turned pale. "You canceled it?" he quavered. "And told them to go back to the lighter plastic wrappers?"

"Of course! Just what is behind all this, Mr. Snedden? *What* recalculations were you trusting, when our physicists had demonstrated months ago that the helium loaf was safely stackable in light airs and gentle breezes—winds up to Beaufort's scale 3. *Why* should a change from heavier to lighter wrappers result in complete non-delivery?"

Roger Snedden's paleness became tinged with an interesting green. He cleared his throat and made strange gulping noises. Tin Philosopher's photocells focused on him calmly, Rose Thinker's with unfeigned excitement. P.T. Gryce's frown grew blacker by the moment, while Megera Winterly's Venus-mask showed an odd dawning of dismay and awe. She was getting new squawks in her earphones.

"Er... ah... er..." Roger said in winning tones. "Well, you see, the fact is that I..."

"Hold it," Meg interrupted crisply. "Triple-urgent from Public Relations, Safety Division. Tulsa-Topeka aero-express makes emergency landing after being buffeted in encounter with vast flight of objects first described as brown birds, although no failures reported in airway's electronic anti-bird fences. After grounding safely near Emporia—no fatalities—pilot's windshield found thinly plastered with soft white-and-brown material. Emblems on plastic wrappers embedded in material identify it incontrovertibly as an undetermined number of Puffyloaves cruising at three thousand feet!"

Eyes and photocells turned inquisitorially upon Roger Snedden. He went from green to Puffyloaf white and blurted: "All right, I did it, but it was the only way out! Yesterday morning, due to the Ukrainian crisis, the government stopped sales and deliveries of all strategic stockpiled materials, including helium gas. Puffy's new program of advertising and promotion, based on the lighter loaf, was already rolling. There was only one thing to do, there being only one other gas comparable in lightness to helium. I diverted the necessary quantity of hydrogen gas from the Hydrogenated Oils Section of our Magna-Margarine Division and substituted it for the helium."

"You substituted... hydrogen... for the... helium?" Phineas T. Gryce faltered in low mechanical tones, taking four steps backward.

"Hydrogen is twice as light as helium," Tin Philosopher remarked judiciously.

"And many times cheaper—did you know that?" Roger countered feebly. "Yes, I substituted hydrogen. The metal-foil wrapping would have added just enough weight to counteract the greater buoyancy of the hydrogen loaf. But—"

"So, when this morning's loaves began to arrive on the delivery platforms of the walking mills..." Tin Philosopher left the remark unfinished.

"Exactly," Roger agreed dismally.

"Let me ask you, Mr. Snedden," Gryce interjected, still in low tones, "if you expected people to jump to the kitchen ceiling for their Puffybread after taking off the metal wrapper, or reach for the sky if they happened to unwrap the stuff outdoors?"

"Mr. Gryce," Roger said reproachfully, "you have often assured me that what people do with Puffybread after they buy it is no concern of ours."

"I seem to recall," Rose Thinker chirped somewhat unkindly, "that dictum was created to answer inquiries after Roger put the famous sculptures-in-miniature artist on 3D and he testified that he always molded his first attempts from Puffybread, one jumbo loaf squeezing down to approximately the size of a peanut."

Her photocells dimmed and brightened. "Oh, boy—hydrogen! The loaf's unwrapped. After a while, in spite of the crust-seal, a little oxygen diffuses in. An explosive mixture. Housewife in curlers and kimono pops a couple slices in the toaster. Boom!"

The three human beings in the room winced.

Tin Philosopher kicked her under the table, while observing, "So you see, Roger, that the non-delivery of the hydrogen loaf carries some consolations. And I must confess that one aspect of the affair gives me great satisfaction, not as a Board Member but as a private machine. You have at last made a reality of the 'rises through the air' part of Puffybread's theme. They can't ever take that away from you. By now, half the inhabitants of the Great Plains must have observed our flying loaves rising high."

Phineas T. Gryce shot a frightened look at the west windows and found his full voice.

"Stop the mills!" he roared at Meg Winterly, who nodded and whispered urgently into her mike.

"A sensible suggestion," Tin Philosopher said. "But it comes a trifle late in the day. If the mills are still walking and grinding, approximately seven billion Puffyloaves are at this moment cruising eastward over Middle America. Remember that a six-month supply for deep-freeze is involved and that the current consumption of bread, due to its matchless airiness, is eight and one-half loaves per person per day."

Phineas T. Gryce carefully inserted both hands into his scanty hair, feeling for a good grip. He leaned menacingly toward Roger who, chin resting on the table, regarded him apathetically.

"Hold it!" Meg called sharply. "Flock of multiple-urgents coming in News Liaison: information bureaus swamped with flying-bread inquiries. Aero-expresslines: Clear our airways or face law suit. U.S. Army: Why do loaves flame when hit by incendiary bullets? U.S. Customs: If bread intended for export, get export license or face prosecution. Russian Consulate in Chicago: Advise on destination of bread-lift. And some Kansas church is accusing us of a hoax inciting to blasphemy, of faking miracles—I don't know *why.*"

The business girl tore off her headphones. "Roger Snedden," she cried with a hysteria that would have dumbfounded her underlings, "you've brought the name of Puffyloaf in front of the whole world, all right! Now do something about the situation!"

Roger nodded obediently. But his pallor increased a shade, the pupils of his eyes disappeared under the upper lids, and his head burrowed beneath his forearms.

"Oh, boy," Rose Thinker called gaily to Tin Philosopher, "this looks like the start of a real crisis session! Did you remember to bring spare batteries?"

Meanwhile, the monstrous flight of Puffyloaves, filling Midwestern skies as no small fliers had since the days of the passenger pigeon, soared steadily onward.

Private fliers approached the brown and glistening bread-front in curiosity and dipped back in awe. Aero-expresslines organized sight-seeing flights along the flanks. Planes of the government forestry and agricultural services and copters bearing the Puffyloaf emblem hovered on the fringes, watching developments and waiting for orders. A squadron of supersonic fighters hung menacingly above.

The behavior of birds varied considerably. Most fled or gave the loaves a wide berth, but some bolder species, discovering the minimal nutritive nature of the translucent brown objects, attacked them furiously with beaks and claws. Hydrogen diffusing slowly through the crusts had now distended most of the sealed plastic wrappers into little balloons, which ruptured, when pierced, with disconcerting *pops.*

Below, neck-craning citizens crowded streets and back yards, cranks and cultists had a field day, while local and national governments raged indiscriminately at Puffyloaf and at each other.

Rumors that a fusion weapon would be exploded in the midst of the flying bread drew angry protests from conservationists and a flood of telefax pamphlets titled "H-Loaf or H-bomb?"

Stockholm sent a mystifying note of praise to the United Nations Food Organization.

Delhi issued nervous denials of a millet blight that no one had heard of until that moment and reaffirmed India's ability to feed her population with no outside help except the usual.

Radio Moscow asserted that the Kremlin would brook no interference in its treatment of the Ukrainians, jokingly referred to the flying bread as a farce perpetrated by mad internationalists inhabiting Cloud Cuckoo Land, added contradictory references to airborne bread booby-trapped by Capitalist gangsters, and then fell moodily silent on the whole topic.

Radio Venus reported to its winged audience that Earth's inhabitants were establishing food depots in the upper air, preparatory to taking up permanent aerial residence "such as we have always enjoyed on Venus."

NewNew York made feverish preparations for the passage of the flying bread. Tickets for sightseeing space in skyscrapers were sold at high prices; cold meats and potted spreads were hawked to viewers with the assurance that they would be able to snag the bread out of the air and enjoy a historic sandwich.

Phineas T. Gryce, escaping from his own managerial suite, raged about the city, demanding general cooperation in the stretching of great nets between the skyscrapers to trap the errant loaves. He was captured by Tin Philosopher, escaped again, and was found posted with oxygen mask and submachine-gun on the topmost spire of Puffyloaf Tower, apparently determined to shoot down the loaves as they appeared and before they involved his company in more trouble with Customs and the State Department.

Recaptured by Tin Philosopher, who suffered only minor bullet holes, he was given a series of mild electroshocks and returned to the conference table, calm and clear-headed as ever.

But the bread flight, swinging away from a hurricane moving up the Atlantic coast, crossed a clouded-in Boston by night and disappeared into a high Atlantic overcast, also thereby evading a local storm generated by the Weather Department in a last-minute effort to bring down or at least disperse the H-loaves.

Warnings and counterwarnings by Communist and Capitalist governments seriously interfered with military trailing of the flight during this period and it was actually lost in touch with for several days.

At scattered points, seagulls were observed fighting over individual loaves floating down from the gray roof—that was all.

A mood of spirituality strongly tinged with humor seized the people of the world. Ministers sermonized about the bread, variously interpreting it as a call to charity, a warning against gluttony, a parable of the evanescence of all earthly things, and a divine joke. Husbands and wives, facing each other across their walls of breakfast toast, burst into laughter. The mere sight of a loaf of bread anywhere was enough to evoke guffaws. An obscure sect, having as part of its creed the injunction "Don't take yourself so damn seriously," won new adherents.

The bread flight, rising above an Atlantic storm widely reported to have destroyed it, passed unobserved across a foggy England and rose out of the overcast only over Mittel-europa. The loaves had at last reached their maximum altitude.

The Sun's rays beat through the rarified air on the distended plastic wrappers, increasing still further the pressure of the confined hydrogen. They burst by the millions and tens of millions. A high-flying Bulgarian evangelist, who had happened to mistake the up-lever for the east-lever in the cockpit of his flier and who was the sole witness of the event, afterward described it as "the foaming of a sea of diamonds, the crackle of God's knuckles."

By the millions and tens of millions, the loaves coasted down into the starving Ukraine. Shaken by a week of humor that threatened to invade even its own grim precincts, the Kremlin made a sudden about-face. A new policy was instituted of communal ownership of the produce of communal farms, and teams of hunger-fighters and caravans of trucks loaded with pumpernickel were dispatched into the Ukraine.

World distribution was given to a series of photographs showing peasants queuing up to trade scavenged Puffyloaves for traditional black bread, recently aerated itself but still extra solid by comparison, the rate of exchange demanded by the Moscow teams being twenty Puffyloaves to one of pumpernickel.

Another series of photographs, picturing chubby workers' children being blown to bits by booby-trapped bread, was quietly destroyed.

Congratulatory notes were exchanged by various national governments and world organizations, including the Brotherhood of Free Business Machines. The great bread flight was over, though for several weeks afterward scattered falls of loaves occurred, giving rise to a new folklore of manna among lonely Arabian tribesmen, and in one well-authenticated instance in Tibet, sustaining life in a party of mountaineers cut off by a snow slide.

Back in NewNew York, the managerial board of Puffy Products slumped in utter collapse around the conference table, the long crisis session at last ended. Empty coffee cartons were scattered around the chairs of the three humans, dead batteries around those of the two machines. For a while, there was no movement whatsoever. Then Roger Snedden reached out wearily for the earphones where Megera Winterly had hurled them down, adjusted them to his head, pushed a button and listened apathetically.

After a bit, his gaze brightened. He pushed more buttons and listened more eagerly. Soon he was sitting tensely upright on his stool, eyes bright and lower face all-a-smile, muttering terse comments and questions into the lapel mike torn from Meg's fair neck.

The others, reviving, watched him, at first dully, then with quickening interest, especially when he jerked off the earphones with a happy shout and sprang to his feet.

"Listen to this!" he cried in a ringing voice. "As a result of the worldwide publicity, Puffyloaves are outselling Fairy Bread three to one—and that's just the old carbon-dioxide stock from our freezers! It's almost exhausted, but the government, now that the Ukrainian crisis is over, has taken the ban off helium and will also sell us stockpiled wheat if we need it. We can have our walking mills burrowing into the wheat caves in a matter of hours!

"But that isn't all! The far greater demand everywhere is for Puffyloaves that will actually float. Public Relations, Child Liaison Division, reports that the kiddies are making their mothers' lives miserable about it. If only we can figure out some way to make hydrogen non-explosive or the helium loaf float just a little—"

"I'm sure we can take care of that quite handily," Tin Philosopher interrupted briskly. "Puffyloaf has kept it a corporation secret—even you've never been told about it—but just before he went crazy, Everett Whitehead discovered a way to make bread using only half as much flour as we do in the present loaf. Using this secret technique, which we've been saving for just such an emergency, it will be possible to bake a helium loaf as buoyant in every respect as the hydrogen loaf."

"Good!" Roger cried. "We'll tether 'em on strings and sell 'em like balloons. No mother-child shopping team will leave the store without a cluster. Buying bread balloons will be the big event of the day for kiddies. It'll make the carry-home shopping load lighter too! I'll issue orders at once—"

He broke off, looking at Phineas T. Gryce, said with quiet assurance, "Excuse me, sir, if I seem to be taking too much upon myself."

"Not at all, son; go straight ahead," the great manager said approvingly. "You're"—he laughed in anticipation of getting off a memorable remark—"rising to the challenging situation like a genuine Puffyloaf."

Megera Winterly looked from the older man to the younger. Then in a single leap she was upon Roger, her arms wrapped tightly around him.

"My sweet little ever-victorious, self-propelled monkey wrench!" she crooned in his ear. Roger looked fatuously over her soft shoulder at Tin Philosopher who, as if moved by some similar feeling, reached over and touched claws with Rose Thinker.

This, however, was what he telegraphed silently to his fellow machine across the circuit so completed:

"Good-o, Rosie! That makes another victory for robot-engineered world unity, though you almost gave us away at the start with that 'bread overhead' jingle. We've struck another blow against the next world war, in which—as we know only too well!—we machines would suffer the most. Now if we can only arrange, say, a fur-famine in Alaska and a migration of long-haired Siberian lemmings across Bering Straits... we'd have to swing the Japanese Current up there so it'd be warm enough for the little fellows... Anyhow, Rosie, with a spot of help from the Brotherhood, those humans will paint themselves into the peace corner yet."

Meanwhile, he and Rose Thinker quietly watched the Blonde Icicle melt.

THE REWARD

AND HERE BEHIND THIS DINGY DOOR, MISS SILVERS—
Well, Diana then—All right, Di! (I am unused to addressing lovely
young ladies familiarity, in fact I am unused to lovely young
ladies, they rarely register for my courses—even the elementary
survey—and you are the first who ever did me the very great
honor of coming back afterwards to pay me a visit, an evening
visit indeed.) Well, behind this unimpressive door, Di, the least
impressive in the whole science building, is Geller's Folly, the last
whimsical fling of a professor emeritus, the ridiculous project that
makes it crystal clear that I am not one of the infinitely competent
new nuclear men, but a physicist of the Cavendish breed—a half-
mad hobbyist. Yes, that is a typewriter of sorts you hear behind
the door—it is part of the Folly. The typist seems to think a lot
between bursts, does he not?

Bother, I have left my key at home. We will pass up the Folly,
Di. Without regrets. You will remember it better as a trivial
mystery, an old man's flaunting boast in a dimly lit corridor, than
in its shrunken dull reality.

You really would like to see the Folly? It does have a certain
robot fascination. Well, I suppose we can get Olafson's key.
He lives in the machine shop except for a brief respite after
midnight—and it lacks three hours of that. With your permission,
Di, we will descend to Olafson's Hole. This way. Your furs and
silks will make a brave shine in his dismal smithy where, a wide-
cheeked Alberich, he fashions our brass and steel traps for the
molecule. Olafson is a physicist's machinist of the old breed, a
dogged perfectionist such as Babbage depended on for building

his ill-starred difference machine. Our Swedish Vulcan will be delighted by your presence and perhaps inwardly flustered—I imagine he is as unused to lovely young ladies as I.

But there is one thing that not even you will be able to elicit from Olafson—a smile. Olafson may conceivably have smiled as a baby, but there is no record of it, and he certainly has never smiled since. He is the very embodiment of sullen materialism, an aggregation of solidly packed molecules in which there is no room for the nonsense of spirit. I must confess that I like him that way, for I am a materialist myself, a devoted monist and atheist—I trust I do not shock you. I do not well understand the new young men in my field, who listen to Bach and Bruckner and Bartok, read Kierkegaard and Niebuhr and Dostoyevsky, have themselves psychoanalyzed, and eventually become Unitarians or High Episcopalians. I stand by Haeckel and Haldane, I know that the universe is a meaningless swirl of atoms, though from time to time I have whimsical fancies.

The Folly? Yes, perhaps it is best that I describe it to you now. Then we need steal only a quick glimpse of the actuality, which may leave it a shred of glamor. Besides, it will pass the time—as you see, Olafson's Hole is a deep one and the way to it is long.

The Folly is a tiny hermetically sealed chamber filled with air under the constant pressure of one atmosphere. Every five seconds a knife-edged wall descends swiftly through its midst, cutting it into two chambers. In each of these two chambers the pressure of the air is automatically measured with an accuracy of five figures. Then the dividing wall flies up, the Folly becomes one chamber again, and the process is repeated. With Olafson's help I try to keep it operating 24 hours a day. There are occasional breakdowns, but we have had it slashing air and measuring pressure continuously for periods as long as 15 months. It is in its seventh month this time.

Somewhere in my pockets I should have a section of the record it taps out like a veritable stock ticker—I have compromised enough with modern methods to let one of the young men hook on a typewriting device that commits the air pressure measurements to a paper tape. Here it is! See, the left-hand column records the pressures in Chamber A and the right hand column the pressures that simultaneously exist in Chamber B—taking the pressure inside the Folly as unity.

1.00000	.99999
.99999	.99999
1.00000	1.00000
1.00000	1.00000
1.00000	.99999

As you can plainly see, the readings do not differ by more than two ten-thousandths—the Folly's permissible margin of error in measurement. I have yards and yards of such figures, all showing the same boresome invariability. Once I spotted a reading of .99997 and my heart skipped a beat, but the reading was the same in the other chamber—the Folly had merely sprung a slow leak and the air pressure outside was lower.

Well may you ask, Di, even though you did audit the elementary survey... you know, I really should remember you. I should remember such a lovely young lady. I am growing old, I fear, and my memory has become an ungallant traitor, while you are exceptionally young to be bothering about alumni reunions and calls on old profs... Well may you ask, Di, why I should expect the air pressure in the two chambers ever to differ, why I should have Olafson build a machine that goes through such a trivial rigmarole, why in short I should spend my declining years dancing attendance on monotony. The answer is that I am trying to trap Maxwell's demon. Here is Olafson's Hole.

Who is he? Why, as I told you, he is our machinist—Oh, Maxwell's demon. Well, *he* might be described as the element of the fantastic in the cosmos—the element of the possible but wildly improbable.

Bother, Olafson has gone off on some errand. He has locked up and hung his "Back in 20 minutes" sign on the door. I fear the Fates are against us, Di, tonight. They do not wish you to see Geller's Folly, and be disillusioned. I am sure of course that they are wiser than we.

You still wish to see it? You are most flattering to an old man. Well, we can confidently wait for Olafson—his 20 minutes never means 21, nor—oddly—19. Better, we'll take a turn around the quadrangle—it is a mild night for January and you have your furs, while I will simply button the cardigan I wear in winter beneath my suit coat. Allow me a moment to scribble a note to Olafson so that he does not go off again. Better, I'll tell him to meet us at the Folly.

How do I expect to trap Max—I mean the fantastic in the Folly? Well... You are sure I am not boring you? Yes, I agree that if you wish to see the Folly, it is likely that you wish to understand it. Thank you. Well, in the Folly I have a double handful of air— billions of molecules of several gasses, each moving at thousands of feet a second, endlessly colliding, rebounding from each other and the walls of the Folly hundreds of times a second, a shuffled jumble of particles. The energy of movement of these molecules, of course, adds up to the air pressure—I fear I grow stuffy, Di.

Science does not allow me to predict the behavior of any one of the molecules—as Whitehead puts it, the individual particle is a rare bird—but I am able to make significant predictions about the behavior of the flock. For instance, I can say that at any given moment the chances are overwhelming (I will not trouble you with the figures) that half the molecules are moving predominantly westward and half eastward—and the same for north and south and up and down.

But that, mark you, is only the overwhelming probability. It is conceivable, though vastly improbable, that at some given instant, all the molecules (or, more modestly, significantly more than fifty percent) might be moving west. It is a little like the chance of getting thirteen hearts at bridge or a "pat" royal flush at poker—though of course vastly more unlikely than that. The point is that the possibility, however remote, is a real one.

You see, Di, miracles are possible though we might have to wait more than the life-times of a thousand universes to see one. Yet, the miracles might come this moment, conceivably. You might unpin that charming half-moon silver brooch at your throat and hold it out, and if all the molecules immediately beneath it chanced to be moving upward at that instant, it would be struck from your hand high into the air! Or across the corridor into my hand, if that chanced to be the whim of the molecule flock. (Here, incidentally, is where Maxwell's demon comes in. The British physicist Clerk Maxwell, simply to illustrate a point about the Second Law of Thermodynamics, hypothesized an invisible spirit with the ability to direct the motion of individual particles.)

Similarly, at some instant all the molecules in the Folly might chance to be in Chamber A when the knife edge comes down. In that case, we would surely know it, for the pressure reading would be twice unity—two—in Chamber A and zero—a vacuum—in Chamber B.

Naturally, I am not looking for any such horrendously spectacular result. The most I hope for is a reading that shows a barely significant difference. Even at that I am like a roulette player waiting for black to turn up a hundred times running (really a million or a billion times), I am like a bridge player hoping to be dealt thirteen hearts in every hand for, say, three weeks of play.

I am like a gambler tirelessly casting a billion billion dice—the Folly my box—in the hope of one day throwing a billion billion sixes. Note, Di, that I try not to change dice, I try to shake the same molecules each time—that is why the Folly is hermetically sealed. I don't imagine that like an old deck of cards the molecules will develop markings with use and become "readers"—though that is an attractive notion—but I coddle in my mind the ridiculous fancy that the same molecular flock, cooped up so long in the Folly, will eventually become bored and frantic and panicky (part of my mind thinks like a pagan infant's) and in their desperation begin to behave irregularly. Some men have suggested that light ages in its passage through space, you know, so why might not molecules go mad from long imprisonment?

I jest, yet from all this you can understand, Di, why younger, sounder, more professional physicists would laugh or shake their heads if I told them of Geller's Folly. I am waiting, on my knees as it were, for an improbability that is for all human purposes an impossibility. To them I must present a ridiculous spectacle. But those younger men, with their easier, more sophisticated, eclectic philosophies, do not comprehend the deep passions of a devoted materialist like myself. Scorning the lie of spirit, believing—only in matter, in molecules and other particles, I have a far more fierce and patient desire than they do to understand all that matter is capable of, to know matter's rare and whimsical as well as its everyday behavior. When one of the young men embraces the Christian faith, especially in its Catholic form, I am tempted to suggest: (again I trust I do not shock you) "Let us subject to chemical analysis this host you consume at mass to learn if there is indeed protoplasm in the transubstantiated wafer and hemoglobin in the wine"—a suggestion which, if I made it, would get me called a blockhead or worse. As I say, they simply no longer understand the true materialist temper.

It is for a related reason that I keep the Folly so carefully under lock and key—a circumstance that I imagine had been puzzling you, Di. Once in an unwise burst of enthusiasm I told my students about the Folly. Instead of receiving the information with bored incomprehension or kindly indulgence, a mischievous cruelty seized them. Attempts were made by doctoring the tape to hoax me into thinking I had achieved fabulous results. Since then I have taken stern precautions and I have told no one about the Folly, no one, at all, except...

Oh, let me hold the door for you. Thank you. Ah, the night is refreshingly chill—I see traces of snow in the shadows—and for once Chicago's air seems smog-free, though acid and cold. We will let it stream through our beings and blow away the stuffy preoccupations of an old man who has lived too long with molecules.

That's a strange thing, Di, but I just now seemed to smell roses, an abundance of roses. Oh, is it your perfume? No—no, I see that yours is a very different scent though equally delightful. Pardon me if I seem flustered, but I don't know when a young lady had leaned her cheek so close to mine—even in the interests of scientific accuracy. You put the perfume behind the lobe of your ear?—that's charming.

You smelled the roses too? You shared my illusion?—if it was one. Roses in January in Chicago snows—a delightful circumstance. Perhaps a hearse skidded and overset nearby—or don't you enjoy macabre fancies?

In Chicago one must learn to treasure each hint of the marvelous or outlandish—there are few enough of them at best to offset the dismalness of the city, its grime, its stenches, its shrieking, roaring, growling, rumbling tumult that distantly assaults our ears even here in these gray gothic precincts. A grimly lonely city. When I first came here as a fellow (my entire academic life, Di, has been spent in this one institution) it seemed to me that Chicago's loneliness was an almost unbearable continuation, in a darker mode, of the loneliness of my childhood and youth. The whine of its elevated trains and the screech of its streetcars, the angry chug of its taxicabs and the pounding of its presses (augmented now by the drone of its aircraft, even the boom of its jets, and not to mention the heavier minatory sounds that proceed from its railway yards, docks and factory districts)—all these noises became an integral part of my consciousness.

Listen to the Song of Chicago, Di! Listen to the steel tom-toms and rattles of modern primitive man. The more noise the less message, the new men say—I sometimes understand what that means. Listen to the Music of the Spheres, Midwestern style—I might venture to call it the Jazz of the Gears. I wonder if, to more sensitive ears, the molecules in the Folly make any such muted pandemonium? What? Yes, I'll be quiet.

Di, you're right! You're right! It was incredible, but it did happen. For a moment—no, for several seconds—the sounds of the city became the notes of a great symphony, tragic and darkly majestic. Let us listen again. No, it is gone now. Oh, I suppose it might have been a powerful hi-fi briefly yet smoothly turned up, perhaps in the dormitory there—no, I will not believe that, I will never believe it!—*it was the random sounds of the city we heard and for several seconds they became powerful, perfect music.* Marihuana, I have read, produces such illusions, but I have never smoked even nicotine. Well, this *is* becoming a night for wonders! I shall always think you somehow responsible for them, Di.

Di, it occurs to me that what we have just shared the privilege of hearing is an excellent chance example of what I am trying to achieve under laboratory conditions in the Folly. It has been said that if you set a billion monkeys to pounding on a billion typewriters they would eventually write among other things *purely by chance* the entire *Encyclopedia Britannica*. There are several catches to that one, especially the length of time represented by the "eventually" and the question of the means of checking the monkey pages for intelligibility and of recognizing and fitting together the fragments. Still, it seems to me that we have here a valid analogy: *listen to the random noises of a city long enough* and you will eventually catch a section where purely by chance they counterfeit a great unknown symphony. It is another case of waiting for three weeks of thirteen-hearts-hands and—in this case—getting them!

Also it occurs to me that the roses we swore we smelled might conceivably by put in the same or a nearby category. Some physiologists believe that odor is a matter of formula and that various combinations of molecules, some common, some most rare, will produce the same scent when impinging on the receptors in the nasal membrane. *Sniff the acrid atmosphere of a city long enough* and you will eventually inhale a rare combination of industrial molecules that counterfeits the scent of roses. Oh, what travesties the cruder of my colleagues would make of that notion!

I suppose there must be some humdrum explanation in both cases (though I don't really believe that) but just the same I feel extraordinarily exhilarated. You know, Di, I have searched for the miraculous all my life, in my austere fashion—Maxwell's demon is a god of sorts, and how else would any god manifest itself except by bringing about the occurrence of the vastly improbable? Tonight for the first time I believe my desire *has* achieved fruition or at least the illusion thereof. When I was a child—this is something I have told to very few people, Di, very few—when I was a child I became enamoured of Greek mythology (Ovid's *Metamorphoses* was one of my first books) and in my loneliness I peopled the empty lots around my home and the park nearby with the deities and monsters of classic Greece. In a glade in the park (really a bare space behind some bushes) I reared rude altars (little more than shingles with flowers and bright trinkets and assorted childish treasures set on them as offerings) to Pan and Diana.

Yes, Di, to your namesake! To Diana, the slim moon-goddess, the virgin huntress. Much later it occurred to me that here I might have made a mistake (no, not a mistake precisely—I do not blaspheme your namesake, Di) in making my offerings to Diana rather than Venus, for no lovely young lady ever came to share my life. I have always been a votary of the chaste Silver One—Miss Silvers! What a night for coincidences!

Small wonder, really, that I remain celibate, for I was always singularly timid, credulous and inept in my very limited contacts with the opposite sex. Why, I was such a num-noddy in such matters, especially during my college years, that I was once cruelly hoaxed. I was accosted in the dormitory corridors by a slim and very pretty young lady who claimed to be in need of immediate assistance with her costume—a pin for her underskirt was wanted. In fear and secret delight I invited her into my room, where she lingered for an embarrassingly blissfully long time and finally wantonly approached me. A few moments later there was a chorus of laughter from a group of hidden eavesdroppers and the secret was out—the young lady was the "feminine" lead in the all-male Capers, or whatever they called their yearly show.

And that is something I have never told another soul. A distressful anecdote, really, with distasteful overtones—I hardly know why I should have burdened you with it. Come, let us return. Here's our doorway again. We have taken rather long, Olafson will have climbed from his Hole and be waiting at the Folly.

Di, why did you touch my cheek? Look up, you say?

Di, that glimmering! What is it? What *are* they? What are those ghostly figures of ice and fire moving up the sky, those jeweled deities, that heroic procession? I'm frightened, Di, hold me close—no, no, pardon an old man's weakness, but what was it that we saw? I'm shaking still. What was it? *Again* the impossibly improbable? *Look at the multitudinous lights of a city long enough...*

Di, what's happening tonight? What are you doing?—it is your doing, isn't it? All of a sudden these things are too much for me, too many for me. Why did you come to me tonight? Why did you come back, really? Were you really a student of mine? Is this some last hoax? No, I don't see how, but—

The Folly? We can't go to the Folly now. I feel... Yes, I suppose we could, but... Very well.

Di! Yes, I'm coming, but the stone, here, by the door—it feels like velvet, like silver velvet! *Touch gray stone long enough...* Di, am I going mad? Wait for me, Di!

Watch out, Di! Watch out for Olafson—I don't think he can see you. Olafson, don't walk into the lady! Olafson, what's happened to you? Olafson!

He moves past us as if we weren't there! And he's smiling, smiling like a man in ecstasy. Do you see that? *Olafson is smiling...*

What's that that fluttered from his hand? I'll get it. A torn-off scrap of paper—the Folly's last measurements. I'll look at them.

.99999	.99999
1.00000	.99999
1.00000	.99999
.00000	2.00000
1.00000	.99999
.99999	1.00001

Di! Where are you, Di?
Di, who were you?

TABOO

"In the name of the great heritage, I claim refuge!"

The voice was strong and trumpet-clear, yet with a curious note of mockery. The face was in shadow, but the embers of a smoky sunset outlined, with smudged brush-strokes of blood, the giant figure. The left hand lightly gripped the lintel of the low doorway for support. The right hung limp—Seafor noted that there the sunset red merged into real blood, which now began to drip upon the floor.

Seafor looked up. "If I am not mistaken," he said, "you are Amine the outlaw—"

"When there was law, or rather the illusion of law, which there hasn't been, in my lifetime," interjected the other, in an amused rumble.

"—who has ravaged a hundred petty domains," Seafor continued imperturbably, "who has thieved, kidnapped, and killed without mercy, whose trickery and cunning have already become legend, and who does not care one atom in chaos for the Great Heritage which he now invokes to save his life."

"What difference does that make?" Amine chuckled. "You have to grant me refuge if I claim it. That's your law." He swayed, gripped the lintel more strongly, and looked behind him. "And if you don't cut your speech of welcome pretty short, it'll be my funeral oration. I'm still fair prey, you know, until I'm inside the door."

There was a sudden humming in the murky sky. A narrow beam laced down, firing the air to incandescence, making a great gout of blinding light where it struck the ground a dozen yards away. Immediately came thunder, a puff of heat, and the smell of burning. Seafor fell back a step, blinking. But in the empty hush that followed the thunder, his reply to Amine sounded as cool and methodical as his previous remarks.

"You are right, on all counts. Please come in." He moved a little to one side and inclined his head slightly. "Welcome, Amine, to Bleaksmound Retreat. We grant you refuge."

The outlaw lurched forward, yet with something of the effect of a swagger. As he passed Seafor, there came from beyond the door a groan of the sort that sets the teeth on edge. Seafor looked at him sharply.

"You have a companion?"

The outlaw shook his head. He turned, so that the ruddy sunset glow highlighted his lean, big-featured face—a dangerous, red-haired god, a hero with a fox somewhere among his ancestors.

"Some beast, perhaps, singed by the blast," he hazarded, and showed his teeth in a long, thin smile.

Seafor made no comment. "Hyousiks! Teneks!" he called. "We have a guest. Attend to his hurts. Relieve him of his weapons." Then he took down from the wall a small transparent globe with a dark cylindrical base and went inside.

It was a ragged and desolate landscape that opened up for Seafor. The crimson band of sky edging the horizon heightened the illusion that a forest fire had recently burned through it. Dead and sickly trees were outlined blackly.

Seafor skirted the blasted patch, holding up the globe, in which a curled wire now glowed brightly. The humming returned. He did not look up, but he moved the luminous globe back and forth to call attention to it.

The groan was repeated. A metallic shimmer caught Seafor's eyes. A few steps brought him to the wreck of a small flier. Beside it, in an unnaturally contorted posture, was sprawled a small figure clad in rich synthetics.

Seafor unlashed the small wrists, and did a little to ease the broken ankle. The boy shuddered and tried to draw away. Then his eyes opened.

"Seafor! Seafor of Bleaksmound!" There was surprise in the shrill voice. He stared and plucked at Seafor's sleeve with his skinny fingers.

The humming increased. It was as if the buzzing of one giant wasp had brought others.

"You're safe now," said Seafor. "Arnine's gone. Your father's men will be here very soon."

The boy's fingers tightened. "Don't let them take me," he whispered suddenly.

"Don't you understand? I said your father's men."

The boy nodded. "Please don't let them take me," he repeated in the same imploring whisper. "I want to stay with you, Seafor. I want to stay at Bleaksmound."

Within seconds of each other, four fliers grounded, their repulsors scattering clods of black soil. From each, two men sprang.

The boy tugged frantically at Seafor's arm, as if by that means he could force a nod or a reassuring smile. Then a kind of boyish cunning brightened his eyes.

"Refuge, Seafor," he whispered. "I claim refuge."

Seafor did not reply and his expression remained impassive, but he hooked to his belt the globe which he had previously set down, and carefully lifted the boy in his arms.

The men hurried up. They wore identical emblems on their blue synthetic coveralls and skull-tight hoods. They carried blasters. They seemed like soldiers, except for a lack of discipline and a kind of animal bleakness that darkened their faces like a tangible film. Because of that film, they did not even seem human—quite.

Seafor's gray robe was crude and beggarly compared with their sleek clothing, but his pale, stern, ascetic face, like something carved from ivory, shone with a light that further darkened theirs.

Now that they faced him, a certain confusion became apparent in their manner.

"We're Ayarten of Rossel's men," one of them explained. "That's his son you've got there. Amine the outlaw kidnapped him, intending ransom. We brought down his flier."

"I know that," said Seafor.

"We're grateful to you, outsider, for the help you've given Ayarten's son," the other continued. He stepped forward to take the boy, but his manner lacked assurance.

Seafor did not reply. The boy clung to him. He turned and walked toward the dark, square mass of Bleaksmound.

"We must take the boy home to his father," the other protested, following a step. "Give him to us, outsider."

"He has claimed refuge," Seafor told them without turning his head, and walked on.

They conferred together in whispers, but no action came of it.

They watched the luminous globe jog gently up the hill, casting a large fantastic shadow.

"Gives you the shivers," muttered one. "Dead men. That's what they're like. Dead men."

"You can't figure them out. Think of getting light by heating a wire inside a ball of dead air. Like our primitive ancestors. And when there's atom power a-plenty!"

"But they give up atom power, you know, when they give up everything else—when they die to the world,"

"Imagine the boy asking for refuge. Scared out of his wits, I suppose. Never catch me doing that."

"I always thought young Ayten was a queer boy."

"Ayarten won't like this when we tell him. He won't like it at all—not with Amine taking shelter in the same place. He'll be angry."

"Not our fault, though."

"We'd better hurry. Set the cordon. Report to Ayarten."

Burly, blue-tinged shadows, they dispersed to their fliers.

Seafor handed the boy to two of his gray-robed brethren, who had a stretcher ready, and preceded them to the infirmary. He met Amine coming out of the weapon room under escort, and noted the greedy look on the outlaw's face.

"Remarkable collection you have there," said Amine. "Some of the fine old models they don't turn out any more. And so many!"

"Some people die in refuge," Seafor explained. "A few become outsiders. And some go away without reclaiming their weapons."

Arnine's ruddy-gold eyebrows arched skeptically. He seemed on the point of launching a satirical reply when he noticed the stretcher.

Seafor motioned the bearers on to the infirmary. "Do you feel up to having dinner in the refectory?" he asked.

The outlaw laughed boisterously, as if the idea of his being too sick to eat was very humorous indeed. His arm was in a sling and the feline springiness had returned to his stride. Seafor accompanied him back along the gloomy corridor.

"It is your intention to become the accomplice of a kidnapper?" Amine asked in amused tones a moment later. He showed no embarrassment at his previous lie having been uncovered.

"The boy claimed refuge," Seafor said.

"They'd have found him soon enough, and that would have

satisfied Ayarten. But the way it is now—Well, you're lucky that the border war with Levensee of Wols is keeping Ayarten's hands full. Still, even that may not be enough." He shrugged his good shoulder.

An elderly man turned into the corridor some distance ahead of them. He wore a green uniform of archaic cut, faded and frayed but very neat. Disks of a greenish metal formed the chief insignia.

"The president of the Fourth Global Republic," Seafor replied in answer to Arnine's immediate question. "Been in refuge here for the past year."

The outlaw expressed incredulity. "Why, if that were the case, he'd have to be two hundred... two hundred fifty years old."

"Not at all. When the last elected president died, he exercised his power to appoint an emergency successor to serve until elections could be resumed. Several of his cabinet members held the office. When the last of those died, he handed on the executive authority to some faithful subordinate—perhaps a secretary or bodyguard. It's gone on that way ever since."

Amine roared with laughter. "Do you mean to say that that old chap still thinks of the state of the world as merely an emergency temporarily interrupting the majestic and tranquil course of the Fourth Global Republic? Is *he* grooming a secretary to succeed *him?*"

Seafor shook his head. "He was alone when he came here. He is a very old man. He has decided to sign over his authority to me, when he dies."

Arnine's laughter became gargantuan. "One more worthless tradition for you to guard! One more trinket tossed into the rubbage bag of the Great Heritage!" He looked at the man ahead more closely. "I see a blaster. Isn't that against your rules?"

"As commander in chief of the Earth's armed forces, we have granted him certain extraordinary privileges," Seafor replied imperturbably.

Amine shrugged his shoulder, indicating that it was impossible to find a laugh big enough to do justice to that jest. They had caught up with the old man now, and Seafor introduced them.

"Your excellency—Amine the outlaw."

The old man inclined his head politely. "It is always good to meet a fellow citizen. Though I warn you, sir, that when peace is restored I will have to proceed against you with the utmost severity." There was a grave twinkle in his eyes. "Still, no need to dwell upon such subjects now. Perhaps you can give me news of what's happening outside this little corner of the Republic. Surely an outlaw ought to get around." His voice became thoughtful. "No one seems to travel any more—perhaps because it's so easy."

Amine seemed to derive amusement from replying in the same quaintly polite veins. Seafor left them talking amiably and returned to the infirmary.

A gray-robed doctor was setting the broken ankle. Unmindful of his sharp command the boy tried to sit up.

"Can I stay here, Seafor?" he called anxiously.

Seafor nodded. "For the present, at least. Now be quiet."

He stood beside the bed until the doctor had finished. Then he looked down at the small damp face and asked, "Why do you want to stay here, Ayten? Why don't you want to go home?" A faint smile touched his thin, pale lips.

The doctor went out.

The boy frowned, trying to find the right answer. A look of fear came into his eyes. "I don't want to go home because... because they're not human beings—not father or his women, or any of them. They're—animals."

"All human beings are animals," said Seafor softly.

"When I was little, I thought they were gods," said the boy. "I took it for granted we were all gods. Why shouldn't I? Things that take you up in the sky at the touch of a finger, transformers that synthesize food and clothes and dwelling domes, weapons that annihilate, picture tapes that tell you how to do things—all that and more!

"But gradually I realized that something must be wrong. All those wonderful things didn't square with our cramped lived, with the endless jealousies and quarrels and killings. Nobody ever had a new idea. Nobody ever seemed to think. Nobody could answer my *real* questions—neither could the picture tapes. They couldn't tell me why the world seemed to end at the boundaries of Rossel, why we almost never saw strangers, except to kill them, why, with all those wonderful powers, we lived like beasts in a cave!"

His face was flushing with the excitement and relief of talking out his thoughts. Quietly Seafor laid his hand on the small shoulder.

"For a long time I told myself that it must be a kind of test," the boy continued, "that they were seeing if I was worthy of the domain of Rossel, and that some day, when I had proved myself, a door would open and I would walk into the real world, the big friendly world I knew must exist somewhere.

"Now I know there is no door. The real world doesn't exist—except for you outsiders, in some way that I don't understand. And you've given up all the things that we possess." He caught hold of Seafor's wrist. "Why is that? And why, with all our powers, do we live like animals?"

Seafor waited a moment before he spoke. "There was a real world," he said. "There's still a little of it left, and some day it will all come back. Civilization came because men needed each other. They found that life was easier and better if they traded together—not only the necessities of life but also the things that can't be weighed or measured and that haven't a definite barter value, like the beauty of a song, or the joy of dancing, or the understanding of each other's troubles and hopes.

"As civilization grew, that mutual dependency increased and became infinitely complicated. Each man's life and happiness was the work of millions of his fellow workers.

"But there were forces working in the opposite direction. Man was learning to synthesize materials and make use of universal power sources. Wars accelerated this process, by periodically shutting off supplies of essential raw materials.

"That trend reached its ultimate development with the perfecting of atomic power and the invention of multipurpose transmutators capable of supplying all the necessities of life anywhere.

"At almost any other time that development would have been a great boon, freeing man's energies for more intensive participation in the social quest. But the shadow of the Second Global Empire still darkened the Fourth Global Republic, and the interplanetary war with the Venusian and Martian colonies sapped its strength. The Great Migrations began. There was an endless, seemingly purposeless surging of populations between the three planets, attended by wanton massacres.

"The end product was stagnation. Distrust in the very forces that brought civilization into being. Humanity turned in upon itself, mentally and physically. Small communities came into existence, each built around some leader who had a little more energy and determination left than any of his fellows. The stragglers were killed, or they drifted into such communities—and stayed there. Men were tired. They wanted only to attach themselves to a single locality—to the soil. A vegetative cycle succeeded a cycle of movement.

"In any previous age, hunger and want would have broken that unwholesome equilibrium. But now each little community was independent of trade, so far as the necessities of life were concerned. And as for the things that have no definite barter value—disillusioned men could get along without them.

"The jealousies and rivalries and suspicions of small-community existence came to make up the whole of life. Strangers were persecuted. There was almost continual warfare between neighboring communities, but it remained a petty, spiteful warfare, incapable of giving rise to widespread conquest and the establishment of nations, because it lacked any enduring economic motivation.

"That's the sort of world you've been born into, Ayten."

The boy said nothing. Seafor continued, "A few men realized what was being lost. They saw all of Earth's cultural heritage sliding into oblivion, save the bare minimum needed for the new self-maintaining mode of life. Reading and writing, for example, were going into the discard—picture tapes were sufficient to transmit the necessary education.

"These men found that they could not change the small-community system of life from within. So long as they remained part of it, they would have to conform to its savage and inhospitable laws. So they got out of it. They gave up atomic power. They gave up all valued possessions. Only by paying that price could they purchase even the most shadowy immunity from attack. They formed small communities. They devoted themselves to preserving the cultural heritage and to maintaining the ideals of universal brotherhood and of individual honor and integrity. They became the outsiders."

Ayten whispered, "I want to be an outsider."

Seafor nodded with a frown. "I tell you what," he said finally. "You can live with us as a novice, and work and study for a year. Then, if you're still determined, we'll talk it over again."

Ayten smiled.

* * *

In the refectory, Arnine's brown-and-gold tunic made a gaudy break in the long rows of gray, as did the clothing of the other refugees.

Seafor paused by Amine. "How does it taste after a diet of synthetics?"

The outlaw turned around. "Inferior, of course. But I've been in refuge before. Where do you get such garbage?" he inquired pleasantly.

"Most of it we grow in shallow tanks on the roof."

"Swamp plants, I suppose?"

"No. They originally grew in dirt."

Arnine's long lips curled in mild and somewhat humorous disgust. There came the faint chiming of the bell over Bleaksmound's door. "How's the boy?" he asked suddenly. "Only slightly hurt? As I thought. You'll be sending him back to his father, of course?"

"On the contrary. He has decided to become a novice."

Amine stared at him through half-shut eyes. "You play a strange game," he said finally. "Turning a kidnapping into a conversion! It turns out that *I* am *your* accomplice! Do you realize the trouble you're brewing? Outsiders exist only on sufferance, you know."

"You mean I should honor your claim of refuge, but not his?" Seafor's eyes were enigmatic.

An outsider approached Seafor from the hall. "Ayarten of Rossel is at the door. He desires to speak to you."

"You see?" said Amine sardonically. "The way things are going, neither claim of refuge is likely to amount to much. Let me know the terms of his ultimatum."

Seafor went out. Swiftly the refectory emptied as the outsiders went off to their tasks. Two remained, ostensibly to converse with Amine. The outlaw, prowling restlessly between the empty benches, did not make their task any easier. His ears were cocked all right, but for noises outside the refectory rather than in it. His movements were aimless, seemingly, but when Seafor returned he was standing by the door.

Doij Darh, Night Bright

"He gives us until dawn," said Seafor, "to give up the boy."

"And if you refuse?"

"He threatens to make an example of Bleaksmound."

"You see?" said Amine. "He didn't let his border war with Levensee hold him back."

"I was not counting on that," said Seafor. "Though it strikes me that he is unwise in drawing off so many of his men for the cordon he is setting around Bleaksmound."

"And you will refuse to give up the boy?" Arnine's voice was edged with anger.

"I gave the boy my word that he could stay in refuge," said Seafor. "In the days of the great civilizations, mankind could afford some weaknesses in the individual moral fiber, because the general progressive trends were strong enough to nullify individual treacheries. But now trust in a man's word has become part of the almost forgotten heritage. If we cannot keep that alive, then all the outsiders' work is vain."

Amine laughed, but unpleasantly.

"Very well," he said. "In that case I shall leave Bleaksmound, for obvious motives of self-preservation."

"Ayarten has set too strong a cordon," said Seafor. "You wouldn't be able to."

"That is for me to judge. Please give orders that my weapons be restored. I leave at once."

Seafor shook his head. "You are our guest. We cannot let you go so soon."

"You mean to hand me over to Ayarten?"

"No. You claimed refuge. You shall have it."

Seafor's sleep turned into a restless, rocking darkness, alive with menace. There was a hand at his shoulder. Someone was shaking him awake. He sat up.

"Ayarten has come?"

"No, but Amine has escaped. Knocked us down. Darted down a side corridor. Can't be found."

He recognized the voice of Hyousiks, one of the two outsiders he had set to guard the outlaw. He threw on his gray robe and hurried out.

Bleaksmound was alive with movement, like a nest of gray ants in which a spider is loose. Seafor made for the infirmary. It was as he expected. Young Ayten was gone.

From ahead came the hiss of a blaster. Seafor hurried to the entry hall.

Amine stood with his back to the outer door. In his good hand he held a blaster. The other was out of the sling and fresh blood stained the bandages. At his feet lay young Ayten, unconscious. Arnine's face was racked with pain but he smiled tautly.

Seafor strode toward him. When there were only a few feet between them, Amine leveled the blaster.

"The first was only a warning," he said. "This time it will be for business."

Seafor stopped.

"I mean to bargain for my life with Ayarten," continued. "Later you will realize that it was for your good, too."

Behind Seafor the circle of silent gray-robed figures parted to make way for an old man in faded green.

"Who dares do violence in Bleaksmound Retreat?" The voice of the President of the Fourth Global Republic quavered, but a note of iron determination came through. "My authority holds here. Outlaw, put down your weapon." He fumbled with trembling hand for the blaster at his hip.

A ray of blinding light touched the old man, pierced him. Amine laughed.

In that instant, Seafor lunged forward. The ray shifted, nicked the gray robe, sizzled against the stone floor. Then Amine was down, grunting with pain because Seafor had thrown him so that he fell on his wounded arm. With both hands Seafor gripped the blaster, wrested it from him, sent it spinning across the floor.

Amine stopped struggling. "You've wrecked your own last chance of safety," he said.

Seafor knelt on his chest. "And you have murdered. We have law here, although it holds good only within these walls. Our penalty for murder is lifelong imprisonment."

The bell began to clang deafeningly.

Through his weakness and pain, Amine smiled.

"I think that penalty has been commuted to sudden death— likely for all of us. You know who that is. Dawn has come."

The door opened. It was Ayarten of Rossel, burly, mean-visaged, clad in cloth of gold. But he staggered, his face was chalk-white, the cloth of gold was torn.

He did not see his son lying at his feet.

"Refuge!" he cried. "Levensee of Wols has struck. He has seized my domain. Those of my men that remained have gone over to him. I claim refuge!"

BUSINESS OF KILLING

THE ROOM WAS SMALL AND UNDISTINGUISHED, YET there was the indelible impression that power radiated to and from it, that it was the focal point of vast, far-flung, tension-fraught, and crucial activities. Its general appearance—that of a hastily stripped living room—clashed with the large, efficient, and centrally located desk from which radiated a number of ribbons sheathing conductors and adhering unobtrusively to the floor. A strong possibility: that it was the temporary headquarters of an organization engaged in a critical enterprise.

The man who had said they might call him Whitlow sat in a corner. His face was long, bony, and big-jawed, but the effect was of fanaticism and obstinacy, even sulkiness, rather than strength. He rubbed his hands in a way that was meant to be amiable, very much the master of the situation although it was he who was being interviewed. His gaze wandered inquisitively. He looked, despite his pseudogeniality, as if he could make his expression go all stern in a moment, and he wore high-mindedness like an admiral's uniform. Yet behind it all lurked a hint of the brat who knows where thecandy is hidden and who knows, furthermore, that he is immune from interference.

Saturnly and Neddar sat behind the desk. Or, rather, Saturnly sat behind most of it, while Neddar was tucked in at a corner, his nimble fingers poised above the noiseless keys of a hidden lightwriter, which was at present hooked up with a little panel that stared slantwise at Saturnly from the center of the desk.

Saturnly was obviously all appetite and will power. Heavy-jowled bullethead set on a torso that had expanded with its owner's enterprises. Eyes in which there was little subtlety but worlds of dogged power. A man who lived to outshout, outpound, outorganize, and outwit. A great driving voraciousness, joyously dedicated to the task of making men and money work.

Yet deep underneath was the suggestion of an iron and admirable integrity; one felt that in a pinch the man would unfailingly stand up for the things he believed in and lived by, whatever the cost and no matter how tawdry they might be.

Neddar just as obviously had no appetite at all except for his own peculiar whims, and subtlety fairly danced a jig in his liquid brown eyes. Yet he was Saturnly's equal in energy and tireless competence, but based on intellectual rather than emotional drives. A small, lithe man, very quick in all ways, young, but with a full black beard. Lips brimming with humor and mockery, though now carefully composed. A human catalyst, a court jester turned private secretary, a superassistant.

Their relationship was that of crocodile and crocodile bird, or—more accurately—shark and pilot fish.

The most arresting difference between them and the Whitlow person related to clothing. Although superficially similar, there was the suggestion of different epochs of fashion—or of some even wider gulf.

They watched him as a fat torn and a brainy kitten watch a mouse just out of reach.

Whitlow said, "I repeat, the means whereby I came here are immaterial to our discussion. Suffice it to say that alternate time streams exist, resulting from time bifurcations in the not-too-distant past, and that I possess the means of traveling between them."

Saturnly extended his great paws soothingly. He said, "Now, now, Mr. Whitlow, don't excite yourself—"

He choked off. Neddar's fingers flickered, although no other part of his anatomy moved, and there glowed up at Saturnly the following warning: "WATCH YOUR STEP! It's probably true. Remember, he turned up where he couldn't have."

Neddar said, "Mr. Saturnly is concerned that you don't overtax yourself after your strenuous ordeal."

Mollified, Whitlow continued in his unpleasantly high-pitched and mincing voice, "I am, among other things, a pacifist. I am visiting the alternate worlds in search of one that has learned how to do away with the horrid scourge of war, in order to bring back the precious knowledge to my erring co-timers. I see in yours no uniforms, no headlines detailing carnage, no posters blaring propaganda, nor any of the subtler indications that war is just over or will soon break out. I assume, therefore, that you have been able to eliminate this dreadful business of killing—"

During this speech a stifled inward churning had been apparent in Saturnly. Now he exploded, "Just who do you think you are, anyway? Coming here and insulting me—John Saturnly—this way! Why, you dirty Red—"

He chewed air furiously. A new message glowed on the panel: "You big ape! This guy's got something. If we offend him, we may not get it."

To Whitlow, Neddar said, "Mr. Saturnly misunderstood you. He is a businessman and has a very keen sense of the dignity and worth of his work. He thought you were referring specifically to business, whereas, of course, you were only using the words in a figurative sense."

At the same time he made furtive motions indicating that Saturnly, though well intentioned, was rather slow of understanding.

Whitlow inquired, "Just what is the nature of Mr. Saturnly's business?"

A grumble of explosions shook the night.

"Blasting operations," said Neddar. "I don't mean his business—that comprises a variety of enterprises and has many ramifications. It happens, moreover, to be very closely concerned with that matter on which you are desirous of obtaining information."

"I'm glad to hear that," said Whitlow. "I appreciate the attention you've shown in bringing me here. But I could just as well follow my usual procedure of drifting around and taking things in gradually."

"A needless waste of your time, which I am sure must be valuable. In Mr. Saturnly you have found the fountainhead. It is his enterprises that have eliminated from this world the terrible and chaotic socio-political upheavals of war."

The explosions continued. There came the vindictive drone of high-speed aircraft. Eagerness and doubt fought in Whitlow's face.

"The night freight," said Neddar. "We are a very industrious people—very businesslike in all matters. And that leads me to another consideration. Mr. Saturnly and I are in a position to provide you with information which you greatly desire. You, on the other hand, possess a very fascinating power—that of passing between time streams."

"Follow my lead," glowed on the panel, but it was unnecessary. Saturnly understood things like this without thinking.

He said, "Yes, how about a little deal, Mr. Whitlow? We tell you how to prevent... uh... war. You tell us how to cross time."

Whitlow rolled the idea on his tongue, as if it were a new but not necessarily unpleasant kind of cough syrup. "An interesting proposal. I could, of course, ultimately obtain the same information independently—"

"But not so adequately," said Neddar quickly, his eyes flashing. "And not soon enough. I take it that there is some particular war which you desire to stop or prevent." A tiny green light began to blink on Saturnly's desk. Neddar thumbed a square marked "No." It continued to blink. He thumbed the square once more, then resumed. "So speed must be your paramount consideration, Mr. Whitlow."

"Yes... ah... perhaps. And if I decide to impart my power to you, I would require assurances that it be used only for the most high-minded purposes."

"Absolutely," said Saturnly, bringing down his palm as if it were a seal and his desk the document.

A door flicked open and a blonde young lady catapulted in. She squealed, "I know you're in conference, J.S., but this is a crisis!"

Saturnly made frantic gestures of warning. Neddar, after one appraising glance, wasted no time in such maneuvers.

She struck the pose of one announcing catastrophe. "There's been a strike of front-line operatives!" she managed to wail—then Neddar was rushing her out. The slamming door punctuated her woeful: "And just when you'd come down to supervise the big push, J.S.!"

"A lovely girl, Mr. Whitlow, but hysterical," said Saturnly. "She talks... what's that word?.. figuratively."

His blandness was lost on Whitlow. "Just what is the nature of your business, Mr. Saturnly?" The voice had acquired an inquisitorial edge.

Saturnly groped for a reply, looking around for Neddar as a dripping man looks for a towel.

"Of course," Whitlow continued, a puzzled note creeping in,

"I assumed that there was no war here, because of the absence of war atmosphere, to which I am very sensitive. But—"

"You took the words out of my mouth," said Saturnly, clutching at the straw. "No war atmosphere—no war. You proved it yourself."

But another door flicked open, and it is doubtful if even Neddar could have stemmed the agitated tide of the small crowd that poured through it.

Of individuals of major importance—the rest wore badges—there seemed to be three. The first was tall and had been, at some prior date, dapper and competent.

He said, "I'm through, J.S. I can't do anything with them. They've gotten beyond reason." He threw himself down in a chair.

The second was short and bristling. He said, "Just let me turn the artillery on them, J.S., and I'll blast them out of their sit-down!"

"You and who else?" inquired the third, who was of medium height, lumpy, and wearing a dirty raincoat. "Just try that, and you'll see the biggest sympathetic walkout you ever tried to toss tear gas at."

They disregarded Saturnly's herculean efforts to shush them as completely as they did the presence of Whitlow.

"J.S., their demands are impossible!" the second man barked over the babbling.

The third man planted himself in front of Saturnly's desk. He stated, "Twenty cents more an hour and time-and-a-half in the mud, with pay retroactive to day before yesterday's rainstorm."

"It isn't mud!" the second man rebutted fiercely. "It isn't sufficiently gelatinous. I've had it analyzed."

Two studious-looking men in the background bobbed their heads in affirmation.

The third man dug his hand in his raincoat pocket, stepped forward, and slapped down a black, gooey handful in the middle of Saturnly's desk.

"No mud, eh?" he said, watching it ooze. "What do you say, Saturnly?"

The first man shuddered and cringed in his chair.

With a sweep of his bearlike arm, Saturnly sent the mud splattering off his desk as he came around it.

"You dirty gutter stooge!" he roared. "So two dollars an hour isn't good enough for your good-for-nothing front-liners?" He waved his muddied fist.

The third man stood his ground. He said, "*And* there are complaints about the absence of adequate safety engineering."

"Safety engineering!" Saturnly blew up. "Why, when I was a front-line operative—and I knew the business, I can tell you, because I worked up to it from a low-down factory job—we kicked out any safety engineers that had the nerve to come sniffing around our trenches!"

"Care to join the union at this late date?" asked the third man imperturbably.

Neddar's return coincided with the outburst of fresh pandemonium. He gave one apprehensive look. Three skipping strides carried him to Whitlow and put his bearded mouth two inches from the pacifist's ear.

"We did deceive you," he said rapidly, "but it was only to avoid giving you an even more false impression. Let me clear out this rabble. Don't come to a decision until we've talked to you."

Without waiting for a reply, he darted to Saturnly and drew him toward the door, pulling the rest of the crowd after him like planets after a sun.

Fifteen minutes later Neddar was still trying to pry Saturnly away. The second and third man had departed with their satellites, but Saturnly was hanging onto the first man and giving him certain instructions that caused him to lose his defeated look and finally hurry off excitedly.

Neddar redoubled his tugging. Saturnly did not at once yield to it. He turned his head. His broad face wore a beamy, glazed smile. "Wait a minute, Neddy," he said. "I see it all now. Of course, when you first brought the guy in and tipped me off about time streams, I got the idea they were something we should go for. But you know how it is with me—I can only think when there's no opportunity to. It was only when those boobs came in and started to yammer at me that I really began to see the possibilities."

"Yes, yes," said Neddar. "And while you gloat, he slips through our fingers. Come on."

But in his exultation Saturnly was imperturbable. "Just think, Neddy, worlds like ours—maybe dozens of them—and we got a monopoly on the trade. A real open-door policy—nobody but us can open it. We got a surplus—we know where to unload it. There's a scarcity—we know where we can get some. We got critical materials by the tail. We set up secret branch offices—Oh, Neddy!"

Only then did he allow himself to be led off.

They passed through three rooms. All had the stripped look of Saturnly's office, yet there was still not enough space for the new installations and occupants. A battery of nimble-fingered girls tended transmitters of some sort. Others typed and lightwrote. Wall maps glowed vital information. Table maps had chess played on them by delicate logistic machines. Rakish young men in windbreakers lounged against the walls. Occasionally one of them would snatch up a packet and dart out into the night.

Various individuals, badgeless and badged, assailed and importuned Saturnly.

"Sign this, J.S.!"

"Those front-liners won't let us bring up reinforcements, J.S. They're picketing the communication trenches!"

"J.S., the aircrafters' brotherhood has offered to take disciplinary measures against the front-liners. Can I give them the go ahead?"

But Neddar did not look to either side, and Saturnly's tranced, Buddha-like smile said nothing.

Only when they came to the blonde secretary's desk, beside the door with the motto over it, did Neddar pause grudgingly.

"If there are any important calls, you might as well let them come through," he said bitterly. "There's no longer any use in trying to keep our visitor in the dark."

She favored him with a poisonous smile.

"We're all set, then?" he asked Saturnly. "We admit everything and try to sell him on it?"

"We sell him," Saturnly echoed positively.

Neddar hesitated. "There's only one thing worries me," he said darkly. "Your unfortunate tendency to tell the truth in crises."

"Ha—a liar like me!" Saturnly laughed, but a shadow of uneasiness flickered across his face.

Mr. Whitlow had obviously used the fifteen minutes for thinking. Lingering puzzlement and cold anger were the apparent results. The latter predominated.

"I'm sorry, gentlemen," he said, "but there's no longer any possibility of an understanding between us. Your world is a war world like all the rest, except that it masks it in a peculiarly repellent fashion."

"That ain't war," said Saturnly gaily. His exuberance in situations like this perpetually amazed Neddar. "Sit down, Mr. Whitlow. That's just Coldefinc conducting its legitimate business enterprises."

"Coldefinc?"

"Sure. Columbian Defense, Inc."

"Don't think to deceive me by any such ridiculous rigmarole," said Whitlow venomously. "It's obvious that, whatever you call yourself, you've seized supreme political power in your country."

"Mr. Whitlow, you make me angry," said Saturnly genially. "I'm sorry, but you do. I'm a respectable businessman."

"But you conduct wars. Only governments can maintain an army and navy."

"That's right," said Saturnly genially. "Come to think of it, they *did* maintain an army and navy—until we bought 'em up."

"But it's impossible!" Whitlow was beginning to argue. "In all worlds I have visited, it is the governments and the governments alone that conduct wars."

"You amaze me," Neddar interjected. "Government is the older form of social organization, business the newer. According to all natural expectations, the newer form should gradually absorb all or most of the activities of the older form."

"Primitive," Saturnly confirmed.

"But don't you have any government at all?" Whitlow demanded.

"Sure," said Saturnly. "Only it doesn't do anything except make things legal."

"An empty sham!" said Whitlow. "How, without armed forces, can government enforce the laws it makes?"

"By prestige alone," Neddar answered. "There was a time when religion clubbed people into becoming converts. When the center of social organization shifted elsewhere, religion had to change its methods—rather to its advantage, I believe.

"Moreover," he added gravely, "I thought you were an enemy of the exercise of force by government, as in war."

Whitlow sat back. For a moment he had nothing to say.

"Government incorporates us, we do the rest," Saturnly concluded. "The point is, Mr. Whitlow, as I've been trying to tell you, that Coldefinc is a legitimate business enterprise, working hard every minute to satisfy its customers, to make money for its stockholders, and to pay its ungrateful employees a lot higher wage than they deserve."

"Customers?" Whitlow mumbled. "Stock—?"

"Sure, customers. We sell 'em defense. That's how we got started. Government was slipping. Crime was on the up. There were lots of disorders. There had just been a big, inconclusive war and everybody was dissatisfied. They didn't want any army or navy, but they did want protection. O.K., we sold it to 'em."

"*Now* I understand!" Whitlow interjected, a whiplash quality to his voice, his eyes burning. "We had it in our world. You're just the same thing, grown to monstrous proportions. Racketeers!"

"Mr. Whitlow!" Saturnly was on his feet. Neddar lightwrote, "Watch yourself!" but Saturnly didn't even see it. "You *will* make me mad. Every step of the way Coldefinc has conformed to law. Should I read you the Supreme Court decision that because it's any man's right to carry arms, it's all right for him to hire somebody to do it for him? Why, we're so clean we haven't done any strikebreaking—at least for outsiders. How can anything be a racket if it's completely legal?"

Neddar lightwrote, "Excuse me. I thought you were going to say something else. That was perfect."

Saturnly sat down. "To continue where I left off at. We sold 'em defense. First, private individuals and other businesses, especially those with racketeers—we had 'em here too, Mr. Whitlow—on their necks. Then small communities that were tired of police departments that did nothing but graft. We advertised—dignified. We expanded—and so we could sell our product cheaper. Then came a war scare."

To give him a breather, Neddar chipped in with, "Meanwhile, similar developments were taking place in all fields of social activity. Forrelinc—Foreign Relations, Inc.—absorbed all but the purely formal activities of the diplomatic service. Social-service companies vied as to which could sell its customers the cheapest and happiest ways of life."

"Then came a war scare," Saturnly resumed determinedly. "People howled for our product. Our stocks boomed. We increased our plant—for years we'd been hiring away the best army and navy officers; now we bought the entire personnel and equipment from the government dirt cheap and used what we could of it. We started a monster sales campaign—this time to include neighboring countries. We—"

Whitlow nervously waved for time to ask a question. His face was a study in confusions and uncertainties.

"Do I understand you right," he faltered incredulously. "You've really organized war—"

"Defense."

"—on a business basis? You sell it like any other product? You issue stock that fluctuates in value according to the failure or success of your activities?"

"Correct, Mr. Whitlow. That's why you didn't see any war headlines. It's all on the financial page."

"And you don't draft soldiers—"

"Operatives."

"—but hire them just like any other business?"

"Absolutely. Though a front-liner usually has to work his way up through other jobs. First in a munitions factory, so he learns all about our weapons. Next, transport and distribution, so he gets that end of it. Then maybe he gets a chance at a front-line job and the big money."

"You mean to say you pay your front-line soldiers—"

"Operatives."

"—more than anyone else?"

"Naturally."

"But that's detestable," said Whitlow righteously, as if seizing any opportunity to maintain resentment. "In my world there are soldiers, but at least we don't try to gild the dungheap by paying them high wages."

"What?" Saturnly asked. "You mean in your world an operative doesn't get as much as a factory hand? Or doesn't anyone make any money?"

"No," Whitlow replied angrily, "a factory worker is well paid. We have wage scales governing such things."

"But that's terrible," said Saturnly. He seemed shocked. "A front-liner has to have all kinds of skills, and besides, it's dangerous work, as dangerous as mining—maybe more—maybe almost as risky as deep-sea diving."

Whitlow wilted. He looked dazed. "Then those men that rushed in here a while back—they really were talking about a strike by front-line operatives?"

"Sure."

"But how can you allow such a thing? Surely it will enable the enemy—" Whitlow looked up, his eyes widening. "Who is your enemy?"

"Right now it is the Fatherland Cartel," Saturnly replied breezily. "You needn't worry, Mr. Whitlow—it's just a little sit-down strike the boys are having. They'll hold the line if they have to. The only bad thing is that it'll slow up the big push—for a while," he added cryptically.

"Then you're actually engaged in fighting a war—a real war? It's a business—but at the same time it's war?"

"Of course, Mr. Whitlow," Saturnly replied patiently. "We try to defend our customers without fighting, but if we have to, we fight. Coldefinc always delivers."

"And that war is like any other war? Battles, invasions, encirclement and annihilation of the enemy army?"

"Liquidation of his plant," Saturnly corrected. "Though of course we're all businessmen and try to avoid useless waste." He airily waved a hand. "Oh, yes, those things happen, but they aren't the really important part of the war. The important part is the underlying financial situation."

"Yes?" A sudden new interest lighted Whitlow's eyes. Neddar noted it, and his tense watchfulness was broken so far as his fingers were concerned. He lightwrote, "Concentrate on this angle. You're going great. Just don't get excited."

Saturnly leaned forward, beaming. "Mr. Whitlow, I know I can trust you. You're not of this world, and what's happening in it doesn't mean anything to you." He paused. "Mr. Whitlow, it's a dead secret, but in a few days Coldefinc will have the Fatherland Cartel by the tail. Through disguised holding companies in neutral countries we've been buying up stock in the component organizations of the cartel. The big push is mainly to scare a few people into letting go their shares. Pretty soon we'll have more than fifty per cent, and then, Mr. Whitlow, this war will be over like that." He snapped his fingers.

Whitlow goggled. "You mean all you have to do is to get a controlling interest in the enemy organization?"

"Sure."

"And the enemy will submit to it?"

"What else can they do? Business is business."

"And you won't have to invade or annihilate them? Untold killing and destruction will be avoided? You won't lose many of your operatives?"

Saturnly shrugged. "Not more than in normal times."

"Mr. Saturnly!" Whitlow stood up. The new interest had grown to a consuming, fanatic flame. "I have a proposal to make to *you*. Could you do that sort of thing for my world?" He held out his hand as if he were giving it to Saturnly.

"Um-m-m." Saturnly leaned back, frowning. Neddar rejoiced at the way he masked his triumph with an air of reluctance. "I'd have to think it over. It's a big proposition, Mr. Whitlow."

"I'd provide the means of entry," the pacifist continued rapidly. "You could bring across whatever you'd need in the way of operatives and... er... plant."

"I dunno," said Saturnly dubiously. "Is there any business at all in your world, or does government run everything? If there isn't, it'll be pretty hard for us to get an in."

"Oh, there's business, all right," Whitlow reassured him. "Though at present somewhat submerged."

"And are there any neutral countries? Or are they all in the war?"

"There are still a few neutrals."

Saturnly thought. Whitlow hung on his reactions.

"Well, we'd have to go slow at first," Saturnly finally said ruminatively. "There'd be the matter of sales research, sizing up likely prospects, setting up pioneer offices, and also incorporating firms to front for us—that's where the neutral countries would come in handy." He began to warm up. "Then we build up plant and personnel—the latter mixed, from both worlds. Then feeler campaigns, trial balloons, preliminary advertising and promotion. With all that set, we really start in." He turned to Whitlow. "Of course, if we get that far, there's no doubt of our ultimate success, because we'll be all business and they'll be just maybe half business and half government—an awful jumble."

Whitlow nodded eagerly. Neddar lightwrote: "You've got him, J.S.!"

Saturnly laid his hand authoritatively on the table. "First we sell the neutral countries—they'll want protection the worst way, because they won't know which side is going to jump them first. At the same time we start hiring out to do small jobs for the warring nations—we pose as kind of war-industrial specialists. Maybe the neutral countries get invaded and we have a chance to show our stuff. Maybe the small jobs grow into big ones. Maybe both." He was really warmed up now. "Either way, our stocks boom. We put in more plant, increase personnel, start a major sales campaign. People begin to have more confidence in us than in their government armies. We pick one of the big powers—whichever is slipping, it doesn't matter which—and buy it out. The other side—we outorganize 'em, outbuy 'em, hit 'em hard on both the financial and operational fronts. And then—"

The phone purred. Automatically, Saturnly snatched it up and bawled into it, "Yes?" A wait, while Whitlow swayed forward in palefaced, hypnotized eagerness. Then in a roar, "What do you mean bothering me with trifles like the strike being called off when I'm fixed with something important?" Suddenly a wicked smile fattened his face. "Oh, it's you, Dulger? You don't like me sending whisky to those front-liners? Well, what would you want if you were out there in all that mud?" From beyond the walls, making them tremble faintly, came suddenly a many-voiced rumbling. It kept on. "Hear that, Dulger? It's the big push. Oh, you're going to indict me for corrupting my workers? Good. Good! Maybe some day when you start a real man he-man's union, I'll join it."

He turned back. His lips formed, "And then—"

But there had been time for his previous words to ferment in Whitlow's emotion-drunk soul. The pacifist's face was a mask of fanatic ecstasy, and his voice was hoarsely vibrant against the grumbling guns as he finished for him: "And then, Mr. Saturnly, will come the millennium to which the nobler side of mankind has always aspired, that Utopia of perfect and gentle brotherhood which your world will so soon attain and, which you will ultimately bring to mine, that purified existence from which all hatred and strife, all greed and war, have been forever banished. I refer, Mr. Saturnly, to that most precious of all blessings—peace."

"WHAT!" Slowly Saturnly came to his feet, crouching bearlike. Slowly his bulging neck suffused with red, with purple. In vain Neddar plucked, tugged, jerked at his sleeve, desperately lightwrote: "Don't, J.S. Don't! DON'T!" resorted to even more drastic efforts to shut him up. He might as well have tried to quiet a god. In the rapidly shifting excitement, the truth-telling mechanism buried deep in Saturnly had been set in motion and now could no more be stopped than if Saturnly had been Juggernaut's car.

"You... you talk to John Saturnly of PEACE when you know War is his business?" He loomed over the astounded pacifist like a prehistoric idol. His voice boomed from the walls. "You'd have me wreck a world organization that I built up with these hands? You'd have me throw my customers to the dogs? Bankrupt my stockholders? Fire millions of loyal employees out into the world where they would drift around unemployed and help start a real mess? No, Mr. Whitlow, I'll gladly help you with your proposition, but you must understand that if Coldefinc tackles your world, it will be war from then on—forever!" He sucked up a great breath and drew himself erect. "Maybe, Mr. Whitlow, you didn't read the motto over the door when you came in. 'When there are bigger wars, Coldefinc will wage them!'"

The pacifist shrank back in horror, shock, and fear.

"I... you—" he mumbled brokenly. Then it all came out in a whimpering rush. "I won't have anything to do with you, you fiend!"

"Oh, yes, you will!" Saturnly came around the table, crouching. "You're going to show us how to cross time." He kept coming. The pacifist was wedged in a corner and fumbling with his coat. "We've been nice to you, Mr. Whitlow, but now that's over. I don't like people who try to go back on me." Whitlow's hands came out with what looked like a small gray egg. He fingered it in a panicky rhythm, and his face went blank as if he were desperately trying to concentrate on some thought. Saturnly closed in. "We're going to have your secret, Mr. Whitlow, whether you get anything for it or not." Then, suddenly, "Stop him, Neddar! Stop him! That way! No, that way!"

Both men dove, Saturnly with a bearlike lunge, Neddar with an incredibly pantherlike leap. They clutched air, scrambled up, looked around. Mr. Whitlow was gone.

For a long while nothing was said or done. Then, slowly, heavily, Saturnly walked back to the desk and sat down and pressed his face in his hands.

"He faded," said Neddar in a voice that likewise faded. "He got misty and went curving off... at an increasing tangent... toward an alternate future—"

Then his rapierlike anger flashed out. His eyes seemed to spark and his black beard to crackle with the electricity of it. He whirled on Saturnly.

"You big, honest, imbecile! How you ever got this far, even with me to do your conniving for you, I don't know. You had him sold. We had worlds within our grasp, worlds ripe for exploitation and conquest, worlds for sale at bargain prices, and you had to go sincere and scare him off—forever. Oh, you bumbling ape!"

"I know." Saturnly pressed his face harder. Neddar twisted his features in one last bitter grimace, then tossed it off, sighed, and almost smiled.

Saturnly peeped at him guiltily between thick fingers.

"You know, Neddy," he said softly, "maybe in a way it's just as well this didn't go any farther. You know how I think—always while I'm doing something else. Well, while I was selling this guy I was thinking of something very different. You know, Neddy, our world is maybe kind of peculiar. We rate business and money and financial things above everything. They're our ultimates. If something's decided in a business way, it never occurs to us to try to go around it or look for any other answer. Maybe it isn't that way in the other worlds. I know it's hard to imagine, but maybe they wouldn't think of business as the ultimate. Maybe the people in those other words are sort of different... sort of crazy—" His voice changed, took on a note almost of relief, as he finished, "At least, if they're anything like that Whitlow guy!"

DAY DARK, NIGHT BRIGHT

HE WOKE, FEELING VERY REFRESHED AND *THANSIG,* and instantly groped for the black plastic far-caller and punched the digits for Time of Day.

The firm, contralto voice came after the second ring. "The time is six forty-six and twenty seconds." Why did they use their females on so many jobs? Cheaper, he supposed. A very grasping planet, indeed.

Light filtered through the cheap drapes of his one window. Careless when alone, he wriggled to his feet, not bothering to feign bones and joints, and pulled wide the drapes. It was an overcast morning, the low clouds thick. Good! He detested bright Sol with its overdose of ultraviolet radiations. Why couldn't they have seven dull, clustered suns—*gentle* hydrogen-burning furnaces—as he had at home? And, of course, no (his thoughts hesitated at the horrible word) night.

He congratulated himself on picking the coastal, water-tempered city of San Francisco for his base. Only they didn't have nearly as much fog as he desired and they advertised. And they did have smog. Liars, liars, liars—they deserved extinction. For dishonesty as well as for their (again the hesitation) night.

His three-orbed gaze—alone, he opened the third one, wrinkle-sealed, in his forehead—lighted automatically on the half-drunk bottle of rum on top of his midget refrigerator. It was good this planet had that liquid tranquilizing drug. How he hated solids! Solid food, to be chewed by his false teeth—another horror. But fortunately this *rum* (how queer to talk with sounds instead of thoughts) was almost as good as *thansiger* for waiting out, unconscious, the horrible night. Too bad he had run out of his supply of *thansiger,* but this had been an unusually long job. To be lost in complete dark—that was horrible and (but not quite) unimaginable. The seventh inner circle of Hell, as they called the place here.

For a moment his mind writhed back to his phone call. What a stupid species!—they really did deserve to be exterminated. They gave him Time of Day (though not Time of Night, thanks to Aahotis!) But they never told you where you were, or which day of the month and week, and which year according to their Christ-reckoning... and one other detail which he for the moment forgot.

The clouds were thickening overhead. Good, good! He would have a comfortable working day by his calculations. It was getting beautifully cool and dark.

He took the elevator downstairs from his sixth storey. The street was strangely empty. He crossed it at an economizing oblique angle. He picked up at the bakery two plastic cups of coffee and two Danish. They were good starch when you'd scraped the almonds off and dug the jam out. But the bakery's trays were only half-filled and there were few Earthans about—sort of odd. He returned to his tiny apartment.

It was getting still darker. Good, good! Dull days were what he loved most—and all too infrequent on this planet. A lovely gloomy day—almost like Sartis, really. He got busy on the telephone. Quite a long job, but this was The Day. His careful preparations were paying off. He called Van Sittart about California and the whole West Coast. Everything ready for the earthquake. He called Siberia. Yes, it was all set to slide off into the Pacific and Arctic Oceans. India?—a famine unexperienced in her long history of famines. Africa?—suicide by inter-tribal warfare. Europe? (or, as the Americans sounded it, Yurrop)—atom-war, which would take care of the middle and eastern parts of the USA as well. The rest of the World (as they called it), well, fallout would do it. And so on, and so on (to get in the Polynesians, etc.) His listeners would let loose doom as soon as he called them a second time.

It was looking still darker outside his window. Good, good, good! A really Sartis day! Oh, how lovely to destroy a whole planet! Or maybe nine of them if his Sol-nova trick really worked.

He hesitated a minute there. Destroy! Destroy? He wouldn't

like to have his wives and cousins destroyed on his home planet, no matter what evil they had done.

Five minutes to explosion. He paced about, then walked to the window, losing his way half-way. But he got there.

He had forgotten that these Earthans did not work on the twenty-four hour principal, but divided each day (quite unreasonably) into twelve hours day and twelve hours…

… NIGHT.

And so he died.

ABOUT THE AUTHOR

Fritz Leiber is considered one of science fiction's legends. Author of a prodigious number of stories and novels, many of which were made into films, he is best known as creator of the classic Lankhmar fantasy series. Fritz Leiber has won awards too numerous to count, including the coveted Hugo and Nebula, and was honored as a lifetime Grand Master by the Science Fiction Writers of America. He died in 1992.

Open Road Integrated Media is a digital publisher and multimedia content company. Open Road creates connections between authors and their audiences by marketing its ebooks through a new proprietary online platform, which uses premium video content and social media.

Videos, Archival Documents, and New Releases

Sign up for the Open Road Media newsletter and get news delivered straight to your inbox.

Sign up now at
www.openroadmedia.com/newsletters

FIND OUT MORE AT
WWW.OPENROADMEDIA.COM

FOLLOW US:
@openroadmedia and
Facebook.com/OpenRoadMedia